I TAKE YOU

I TAKE YOU

ELIZA KENNEDY

Jonathan Cape
London

Published by Jonathan Cape 2015

2 4 6 8 10 9 7 5 3 1

First published in the United States in 2015 by Crown Publishers,
an imprint of the Crown Publishing Group, a division of Random House LLC,
a Penguin Random House Company, New York.

First published in Great Britain in 2015 by
Jonathan Cape
Random House, 20 Vauxhall Bridge Road,
London SW1V 2SA

www.vintage-books.co.uk

A Penguin Random House Company

global.penguinrandomhouse.com

A CIP catalogue record for this book is available from the British Library

ISBN 9780224099721 (hardback edition)
ISBN 9780224099738 (trade paperback edition)

 Penguin Random House is committed to a sustainable future for our
business, our readers and our planet. This book is made from Forest
Stewardship Council® certified paper.

Printed and bound in Great Britain by Clays Ltd, St Ives PLC

For Joshua

I TAKE YOU

SATURDAY

I'm getting married.

He's perfect!

It's a *disaster*.

"You're crazy," Freddy says as she hands me another drink. "Will is adorable. He's got a cool job. He cooks. He's super sweet."

"He's everything I'm not," I say. "He cancels out all my flaws."

"Ha ha!" Freddy says. "Nope."

We're at a club downtown. It's dark, hot, crowded and insanely loud. Nicole is playing with her phone at the other end of the table. The rest of the girls are dancing by the DJ booth.

"You're a pig in a poke!" Freddy shouts over the music. "You look good on the outside, but buy you and bring you home?" She tosses back her drink. "Forget it."

I sigh. "I'm not even sure how things got to this point."

"Is that right?" She jabs at me with one of her pointy purple nails. "Did he trick you into saying yes? Did he distract you with, like," she waves her hands in my face, "whoo! whoo! pretty lights? Then shove the ring on your finger?"

"It was very romantic!" I protest. "The moonlight, the museum!"

She nods thoughtfully. "When Patrick proposed, he hid the ring in the mouth of his bearskin rug."

"The one in the foyer?"

"The one in the media room."

"Why have I not heard this story before?"

"He made me crawl around on the ground, searching for it," she adds. "Stark naked."

I miss Patrick.

"Also handcuffed," she says. "Which, you know. Helped."

I'm about to follow up on this little tidbit when someone sits down next to me. He's cute. I smile at him. He smiles back.

"I can kill people with my mind," I tell him.

He laughs and says, "Can I buy you a drink?"

He's British. I fall deeply in love.

I reach up and touch his curly hair. Soon we're kissing. He tastes like smoke and bourbon. I could kiss him all night, but Freddy pulls me onto the dance floor. We weave and twist and shimmy. We twirl and bob. We spin each other around.

"Did you bring *las drogas*?" I shout.

She looks surprised. "I thought we were cutting back."

"Winifred! Tonight of all nights?"

She grabs her purse from our table and leads me to the bathroom. When we get back, the cute British guy is gone. Nicole is still texting. Leta and Chelsea and Joy are bouncing up and down in their seats like maniacs, shrieking along with the music, their drinks flying everywhere.

I *love* this. I am so happy right now. I want to have a bachelorette party every week.

"Let's make prank calls!" I say.

"Let's go to a strip club!" Freddy says.

"Yes!" we all yell, except for Nicole, who is still goddamned texting.

My phone pings. It's a message from Philip.

—Wilder. I need you to come in right away.

I stand up, a little wobbly. "Kiss Mommy good-bye, girls!"

"Now?" Freddy cries in disbelief. "They can't do this!"

I pat her on the shoulder. "I'll be right back."

Ha ha! Nope.

The office is a madhouse. Paralegals racing through the halls with stacks of binders and file folders, night secretaries printing and photo-copying like the fate of the world hangs in the balance. I've never shown up to work in this condition before, so everything is strange and new and a little hilarious. I start to laugh, which gets me some dark looks. Then I hit an unexpected pocket of turbulence in the hallway. Oh no—

I'm going down! Fortunately, a wall saves me. You know what? Thank God for walls. Whoever put them in this hallway had a lot of foresight. Whoever *invented* them was a freaking—

I slip inside a bathroom and splash water on my face. That's better.

I head for my office. The light is on in Lyle's room, so I stop by. There he is, surrounded by piles of paper and greasy take-out containers, banging away at his laptop, looking all sweaty, pale and infarcted. Lyle and I work on the same litigation team, for the same partner. I'm in my second year at the firm, he's in his fifth. You could say we're friendly rivals. Kindred spirits. Just super, *super* close.

"Go fuck yourself," he says.

I drop into a chair. "What's up, Mighty Mouse?"

He sighs heavily. "How many times have I asked you not to call me that?"

"Eleven. What's going on around here? It's after midnight."

"The plaintiffs in the Lucas case filed a motion for a preliminary injunction." He's still typing furiously. "We have forty-eight hours to respond. Can you help?"

I flick at a piece of sparkly club confetti stuck to my dress. "Afraid not."

Lyle reads through what he's typed, hits return, hits it harder, shouts "Fuck God!" at the screen, hits return really hard, exhales, cracks his neck and turns to me. "She. Cannot. Help." He's doing his annoying third-person zombie monotone thing. "Why. Is she. Here?"

Pesky confetti—I flick at it again. "Because Philip. Texted. Her."

Lyle frowns. "He's here?"

"Apparently, Wee One."

"Philip doesn't know how to text."

I shrug. "Maybe his secretary taught him."

"Betty's ninety. Why did he text you?"

"Lyle is. Troubled. Lyle wonders why the partner. Did not text. Him. Lyle fears. He is out. Of the loop."

He picks up a pen and grips it tightly.

"There is so much love in your eyes right now, Lyle." I hold a hand to my heart. "I can hardly stand it."

For a second I think he's going to lunge across the desk and stab me in the eye, but he manages to rein it in. "Out," he says, pointing at the door with the pen. "Now."

I walk up two flights to the forty-fifth floor, where the partners have their offices. The lighting is dim and expensive, the carpeting plush. Even the air smells better up here—crisp and fresh, like it was just imported from the Alps, which, who knows? I stroll the hallway, admiring the expensive art and framed artifacts from the firm's glorious past. Sepia-tinted photographs of the founding partners. Thank-you notes from robber barons and titans of industry. A letter from Theodore Roosevelt bitching about his bill.

Philip is reading a brief, feet up on his desk. I pause in the doorway. I oh-so-casually lean against the door frame. I kind of miss. So I knock and say, "Yeth, Mathter?"

He glances at me over his reading glasses. "Wilder. Come in."

He's wearing a tuxedo. "I just came from a charity function," he explains.

"Whoa." I hold up my hands. "Hey. A charity function. Let's not get so specific, okay?"

He regards me silently for a moment, then returns to his reading. I perch on the edge of one of his wing chairs and wait.

It's a nice tuxedo.

I shift my attention to his desk. It is massive, baroque, intimidating. I get completely lost in its swirls and whorls and ornate floral motifs. I wonder who carved them. Orphans, probably. Eighteenth-century French orphans. I picture them toiling away at the workhouse, their tiny, chapped hands trembling in the cold wind sweeping across the plains of . . . wherever. Someplace French. Fumbling for their woodworking tools, dropping them, lopping off a finger here, a toe there. Tearing strips of lace off their smocks to make chic little tourniquets, then getting back down to business.

I start to ask Philip about them. I think better of it.

I fold my hands in my lap. My dress is riding up. Way up. Red zone! I tug at the hem. Something rips.

Philip tosses the brief on his desk. "So," he says. "You're getting married."

"Yeppers!" I give him two dorky thumbs-up. Why? And why am I here? I really shouldn't be. "We're flying down to Key West tomorrow."

He smiles. "Congratulations."

"Thank you!"

"We need you to cancel it."

"Sorry?"

"Postpone it, rather." He lifts his feet off the desk and sits up. "Just for a few months."

I'm outraged. They can't do this! I want to get married! Will and I are soul mates!

"No way," I say. *Je refuse.*

Philip is sifting through a pile of papers, searching for something. He stops and looks up. "This is your first marriage?"

"Yes, and—"

"I remember my first." He goes a little misty. "It's true what they say. The first marriage really is the best."

"Good to know, but—"

"The next deposition in the EnerGreen litigation is scheduled for Friday." He's consulting a sheet of paper plucked from the disarray. "The witness is an accountant. Peter Hoffman."

"Hoffman?" I say. "The guy with the e-mails?"

"According to Lyle, Mr. Hoffman is not ready to be deposed. We need someone to prep him." He glances at me, eyebrows raised.

Oh. Philip's just confused. "That's the fraud part of the case," I remind him. "I work on the environmental claims." I cross my legs and smile at him. Problem solved.

But he frowns and shakes his head. "Lyle says that you know the documents. You know the record. It has to be you."

I should have known who was behind this. "Lyle is lyling—I mean, he's *lying*, Philip! He's trying to ruin my wedding. He—"

Philip looks at me over his reading glasses. He's all stern schoolmaster to my unruly little student. I'm totally digging it. I lift my chin and stare back at him defiantly. I try propping my elbow on the arm of the chair, but it's really slippery, which is weird for brocade. I fold my arms instead. "You're going to have to find somebody else."

Philip launches into this big speech about how EnerGreen is the firm's most important client . . . this is a historic case . . . billions of dollars at stake . . . furious government agencies breathing down our necks . . . so much public scrutiny since the oil spill . . . the true test of a lawyer's commitment is her willingness to make sacrifices for the good of the client . . .

Honestly? I can't focus. His voice is so smooth and measured. Almost hypnotic. And I'm distracted by how the light from the desk lamp makes his silver hair gleam. Philip has good hair. Great hair. But then, he's a good-looking man. He—

"—because this witness's documents are rife with potential pitfalls, he *must* be well prepared for his deposition, and you, Wilder, must be the one to prepare him. I have some information that you should find welcome, however. By a happy coincidence, Mr. Hoffman is vacationing in the Florida Keys this week. He wishes to be deposed there, and the plaintiffs have consented." Philip smiles at me.

The tuxedo, plus the reading glasses, plus the smile?

He's *killing* me right now.

"This, then, is our plan," he continues. "You will meet with Mr. Hoffman on Tuesday at his resort, a place called," he glances down at the sheet, "Tranquility Bay. Doesn't that sound charming. I will fly down Thursday evening. On Friday, I will defend the deposition," he glances up, "with your assistance, of course. By Friday evening you will be free to enjoy your well-deserved time off."

I think this through. "So I don't have to postpone the wedding."

"Correct."

"Then why did you say—"

"Because I love how outrage focuses your attention." He smiles again.

I close my eyes. "Send someone else," I say faintly.

"Very well, I will," Philip says. "On one condition."

I open my eyes. We gaze at each other in silence.

I stand up and shut the door. "Dress on or off?"

He comes around from behind his desk. "What a question."

I reach back for the zipper. "I want you to spank me again."

"You enjoyed that?" He stretches out on the long leather sofa. I climb on top of him.

"No," I say, my mouth close to his ear. "I *hated* it."

Afterward, I lie beside him and rest my head on his chest. That was exactly what I needed. And exactly why I left my party. Maybe that was obvious. It wasn't obvious to me. Not right away.

I feel his hand on my head, his fingers combing through my tangled hair. Philip has a lot of stamina for an old guy. I think about old guys. They're all right. They're all so very, very—

"Wilder?"

"Yes, sir?"

I love calling him "sir." It's making me excited all over again. Subservience!

"Something is troubling me," Philip says.

"I'm sorry to hear that, sir."

I feel him separate one curl from the rest, twirling it around his finger, tugging it gently. "The fact is, I may have misled you just now."

"In what way?"

"You still have to prep Hoffman."

I sigh contentedly and pat his chest. "I know."

He raises his head to peer at me. "You do?"

I sit up and stretch. I start gathering my clothes. "Of course. And I don't mind." I look down at him. "Although it was wrong of you to try to coerce me."

"I know." He smiles. "Wasn't it wonderful?"

It really was. So I let him coerce me again. Then I coerce him for a while. Then I get dressed and get a cab and go home.

Will and I live in a loft on North Moore Street. Before he moved in five months ago, the place was spare and chilly and barren—much like my soul, as Freddy likes to say. Now it's cozy and inviting, full of Will's old furniture and art and the beautiful things he picks up on his travels.

He must have heard me stumble out of the elevator, because he's waiting at the door. In a t-shirt and pajama pants, his hair all tousled from the shower. Freddy's right—he's so cute.

He yawns and smiles at me. "Hi, Lily."

"Baby! You waited up."

Logs are crackling in the fireplace. Soft music is playing. I collapse in his arms. He searches my face with loving eyes. "Do you need the bucket?" he asks tenderly.

"Not yet," I whisper.

He helps me to the sofa and hands me a glass of fizzy water. Aspirin. A mug of tea. He had it all waiting for me.

I stretch out and rest my head in his lap. He covers me with a blanket. "Did you have a good time tonight?" he asks.

I don't deserve him. I know this.

"It was okay."

He brushes a few strands of hair from my forehead. "You look beautiful."

The fact that I acknowledge that I'm a terrible person doesn't make me any less terrible. I know this, too.

I gaze up at him hopelessly. "I'm a pig in a poke, Will!"

"I love you just the way you are," he says.

"Oh, ha," I say weakly. "Ha ha."

I'll be better. I will!

I'll find a way to be worthy of him.

"We have an early flight," he says. "Let's get you to bed."

"I love you, Will!" I cry. "I love you so, so much."

And at this moment, I do. I really do!

He grins at me. "Then I have a great idea."

"What's that?"

"Let's get married!"

Oh, Jesus.

I close my eyes. "Okay!"

What am I doing? What have I *done*?

Stop. Just . . . calm down.

It's going to be fine. Totally fine!

How? Not sure. Really not sure about that. But it is. I know it is.

Everything's going to be fine.

SUNDAY

2

The drive to JFK is tough. I have to use my bucket twice. Check-in and security are special little hells. Will coaxes me through the terminal. I basically crawl down the aisle of the plane and collapse into my seat.

The woman next to me is whimpering, her head between her knees. I touch her back gently. "Are you okay?"

"I'm so friggin' sick!" she moans.

"Hey, me too! I had my bachelorette party last night."

She lifts her head. "Get outta here!"

Her name is Lola. She's getting married in Boca Raton in three days.

"Marry on a Wednesday," Lola informs me, "and you're less likely to divorce. Like, way less."

"No kidding?"

"They proved it," she says solemnly. "With *statistics*."

Naturally, we start swapping war stories.

"There's one tuxedo shop on the island," I tell her. "Our wedding planner drops off the deposit, and a few hours later the place is robbed. At gunpoint."

"I might know the guys who did that," Lola says.

"They were caught a couple of days later."

"Oh," she says. "Then no."

I lean across Will to look down the aisle. "When do you think they're going to start the beverage service?"

"We haven't left the gate yet," he murmurs.

"This formalwear bullshit is bullshit," Lola says. "Bettina, my maid of honor? She's, like, one of those all-natural girls? Doesn't buy paper towels? Eats the shit out of kale?"

"Oh yeah." I nod sympathetically. "I know the type."

"I choose this strapless dress for the bridesmaids, right? Gorgeous." Lola purses her fat little shrimp-colored lips. "Now Bettina says she won't shave!"

"Yikes!"

"It's disgustin'! All brown and tufty?" Lola shudders. "Like she's stashin' a couple of those animals up there. You know the ones?"

"Hamsters?"

"No. Olinguitos."

"Olinguitos?" I repeat.

"They're from Ecuador." She shakes her head. "Cross-eyed little fuckers."

I try to steer the conversation back on track. "The first resort we booked for our guests was super eco-conscious, like your friend," I say. "Solar powered, carbon neutral, zero emissions, you know?"

"Like with the crappy lightbulbs?"

"Exactly. But get this." I lean closer to her. "It closed down last month, after they found a dead hooker in the cistern."

"Oh, *shit*!" Lola cries.

"Right?"

"That's so nasty!"

"I know!"

She picks thoughtfully at a bit of orange skin flaking off her nose. "I got these girl cousins comin' to the wedding? Identical twins? Real heavy?" She pauses. "They're totally doin' it."

I feel my mouth drop open. "With each other?"

"Always sneakin' off during family functions, like to the garage? Writin' these weird poems to each other?" She takes her phone out of her bag and starts scrolling through her photos. "Lemme see if I got a picture. You won't believe how gross."

Will mutters, "She's kicking your ass at this game."

I turn to look at him. He's hunched over his phone, his long body pretzeled into the tiny seat. He's wearing a hooded sweatshirt and a faded green baseball cap pulled low over his unkempt hair. He hasn't shaved, and he's so absorbed in whatever he's typing that his glasses have slipped to the very end of his nose. Basically, he looks like a handsome vagrant, not someone who speaks four dead languages.

I nudge him. "They just closed the door. You can't text in here."

He nudges me back. "Try to stop me."

I snatch his phone away. He grabs for it, but I hold it out of reach. "I need that!" he protests.

"You are so addicted to this thing."

"Addicted," he says. "*I'm* addicted."

"Please. I'm an amateur compared to you."

He reaches for it again, but I hold it tight. "Ian has a question about my research proposal," he says, laughing. "I have to answer!"

"The first step toward recovery," I tell him, "is admitting that you have a problem."

He folds his hands in his lap. "I have a problem."

"A serious problem."

"I'm a very sick person," he says obediently, "and I need help."

"Good boy." I look at the phone more closely as I hand it back to him. "Wait—is this new?"

"It's my work phone," he replies, finishing his text.

"The museum gave you a phone?"

"For when I travel." He powers off the phone and slips it into his pocket. "All the curators get one."

"That makes sense," I say. "In case one of those burning archaeological emergencies crops up."

Will sighs. "Here we go."

"Like if those pesky Nazis try to steal the Ark of the Covenant again."

He takes my hand. "Have I ever told you how much I appreciate the respect you have for my work?"

I kiss his cheek. "You're welcome, baby."

We finally take off. Lola and I have a friendly-but-sort-of-not tussle over the shared armrest. I doze for a while. An elderly woman comes out of the restroom. I unbuckle my seat belt.

Lola eyes me dubiously. "You goin' in there?"

"Sure. Why?"

"I never use the toilet after some old lady."

"Seniors," I say. "They're so tidy."

"They're filthy sluts," she informs me.

I slap her leg. "Lola, you crack me up!"

"What do they give a shit about STDs? They're basically dead! My great-aunt Rita, she's eighty-four? She's got a colostomy bag, and, like, rickets? Had gonorrhea three times!"

"Poor lady!" I say.

Lola snorts. "Auntie Rita ain't no lady, honey."

Will sticks some kind of bran muffin from hell in my face. "Why don't you try to eat something?"

Looking at it makes my stomach churn all over again. "I don't think I can."

"One bite?"

I take one bite, to please him.

"He's a keeper," Lola announces. "He's a prize."

I rest my head on his shoulder. "I know."

"Mine impregnified a stripper at his father's bachelor party," she continues.

"Wait," I say. "His *father's* bachelor party?"

"Fourth marriage," Lola explains.

"Sounds like my family. Was this before you guys met, or . . . ?"

"Nah. Benny and me been together since high school. But he made it up to me. See?" She shows me her engagement ring.

"Beautiful," I say.

"Big-ass," she agrees.

"What happened to the baby?"

"Cordelia's almost three," Lola tells me. "So cute! Gonna be the flower girl." She picks up her phone. "Lemme see if I got a picture."

We have a layover in Miami. Our plane to Key West is smaller, and the rows have only two seats. I have no one to talk to but Will, and his nose is buried in a book.

I nudge him. "What are you reading about?"

"Epictetus," he says, not looking up.

"The suburb of Cleveland?"

Will turns a page. "That's the one."

I nudge him again. "I'm bored. Talk to me."

"Why don't you read a book?"

"I'm not *that* bored. Tell me about Epictetus."

He closes his book and adjusts his glasses. "He was an ancient philosopher. A Stoic. He was born into slavery in the first century AD, in what's now Turkey. But he lived most of his life in Rome and Greece."

I snuggle into my seat. I love listening to Will talk about his intellectual interests. He's so adorably precise and methodical. Long, complicated sentences roll right out of him. It's kind of like being engaged to an audiobook.

I pick up one of his hands and start to play with it.

"Epictetus believed that our capacity for choice is our greatest strength and the source of our freedom. It allows us to recognize the very limited number of things in life that are within our actual control."

I like Will's hands. They're strong and calloused—from all his field-work, I guess. He's got long fingers with big knuckles. Bony wrists. I hold one of my hands up and compare them, palm to palm.

He breaks off midsentence. "Are you trying to distract me?"

"Of course not!" I let go of his hand. "Why, is it working?"

"Always." He smiles down at me. "Where were we?"

"Choice. Freedom. Control."

"Right." He collects his thoughts. "Epictetus believed that all human suffering is the result of our futile attempts to control things that are not within our power to control. Our bodies, our possessions. External events. Other people."

"Epictetus was anti-suffering?" I say. "What a coincidence—*I'm* anti-suffering!"

"Only by renouncing our desires and attachments can we obtain a measure of inner peace and live in harmony with the universe."

"I'm *really* thirsty," I say. "Would you mind renouncing your attachment to that orange juice on your tray?"

"Why don't I renounce it onto your head?"

"I don't think that would be harmonious with the universe, Will."

"True," he agrees. "But it would provide me with some much-needed inner peace."

By the time we land in Key West I'm feeling a thousand times better.

I spot Mom the instant we walk into the terminal. She's leaning against a wall with her hands shoved deep in her pockets, saying something to a little grey-haired woman who's hopping from one foot to the other, scanning the new arrivals anxiously. Mom's faded auburn hair is pulled into a messy ponytail, and her ivory skin—the sign of a true Florida native—seems to glow amid the peeling tourists in their tropical shirts. She looks relaxed and natural. Nowadays I only see her when she and Gran visit me in New York. She looks so out of place there, an anxious, scruffy stray among the hyper-groomed lynxes prowling the streets of Manhattan. Here, she belongs—which explains why she never wants to leave. That and her business. She renovates old buildings, historic Florida architecture, mostly. She's become a real expert. She dresses the part, too: paint-spattered cargo shorts, old t-shirt, work boots.

Mom sees me and launches herself off the wall. She throws her arms around me, already sniffling. What a softy.

"Lily! You're really here!"

"I'm here," I say into her hair, which smells like lemons and sawdust.

She releases me, laughing and wiping her eyes, and we both turn to Will. "This is my mother, Katherine," I tell him. "Mom, this is Will."

Yes. They're meeting for the first time.

Mom's speechless. She turns pink. "This is . . . I'm so . . . this is amazing!" She ignores his outstretched hand and hugs him, too.

The grey-haired lady is hovering around us. "Oh, sorry!" Mom says. "I forgot! Lily and Will, this is Mattie."

Mattie. Our wedding planner. Mom hired her five months ago, when Will and I got engaged and decided to have the wedding down here. Although "hired" might be the wrong word. Liberated from an asylum? Rescued from a storm drain, where she was adjusting the antenna on her mind-control helmet and crooning to the manatees? Because Mattie is completely—

"Thank *goodness* you made it!" She clutches my hand in her skinny little paw. "I was so *worried*. The weatherman said there was a low-pressure zone over the Southeast, and a storm building over the Atlantic. All I could think about was you and Will, trapped on a *plane*!" Her bright blue eyes widen. "There was a flight stranded last year in Minneapolis for twenty-eight hours! A seeing eye dog had a *seizure*! What if that happened to *you*?"

Help me, Epictetus. Luggage finally starts tumbling onto the carousel. Mattie is standing right next to me. I edge away. She fidgets closer. I'm about to tell her that she's going to need a flashlight pretty soon when she clears her throat and says, "Lily? Did you get my . . . my thing?"

"Your thing?"

"Yes, my, my . . . oh, God bless it!" She slaps her forehead. "What's the word? My . . . you know . . . with the . . . ?" And she wiggles her fingers.

"Piano?" I say, taking a wild stab.

"No no no, it's the thing with the . . . and you use the . . . ?" She's still doing the finger thing.

"Gloves?" I say. "Fake fingernails? Little baby worms?"

"*E-mail!*" she cries. "Did you get my e-mail?"

Mattie has a bad memory. It made our phone conversations a challenge. "No," I say. "Nothing today."

She frowns. "Aren't computers so unreliable?"

"Actually, they're pretty—"

"I'll just tell you what I wrote. I wrote—" She breaks off and starts whirling around. "The gown! Where's the wedding gown?"

"It's okay," I say, trying to calm her down. "Freddy's got it."

"Well, he'd better give it *back*!"

My hangover is threatening to return with a vengeance. Fortunately Will steps in. "Freddy is Lily's maid of honor. She made the dress. She's flying into Miami this afternoon and driving down with another bridesmaid."

Mattie nods slowly. "I see. That's . . . well, I don't want to question your judgment, but I don't think that's a very good idea. There's that low-pressure zone, and you know how inexperienced drivers skid right off Seven-Mile Bridge *all* the time. . . ."

Our suitcases finally appear, and we head out to the parking lot. I glance at Mom.

"Don't," she says.

I hold up my hands. "I didn't."

"Our options were very limited," she points out.

"I didn't say anything, Mom!"

She ignores me, getting all worked up. "This is what happens when you're in such a rush to get married!"

I tilt my face to the sun. The sky is a brilliant blue, and a breeze off the ocean rustles the leaves of the tall palms circling the parking lot. Hard to believe that only five hours ago Will and I were in slushy, grey New York. "Relax, Mom. Mattie's a gem. She's going to be a wonderfully Zen influence on us all."

We both laugh. Then she asks, "Are you happy to be home?"

I hear the concern in her voice. I turn and see it in her eyes. I throw my arm around her shoulders and kiss her cheek. "Very."

She looks like she's about to say more, but instead she starts helping Will load our suitcases into the trunk of Mattie's car.

"Now, Lily." Mattie glances at me in the rearview as she steers out of the lot. "First thing tomorrow we need to go to Blue Heaven and review the menu for the rehearsal supper."

"Aye aye, Cap'n."

"Oh, I'm not the captain of this ship!" Mattie laughs. "I'm just the . . . the . . ."

"Bosun?" I say.

"Swabbie?" Will suggests.

"Master gunner?"

"Powder monkey?"

Mom turns around and gives us a look like Children, please.

"*First mate,*" Mattie says brightly. "You're the captain, and I'm the first mate. But about the rehearsal. We have a number of options. We can do fish, or we can do pasta, or chicken, or chicken with pasta, or fish and chicken *together,* although I'm not sure that's wise. . . ."

We're driving along the south shore of the island. To our left is Smathers Beach. Sails dotting the horizon, volleyballs flying through the air, pale bodies littering the sand. Bicyclists and skateboarders and drunks clutching paper sacks. Standard Florida wintertime fun.

"They do an excellent appetizer. It's called . . . oh, I forget what it's called. Something to do with raw seafood. But perhaps that's not a good idea, now that I'm giving it a little bit of a think. Perhaps not. After all, you wouldn't want to *poison* everyone the night before the wedding. . . ."

"Not everyone," Will says agreeably.

We pass a block of shabby pink condos, a scrubby park, a motel. We could be anywhere—anywhere poor and southern and sad—except that to our right, visible between buildings and through rusted chain-link fences, are the salt ponds, long abandoned, slowly being reclaimed by the mangroves, and the feeding pelicans, and the silence.

I lean forward and tap Mom on the shoulder. "When do Jane and Ana get here?"

"They arrived last night," she replies.

"Really?"

"Yep!" She quickly turns to Mattie and asks her a question.

"Your stepmothers?" Will asks. I nod. The wedding isn't for six more days. I wonder why they're here already.

Mattie takes a right, then a left onto Truman. We pass an auto-parts store, a self-storage lot, a supermarket. A large strip club, its parking lot empty this early on a Sunday. All at once, things get lush. The vegetation takes over, crowding the ramshackle buildings on their tiny lots. Palm and banana-flower trees, snow bushes and oleander, hibiscus. A million other trees and shrubs whose names I don't remember, or never knew. And bougainvillea everywhere, trailing along the white picket fences and climbing the low concrete walls, crazy and pink and relentless.

We're on White Street now, entering my old neighborhood. Bring on the quaint! The streets are narrow, some only one-way alleys dark with foliage. The sidewalks are cracked and weedy. But the homes—tiny shotgun cottages, towering Victorians, pastel conch houses—are beautiful. They flash by, only a detail springing out here and there. A set of tall white shutters. A sloping tin roof. A porch ceiling painted sky blue.

I relax into the backseat and squeeze Will's hand. I thought it would be strange, coming home. I thought it would be hard after so long. But it feels natural. It's like a warm embrace.

Meanwhile, Mattie has barely paused for breath. "Martin has recommended gardenias for the centerpieces, but I wonder whether that strikes the right tone."

"Who's Martin?" Will asks.

"The florist," Mattie says. "He's very talented, but I'm worried that he's not quite . . ." She taps her forehead. "*All there,* if you know what I mean."

A scrawny chicken darts across the road. Two kids on bikes appear out of nowhere, racing alongside the car. A girl and a boy, maybe ten, maybe twelve. My heart stops. It's me and Teddy. For an instant I'm sure of it. The boy has sun-streaked, shaggy hair. The girl is all arms and legs. They're screaming with laughter, swerving around potholes, banging into each other. The boy glances over his shoulder and starts pedaling faster. They veer down a side street, skidding, almost crashing. The boy hollers. The girl shrieks. Our car keeps moving.

I twist around, craning my neck to look out the back window. But I'm too late. They're gone.

Will is watching me. "Friends of yours?"

I try to think of an answer, but I can't. So I shake my head, and smile, and say nothing.

3

A few more turns, a few more beautiful old Florida blocks, and we're home. Our bags are barely out of the trunk before Mattie tears off, muttering something about napkin rentals. I gaze up at the house. My house. It's an old island Queen Anne with a double-decker veranda and a round tower on one side. Lavish scrollwork drips from every available surface, barely visible through the palms and the banyans in our tiny front yard.

Will looks impressed. "You grew up here?"

"It seemed so much bigger back then," I say.

"Maybe the new color makes it look smaller," Mom suggests. "Do you like it? I did a little research at the preservation commission last year—this is the original yellow."

Will turns to her with amazement. "How did you match it?"

Mom launches into an earnest explanation as he listens, rapt. He's not kissing her ass, either—he lives for random historical details like this. I push through the wooden gate and run up the steps.

Ana is hovering just inside the front door. "Lilybear!" She hurls herself at me like a tiny tornado. "How the hell are you? How was the flight? Look at your hair—good Christ!"

Will follows me in. "Is this Will?" Ana says. "Listen to me—what a moron. Of course it's Will!"

"Will, my stepmother Ana. Ana, Will."

He holds out his hand. "This is such an honor."

She takes his hand in both of hers and gives him a dazzling smile. "I can't tell you how much I appreciate that, Will. I get far more death threats than compliments. Last week, I—"

"Ana. You're tearing his arm off."

"Sorry!" She lets loose with her raucous laugh. "Professional hazard."

Will laughs, too. He seems totally comfortable around her, which is a relief. Ana tends to intimidate people. She's in Congress—serving her eighth term in the House, one of the distinguished gentlewomen from California—so she's got a real aura of power about her, which is somehow magnified by the fact that she's barely five feet tall. She's fierce and scrappy—famous for her tirades on the Sunday talk shows and for antagonizing her constituents at town-hall meetings. She'll say anything, to anyone, which tends to provoke either fanatical devotion or homicidal rage.

She looks wonderful. I haven't seen her since July, when she was in New York for a fund-raiser. There, she was dressed in one of her ugly power suits and all cranky from having to ask rich people for money. Here, she's the real Ana—long hair loose, eyes twinkling. I hug her again. "I'm so glad you're here," I whisper.

She whispers back, "We need to talk."

"Lily darling." We all look up as Jane descends the staircase. She's wearing a shimmery blue dress and scary-high heels. Her perfectly straight, perfectly platinum hair floats gently around her. She zeroes in on Will, showing him her expensive teeth. The poor boy is going to go blind from all this smiling.

"Will, this is my stepmother Jane," I say. "Jane, Will."

She holds out an elegant hand. "I hope your flight down wasn't as wretched as mine," she says, in her flat, slightly bored voice. She's looking him in the eye, but I know she's also appraising every inch of him—clothes, shoes, haircut.

"Oh, no!" Will says, sincerely concerned. "You had a rough flight?"

But she's already turned to me, all business. "Let me see it."

I give her my left hand. She scrutinizes the ring from a distance, then closer. She turns it on my finger. Her brow would be furrowing right now, except that it hasn't done that in years. She looks up at me at last. "Where is the diamond?"

Will clears his throat. "There isn't one. It's a replica of a Roman ring in the British Museum. The Romans didn't use gemstones in their—"

"And why is it all . . . scratched like this?" Jane asks, picking at the ring with a sharp fingernail.

"I had an inscription added," Will says hopelessly. "In Latin."

I pull my hand away. "Give it a rest, Janey. I love my ring."

"So do I," says Mom, coming through the front door. "It's very artisanal."

I can feel Will cringing. He hates that word. Jane gives me a look of boundless pity, then drifts toward the living room. Will watches her go. I squeeze his arm sympathetically. I always marvel at how Jane is the opposite of Ana, in almost every way. She's cultured and poised. A fancy society type who spends her time organizing galas and minimizing her cleavage wrinkles. Condescending to maître d's and pretending to care about art. Hiring huntsmen to lead all the younger, prettier women into the woods and . . . you know.

"Gran!" I yell.

"Kitchen!" she yells back. Something crashes in the distance.

I turn to Ana, who's typing on her phone. "She's not cooking, is she?" Ana nods grimly.

"Is that a bad thing?" asks Will.

Before I can answer, Gran shoots through the dining room with crazy hair and flour on her nose. "Finally!" she growls. I get another crushing hug. Then she leans in to smell my breath.

"Cut it out!" I whisper, pushing her away. "Gran, this is Will. Will, this is my grandmother Isabel."

Gran looks him up and down while she takes his hand. "What a pleasure," she says. "I've heard *so little* about you."

He laughs. "I've heard a lot about you."

I clap my hands together. "I have an idea—let's go out for lunch!"

Gran yanks on a lock of my hair. "Nice try. Food's ready."

We file into the dining room and sit down. The table is a crime scene. There's a sickly looking salad, slabs of greyish meat heaped on a platter and a tureen filled with . . . I don't even know what that is. Gruel, maybe? We fill our plates dutifully. Silence descends, interrupted by occasional gagging noises.

"Thank you, Isabel," Will says. "This is delicious."

Ana smothers a laugh. Mom sighs. Jane shakes her head sadly.

Gran points her fork at Ana, who's checking her phone. "Put that machine away before I toss it into the fucking street."

"Mother, please!" Mom says. "We have a guest!"

"I'm expecting an important e-mail," Ana protests.

"Do it, Izzie," Jane drawls. "You'd be performing a public service."

I catch Jane's eye and hold up my lemonade glass. I mouth, *Vodka?* She pretends not to understand.

Sunlight is filtering through the tall windows and bathing my mother figures in a heavenly glow. I'm so happy to see them—they're rarely all in one place like this. I look over at Will. He's fidgeting in his seat and moving his silverware around, aligning it with the edge of the table. He steals a glance at them across the table, then looks away. But when Mom leans toward him to say something, he responds with a big, goofy grin. So he's not too overwhelmed. Good.

"Why are you guys here already?" I ask Jane and Ana.

Jane smiles serenely. "Lovely to see you too, darling."

"Seriously. The wedding isn't for a week."

She shrugs, touching the glittering pendant of her necklace. "You know I can't stand New York in February."

"A likely story." I turn to Ana. "What about you?"

"The House is in recess."

"There's nobody running the government?" I widen my eyes. "How is anything going to get done?"

She chucks a roll at me. "Aren't you funny."

"So, Will," Gran says sharply. He snaps to attention. "Lily tells me your mother is Anita Field."

"Yes, ma'am."

"Anita Field," Ana says. "How do I know that name?"

"She's the United States Attorney in Chicago," I explain. Ana nods and rises, picking up her empty glass. I raise mine. *Vodka?* She rolls her eyes and disappears into the kitchen.

"A federal prosecutor for a mother," Jane remarks. "How was that, growing up?"

"A little like Guantanamo," Will says cheerfully. "Before they banned torture."

"Your mother has an excellent conviction rate," Gran allows.

"Did you ever try any cases against her?"

"Never," Gran says. "And now I never will."

Will looks puzzled. "Izzie retired in December," Jane explains.

Gran snorts. "Retired, my ass. Forced out is more like it."

"Oh, Mother," Mom says. "You know it was time."

Gran is—was—a criminal defense attorney. One of the best in south Florida. She opened her own practice right after law school, when none of the good old boys would hire her. It wasn't work for a woman, they said, but she quickly proved them wrong. She was smart and tenacious and hardworking. And she won—a lot. She quickly moved on from representing petty criminals to really big cases—drug smuggling, police corruption, capital murder. She built her own firm from the ground up, hiring and training other lawyers, working all over the state.

When I was little, I used to sneak in and watch Gran at work. You could do that in the courts in Key West back then. She held juries in the palm of her hand. She tied witnesses up in knots. She stood up to other lawyers—often smug, self-righteous men—and outsmarted them, over and over again. It looked like so much fun.

Unfortunately, Gran had been slowing down for a few years. She was crankier than usual. Forgetting things and making mistakes. Her partners finally intervened. She wasn't happy about it, but she couldn't deny the truth of what they were saying. So she very reluctantly stepped down.

"I can't imagine what life would be like without work," Will says to her. "It must be a hard transition."

Gran is touched by his sympathy. She hides it by jabbing me with her fork. "Elbows off the table! You've got the manners of a damn hillbilly."

Ana reappears from the kitchen and sits down. She looks at her plate, moving the food around warily with her fork. "What are we eating? Chicken?"

"I think it's pork," Mom says.

"It's fish," Gran says.

Will says, "I love the rice."

Gran says, "It's polenta."

"How is that possible?" Jane murmurs.

Gran throws her fork down. "Goddammit! I used a cookbook this time!"

"Think positive, Iz," Ana says. "Your kitchen skills could jump-start a new career. The legal profession's loss might be the prison food industry's gain."

We laugh. "To hell with all of you!" Gran shouts, but she's smiling.

"Seriously," I say, "it's hard to believe I haven't eaten this badly in thirteen years."

Will turns to me curiously. "What?"

The chatter at the table dies away. "I, um, haven't been back in a while," I explain.

"In thirteen *years*?"

Everyone is watching now. "More or less. Since I moved north to live with Dad and Jane. I sure have missed Gran's home cooking!" I give him a big, diversionary grin. It doesn't work.

"You never came back? Not even to visit?"

Mom saves me. "We don't give her a chance, Will. We're too happy to come to her." Gran nods in agreement, her fierce little eyes fixed on me.

"Tell us what you do, Will," Ana says quickly. "Something with museums, right?"

"I work at the Metropolitan Museum of Art," he replies, with a touch of pride that's totally adorable. "I'm an associate curator in the Department of Greek and Roman Art."

They look suitably impressed. At my urging he explains a bit more about what he does, some of the digs he's been on and articles he's written and exhibits he's designed. They're hanging on every word.

"I am astonished that we haven't met before now," Jane says. She turns on me. "Why haven't you brought Will uptown?"

I frown apologetically. "I wanted to, but there's that new ordinance."

"What new ordinance?"

"You can't travel north of Fifty-Ninth Street unless you have a white-hot poker shoved up your ass."

"Lily," Mom says. "Your language."

Jane just smiles. "Classy as ever, darling. Still, I expect to see you at my benefit in April. It's at the Pierre."

"Is it black tie?"

Jane looks appalled that I would even ask. "What other kind is there?"

I do like men in tuxedos. "We're so there."

I reach for another handful of potato chips. Jane catches my eye. "Remember, darling, marriages come and go, but wedding photographs are forever."

"Leave her alone," Ana snaps. "She's too thin as it is."

"It's those ridiculous hours," Mom adds.

"She needs to put in long hours if she wants to be a good lawyer," Gran says.

"Hello?" I wave at them. "She's right here in the room with you. Feel free to address her directly."

"When are you going to quit that awful firm?" Mom demands.

"When Ana hires me."

Ana chuckles. "Good one."

"We'd have so much fun! I want to be quoted in all the newspapers as Representative Mercado's 'trusted aide' and 'longtime political operative.'"

"Never going to happen, Lilybear," Ana says. "You'd be a huge liability."

"Exactly!" I say enthusiastically. "I'd distract the press from all your *real* scandals."

Ana only laughs.

"Why would Lily be a liability?" Will asks.

There's the briefest of awkward pauses before Ana says, "I'm only teasing! Great lemonade, Izzie!"

"Delicious," Jane agrees.

I head into the kitchen to find the damn vodka myself. When I come back, Will is saying, "Did you renovate this house yourself, Katherine?"

Mom blushes. "Almost twenty years ago. It was my first full restoration. That's why it looks so awful."

"It doesn't!" Will protests. "It's beautiful."

She waves him off. "I was such a rookie. I just cringe whenever I look at the joinery."

"Me too," Ana says. "I always think, nice place, but what's with the fucking joinery?"

"Oh, Ana," Mom sighs. She tells Will, "We don't usually curse this much."

"That's true," I say. "We reserve profanity for special occasions. Like divorces."

Will laughs. He likes them. And they like him, too—I can tell. He props his elbows on the table. "So, speaking of divorces . . ."

They all laugh—they've been waiting for this. "You want to know the batting order."

Will points at Mom. "I think . . . you were first, Katherine?"

"That's right," she says. "Then Ana, then Jane."

"I was followed by Annette," Jane explains. "But," she pauses delicately, "we're not close."

"Henry is currently married to Ekaterina," Ana says. "The mail-order bride."

"That's cruel," Jane says. "You know he paid extra for DHL."

They all laugh. "Trina is super sweet," I tell Will.

"Lily!" Ana cries. "She's three years younger than you are."

"She's so awesome! She set up my wireless."

"Have you met Henry?" Mom asks Will.

"Not yet. I'm a little nervous. Any words of wisdom?"

"Don't get in a drinking contest with him," Ana advises. "You'll lose."

"Don't let the British accent fool you," Gran says. "He's as dumb as a post."

"And whatever you do," Jane tells him, "don't look too deeply into his eyes. He'll hypnotize you. Like a snake."

Mom, Jane and Ana glance at one another, then dissolve into laughter. Gran snorts contemptuously and stands up to collect our plates.

"You all get along so well," Will marvels. "How did that happen?"

My mothers exchange another look, half proud, half bashful. "What's the quote, Kat?" Ana says. "Something like, before we could call each other sister, we had to call each other a lot of other things first."

"Before the laughter came the tears," Mom agrees.

"And the lawsuits," Jane notes.

"The restraining orders," Ana says, "the reconstructive surgeries."

Mom smiles. "Now we're one big, happy family."

"With one wonderful thing in common," Jane says.

They all look at me. "Aw," I say.

We choke down pie on the veranda while Mom shows Will around the house. They get into a real nerd groove talking about foundation piers and heart pine—I can hear them laughing upstairs. Eventually I call a taxi so that we can take our bags to the hotel.

Jane puts a hand on my arm. "Stay behind a minute. We'd like to speak with you about something."

I walk Will to the door. "Was it hell?"

He laughs. "Are you kidding? I'm in love with all of them."

"You can stop, idiot. They can't hear you." I reach on my tiptoes to kiss him. "See you at the hotel?"

"I'm meeting Javier at the airport at five. We'll find you after."

He leaves. I wander into the living room and stop short. They're all there, composed like some Victorian portrait: Jane and Gran on the green velvet sofa, Mom and Ana standing behind them. Everybody staring at me, looking dire and a little constipated.

"Do I have something in my teeth?" I say.

"He doesn't know a damned thing about you, does he?" Gran demands.

"Who, Will?"

"No," she snaps. "Mr. Clean."

Mom clears her throat nervously. "What your grandmother is trying to say, honey, is that we've talked it over, and—"

Ana cuts to the chase. "We think you should call off the wedding."

I sink slowly into a chair. "What?"

Jane leans forward and takes my hands in hers. "We love you, darling. You know that."

Ana nods. "But you're not exactly marriage material, are you?"

I have to laugh at this. "Are you serious? I'm getting a lecture on marriage from a bunch of divorcées?"

"Who better?" Jane counters. "We all know exactly what it's like to be married to someone who is, let's just say, constitutionally unsuited for it."

She looks at me meaningfully. I roll my eyes.

"Will seems like a very nice young man," Gran says.

"He's charming," Mom agrees.

"And kind, and intelligent," Jane adds. "And normal."

"He's all wrong for you," Ana says.

"Gosh, thanks."

"No no no, honey! That's not what we mean. It's just . . ." Mom pauses, struggling to articulate. "It's just that you're such a . . . a free spirit!"

"A live wire," Ana suggests.

"A brazen slut," says Jane.

The others glare at her. She shrugs as she adjusts a bracelet. "I really don't see the point in mincing words."

"Lilybear, we don't think you're ready. We don't want Will getting hurt. Or you, of course."

"You guys make me sound like a real nightmare."

"You're a very sweet person," Mom says. "You're the light of our lives. You're so full of joy, and fun—"

"And love! For Will!" I cry. "I'm so full of it!"

"Are you?" Ana fixes me with her no-bullshit stare. "Are you really?"

I stare right back. "So this is why you and Jane came down early. To stage a little intervention."

Gran starts jabbing one of her gnarly fingers at me. "Don't change the subject, Lillian Grace! You've been engaged for what, five months now? How long have you even known this boy?"

"Six months."

Gran shakes her head slowly. "What is the damned rush? You aren't pregnant, are you?"

They all freeze with these looks of complete horror on their faces.

"Of course not!" I retort.

They breathe a huge sigh of collective relief. Then they start right back up.

"Izzie's right," Ana says. "Do you really know Will? And does he know you?"

"Does he know about your . . . your various interests?" Mom asks delicately. "Your . . . you know, your habits?"

"He knows me well enough."

"He can't," Jane insists. "He wouldn't be here if he did."

"You obviously didn't tell him this is your first time back," Ana adds. "Does he know why you left?"

"No," I admit.

Gran scowls and throws up her hands.

"Ladies, ladies," I say breezily. "Aren't you being a bit dramatic about this?"

"No!" they all cry.

"Will and I are great together. Can't you see that? We have chemistry. We have good patter."

"Patter," Ana repeats. "You're marrying him because you have good patter."

"He's cute. He's sweet. He . . . he cooks!"

"Lily." It's Jane's turn to lock her eyes on mine. "Be serious, for a moment. Why are you doing this? Why marry someone you barely know?"

I don't answer.

"We think we have the right to ask," she adds.

I try to explain. But I have a hard time gathering my thoughts. Finally, I say, "Will is a really nice person. He's fun to talk to. We have a great time together."

"Those sound like reasons why he'd make a fine boyfriend, Lillian Grace," Gran says, with uncommon gentleness. "But they aren't reasons to marry him."

"Do you understand what marriage means, honey?" Mom asks. "It's not some joke. We're very concerned. We don't want to see you turn out like your—"

"Don't, Mother," I warn her. "Don't say it."

"You need to be honest with him about who you really are," Ana tells me.

"Or we will be," Jane adds.

I smile sweetly and give them the finger.

"Enough." Gran stands up. "We've said our piece. Please do us the courtesy of thinking it over." She heads for the kitchen, but stops. "By the way, I asked around about your future mother-in-law."

"And?"

"Watch yourself. She's a killer." With that, Gran vanishes through the swinging doors.

4

After another vodka lemonade and a few more attacks on my character, I escape my mothers and wander upstairs to my old bedroom. I guess I expected it to remain unchanged all these years, my relics preserved intact: the mangy patchwork quilt covering my narrow bed, the poodle lamp, my Harry Potter books. But no. My room is now an exercise studio. There's a treadmill, a mirrored wall and one of those exercise poles that women use for—

Oh, Lord. I really didn't need that image.

Still, the ghost of my old room lingers, in the height marks penciled on the door frame and the stickers plastered on the inside of the closet door. In the dozens of small cuts in the ceiling above the bed, from the hours Teddy and I spent lying on our backs, throwing knives and trying to make them stick.

I finally slip out of the house and head for the hotel. I take the side streets, dusty little alleys where working folks used to live. When I left Key West, a lot of these houses were pretty ramshackle—rotting wood siding, peeling shingles, scrubby yards. A few are still like that, but most have been renovated into blinding pastel perfection, with artfully disheveled landscaping and German cars parked in front. The fishermen and cigar makers wouldn't recognize their old homes. I guess it's progress.

It's a hot, still Sunday afternoon. Close by, a rooster crows. A man swears at it. A moped revs up in the distance. And just like that, I'm fourteen again. I've climbed out my bedroom window and shimmied down the Indian almond tree in the side yard, escaping yet another grounding. An endless Sunday afternoon stretches before me. I turn a corner, expecting to see Teddy leaning against a fence, waiting for me.

My phone rings, shattering the illusion. I glance at the display before I answer. "We were just talking about you."

"Darling, forgive me! My plane is delayed. I'm sitting in some vile airport bar, but all I can think about is how soon I'm going to be holding you in my arms."

My father's voice is ardent, eager, breathless. For about three seconds I am deeply confused.

Then I get it.

"You speed-dialed wrong, Dad."

There's a long pause. "Who is this?" he asks suspiciously.

I laugh. "How many people call you Dad, Dad?"

"Oh, *Lily*!" He laughs too. "Sorry, darling—I meant to call someone else."

Master of the obvious. "Should I ask who?"

He hesitates. "I think not."

"Right. Let me let you go."

"No, no, wait!" I hear ice cubes rattling in a glass and the murmur of nearby conversation. "I'm bored, little one. Amuse me. Tell me the news."

I turn a corner, trailing my hand along a picket fence. "Get this. They want me to call off the wedding."

"What?" he cries. "Who?"

"The coven. They say it's not fair to Will. That he doesn't really know me."

"As if that's a reason not to marry a person," Dad scoffs.

"So . . . you don't agree?"

I hear him say, "Another of the same, please." Back to me: "Of course not! Those women haven't a clue what they're talking about. Think about it, Lily. The human heart is the darkest of all mysteries. Who among us can honestly say he knows, *truly* knows, anyone else? Who even knows himself? Not you. *Certainly* not me. Why, the other day I found myself . . ."

I close my eyes and let it wash over me. My father has the most beautiful voice. It's low and melodious. Posh. Like melted English toffee.

"Can you imagine what would happen if people *knew* their spouses properly before marrying them?" he's saying. "It would be a calamity!

The institution would wither and die. The family unit would disinte-grate. Humanity," he concludes grandly, "would *perish*."

I open my eyes. "But Dad. What if Will and I get married and real-ize later that we're not suited for each other?"

"Darling," he chuckles. "What do you think divorce is for?"

I try to break it down for him. "Look, Henry. I can't get married thinking that if it doesn't work out, I can walk away. The moms put on this big, jokey act for Will just now, pretending that the divorces were no big deal. The divorces were mini Hiroshimas. I never want to get divorced. What if I have children?"

Dad says, "Thank you, that's lovely, cheers." Then he sighs heavily into the phone. "I find all this talk of children so fatiguing. We're ob-sessed with children nowadays. Think about the children. What about the children. Suffer the little children. What people don't realize is that divorce is *wonderful* for children."

"What?"

"Divorce prepared you to face the world, little one. It taught you about the fundamental instability of the universe. The inevitability of change. It showed you that the only thing you can depend on in life is that nothing will remain the same."

"So the horrific breakups were all for my benefit? Wow, Dad. That's—"

He doesn't even hear me. "It doesn't surprise me in the least that gay people want the right to marry. They simply want their children to have the same advantages that the children of heterosexuals have."

"The advantage of being from a broken home?"

"Precisely!"

"This isn't exactly helpful, Daddy."

More rattling ice cubes. "Lily, don't you know I'm only joking?"

"You are?"

"Well, no," he admits. "I suppose I'm quite serious."

"Dad . . ."

"I'm *sorry,* darling. You know I'm rubbish at these emotional conver-sations. If you're asking my opinion, I think you ought not to take it all so seriously. You should just . . . keep your chin up, and all that. Go with the flow, follow your heart, and . . . et cetera, et cetera."

I don't say anything.

"Look," he continues. "Don't do anything drastic, and stop letting those women fill your ear with poison. I'll be down there in a few days, and I'll stand by your side. We'll fight off whatever they throw at you. What do you say?"

"Yeah, Dad. Sounds super."

"That's the spirit! Cheers, love! Bye!"

We hang up, and I turn onto the walkway to our hotel. It's an old 1930s place with a tiled roof and creamy stucco walls, perched on the south end of the island. Sharing my fears with my father hadn't exactly been comforting. But what was I thinking, asking him for guidance? This was the man who'd urged me to go to Harvard Law School instead of Yale based on a single night he'd spent in Cambridge years ago, drinking perfect martinis at the Charles Hotel. Good judgment isn't exactly his strong suit.

Also, the martinis at the Charles? Way too weak.

I wonder what Will's going to make of Henry. My father has organized his entire life around a single principle: maximizing his own pleasure. He's carefree. Uncomplicated. Doesn't overthink things. Arguably doesn't think at all. He has no fears for the future, no regrets about the past. He simply goes where his inclinations take him. Thanks to a few hardworking ancestors who spent the nineteenth century sailing around the world, buying and selling (and stealing) things, Henry never had to earn a living. After getting kicked out of Oxford, he decided to become a novelist, so he moved to Key West, where he met Mom. He never finished the book—he liked the drinking and fishing parts of the Hemingway myth more than the backbreaking hours at a desk. So he decided to get into the movie business, which took him to L.A., where he met Ana. When that didn't work out, he headed for New York to try his hand at philanthropy—and, it turns out, Jane.

It's a little hard to explain Henry to someone like Will, who's so serious and intellectual, so focused on his career. Their meeting should be interesting.

The lobby of the hotel is cool and pleasant, with rugs scattered on the mahogany floors and ceiling fans turning lazily above. French doors along the back wall are open to the beach. A package from the firm is waiting for me at the front desk. Good—I could use some professional distraction.

I find our room, which is airy and bright, with a balcony overlooking the water. The package contains a binder and a note from Lyle: "Enjoy the first two e-mails."

I open the binder. I read the first two e-mails. Lyle picks up on the first ring. "What."

"Are you kidding me with this shit?"

"Will you guys give me a minute?" Lyle says to someone. To me: "I don't have a lot of time, so shut up and listen. Here's what you have to do. Meet with Hoffman. Do a standard deposition prep. Then, help him come up with a plausible explanation for why he's such a stupid son of a bitch."

"Can we back up a minute?" I say. "I don't work on this part of the case. I work on the environmental claims, remember? I don't know anything about Hoffman or this accounting stuff."

"It's deposition prep, Wilder. Not rocket science."

"Right." I stretch out on the bed and start flipping through the rest of the binder. "And I'm sure you would love to see me screw up and look bad in front of Philip. But do you think maybe you could clue me in a little bit, so that this deposition isn't a complete disaster?"

"Fine." I hear his chair creak as he leans back. "Where do you want to start?"

"Explain why the plaintiffs want to depose an accountant in a lawsuit about an oil spill."

"Oil spill," Lyle repeats. "I'm not familiar with that term. Perhaps you're referring to the alleged industrial accident on an offshore oil rig that allegedly caused the dispersal of certain quantities of unrefined petroleum into the Gulf of Mexico?"

"Whatever, Lyle. The rig exploded, millions of barrels of oil spewed into the Gulf, and plaintiffs are suing EnerGreen on behalf of all the people whose lives were ruined by this colossal fuckup."

"Alleged colossal fuckup," he says.

"Where does the accounting come in?"

I hear muffled voices. "No," Lyle says. "I said double-sided. This is useless to me. Do it over." Back to me: "So, after the *alleged* incident, our client, EnerGreen Energy, took a big hit on its financial statements, based on losses it anticipated from the spill."

"Compensation to the victims, fines, et cetera, right? It was fifty billion or something insane like that." I get up and carry the binder out onto the balcony, where I drop into a chair.

"Right," Lyle replies. "But according to the amended complaint filed last month, EnerGreen allegedly inflated that figure to hide losses suffered in another part of the company. The plaintiffs are now claiming that EnerGreen exploited a horrific environmental disaster to conceal unrelated wrongdoing."

I'd read those new allegations, but assumed it was all a bunch of empty rhetoric to make EnerGreen sound worse than it is. "Do they have any proof?"

"Solid proof?" Lyle says. "No. But there are discrepancies in EnerGreen's financial statements that seem to support the plaintiffs' argument."

"What discrepancies?"

"It's some technical accounting thing," he says dismissively. "Urs says the finance people can easily explain it. But it looks shady, which is all the plaintiffs care about."

I prop my feet up on the railing and look out at the water. There's a fishing boat anchored close to shore, and a man standing in the bow casting for bait. With one long, graceful sweep of his arm, he sends the net spinning lightly onto the waves. Seagulls circle hungrily. Thirty yards out, the turquoise water turns darker where the ocean floor drops away.

"So what's Hoffman's role in all this?" I ask.

"He reviewed EnerGreen's financial statements before they went to the outside auditors. He's the person who would be responsible for catching any mistakes or shifty accounting tricks." Lyle pauses. " 'Midlevel CPA nobody' is his official title. But as you've seen, he also holds the unofficial post of immortal poet of the golden age of e-mail."

I open the binder and read Hoffman's first e-mail out loud:

> From a financial reporting perspective, this oil spill is the best goddamn thing that ever happened to us.

"Gives me shivers," Lyle says. "Every time."

I turn to the second e-mail:

> I'll give these loss estimates a good old scrub-a-dub before
> they go to Ernst & Young. It's kind of a scam, but who's going
> to notice?

"It's kind of a scam," Lyle repeats dreamily. "Not a full-blown scam, not a big scam, or a little scam, but . . . *kind of* a scam. The ambiguity is thrilling."

"So are the plaintiffs right? Did EnerGreen commit fraud?"

"Come on, Wilder," he says impatiently. "You know how this works. Some idiot dashes off a terrible e-mail, and random plaintiffs take it completely out of context to show that the whole company is a massive criminal enterprise. Hoffman's an idiot. A drudge. He doesn't know anything."

"Good."

"But EnerGreen still doesn't want him testifying about the e-mails. If there's the slightest suspicion that something funny is going on with their financial reporting, the DOJ and the SEC will be all over them. Add that to the ongoing PR nightmare of the botched cleanup efforts, the protesters, the lost business? Forget it."

I watch a couple of windsurfers skidding across the surface of the water. Looks like fun. "Why doesn't EnerGreen just settle?"

"Because they're rich Texas assholes who don't want to pay twenty billion dollars to a bunch of shrimp-boat captains."

"Urs isn't an asshole," I point out. "Or Texan."

Urs is the EnerGreen in-house counsel assigned to our case. He's a transplant from the company's European division, which is based in Geneva. He's supposed to be supervising our work, but he's terrified of Philip and has no idea how American-style litigation works. Another sterling example of our client's negligence—assigning a foreign regulatory attorney to a $20 billion lawsuit. Not that it matters, in this case— they have Philip.

"Just keep it simple, okay?" Lyle says. "You need to prepare Hoffman to deal with aggressive questioning by skilled opposing counsel. You

need to teach him how to listen and how to answer without actually saying a damn thing. He needs to sound calm, friendly and credible. After
you do all that, you need to help him explain those e-mails. Maybe they
were a joke. Maybe he was hacked. Maybe he accidentally took his wife's
Xanax instead of his Lipitor and spent the day writing schizo e-mails to
the entire office. Whatever. He needs a coherent story that establishes
why the e-mails aren't relevant to the lawsuit. Philip will take care of the
rest at the deposition itself."

"Gotcha," I say.

"Good. Don't fuck this up." Then a click, and he's gone.

5

I walk back inside the room and flop onto the bed. I'm drifting off when my phone pings with a text.

—here thirsty come now

I find Freddy and Nicole sipping frothy drinks by the pool. Freddy is wearing a yellow muumuu and cat's-eye sunglasses, her shiny black hair in a knot at the top of her head. Nicole is slouched across from her, texting, of course.

"Bridesmaidens!" I cry. "How was the drive?"

"Heaven!" Freddy gushes. "Ninety miles of shell shops and tacky souvenir stands. We stopped at an amazing state park for a swim."

"I got stung by a jellyfish," Nicole mutters.

"Poor Nickie!" I rub her arm sympathetically, but she barely looks up from her phone.

"We had conch fritters for lunch," Freddy says. "Delicioso!"

"A little less grease would have been nice," Nicole remarks.

"This hotel is fantastic!" Freddy adds. "We're right down the hall from you."

"You guys are sharing a room?"

"Why not?" Nicole replies. "This wedding is costing a fortune. And it's not like I'm going to meet anyone here."

She gazes gloomily at the happy people splashing in the pool. Freddy catches my eye and mimes hanging herself, then shooting herself, then stabbing herself in the face.

Nicole finishes her drink and hauls herself upright. "Early flights kill me. I'm going to take a nap."

We watch her shuffle into the hotel. "Was she like that the whole way down?"

"She was worse," Freddy replies.

"Sorry."

"It was okay. I spent most of the drive planning a nice little murder-suicide scenario for us."

The bartender arrives. "Another pink squirrel?" he asks Freddy. She nods.

I smile up at him. "Make it two, Lloyd." We watch him walk away.

"After a lot of thought, I decided to bust through a guardrail and drive off a bridge," Freddy says. "It was going to be like *Thelma and Louise,* except less about female empowerment and more about Thelma just wanting Louise to shut the fuck up."

"What stopped you?"

"Your wedding dress. It was in the trunk of the car."

I pat her hand fondly. "The sacrifices you make."

She shrugs. "We're driving back together. I figure I have another shot."

Our pink squirrels arrive. We clink glasses. We drink.

"Hey!" She kicks me under the table. "You bailed on us last night."

"Sorry. Work was . . ." I shake my head. "Crazy."

"Was your boss there?"

"No," I say quickly. "Definitely not."

She scrutinizes me over the rim of her glass. "Is that right."

Time to change the subject. "Get this!" I tell her. "I'm not even on vacation yet. I have to prep a witness."

"You have to what a what?"

"It's for my big environmental case, the one about the oil spill in the Gulf a few years ago? There's this accountant who's going to be de-posed, and—"

Freddy holds up a hand. "Stop. I just died of boredom. Also, why are you pretending to be outraged? You love this. You're totally delighted."

I sip my drink. "I like my job. That's a crime now?"

"It should be." She gestures for another round. "You know who gets to love their jobs? Scotch tasters. Zookeepers. Elvis impersonators. Law-yers? It's not natural. There's something wrong with you."

"Probably." I check my phone. Nothing from Will. I text him:

—where u

He writes back:

—Javier just arrived. We'll be there soon.

—hurryup!!

—I will.

I toss my phone back in my bag. "Freddy?"

"Yes love?"

"Do you ever think Will seems a little too good to be true?"

She sets her drink on the table. "Nope."

"He's so perfect, he's so wonderful, he's so this and that and the other thing." I tilt my head back to catch the final pink dregs at the bottom of my glass. "He can't be all that."

"Yes he can," she says. New drinks arrive.

"You marry him, then."

"He's not my type. And anyway, he wants *you*. He's crazy about *you*. You walk into a room and his eyeballs fall out of their sockets and start rolling around on the floor like spastic little puppies."

"He met the moms at lunch."

"How did that go?"

"Amazingly well. I was sure he was going to get all nervous and dork out, but he was super charming."

"Will isn't that dorky, you know."

"Sure he is." I smile. "That's why I love him."

"A minute ago he was too good to be true," she says. "Now you love him?"

"God, Freddy, I don't know! Can't I not know? Who among us can say, with absolute certainty, that they love, *truly* love, the person they think they love?"

"Most people," Freddy says promptly. "No, wait. The vast majority of people. No, wait. Everybody."

I poke my straw around inside my glass. "They ambushed me afterwards. They think I should call off the wedding."

"Let me guess," she says. "That only made you more determined to do it."

I don't answer. She hails a waiter and asks for another round. Somewhere close by, a creature starts shrieking in agony. I look up to see a father hauling a flailing toddler out of the pool. "Cute," I say.

Freddy looks appalled. "The child?"

"Jesus, no! The dad."

"You scared me for a minute." She watches him, head tilted appraisingly. "Nah. Too skinny."

"They all talked as if it's *so* easy. Just," I snap my fingers, "stop the wedding."

"It is easy," Freddy tells me. "I've done it three times."

"Twice," I correct her. "Norman dumped *you*, if I recall."

"Only because he caught me with Zoe," she reminds me. "That makes it a tie."

"Why do you keep getting engaged to men? You can marry whoever you want now."

"Doctor Boog thinks I'm still seeking my parents' approval," Freddy explains.

"Interesting. Doesn't he know your parents are dead?"

"That doesn't matter, apparently. I have a general idea of what they'd like. He also says my efforts are doomed because I'm unrealistically optimistic about my capacity for change."

"He sounds fun."

A breeze rustles the palms above our heads. A waiter arrives with more pink squirrels. He sets them down. We watch him walk away. We clink glasses.

"So what are you going to do?" Freddy asks.

"About Will?"

"No," she says. "About the Israelis and the Palestinians."

I sip my new drink. "I'm going to see how things play out. I think it's going to be fine."

She yawns and stretches her arms over her head. "Well, you've got plenty of time to think it over."

"Do I?"

"No, idiot. You have six days."

"But they're the six days before my wedding," I say. "That makes them super long. Like dog years."

Freddy nods. Then she stops nodding. "You mean the opposite."

"What?"

"Dog years are short," she says. "Like, there are nine dog years in a human year. A dog that's seven is really ninety-six."

I think about that. "Nine times seven is eighty-one. Not ninety-six."

"You know what I mean."

We sit and watch the last of the sunbathers pack up their things in the dying light. A young couple strolls past us, hand in hand. A steel drum band starts playing at the bar. More drinks arrive. I smile at the new waiter. He smiles back. I watch him walk away.

"Now that guy," I begin.

"Is gay," Freddy finishes.

I sip my drink. "Maybe Will is marrying me for my money."

"The Wilder millions?" Freddy removes her sunglasses and polishes them with a napkin. "I thought your share was all tied up in trusts."

"That's the genius of his plan. He marries me now, waits until I'm fifty and come into my inheritance, and then—*bam!*—feeds me to the fishes."

"Twenty-three years is a hell of a long time to put up with you," she observes.

"He's patient. Patient and devious."

"I'm not buying it. Where is the lucky fella, anyway?"

"Picking up Javier at the airport."

"Javier," Freddy sighs. "At last we meet."

Freddy has spun an enormous fantasy around Will's best friend, based entirely on his name. "You are going to be so disappointed," I tell her.

She gives me a pitying look. "Jealous much?"

"He's whiter than I am!"

"Please," she scoffs. "You need to face the fact that my dusky Latin lover and I are going to make beautiful, pan-ethnic love all week, while you're stuck with the boring white dude. Again."

"I'm not only into white guys!"

"Racist!" she sings. "Honky lovah!"

"What about that Indian guy? The graduate student."

"Stalkers don't count," she replies.

"My point, Winifred, is that I thought he was cute."

"My point, Lillian, is that was only because he was a stalker."

"The black guy, then," I say. "The pickle maker. Lived in Brooklyn? He had an amazing—"

"Here's Will!" Freddy says brightly.

"Baby!" I leap up and kiss him. "And here's Javier! Javier, meet my best friend, Freddy. You'll be walking down the aisle together."

"Pleased to meet you," says blond, blue-eyed Javier Collins of Schaumburg, Illinois.

Freddy stares at him, speechless.

"Who's hungry?" Will asks.

Freddy takes my arm as we leave the bar.

"His mom's from Barcelona," I whisper. "One of those fair, northern Spaniards."

"I'll get you for this," she hisses.

"Don't be racist," I warn her. "Don't be a honky hater."

She pinches me. "I call this some bullshit false advertising."

I put my arm around her. "Whatever you say, Korean woman named Freddy. Whatever you say."

We drag Nicole out of bed and have dinner at an old-school Cuban restaurant on Catherine Street. At a bar down the block, a waitress tells us about a new place on William. We have a few drinks there, until Freddy decides she needs to go where Ernest Hemingway drank. We wander down Duval, the trashy neon heart of the island. Even on a Sunday night, the sidewalks are packed with herds of young people staggering around all drunk and shouty, drag queens, drugged-out hippies and ordinary people gazing openmouthed at the show. We pass strip clubs, Irish pubs, the occasional hookah lounge. Dive shops, hat shops, shops selling kitschy gifts made out of coconuts and palmetto leaves and conch shells, raunchy t-shirts, tacky lingerie, shot glasses, key chains.

And chicken art. So much chicken art.

We pass a juggler, a mime. Someone dressed as Darth Vader, playing a banjo. The restaurants are wide open to the warm, humid night. Live music pours out of some of the bars and clubs. Barely dressed women beckon from others. Cars race up and down the street, thumping with bass.

We drink at Sloppy Joe's for a while. A biker there tells us that if we really want to see where Papa drank, we should go to a place on Eaton Street. By midnight, we're at our fourth "Hemingway bar." Will goes to the bathroom. Javier and Freddy are talking with a couple of German tourists at the next table. Nicole is . . . I look around. I don't know where Nicole is.

I feel so relaxed and happy. It's great to be home.

Will comes back and sits down. He runs his hands through his hair, making it stick up in funny ways. But then, it usually sticks up in funny ways. Still, he seems nervous. I put a hand over his. "Are you okay, honey?"

"Yeah, I'm fine."

"Your parents arrive tomorrow, right? Are you worried?"

I haven't met my future in-laws. I was supposed to go to Chicago for Christmas, but an emergency in one of my cases intervened. Will gets a little tense whenever he talks about them—I think there must be some drama there.

"Worried? Not at all." He squeezes my hand.

"It's going to be great," I assure him. "Parents love me."

He smiles and kisses the side of my head.

I watch a rowdy bachelor party barge through the door. I go up to get another drink.

The in-laws, arriving tomorrow.

The wedding, six days away.

I look around. This place is boring. I leave.

I find myself in the restaurant next door. There's a super-cute guy sitting at the bar. He's got dark hair and a few days' worth of stubble. I sit down next to him. I smile at him. He smiles back.

"Okay okay okay." I hold up my hands in surrender. "You can buy me a drink."

He laughs sheepishly. "I'd love to. But . . . I'm married, just so you know."

"I'm engaged," I say. "Officially, that's a tie."

He looks puzzled. "Don't overthink it," I advise him. "Overthinking is overrated."

We start talking. His name is Tim.

"So Tim," I say.

"Tom," he says.

Maybe it's Tom.

"This marriage thing," I say. "How's it working out for you?"

He shrugs. "You know. It is what it is."

Quite the conversationalist. But with those eyes, who cares? We have another drink. I put my hand over his on the bar. He doesn't pull away. I turn his hand over. I stroke his palm lightly with my fingers. I brush my fingers across his wrist, feeling his pulse. I look up at him. "Where is this alleged wife of yours?"

He shifts in his seat. "She flies down in a few days. A friend of mine is getting married."

I smile at him. "What a coincidence. I'm here for a wedding too."

We're facing each other on our stools. I catch one of his knees between mine and hold it. I lean toward him. "Hey, Tom. Do you want to know a secret?"

He hesitates, then he looks me in the eye, and I know I've got him.

I lean closer, placing my hands on his thighs. "The state of Florida doesn't recognize marriages performed outside its borders."

He raises his eyebrows and smiles. "Is that true?"

"That is true." I slide my hands up his legs. "So unless you and your wife tied the knot here? You're not *actually* married right now."

He looks down, shaking his head, but he's still smiling. I stand and place my hands on his shoulders. I look into his eyes.

"You can trust me on this, Tom. I'm a lawyer."

He laughs, and I lean closer. He smells like the beach, like salt and sand and sunscreen. I slip a hand around the back of his neck, into his hair. I let my lips brush his ear. I say, "Let's go somewhere."

There's a tap on my shoulder.

"Come on, Noreen," Freddy says. "Time for your injection."

"Go away!" I hiss.

But of course she doesn't. Eventually I let her take my arm and lead me out the door.

"I don't know if you've heard, Winifred, but there's a special place in hell for women who don't help other women."

"You're lucky I'm the one who came looking for you and not Will," she says.

"I am lucky. I'm a lucky, lucky girl. And you're a good friend. A great friend. The bestest ever." I throw my arm over her shoulders.

A giant shard of concrete rears up and attacks me. I stumble. Freddy catches me.

Metaphor!

We return to the first bar. "Great, you found her," Will says. "Let's go."

Will and Javier hustle us into a pink taxi. Freddy rests her head on my shoulder. Javier is up front, talking to the driver. I lean back and look at Will's profile, flickering in and out of the light cast by the streetlamps as we drive up Duval. He's holding my hand, absently brushing his thumb back and forth across mine.

Why did I leave, why did I go roaming when I have this, right here? And I had to pick a *married* man, of all people? Classy, as Jane would say. She should talk, though. My moms have a hell of a lot of nerve, presuming to tell me who is and who isn't marriage material.

But . . . do they also have a point? What exactly am I doing? Is this me changing my mind? Is this me never having made up my mind in the first place? Do I want to call this off? Do I want to get caught?

Do I love Will?

Henry was right about one thing. People are unknowable. I am a complete mystery to myself. But Freddy's right, too—how can I *not* know whether I love him? Can Freddy and Henry both be right? That would wreak some serious havoc with the harmony of the universe. Speaking of which, what would Epictetus say about all this?

Nothing, probably. He'd just gather a bunch of rocks in his toga and stone me to death.

Because I should love Will. He's such a wonderful person. So very lovable. He possesses so many wonderful, lovable, admirable qualities. There's only one quality that he lacks. The quality of being more than one man.

So many qualities, but just one body! If only he had more bodies. He could divide up all of his qualities. Parcel them out. It would be more egalitarian that way. A quality for every body. And maybe a few extra bodies, without any qualities. Those would probably be my favorites.

I lean my head back on the seat. He smiles down at me. "Tired?"

"A little."

But . . . *marriage*? I'm *marrying* him? Am I out of my *mind*? I mean, it wouldn't be a problem if the situation were different. Like if we were characters in that one Greek myth, and every night when the moon rises and the lamps are lit my husband turns into a different man, and at dawn turns back into Will.

Is there such a Greek myth?

Don't think so. Should have been. Greeks might not have gone extinct.

Did Greeks go extinct? They aren't dinosaurs. Just very indebted.

Why am I thinking about the Greeks? Why am I thinking at all?

It's okay. It's been a long day. I've still got time to sort everything out. Plenty of time. Dog's years. Or donkey's. Whatever.

Tomorrow will be better. I'll be better. Tomorrow.

"Close your eyes," Will says. "I'll wake you when we get there."

MONDAY

6

I feel his hand first. Near my knee, stroking gently. Tracing a pattern on my skin. I shiver.

I'm on my back, one arm flung over my eyes. Where are we? There's a breeze. Scent of the ocean. A brightness in the room.

Key West. I'm home.

His hand slips under my knee, lifting it up. He parts my legs. His fingers trail up the inside of my thigh, pushing the thin silk of my slip out of the way.

"Lily," he whispers.

I feel the heat of his body next to mine, his weight on the mattress drawing me toward him. I resist, leaning away slightly. His hand brushes across my stomach. I murmur and stretch, pretending that I'm still asleep. I turn away from him, but he pulls me back, gently pushing my shoulder into the pillow. He sweeps my hair out of my face, his fingertips on my cheeks and forehead. I keep my eyes closed. His breath is warm and smells sweet. He kisses my temples, softly. I inhale deeply as his throat brushes against my mouth. He kisses my ears. My eyebrows. My nose. The line of my jaw. I lift a hand and push him away sleepily. He takes it and kisses the inside of my wrist, my forearm, my elbow. He bites a finger.

It is *so* hard not to respond, but I want to see what he's going to do. He's kissing my shoulder. His mouth is warmer, moving urgently now. I groan a little and shift away, but again he pulls me back. He slides the straps of my slip down my arms. His lips are on my throat, my collarbone. My right breast. My left. Kissing and licking and biting gently. I slowly reach down and find his cock, stroking it lightly with my fingers.

He puts a hand between my legs now, a finger inside me, then two. I dig my heels into the mattress and press against them.

"Lily," he whispers.

Then, just for fun, I push him away, hard, and start to sit up.

That's when Will grabs me and throws me back down on the bed. I try fighting him off, but he pins my wrists above my head with one hand, parts my legs with the other and enters me in one long thrust. I don't expect it, it's happened too fast, and it's *amazing*. I gasp, my eyes wide open now, but Will's are closed. His mouth finds mine. He kisses me deeply. Desperately. His mouth is insistent and unbearably hot. I can't stop kissing him. He pulls out and enters me again roughly, and again and again. I cry out. He only thrusts harder. I say, "Will?"

And he says, his lips close to my ear, "Shut up."

He releases my wrists and I wrap my arms around his neck. His hands move down my body until he's clutching at my hips, pulling me up to him, over and over. It's passionate and exciting and . . . what? Untender. And perfect. I bury my fingers in his hair and kiss his mouth, his cheeks, his stubbly throat. I bite his tongue. I bend my head and catch a nipple between my teeth. I move my tongue around it, swirling, tasting salt on the delicate skin.

Then he's kneeling on the bed and pulling me on top of him. His hands are on my hips again, his fingers digging in, as he guides me up and down. I lean over him so that my breasts brush against his mouth. I close my eyes and move with him, slowly, then faster and faster until I can't take it anymore, warmth spreads through my entire body and I come, calling out, crashing down onto him over and over as the world goes a little dim.

We're still for a minute, me on him, him stroking my hair, still hard inside me. Then he pushes me off, turns me over and pulls me to my knees. I'm a little dazed, a little helpless—not that I would stop him from doing anything right now. Or ever. He enters me from behind, one hand on my hip, another in my hair. Moving slowly and deliberately. After a while I come back to myself a little. I can think.

It's our first three days, all over again.

Just when I thought they were gone forever.

I push back against him, wanting as much of him in me as possible.

Everything, muscle and skin and blood and bone. He pulls all the way out and plunges back in, faster now, again and again. He slaps my ass, hard, and I cry out, and he does it again. I look at him over my shoulder. His eyes are closed, his face rapt. He's saying my name, over and over. Pushing himself so deeply into me that I can't catch my breath, and just when I think I can't take it anymore, he reaches around and touches me and I come again, long and loud, a glorious, whole-body, tingling thing. So does he.

We collapse together on the bed, the sheets twisted up beneath us. I'm drifting away on a cloud of pure happiness.

"Will?" I whisper.

"Hmm?"

"Holy shit!"

He laughs softly. "You're welcome."

I can feel him smile against my skin. He kisses the back of my neck. His hand rests lightly on my hip.

I turn my head so that I can see his face. "Can I ask you a question?"

"No."

We start laughing. I roll over so that I'm facing him. My laughter dies away, and so does his. We're looking into each other's eyes now. Will's are so dark that when I'm close like this I can see my reflection. But I'm seeing something else now. I'm seeing past his eyes, right into him. I'm seeing all of him, all at once. I'm seeing—

There's a knock at the door.

I blink. I start breathing again. "God. Who could that be?"

"The paramedics," Will says, brushing the hair from my forehead. "Responding to multiple 911 calls."

We laugh again. "Lily?" Mattie calls out. "We're going to be late!"

"Go away!" I holler.

"Blue Heaven? The rehearsal dinner? Whether we're going to serve chicken, or pasta, or chicken with pasta . . ."

We eventually crawl out of bed and pull on some clothes. Will catches up to me as I'm about to leave. He pushes me against the wall, and his hand goes up my skirt. I reach inside his pants. He's already hard again.

He says, "Don't forget. We have lunch with my parents today."

"Oh, baby," I whisper. "I love it when you talk dirty."

He laughs and tugs my panties down. "One o'clock."

I press myself against his hand. "What happens if I'm late?"

"Bad things." He starts unbuttoning my blouse. "Very bad things."

"Oh my God." I lean my head back against the wall. "Who *are* you?"

"A fool." He kisses my throat. "I'm a fool in love."

We do it again, quickly, right there by the door. Eventually I go down to the lobby, where Mattie is waiting. She hands me a steaming cup of coffee.

"Mattie! Bless your event-coordinating little heart!"

"Don't drink too much," she warns. "We don't want you to have horrible stained teeth in the photographs."

"These puppies won't stain," I tell her, tapping my teeth. "They're one hundred percent false."

She looks shocked. "They are?"

"I did *way* too much meth in law school."

She stares at me.

"I'm joking."

"Oh!" she says. "Oh. That's funny."

We head out to her car. She unlocks the doors and we get in. "How are you this morning?" she asks.

"Never better, Mattie. Never. Better." I raise my face to the sunshine streaming through the windshield. "It's a beautiful day. I'm surrounded by my family. I'm marrying the perfect man. Life is good."

"I'm delighted to hear that." She pulls out of the lot, swerving to avoid a brilliantly plumed rooster strutting across the road. Chickens run wild in Key West—they're our squirrels, basically.

"So many brides find the week before the wedding to be one of the worst of their lives," Mattie continues. "It's tragic! They should be at their happiest, and instead they're stressed out and miserable."

"Not me, Mattie. I mean, I've had my doubts recently, okay? Not anymore." I lean back against the seat and sip my coffee. "I hit the fucking jackpot with this guy."

She glances at me uncertainly. "Yes, he seems—"

"Fucking," I catch her eye for emphasis, "*jackpot.*"

"Goodness!" she laughs. "You're a real New Yorker, aren't you?"

I put my hand out the window, feeling the warm air push against it. I'm still basking in the afterglow.

It's back. I can't quite believe it, but the great sex with Will is back.

On a Thursday night back in August, I was at Walker's Pub, down the street from my apartment. I was on a date with someone I'd met at a party, a banker. Hot, but a little predictable. I got up to go to the bathroom. There was a guy standing in the back hallway. He was tall and skinny. Light-brown hair. Glasses. Dressed a little carelessly. Normally, somebody I wouldn't have looked twice at.

What am I talking about? I look at everyone twice.

But here's my point: as I got closer, I noticed something unusual about him. He was still. Perfectly still. Leaning against the wall—not futzing with his phone, not fidgeting, not looking around. But not bored or spaced out, either. He looked like he was having an interesting conversation with himself.

I put my hand on his arm, and he turned and looked at me politely. He had brown eyes and thick, expressive eyebrows.

I said, "Are you in line for the bathroom?"

"I am, yeah," Will said.

"Okay," I said. "But I was here before you. Just so you know."

He gave me this slow, shy smile. "Is that right?"

"I was here last night," I said. "And the night before that."

"You come here a lot?"

I nodded gravely. "I practically live here."

We heard the toilet flush. Someone stepped out. Will gestured gallantly toward the open door. "Please."

When I came out, he gave me a quick smile, ducking his head as he passed me to go in.

When he came out, I was still waiting. "I forgot something in there," I explained.

He looked surprised. "What was it?"

I smiled at him. "You."

He burst out laughing. Will has this great laugh, really sudden and happy. The kind of laugh you feel proud to have inspired, the kind that you want to keep hearing. I went to say good-bye to the banker. Will went to say good-bye to his friends. We met up at the restaurant across the street.

He was a little shy at first, but not for long. We talked for an hour. He told me he was an archaeologist. I told him I was an astronaut. He said he was serious. I laughed at him. He showed me his museum ID to prove it. Then he told me all about his job, and he was so earnest and charming. I told him what I did, and he pretended to be interested. I asked him to speak Latin, and he did, but he wouldn't translate what he said. Then he spoke a few more languages—Aramaic and ancient Greek, I think. Then we were kissing. Then we were leaving. My building was a block away. We barely made it into the elevator before we started tearing each other's clothes off. Once we got inside the apartment, we didn't leave again for three days.

The sex was amazing. The best I've ever had. Ardent and intense and dirty and . . . honest, is the only way I can describe it. We knew how to communicate with each other, right away. And it was so much *fun*. When I wasn't coming, I was laughing. And I mean, *this* guy? This sweet, brainy guy? Will is good-looking, but he's totally unaware of it. He wasn't at that bar to pick up women. He wasn't one of those men who are so impressed with themselves, so eager to telegraph their prowess. And yet he turned out to be this gifted, uninhibited sex maniac.

It was such a surprise. And I *love* surprises.

Sometime in the middle of that first night, I woke up, aware that Will was touching me. Not like he had in the hours before, when it had been frantic and wild. Now it was slow, careful. Reverent. The light was on, and he was studying my body, inch by inch. Dwelling on my face. Combing his fingers through my hair. It was like he was memorizing me.

"You're so beautiful," he said softly.

I'm not, really I'm not, but who am I to contradict? Instead I raised my face and kissed his mouth and pulled him down to me again.

It came to an end, eventually, as it had to. I got dragged back into work on Monday, when the opposing side in one of my cases filed an emergency motion. I pulled an all-nighter at the firm, then another. I flew to California with Philip and Lyle for a hearing. By the time I got

back, Will had left for an academic conference in London. He was gone
for a week. We'd been talking and e-mailing whenever we could, but
I was swamped, and things kind of trailed off. Freddy and I went out
one night while Will was gone. I met someone—the pickle guy. I went
home with him. It was pretty great, which made me feel weirdly guilty.
I barely knew Will. He had no claim on me. I had never felt bad before.
Still. I did.

Two weeks after we first met, Will and I got together again. We
went out to dinner, then back to his place and straight to bed. And it was
nice. But not the same. He was reserved. Almost awkward. The same
thing happened a few nights later, and the night after that. It was sweet,
and tender, and romantic, but . . . a little dull. I didn't say anything, expecting things to go back to the way they were. And I *really* liked him,
so we kept seeing each other.

Two weeks after that, he proposed. He told me he'd had the ring
made while he was in London, because even then he knew.

He knew! How crazy is that? No one had ever wanted to marry me
before. I'm so not that kind of girl. But Will did. He loved me. I was
shocked. I hated the thought of disappointing him. So I said yes.

Our sex life never reached the same heights, although I kept chasing
those first three days. I finally concluded that Will didn't have a very
strong sex drive. Some guys are like that, I guess. I didn't push matters.
We're busy people, we both work long hours—it's just not a priority for
him. Could I have forced the issue, demanded that we talk about it?
Could I have initiated sex more? I suppose, and part of me is still mysti-
fied about why I didn't. Maybe I was holding back a little. Or a lot. I didn't
want him to get the wrong idea about me. Or the right idea. Whatever.

It doesn't matter. After this morning, every average thing about our
sex life is in the past. We're back to where we started, and I couldn't be
happier. I'm not going to waste time wondering why. Maybe it's the fresh
ocean air. Maybe it's the sultry surroundings. Maybe he couldn't let loose
and regain his lustfulness until now, the eve of our wedding.

I think the Amish are like that.

Bottom line? I am done, *completely* done, with questioning my decision to get married. That business last night? The uncertainty, the

worry, the random flirtation and—let's face it—mindless panic? So silly. So pointless. My initial instincts were right all along.

Everything's going to be fine.

I sip my coffee. "What's on the agenda this morning, Mattiecakes?"

"I've kept it light," she replies, turning onto Whitehead Street. "After the restaurant we just have to stop by the new florist and go over the plan for the reception."

"Great!" I say. "Wait. We have a new florist?"

"Yes. I fired the old one."

"Really?"

Mattie sighs regretfully. "He wasn't doing his best work."

I think this over. "Shouldn't I have been consulted?"

She turns to me, horrified. "Did you like Martin?"

"Well, no," I admit. "I mean, I don't have any idea what he was doing. And I probably would have gone along with whatever you wanted me to do. But . . ."

Why am I objecting? I've always given Mattie free rein. I need her to have free rein. Maybe I don't like the pointed reminder of how uninvolved I've been in these proceedings. How disengaged.

Mattie pulls up in front of Blue Heaven, a funky island café on Thomas Street. She switches off the ignition and bursts into tears.

"I'm letting you down!" she wails.

Oh, Jesus. "Of course you're not!" I assure her.

"Planning this wedding has been utterly overwhelming," she confesses. "Your family is very . . . *unusual*. And everything has been so last minute! I want it all to be perfect, but I haven't gotten a great deal of direction from you. And now I've overstepped my bounds!"

"No no! You're doing an amazing job, Mattie."

She blows her nose and glances at me hopefully. "Really?"

"Absolutely," I say. "This is my fault. I haven't always responded as quickly as I should to your e-mails and texts and voice mails and Facebook messages and . . . everything else. But that's going to change. Starting now."

"Are you sure, dear?"

"Whatever you need me to do, Mattie, I'm here. Lay it on me. Let's do it. Let's *plan* this wedding, okay?"

"Okay!" she warbles happily, and hops out of the car. We walk into the restaurant's open-air courtyard, total besties. I realize I'm starving, and the owner is kind enough to give me a plate of fruit and a delicious Bloody Mary. We pore over the menu for the rehearsal dinner, and with the assistance of a second Bloody Mary, I make a number of critical bridal decisions (chicken *and* fish, bitches!). After a third, valedictory Bloody Mary, I follow Mattie back to the car.

"Key West has changed so much since you grew up here," she tells me as she steers us back toward Duval Street. "We're very cosmopolitan now. That's an interesting shop over there." She points at a cheerful yellow cottage. "It opened in November. They make . . . oh, what do you call it?" She snaps her fingers. "God bless it! Why can't I remember? Comes from a cow."

"Milk?"

"No," she says. "Harder."

"Ice cream?"

"No, it's not sweet."

"Cheese?"

"*Cheese!*" she cries. "They make their own cheese."

"You forgot the word for cheese?"

"My memory is terrible these days," she laments.

"Do you maybe need to, I don't know, get that checked out?"

"Doctors can't do anything for me, dear. It's the Change."

"The Change?" I repeat. "That sounds very dire."

"Menopause. It's relentless. The hot flashes. The metabolic shifts. The forgetfulness." Her hand flutters to her forehead and flutters away again. "My mind is . . . oh, what do you call it? The thing with holes."

"A sieve?"

"Yes! A sieve."

I laugh. "You forgot the word that you wanted to use to describe how forgetful you are. That's funny."

She just looks at me.

"You're right," I say. "It's not funny."

Duval Street looks a lot less seedy in the morning light. The bars are shuttered. Tourists wander around sipping smoothies and Cuban coffee. The sidewalks are damp and clean.

"Do you see that church over there?" Mattie says, pointing at a white clapboard chapel.

"I have an idea! Let's have Bloody Marys at the rehearsal dinner!"

Mattie cocks her head. "Isn't that more of a morning beverage, dear?"

"Maybe we could do a breakfast-for-dinner theme," I suggest. "With pancakes!"

"No," she says. "Now, as I was saying. There's a new pastor at that church. People adore her. I thought you might be interested in having her officiate on Saturday."

Mattie launches into a story about the pastor while I watch a family of tourists buy palmetto hats from a ragged hippie. Teddy and I wove hats one spring break, when we were eleven or twelve. Our hats were terrible, but we were so cute. We made a killing. Then we blew all our earnings on ice cream and firecrackers.

"Lily?" Mattie says.

I turn. She's waiting for me to say something. "Sorry. Don't we already have a pastor?"

"Yes," Mattie says reluctantly. "Leonard Garment."

"Right. Will talked to him on the phone. He really likes him." Actually, I think Will just wants our marriage certificate to be signed by someone named Reverend Garment. But he made the decision—I can't overrule him.

"The last thing I want to do is second-guess your choices," Mattie says. "But I think Len would be a serious mistake."

"Why?"

Mattie slams on the brakes just in time to avoid crushing a small electric car puttering ahead of us. "I see your wedding as an elegant, storybook kind of affair," she replies. "Quite formal and traditional."

I have to laugh. "You've got me pegged, sister."

"Len is so . . . countercultural." Mattie frowns. "He's very irreverent. I think he'll send the wrong message."

I gaze out the window while she keeps talking. We're on Margaret Street now. Marriage certificates. Officiants. It all sounds so very . . . official.

"Lily?" Mattie is looking at me intently.

"What? Oh, sorry." I roll down the window. It's really warm in here all of a sudden. "If you think it's a big deal, I'll talk to Will about it."

"Wonderful! You'll be glad you did."

My phone rings. I answer. "Hola, madrasta bonita!"

"If you marry that poor boy, you're both going to regret it for the rest of your lives," Ana says.

I lean back against the headrest. "Will you please fuck off?"

Mattie jumps a little in her seat. "Sorry!" I whisper. Back to Ana: "I'm not changing my mind. Deal with it."

"Then how about this," she says. "Postpone. Give yourselves time to get to know each other better. If you still want to get married, we all reconvene here in six months. What do you say?"

I have to be careful—Ana's persuasive as hell, and her inner conviction can be contagious. When I was little, she was always conning me into doing things I didn't want to do—attending rallies, campaigning with her, trying weird foods. She's passionate and dramatic and always, always right. Which often makes her very, very annoying.

"Sorry," I say. "Not doing it."

"Dammit, Lilybear. You're so stubborn."

"Wonder where I learned that."

"You worthless piece of shit!" she cries loudly.

I hold the phone away from my ear. "That's a little harsh, don't you think?"

"Not you," she says absently. "I'm reading an e-mail."

"Yeah? Glad to know you're maintaining a single-minded focus on my concerns."

"This is *ridiculous*," she hisses, and I hear the clatter of keys as she starts typing angrily.

"Is there anything else I can help you with?"

"No," she says, her mind clearly elsewhere. "I mean yes. Give me your friend's number. The designer. I need help finding a dress."

"You don't have a dress for the wedding?"

"When do I have time to shop?" she protests. "And frankly, I didn't think you'd actually go through with it."

I give her Freddy's number.

"Now," Ana continues, "if you start having second thoughts—"

I hang up on her as Mattie pulls up to a weather-beaten grey house with purple trim. The crooked front porch is bursting with plants and flowers. The hand-painted sign reads ROSE'S FLOWERS AND GIFTS.

"Here we are!" Mattie chirps.

I gape at her. "You brought me to a sex shop?"

She looks mortified. "No no no! This is—"

"Mattie, that's disgusting! I don't go for that sort of thing!"

"I would never—"

I pat her thigh. "Relax. I'm only teasing you."

"Oh," she says, slightly mollified. "Well, that's—"

"This is obviously a funeral parlor," I say.

"What? No!"

Three drinks on an empty stomach and I'm tormenting this poor woman. I apologize, and we go inside, where I meet Rose, a pleasant woman with pink cheeks and a halo of frizzy white hair. She has a folder of paperwork spread on the counter in front of her.

"These are the plans Martin worked up," she says. "It's a lovely start. But I think I can make a few improvements."

Rose and Mattie bend their heads together. I check my e-mail and work voice mail. My phone pings with a text.

—Hw do I tzpe on ths fubking thig,

It's Gran. I type back:

—pls stop spamming me

About five minutes later, I get:

—Y7 idio8

This is fun.

—youre one of those internet perverts, arent you. im going to report you to the FTC

—ths sht

—youre sick, mister, you know that? sick

She finally calls, sputtering with rage.

"Texting is supposed to save time," I tell her. "It doesn't make any sense for someone in your condition."

"What the hell?" she snaps. "What condition?"

"One foot and all ten fingers in the grave." I pull a couple of sprigs of baby's breath out of a vase and start crumbling them between my fingers. "What's up?"

"I need to add a guest. Assuming you're still going through with this wedding nonsense."

"Of course I'm still going through with this wedding nonsense!"

Mattie and Rose stop talking and look up. "Prank caller," I explain. To Gran: "Sorry, aged relation. We're at capacity."

"You can fit one more," Gran insists. "My all-time favorite client just got paroled."

"Mazel tov. What was he in for?"

"She," Gran replies. "Ran her husband over with a speedboat."

"Did he deserve it?"

"They all deserve it," she says darkly.

I start poking holes in a block of dank, squishy green florist's foam. Rose is eyeing me. I make a *Sorry!* face and push it away. "Your friend sounds like a super-fun addition to the party, Gran, but—"

"Dawn's a gas. And she's lonely. I thought maybe she could meet someone."

"You want to use my wedding to help a murderer find a hookup?"

Rose and Mattie look up again.

"Manslaughterer," Gran says. "She took a plea."

"Oh!" I say. "That's fine. Consider it done."

We gab awhile longer, then I hang up. Mattie is in raptures over whatever floral wizardry Rose is performing. I listen to them idly. Rehearsal dinners. Stepmother-of-the-bride dresses. Last-minute guests. Since the moment Will and I got engaged, the wedding has been a little bit unreal to me. Slightly theoretical. I was in New York, working hard, living my life. Most of the planning was going on down here, in the hands of people I'd never met. All I had to do was send guest lists, listen to Mattie yak, and say yes, or no, or let me ask Will.

Now it's all very real.

"—and a lovely spray of daisies here," Rose says, sketching rapidly. "Some people say that peonies brown too quickly, but I entirely disagree, so we could have some *there* . . ."

Real! That's good! Realness is a good thing. I think about Will, how he was in bed this morning. If it takes a wedding, with its vows of faithfulness and constancy, to get a lifetime of that? No problem. No problem at all.

"I have something else to show you." Rose leads us to a small table covered with scraps of cloth. "Mattie said that you need gauze bags to hold the wedding favors."

"The what?"

"Candied almonds, stamped with your and Will's initials," Mattie explains. "In a drawstring bag sealed with a ribbon and a spray of silk flowers. I left you a voice mail about it?"

"I picked out a few fabric samples," Rose says, "but I wasn't sure which one matched the bridesmaids' dresses."

"Do they have to match?" I ask.

"Everything matches," she replies.

"Everything?"

"From a visual perspective, a wedding is all about symmetry and cohesion and continuity," Rose says earnestly. "That's why we want the flowers at the ceremony and the reception to be foreshadowed by the flowers at the rehearsal supper, and to be echoed, you might say, by the flowers on the tables at the Sunday brunch."

Foreshadowed? Echoed?

Brunch?

Mattie chimes in. "That's also the reason why the font used in the programs matches the font on the invitations and on the place cards for the meals."

"So," Rose continues, "the fabric used for the wedding favors should match the color of the bridesmaids' dresses."

"Which also matches the lining of the envelopes that held the invitations," Mattie concludes.

They're staring at me.

I'm staring back.

I've been kidnapped by a couple of obsessive-compulsive space aliens.

They're waiting for me to say something.

"Ladies?" I clap my hands together. "Let's match some motherfucking gauze!"

Rose looks a little startled, but recovers and presents me with six squares of champagne-colored fabric.

I gaze down at them. "These are completely identical."

"No they're not," Rose says.

I turn to Mattie. "Rose be trippin'."

"Take your time," Mattie urges me. "Hold them up to the light."

I look at her, then at Rose. "Ladies? To say that I do not give two shits about this vastly overestimates the value I place on shits."

They puzzle that one out for a moment. So do I. Those Bloody Marys must have been pretty strong.

"It's the second swatch," Mattie tells me.

"It's the second swatch," I tell Rose.

She sweeps the others away with a smile. "You're an easy bride."

"Honey," I laugh, "you have no idea."

"I have a few thoughts about how to decorate the restrooms at the Audubon House," Rose continues.

"Where?"

"The Audubon House," Mattie murmurs. "Where you're holding your reception."

"Right!" I cry. "Wait. We have to decorate the bathrooms?"

"It's customary," Rose informs me. "Tea candles, scented soaps, embroidered hand towels. Perhaps a posy."

"A posy." I nod. "But only perhaps."

She's rooting around in a plastic bin. "I have just the thing."

My phone pings with a text from Will.

—Where are you?

It's one fifteen. I'm late for lunch.

7

I leave Mattie with Rose and hurry to the restaurant. As I turn onto Simonton Street I nearly collide with a woman leaving a salon. She's wearing shorts and flip-flops, but her hair is swept up elegantly and topped with a veil. Another bride, doing a dry run for her big day. She looks so happy.

My phone rings. I answer. "Yo, dawg!"

"Lily?" Jane says. "I need a favor."

"For you, mon cherie? Anything."

"I take it you haven't changed your mind about the wedding?"

"Why does everyone keep asking me that?"

"We suffer under a collective delusion that you might someday do something sensible."

"Ha! When pigs freeze over. When hell flies."

"Indeed," Jane says drily. "Now please listen carefully. Two couples are coming to the wedding. They're friends of mine. The Gortons and the Heydriches. They need to be seated at separate tables."

"Uh-oh! Who bonked who?"

"Whom," she corrects me, then hesitates. "Donald Heydrich and Mitzy Gorton."

"No!" I cry. "Not Donald and Mitzy!"

I actually have no idea who these people are. I don't know half the people my parents have invited to the wedding.

Jane sighs. "I'm afraid so."

"You run with a fast crowd, Janey. Hey, that reminds me. Are the swingers coming?"

"As I've told you numerous times, Bob and Gloria are *not* swingers," she says sternly. "It's a vicious rumor started by that insufferable Sloane Kittredge."

"I hope so. I'm trying to run a clean family wedding here."

"Have you been drinking?" she demands.

"Oh, Jane!" I laugh uproariously. "The very thought!"

"Let me finish, please. The worst is over now, thank God. It was all so tiresome—the tears, the recriminations." Jane sighs again, and I can just picture her, reclining on the sofa at Gran's house, hair fanned out on the pillows. Admiring the rings on her fingers, looking down her long, elegant nose at these naive little people and their tedious tantrums. When I first met Jane, I thought of her as the Snow Queen—the beautiful fairy-tale bitch who steals children and makes them forget their friends and family. I thought she was deliberately wrenching me away from Ana, but of course that's not what she was after at all. Eventually, she became fascinating to me—I'd never met another woman like her, so urbane and knowledgeable about things I'd never taken an interest in: power and money and beauty and relationships between men and women.

"You would have thought it was the end of the world, instead of some silly fling," she continues.

"People can be so dramatic," I agree.

"Now, their spouses have forgiven them, and everyone is moving on. Nevertheless, I promised that I would do my best to minimize contact among them this weekend. Can you help me?"

"No problemo."

"Of course, the entire issue is moot if you—"

"The wedding is happening, Janey. I'm not changing my mind."

"But Lily darling, think of—"

I've had enough of this for one morning. I hang up and turn onto Duval, where the heavy foot traffic slows me down. There's a middle-aged couple walking ahead of me. They're daytrippers off one of the big cruise ships. He's wearing a Cubs hat, a camera slung around his neck. She's got one of those no-nonsense midwestern haircuts. They're fighting. I can tell. Walking side by side, but with six inches of militarized distance between them. Not speaking, not touching, not looking at each other. They should be enjoying themselves. They're on vacation, for God's sake!

I bet Mitzy and her husband had ragingly hot morning sex at first. I bet Donald couldn't get enough of his wife in the early years. These two ahead of me? Probably went at it like bunnies during those first heady days in Milwaukee or wherever. So what happens? Time passes. Boredom grows. The pressures and routines of daily life flatten the romance. And one night, after a few too many glasses of chardonnay at some fancy shindig, Mitzy glances at Donald across a room, and he glances back, and a spark ignites.

Or maybe it's even worse—not physical temptation, but the slow, relentless accretion of slights and misunderstandings and annoyances and accommodations, until you find yourself walking down a street in paradise next to a stranger who you kind of hate. Love, gone. Affection, gone. Whatever brought you together in the first place, gone.

Jesus. Kill me now.

I find the restaurant and stop in the bathroom to freshen up. I have a quick drink at the bar to steady my nerves. From where I'm standing, I can see Will sitting on the deck with a pleasant-looking bald guy and a dark-haired woman in pink capris. Will says something, and his mom smiles widely. Gran wasn't the only one to warn me about her. A few of the partners at my firm have gone up against Anita Field in white-collar cases. They told me to watch out for that smile. It's how she bares her fangs.

I have one more drink and head out.

Halfway across the deck I bellow, "Hi there!" The men rise. The toe of my sandal catches on a slat and I pitch forward. Will catches me. He smiles as he guides me to my seat. "Easy, tiger," he whispers.

We introduce ourselves. Will's dad, Harry, seems like an amiable, easygoing guy. His mom is more high-strung, but pleasant. Hardly a— what was it? A killer? That was just the defense lawyer in Gran talking, with her reflexive mistrust of prosecutors.

"I'm sorry I'm late," I say. "Our wedding planner had me running all over town."

Will's mom laughs. "I remember that so well," she says. "Harry and I had a much smaller wedding than you two—only fifty guests or so. But the planning was endless! And it's all up to the woman, right, Lily?" She zeroes in on me with her blue eyes.

She's a pussycat! I begin to relax. "That's right, Mrs. Field," I say. "It's so unfair."

"Please," she says. "Call me Anita."

I smile. "Okay, Anita."

She smiles back.

"Anita," I repeat. "Ah. Nee. Tah. Ahhhhneeeeetaaaahhhh."

She looks puzzled.

"Anita Bobita." I bob my head. "Super Beeta."

Why am I doing this?

"Lily?" Will says in a low voice.

I can't seem to stop.

"Anita." I go deep. "*Yeah.*"

Will is staring at me. I give him a reassuring smile.

Our waitress arrives. Anita orders the salmon, Harry has the tuna, Will has the grouper. "Scotch on the rocks," I say when it's my turn.

"And for your meal?" the waitress asks.

I smile up at her. "That is my meal, sweetheart."

Will takes my hand. "You should order something." He turns to his parents. "Lily works so hard she sometimes forgets to eat!"

"I'll have a steak," I tell the waitress. "Rare."

"A steak!" Harry chuckles. "That's how we know you're a native Floridian."

I smile at him. "I had enough fish in my first decade to last a lifetime, Harry. I'm up to here with the omega-3s."

Anita is watching me closely. "Omega-3s," she remarks. "Excellent for brain power."

"Which I need, to keep up with your brilliant son," I tell her.

We make some more idle chitchat. The waitress returns with our drinks. I help her out by taking mine right off the tray.

"The waitstaff is gorgeous here," Harry remarks after she leaves again.

I slap him playfully on the arm. "Bless you, Harry. She's a tranny!"

He freezes for an instant, then chuckles. "I suppose I forgot where we are."

"You blush just like your son!" I cry. "Do you know that this morning, when he was—"

"Before you got here," Will says quickly, "I was telling my parents the story of how we met."

"In the bathroom," I say.

"In the bar," he says.

"In the bathroom of the bar," I say.

Will reaches for my hand but knocks over a glass of water. Or maybe I do. Either way, we sop it up with our napkins. His mother is silent, studying me.

"Like I said, Lily works so hard," Will says. "She barely gets any sleep at home. I think she really needs this week off before the wedding to," he looks at me with a fixed smile, "chill out. Relax."

"I remember those days," Anita says, after a longish pause. "Before I joined the U.S. Attorney's Office, I spent eleven years at one of the biggest firms in Chicago. What a life." She launches into some anecdote, but I can't concentrate. I'm too distracted by her perfect hair. The breeze is stiff out here, but there's not a tendril out of place. It's superhero hair. I bet it could deflect bullets.

I start laughing. She stops talking.

"Sorry?" I say. "What?"

"I understand it's even worse now," she concludes, kind of grimly.

"The hours are long," I agree. "But I love the work."

She looks surprised. "It's rare to hear someone in our profession say that. Most young lawyers—"

"Lily," Harry leans forward. "I think your nose is bleeding."

I feel my lip. He's right. "Sorry!" I say, standing up. "This happens sometimes. I have a nervous septum."

Anita frowns. "A what?"

I excuse myself and clean up in the bathroom. I stop at the bar on the way back. "Triple pink squirrel please, Lloyd."

The bartender looks up from her phone. "What?"

"Or a bourbon," I say. "Neat."

She takes a glass down from the shelf.

"Future in-laws," I tell her, jerking my thumb toward the deck.

She pours a stiff one and pushes it toward me. "On the house, sugar."

I come back to the table and sit down, a little too hard. Anita clears her throat. "Will told me you attended Harvard Law School. I've hired some of my best prosecutors from Harvard." She says something else, but I don't catch it because I'm totally hypnotized by the way her jaw doesn't move when she talks.

"Lily's a genius," Will says.

I wave the compliment away. "Getting into Harvard was easy. I just had to blow the Dean of Admissions."

Anita stares at me. "I beg your pardon?"

"She's joking," Will says, covering his face with his hands.

"I am! Joking!" I say. "Sorry. Totally a joke. That definitely did not happen."

Anita's fingernails are tapping the table slowly. They are a deep, bloody red. I am completely entranced by them.

"We're looking forward to dinner with your family on Thursday night," she says. She's relentless with the conversational topics, this one. Sister's like one long, boring, conversational-topics steam train. But now she's giving me this nasty little smile. "You certainly have an unusual number of parents. When I opened the newspaper yesterday, I wasn't sure whether I was reading your wedding announcement or a review of some reality-television program."

"Meow," I say.

"Mom," Will sighs.

I'm not going to let her rattle me. No sir. I will maintain my dignity and composure.

"Did the announcement run?" I say. "How is it?"

For some reason I've adopted my father's British accent.

"It's very nice," Harry says.

"Capital," I say heartily. "Capital, capital!"

"Got Will's name wrong, though," he adds.

"Crikey! How?"

Will jumps a little in his seat. "It's no big—"

"His first name isn't William," Harry tells me. "It's Wilberforce."

"No it isn't," I say automatically.

"Yes," Anita says, "it is."

I stare at Will.

"I never said my name was William," he insists.

"Wilberforce?" I burst out laughing. "Good old Wilberforce!"

"Wilberforce was my father's name," Anita says.

I nod solemnly. "Mine too."

Anita stands abruptly and leaves. Will leans toward me. "Lily? I think you should go back to the hotel."

"Why? I'm fine!"

"You're not fine," he says. "You're nowhere near fine."

"I just need to eat something. Look! Here comes food."

Will, Harry and I dig in, and the atmosphere at the table relaxes. Anita doesn't come back.

"I hope your mom didn't get stuck in the bathroom," I say. "The toilets in this restaurant are extra . . . extraord . . . I mean they're really—"

"Forget the toilets," Will mutters. "We don't need to talk about the toilets."

"So Lily. How long have you lived in New York?" Harry asks.

"Technically since I was a teenager. That's when I went north to live with Dad and my stepmother Jane. But they packed me off to boarding school pretty much right away. I only spent vacations and holidays in the city, until I moved there after law school."

"And are you as happy with the city as Will is?"

"I love New York. It's the greatest place in the world."

He smiles. "How do you like the Upper East Side?"

"I hate it. It's the suckpit of the universe."

Harry looks confused. "Then why do you live there?"

"I don't. I live downtown with Will."

Harry looks shocked. I glance at Will, whose face has turned pink.

"Oh, wait!" I slap my forehead. "Ow. I do. I do live on the Upper East Side. We . . . we call it 'downtown.' It's a real estate thing. Anything below Ninety-Sixth Street is 'downtown.' Property values. It's . . . kind of crazy."

Harry stands up. "I should see how your mother is doing." He leaves.

I have another bite of steak. It's so good! I should eat food more often. Will tosses his napkin onto the table. "That went well."

"You think?"

"Fuck no!" he cries.

I'm so startled that I drop my fork. Will almost never swears.

"Will, I—"

He's staring at me, aghast. "What were you thinking, Lily? Were you trying to ruin that?"

"Of course not!"

"It was a *disaster*. I don't even know what to say." He's furious. He's never talked to me this way before. And he's right. Of course he's right. I see that now.

"I'm sorry." I touch his arm, but he doesn't respond. He's staring at nothing. "I wanted to make a good impression," I say. "I talk too much when I'm nervous."

Will beckons the waitress over and orders a drink. He runs his hands through his hair. "What they must think," he laments.

I try to cheer him up. "Who cares? They're only your parents."

He shakes his head. "It's more complicated than that."

"Really? Are they also," I pause dramatically, "your *brother and sister*?"

"Goddammit, Lily!" he shouts. "This isn't funny!"

"Sorry sorry sorry." And I am. I didn't mean for it to turn out this way. Things got out of hand. And now Will is despondent. I feel terrible.

"My relationship with them is . . . challenging," he says. "It's important to me that they like you, that they approve. Otherwise . . . never mind. It's impossible to explain."

He sounds so grim. Can it really be as bad as that? "Tell them I'm not usually like this," I suggest. "Say it's stress from the wedding, or work, or whatever. Tell them it's driving me bonkers. And I drank too much on an empty stomach." I reach out for his hand. "I'm sorry, baby. It won't happen again."

Will thinks this over. His drink arrives. "Wedding stress," he says. "It might work."

I let him ponder that. I'd love to order a glass of red wine to go with my steak, but I don't.

Maturity!

"You could have warned me that they didn't know we live together," I say.

He glances at me ruefully. "I meant to tell them this morning. I didn't get the chance."

"Is it such a big deal? I didn't think people cared about that sort of thing anymore."

"Lots of people do," he says. "Including my parents. Not everybody's family is as unconventional as yours."

"I guess. But . . . did you really have to tell them I lived on the Upper East Side? That's like a knife, Will." I tap my chest. "Right to the heart."

He half smiles. "What was I thinking?"

"It's okay." I pat his hand. "It just means we're even now."

He puts his head in his hands.

"Will? I was kidding!" I tap his shoulder. "Will? Will?"

8

Will's parents don't come back to the table. Eventually he calls his dad and finds out that they've gone back to the hotel. I talk him into renting a scooter so that I can show him the island. He drives (obviously!) while I give him a tour of all my favorite places: the rocky beach at Fort Taylor, the quiet stretches of Louisa and Royal where I used to ride my bike. Bayview Park, where Mom played softball. The Bight, where sailboats from all over the world knock gently against the weathered docks. The parking lot of the federal courthouse, where an unhappy client put a Santeria curse on Gran using some chicken bones and a vial of goat blood.

I rest my cheek against Will's sun-warm back as we putter through the streets. I can feel him relaxing.

"Down to our right is the southernmost point in the continental United States," I tell him. "From there it's only seventy miles to Cuba."

"Is it worth seeing?" he asks.

"If you like that sort of thing." I pause. "The monument looks like a giant red-and-yellow suppository."

He takes a right. "Can't miss that."

We stop and take a few pictures of each other, and ask someone to take a picture of the both of us. Then we head back in the direction of Old Town.

I try to guide him to the cemetery, but I get confused. "Turn left here."

"No, I think it's to the right," he says. He turns, and in a block we're there. We stroll around for a while, reading the bizarre epitaphs, admiring the stone carvings. Then we scooter back up Duval. There's a cluster of women outside Margaritaville. The drunkest and loudest is wearing a feather boa and bright-pink sash that screams *Bride!*

Will drops me at the hotel and heads out to meet some college friends who arrived last night. I change into my bathing suit. The bartender at the pool tells me that Freddy is on the beach. I order two more of whatever she's drinking and head out.

She's huddled on a chaise lounge under an umbrella, wearing a floppy hat and enormous sunglasses and wrapped in a white hotel bathrobe.

I look down at her. "I hope the skin grafts are healing nicely."

"It's freezing out here!" she cries. "What is wrong with these people?" She waves an outraged hand at the swimmers, the loungers, the frolicking children.

I flop into the chair next to hers. "They're enjoying life. You should try it."

Our drinks arrive, in steaming mugs. "Irish coffee," Freddy explains.

I sip mine and gaze out at the horizon. "Brides. They're everywhere. What do they know that I don't?"

"So very, very much," she replies. "How was your morning?"

I describe my planning activities and the calls I fielded from Ana, Gran and Jane. "Then I had lunch with Will's parents."

"How was that?"

I hesitate.

"Uh-oh." She gestures to a passing waiter for another round. "What did you do?"

I tell her everything. New drinks arrive. When I finish, she says, "It doesn't take a genius to figure out what you're doing."

"No? Glad I came to you, then."

"Hold up there, missy!" A warning finger emerges from her terry-cloth cocoon. "Please recall that I am, officially, smarter than you are."

"Whatever, lady."

"Whatever with your whatever," she scoffs. "I beat you in that online IQ test."

"Well I beat *you* in that online quiz that shows your real age."

She looks skeptical. "How did you beat me? It said you're fifty-three."

I clink my mug against hers. "Age before beauty, my love. Age before beauty."

Freddy takes a towel from a nearby chair and wraps it around her feet. She takes a polka-dotted scarf from her bag and twists it around her neck. She blows on her hands. She settles back in her chair. "So," she says. "Lunch. You did it on purpose. I bet you weren't even that drunk. What did you have, five or six drinks in the space of a few hours? That's nothing. That's like back to baseline for you."

New drinks arrive. "But maybe I did it because I was nervous, not because I don't want to get married. And if I'm nervous, that means I genuinely love him. And if I genuinely love him, that means we should get married."

"Do you really want my opinion?" Freddy asks.

"Is it one I want to hear?"

"No," she says.

"Then no," I say.

"You should call off the wedding."

"No way! We had the most incredible sex this morning."

"Oh, then marry him, by all means," she says lightly. "Wouldn't want that to stop."

We order another round. I know Freddy is waiting for me to stop joking and tell her honestly what I'm thinking. She always does this: she nudges me in one direction or the other, never pushing me too hard, always trying to help me come to my senses on my own. And I want to explain it to her, I really do. How this morning I was so convinced that marrying Will was the right thing to do, and how that conviction slowly ebbed throughout the day.

But I'm tired of talking about it. I'm tired of thinking about it. There's plenty of time for that later. "Where's Nicole?" I ask.

Freddy rolls her eyes. "Moping around somewhere. She's such a drag, Lily. Why are you even friends with her?"

"Law school. All those late nights. It was a bonding experience."

"She's so annoying. And she says such shitty things about you."

"She's usually not this bad," I explain. "She hates her job. And her boyfriend dumped her. And her apartment has bedbugs."

Freddy looks appalled.

"Had!" I say quickly. "*Had* bedbugs."

"You bitch!" she cries. "How could you not tell me?"

"How was I supposed to know you were going to share a room? This isn't band camp!"

"I'm poor!" Freddy wails. "And now I'm going to have bedbugs!"

"The guy came and cleaned. The bedbug guy. With the dog! She's totally cured."

"She'd better be. Do you want another drink?"

"Do you have any . . . ?" I tap my nose.

Freddy gathers the folds of her bathrobe and struggles to her feet. "Come with me."

As we pass the front desk, the clerk hands me an envelope. We go up to Freddy's room and do a couple of lines. I open the envelope. It contains the guest list, an empty seating chart and a long, complicated note from Mattie. "Help me with this," I call out to Freddy, who's changing. "It's the seating arrangements for the reception."

She comes out of the bathroom and examines the list. "How do you decide where to put people?"

"No idea. All I know is that the Gortons and the Heydriches must be separated."

"Gortons?" she says. "Like the fish sticks?"

"Sadly no. I think this one runs a hedge fund."

"I *loved* those when I was little," Freddy says.

"Hedge funds?"

"Fish sticks! 'Trust the Gorton's fisherman!'" she sings.

"We should serve them at the reception!" I take out my phone and text Mattie.

—Pls investigate poss of srvg fish stx at wddng asap stat thx

"I wish we had some right now," Freddy says dreamily.

I dial room service and demand two dozen fish sticks. Then I tell Freddy the tale of Donald and Mitzy's forbidden passion.

"And you're supposed to keep them apart?" she says. "That's bullshit."

"You think?"

"Hell yes I think!" she cries. "Who are you to come between them? Who the hell are you?" She's all up in my face. "Think about Donald's

heart, Lily. You think it doesn't beat like yours? Because it does. Feel it.
Feel your heart."

"I don't need to—"

"Put your hand up and feel it right now."

"I really—"

"*Feel it*, goddammit!"

Freddy gets like this on coke sometimes.

I put my hand on my heart.

"We're not gods, Lillian. We can't interfere in the course of true love.
Do you think Donald is dead inside? Do you think he doesn't feel a
little thrill when the first breezes of spring waft through the windows
of his penthouse? Making his thinning hair dance? Ruffling his piles of
money? You know what Thoreau said about this."

I think about that for a minute. "'Drink the drink, taste the fruit?'"

"No."

"Yes, he did. I saw it on a poster at Starbucks."

"'In the spring,'" Freddy recites, "'a young man's fancy lightly turns
to thoughts of love.'"

"Using Thoreau to sell shit." I shake my head. "It's like, hats off, cap-
italism. Who are you going to hijack next—Karl Marx?"

Freddy starts jumping up and down on the sofa. "'We looked at each
other with a wild surmise! Silent, on a peak in Darien!'" She leaps off,
landing on the floor with a thud.

"Hey, workers of the world! Drop your chains and pick up our new
Acai Caramel Salted Burrata Latte!"

"Love über alles!" Freddy shouts, grabbing the seating chart. She
puts Mitzy and Donald at one table, their spouses at another, far away.

"Four down, two hundred and eighteen to go," I say.

"Let's do more coke," Freddy says.

We do.

"Let's rearrange the furniture," she says.

We can only move the sofa and the end tables. The beds are bolted
down. We pull the mattresses off the beds and make a fort. Inside, we
look at the guest list again.

"Time to focus," I say.

We put all the lawyers at the tables closest to the bandstand. We put Gran's ex-con with the federal judge I clerked for after law school. We decide to seat all the left-handers to the right of right-handers.

"How can we tell which is which?" Freddy says.

I text Mattie.

—pls send mass email inquirining re handedness of all guests fyi thx btw yolo tgif

"I'm going to cannonball into the pool," Freddy announces.

"From the balcony?"

"Where else?"

"You'll die."

"I won't."

"You will."

"I'm petite," she says.

"Your death will be small and final," I say.

I get a text from Mattie:

—I think you've sent me two texts that were intended for someone else.

—they were intendeded, my dear, for posteriyt

—Sorry?

There's a knock on the door. "Fish sticks!" we yell, and burst out of our pillow fort.

"I'll give you a thousand dollars if you seduce the room service waiter," I tell Freddy.

"Done!" She whips off her dress and flings opens the door.

Nicole is standing there.

"I forgot my key," she says. "Why are you in your underwear?"

"Global warming," Freddy says.

Nicole looks around the room. "What happened to the furniture?"

"Air raid," I say.

She rolls her eyes, finds her key and leaves.

Freddy and I huddle over the seating chart again. We put all the bald men together. All the known redheads. All the young children at one table with Will's mom. We finally get bored and fill in the rest of the names at random.

"We're done!" I throw down the pen.

"I love wedding planning," Freddy says. "Let's do some molly and get started on your thank-you notes."

Tempting! Instead, I wander back to my room and flop on the bed. I pick up the binder for the Hoffman prep. I'm not actually going to work—surely there's an ethical rule against billing under the influence. Although, wasn't Sherlock Holmes all coked out when he solved his cases? Maybe I can crack this thing wide open! I open the binder and read the complaint again.

Nope. As far as the environmental claims go, the plaintiffs have pretty much nailed it. EnerGreen employees doctored the maintenance logs on the oil rig in the months leading up to the explosion. They racked up dozens of safety violations and chose to pay the fines rather than correct the problems. When the rig blew, they lied to state officials about how much oil was gushing into the Gulf. They deserve to fry for what they did, and I really wish they'd suck it up and settle.

I dial Lyle's number. He answers. "What."

"I have a question." I lean back against the headboard with the binder in my lap. "What's stopping the plaintiffs from giving Hoffman's e-mails to the DOJ right now?"

"They can't disclose them without violating a court order. The confidentiality stipulation states that the plaintiffs can't show our documents to anyone who isn't a party to the lawsuit."

I remember now. "Unless that document is used at a deposition or at trial."

"Right. If the plaintiffs properly offer the e-mails into evidence at Hoffman's deposition, they effectively enter the public domain. Plaintiffs can then show them to the court, to the media, to the DOJ."

"How's Philip going to stop them?"

"He's going to be Philip," Lyle replies impatiently. "Daniel Kostova, plaintiffs' lead counsel, is good, but Philip is better. He'll fill the record with objections. He'll ensure that Hoffman's testimony is evasive and confusing, or that it repudiates the e-mails so clearly that if plaintiffs try to publicize them they'll come off looking like misleading scumbags.

And he'll do it all with perfect courtesy and completely by the book, so the plaintiffs can't cry foul."

"But—"

"Why are you wasting my time?" Lyle demands. "You want to know what Philip's going to do? Ask him yourself. Judging from what I overheard Saturday night, you know him a lot better than I do."

I don't say anything.

"I went up to his office to discuss the brief I was working on," Lyle continues. "You weren't exactly being discreet in there."

I take a minute to think about that. I started sleeping with Philip a few months ago, when we were traveling together for a different case. It's only happened a few times. It's fun and exciting and meaningless— just the way I like it. Would I prefer that people at work not know about it? Of course. So this is unfortunate. But not a disaster. Lyle is my senior associate—he can make my life miserable, but he already does that. He can gossip, but so what? I haven't broken any rules. God knows I'm not getting any preferential treatment from Philip—look at how I'm spending the week before my wedding.

This is my business, not Lyle's. And the best way to deal with someone who doesn't know something is none of his business is to let it go. So I do.

"I still don't understand why we're not settling," I say. "Doesn't Ener-Green know how bad this looks?"

"Urs keeps urging his higher-ups to settle, but they won't listen to him. They have a lot of faith in Philip."

"Can I ask you one more question?"

"No," Lyle says, and hangs up.

9

I spend a little more time skimming through my binder, eventually dozing off. I wake up when Will comes in. He stretches out beside me on the bed and starts telling me about the friends he met up with. I hike up my skirt a little bit. Their names are Jason and Thomas. They were his roommates freshman year of college. I unbutton the top button of my blouse. He launches into some story about an archaeological dig in Crete one summer. I'm about to abandon the super-subtle moves and just jump him when he says, "I talked to my dad, too."

I sit up. "You saw him?"

"He called," he says. "Mom is really upset. I tried to explain how much stress you're under, and Dad seemed understanding. He's going to try to bring her around."

"Good!"

He smiles at me. "Want to go out? Just the two of us?"

We make it to Mallory Square in time for the sunset freak show. We watch a man walk across a tightrope juggling knives. A woman with a litter of trick kittens. An escape artist. A whole bunch of spray-painted people Standing Very Still. Fortune-tellers, bagpipers, drummers, dancers, acrobats. This scene was a whole lot dirtier and grittier when I was a kid—homeless people, panhandlers, drug dealers loitering at the outskirts of the crowd. The modern version has been sanitized for the cruise ships. But Will is getting a kick out of it.

We find a place to eat just off Duval. A waitress leads us to a booth and starts telling us about the specials. She's beautiful—tall and curvy, with blonde braids piled on top of her head. And she's *quite* taken by my fiancé. She keeps glancing at him while she talks. He's studying the menu, oblivious.

"That was a special little smile you just got," I tell him after she walks away.

He looks up. "Really?"

"Really." I pause. "She must have noticed you checking her out when we walked in."

"I didn't check her out!" he cries, blushing furiously.

"I'm not blind, Wilberforce. And neither are you, apparently."

"I don't know what you're talking about," he insists. "And please don't call me that."

"Admit it."

"No!" But he's cracking a smile.

"Liar!" I cry. "Admit it!"

He hesitates. "Maybe a little."

"Aha!"

"She reminds me of a famous statue," he says. "The Athena Parthenos."

I crane my neck to look at her. "She also has a really nice ass."

He nods. "That too."

We pick up our menus again. I wonder if Will is going through some sort of sexual reawakening. First there was the business in bed this morning, and now he's ogling the waitress right in front of me? Maybe he's finally exploring the lusty side I glimpsed when we first met. Freeing himself from all those enlightened, egalitarian ideas about sex that make sleeping with educated, sensitive men like him such a snorefest most of the time.

God, wouldn't that be something?

He looks up from his menu. "Lily?"

"Yeah?"

"How many guys have you been with?"

"Three," I say.

"Ha ha," he says. "Seriously, though."

So much for a sexual reawakening. I really hate this question. I find it reductive and judgmental. I also have no idea what the answer is.

I put down my menu and take his hand across the table. "Let's not talk about it. Who we were before we met, what we did—who cares?"

"I think we should talk about it," he says, drawing his hand away. He sets his menu on top of mine and squares them, aligning them with the edge of the table. "Not necessarily about that—that's just one question that occurred to me. But there's a sense in which we don't know each other all that well." He looks up at me. "I mean, I know you, but there are things *about* you that I don't know. And things about me that you don't know. Pasts. Experiences. We met, what, six months ago? A lot of people would say that we rushed into this."

"But Will, you're the one who proposed to *me*."

"Absolutely," he says quickly. "Because I wanted to. And you wanted me to. And it was exactly how it should have been. But I sometimes think—"

The waitress returns and takes our order. She scoops up our menus and leaves. Will starts fidgeting with the napkin holder.

"Are you having second thoughts?" I ask him. My heart thumps once, hard.

"No!" He takes my hands across the table. "I'm asking because I'm *not* having second thoughts. Like I said, I know you. But I want to fill in the blanks." He smiles. "I'm a scientist, after all. I need data. I don't know anything about your childhood, for example. You must have been exposed to a lot of craziness, growing up down here. Drugs and sex and all that?"

"I don't know," I say slowly. I'm trying to find my footing in this conversation. What is he driving at? Did I do something this morning that made him suspicious? Did my behavior at lunch make him afraid of what other surprises might be in store? "I guess I was never really aware of it as crazy. It was just . . . what adults did. Naked people running around, weirdos on drugs. Men dressed as women. People having sex outside. We were always stumbling on people going at it on the beach, or in the park."

Teddy and I loved to sneak up and steal their clothes. Once, we were chased down the street by a guy who—

"We?" Will asks.

"Me and my . . . my friends. But like I said, it didn't really affect me. My life was school, and homework, and, you know, typical kid stuff. It might not seem like it, but Key West is a really small town. We're one of the old families, and everybody knew us. And then there was Gran's work. In fact, the weirdest part of growing up here was probably hanging around with her clients. Drug dealers and gangsters calling the house, showing up at all hours."

"Why did you leave?"

"It was time for me to go," I say. "As I got older, everyone began feeling apprehensive about the influence of this place, especially on a girl. And the school system sucks."

All true. Totally incomplete, but true.

Our food arrives. "Your turn!" I say. "I want to know everything about life in the 'burbs with Anita and Harry, and science projects and skipping grades in school."

He smiles. "It wasn't exactly like that, you know."

"Sure it wasn't," I laugh. "Come on. Give me the details. I can take it."

"Okay." He takes a deep breath. "Okay. It's just that I . . ."

And he gives me this strange look. There's something in his eyes that I can't read. Indecision? Fear? Something else?

"Will?"

He doesn't say anything.

"Will, did . . . something bad happen to you?"

"No! No, not at all." He laughs. Then he tells me all about the suburban hell where he grew up.

"I was so shy," he says. "Painfully shy. And awkward. I even had a stammer."

"That's so cute!"

"You wouldn't have thought so," he replies. "The library was my only refuge. I loved to read. I loved to study. I was fascinated by archaeology and classical languages, and I spent most of my time lost in the ancient world. It was a lot more fun than junior high."

He proceeds to describe life with what sounds like the tiger mom from hell. "Anything that wasn't academics was a waste of time, as far as she was concerned," he says. "In one sense it was perfect—that was the direction I was heading in anyway, and she instilled a great work ethic in me. But anything else I wanted to pursue—hobbies, or sports, or . . . girls," he glances shyly at me, "I basically had to keep secret from her."

"What a drag."

"I didn't want to disappoint her. I should have been more honest. I still have a hard time communicating with her." He pauses. "Maybe I should get plastered and meet them for breakfast tomorrow. Give them a taste of the real me."

I cringe. "I'm so sorry, Will."

He takes my hand across the table and kisses it. "I know."

After dinner we walk down to the docks. Will stops to examine a weedy patch of soil in front of a bar. He's always doing something like that—scuffing through dirt with his shoe, absentmindedly gazing down at the trash in the subway tracks. Professional habit, I guess. Now he plucks out a few long blades of grass and tugs at them like he's testing them for strength.

"Did you run out of floss?" I tease him. "You can borrow some of mine."

He only smiles at me and slips them into his pocket.

We share an ice cream cone on the way back to the hotel. Guilt is nagging me. He told me so much about his childhood. Shouldn't I have told him the truth about what happened when I was fourteen? Why I really left?

But it's ancient history. He can't know me from my past. As an archaeologist, he might quibble with that statement. But it's true. Will knows the important stuff. Most of it, anyway. Or he will. After we're married.

Because we're getting married.

I'm done with the dithering and the indecisiveness. Symmetry, cohesion and continuity. That's what I want.

Okay, but the lying. The lying is bad. Still, I can change. I've been in an adjustment period, and now it's over. No more cheating, no more lying. No more feeling bad about the cheating and the lying. It's goodbye to the old me. Everything that came before, up to this very moment? It's in the past.

And the past doesn't matter.

We walk up the drive of the hotel. "What should we do now?" Will asks.

I smile up at him. "You really have to ask?"

He laughs and holds the door open for me. "This morning wasn't enough for you?"

Here we go—the perfect opportunity to try out my new approach! We walk into the lobby. "That's actually something I wanted to talk to you about."

Then I stop.

There's a man sitting on a sofa, a man in a suit. I can't see his face—he's half turned, as if something in another part of the room has caught his attention. He's rubbing his head absently, his hand moving back and forth over his short hair.

He looks nervous. He never used to look nervous.

Now he turns toward the door and sees me. He stands up. My stomach drops. I have this overwhelming urge to turn and run toward the elevator, but somehow I resist.

We're watching each other. Waiting it out.

"Hi," he says at last.

And with that one syllable, the spell is broken.

"Teddy!" I run up to him and practically jump into his arms. He stiffens, then gives in, his arms encircling me reluctantly. "What are you doing here?"

"I—"

"Will!" I cry, turning to look for him. He's standing right next to me. "There you are. Will, this is Teddy! You were asking about my friends. Teddy was my friend, growing up. My best friend in the whole world. Teddy, this is Will."

They shake hands, both doing that wary man-nod thing.

"We're getting married, Teddy!"

He turns back to me. "Yeah, I heard you—"

"Do you want to come?"

Will laughs. "Let the guy breathe, Lily."

I stop talking. Teddy doesn't say anything. How did I recognize him? He looks so different. I used to have two or three inches on him. Now he's the tall one. His hair is darker. And so short. Why is it so short?

At the same time, he hasn't changed at all. Same face. Same big ears. Same grey eyes, giving nothing away.

"Let's get a drink," I say. "Catch up."

"I can't. I'm working."

He's watching me steadily. Is he as calm as he looks? I keep talking, desperate to fill the air. "What do you do?"

"I work for the FDLE," he replies.

I burst out laughing, but his expression doesn't change.

"Seriously?"

He pulls out his wallet with the air of amused tolerance I remember so well. He has a badge. Special Agent, Florida Department of Law Enforcement. "And you live here?" I say, examining it. "You're back?"

"For the last six months. Stop looking through my wallet."

I take one of his business cards and hand the wallet back. "How's being home?"

"You know. It's home."

I look at the card, then up at him. He's still watching me.

"I'm beat," Will says, startling me. I'd almost forgotten he was there. To Teddy he says, "It was great to meet you." He gives me a quick kiss on the cheek and heads for the elevator.

Teddy and I sit down. He's so grown up, so professional-looking. He's wearing a suit, for God's sake.

It's impossible. Any second now he's going to toss the badge and the awful tie and say, "Had you going there!" And then we'll have a good laugh.

Because Teddy can't be a cop. He just can't be.

"What are you doing here?" I ask him. "I mean right now. At the hotel."

"Meeting someone," he says.

"A girl?" I ask, before I can stop myself.

"A witness. Someone I need to interview." He looks around, as if the witness might be lurking somewhere in the room.

"I can't believe you're a cop."

He turns back to me, the ghost of a smile on his face. "I can't believe you're a lawyer."

"Touché. How'd you know?"

He shrugs. "Word gets around."

Chatty as ever. The ice is thawing, though. If ice is what's between us.

"It's so good to see you! How have you been?" I reach out and touch his knee.

He yanks it away. "Don't, Lily."

"What?"

He stands up. "This was a mistake."

"What was a mistake?"

"I have to go."

"What about your witness?"

"There's no witness," he says. "I wanted . . . forget it. I'll see you around."

"Teddy, wait!"

But he's walking away, he's pushing through the door. He's gone.

I poke my head into the lobby bar, but I don't see anyone I know. I wander outside. The pool is empty, a breeze whipping up little waves on the surface. I walk down to the beach and sit on an empty chair, watching the water.

When I get up to the room, Will is just coming out of the shower. I stretch out on the sofa. "Do you want something to drink?" he asks.

"No thanks."

He opens a beer. "So, Teddy."

"Teddy."

"Were you guys boyfriend and girlfriend?"

"Nope." The door to the balcony is open, and it's chilly in here. I pull my sweater more tightly around me.

"No?" Will asks. "I thought I detected . . . I don't know. Something."

I smile at him. "Jealous?"

"Absolutely. He knew you when you were all pimply and moody, and I didn't."

"I was a real prize back then." I lean my head back against the arm of the sofa and look out at the night. "But no. We were just friends. I left, and we lost touch. That's it."

TUESDAY

10

I open my eyes. Freddy is standing next to the bed.

"You have to help me," she whispers.

"Okay," I whisper back.

"I wake up this morning? And some psycho is, like, looming over me."

"Sounds scary."

"She looked like a hamster."

"Oh!" I sit up. "That's just Mattie."

"She dumps these shopping bags on my bed," Freddy continues, holding them up to show me. "Then she says she hopes I brought my own glue gun."

Deep from under the covers, Will groans.

"I mean, I did," Freddy says, "but who acts like that, right?"

The shopping bags contain candied almonds, fake flowers, champagne-colored gauze bags and a long note, which I skim. "She wants us to assemble the wedding favors."

"Yay, crafting!" Freddy hops onto the bed. "Let's order room service."

"How did you get in here?" Will asks groggily.

"I went out with one of the desk clerks last night." Freddy yanks the cord of my bedside lamp out of the socket and plugs in her glue gun. "Let's just say her gratitude knows no bounds."

Over breakfast, Freddy and I fill bags with almonds while Will reads the paper. "Listen to this," he says. "A man was arrested on Southard Street for jumping through a window, tackling a homeowner, emptying a vacuum cleaner canister onto the floor and masturbating on a pile of clean laundry. Stark naked the entire time."

"Florida." I smile. "Home sweet home."

Freddy points the glue gun at a pile of sea grass drying on the windowsill. "What's with the dying foliage?"

"Will's been collecting it. He won't tell me why."

She looks at him. "It's a secret," he says.

A cell phone rings. "Whose is that?" she asks.

"It's my second phone," Will replies, silencing it.

"Yeah? For your second family?"

He laughs. "It's for work."

"Will has a double life," I tell Freddy. "By day, he's a brilliant, mild-mannered archaeologist, but when the sun goes down, he reveals his true identity as—"

"Wait wait! Let me guess." Freddy peers at him. "A cold-blooded CIA killer."

"A high-flying drug dealer," I say.

"A mutant superhero," she suggests.

"Pope Francis!"

"Both!"

Will smiles as he powers off the phone. "You're not even close."

Freddy and I finish the favors, and she leaves for the pool. I sit down next to Will on the sofa.

"Hi," I say.

He folds the paper. "Hi."

I curl up to him. He reaches for me. We start kissing. I slide my hands underneath his t-shirt and up his back.

He breaks off and checks my phone. "Look at the time."

Ugh, he's right. I'm going to be late for my prep.

We get up. He heads into the shower while I dress. "I should be done by two," I say through the bathroom door. "Meet me back here?"

"I'll try, but I've got a busy day. Lunch with the groomsmen. Picking up the tuxedos. And tonight's my bachelor party. I might not see you." He pokes his head out. "Good luck with work."

He kisses me and disappears. I loiter around for a minute, but all I hear is running water. I guess a repeat of yesterday morning isn't going to happen.

I go downstairs and stop at the front desk, next to a sign that says RENTAL CARS AVAILABLE.

"I need something sporty," I tell the man behind the counter.

"So do I," he says.

"Do you have a Jaguar?"

He taps at his computer. "Got an XK. A convertible." Tap tap tap. "It'll run you four hundred ten dollars a day."

"Perfect!" I hand him my license. "Go ahead and give it to me for the week."

"Room number?"

"I'm going to put it on my corporate card." I pause. "Actually, would you mind writing on the invoice that it's a Ford Focus?"

He looks at me over the top of the screen. "That the Jag is a Ford Focus."

"Yes," I say.

"But you want the Jag."

"Yes. But I want you to say it's a Ford Focus."

"That's a pricey Ford Focus," he remarks.

"Maybe it's a turbo."

"They don't come turbo," he says.

"Are you going to do this for me or not?"

He thinks about it for a second. "Not."

"Whatever." I hand him my corporate card. "Lyle will just have to deal."

I drive north on U.S. 1 toward Marathon Key. I'm passing through Sugarloaf when Mattie calls. "The wedding favors are waiting for you at the front desk," I tell her.

"Oh, *wonderful*! I felt terrible asking you to do it. I know how busy you are. In two days I've seen how your life is . . . it's so . . ."

"Hectic?"

"Well, yes, but more—"

"Harrowing?"

"Oh, I don't know if—"

"The stuff of legend?"

"*Complicated,*" she says. "I hate burdening you with something minor like this, but I didn't have a moment to spare."

"No worries," I say. "It was a laff riot. It was a long ride on the chuckle truck."

"Sorry dear, what?"

"It was fine," I say. "Freddy and I had fun."

She yammers on about a few other things, then we hang up. I put the top down and turn up the radio. It's another beautiful day. Too bad I have to spend it indoors.

Not too, *too* bad, though. I told Will's mom the truth yesterday: I like my job. And I'm pretty good at it. I'm a decent analytical thinker, I'm quick on my feet and I have a good memory. I'm especially talented at prepping witnesses for deposition. I ought to be—I've done it dozens of times. At a big firm like mine, junior lawyers aren't allowed to do the fun stuff, like appearing in court or actually taking depositions. Preparing witnesses is about as much responsibility as we get. And for good reason: nobody graduates from law school knowing anything about being a lawyer. A recent law grad is like a newborn panda, mewling and useless. She needs a few years of growth and experience before she can be released into the wild without getting eaten. I chose my firm because it's one of the best at training lawyers. And I'm learning a lot.

I just wish it wasn't in the service of EnerGreen. Some people are on the side of angels? I'm right here, next to the red dude with the big fork. Not always—not all the firm's clients are evil—but EnerGreen is. I have to keep reminding myself that my purpose right now is essentially selfish. If I don't become a decent lawyer, I'm of no use to anyone. After a few years, I can leave the dark side and use my amazing legal skills to do something useful.

Because being a lawyer is great. It's mentally engaging and competitive and fun. Work is really the only time that I feel focused.

That's not true. One other thing focuses me. But I don't get paid for it.

That's not true. I got paid for it once.

Misunderstanding!

Anyway, I'm good at prepping witnesses because I'm good at reading people. That's a little gift I inherited from Gran. It's what made her such a great lawyer—intuition that allowed her to size up clients, connect with witnesses and persuade judges and juries. Like her, I always know when someone is lying. I can divine a person's true intentions and motivations.

So what motivates Peter A. Hoffman, certified public accountant?

Fear.

Fear and doughnuts.

He's attacking a plate of them when I walk into the conference room at his resort. "Help yourself," he says with his mouth full. "I ordered us some coffee, too."

I sit down across from him. I pull out my binder and a legal pad and place them on the table. I take my laptop out of my bag.

"My family's at the pool," he tells me. "How long's this gonna take?"

I uncap my pen. "Most of the morning."

"The whole morning?" he whines. "Why?"

I set my pen down and regard him for a moment. He's a squat man with a balding buzz cut and doughy cheeks. He's wearing khaki shorts and a Hawaiian shirt sprinkled with powdered sugar.

"Mr. Hoffman. Pete. Your employer, my firm's client, EnerGreen Energy, is the defendant in a lawsuit. A multibillion-dollar lawsuit. You are aware of this, correct?"

"EnerGreen Energy isn't my employer per se," he says. "I work for a subsidiary."

"Fine. But you know that there's a case arising from the collapse of the Deepwater Discovery oil platform in the Gulf of Mexico two years ago. You know that the plaintiffs—residents of the coastline of Louisiana and Mississippi—are seeking twenty billion dollars in damages from EnerGreen for injury to the environment, loss of tourism, medical expenses, loss of their livelihoods. Right?"

"Of course," he says.

"Good," I say. "Right now, we're in what's called the discovery phase of the lawsuit, when the parties gather information from each other. The plaintiffs are looking for evidence to prove their claims, and we, EnerGreen, are looking for evidence we can use to defend ourselves.

The plaintiffs asked EnerGreen for a lot of documents, some of which we gave them. Now they want to ask questions of the people they think may have knowledge of the matters in dispute."

"Right," Pete says. "Like an interview."

"Pete," I say sharply. "This is not just some interview. This is legally binding testimony. You're going to be sworn in by an officer of the court. That means that if you do not tell the truth, you're committing perjury. You could go to jail."

At last he looks worried.

"The plaintiffs' lawyer is going to ask you questions. He's not Matt Lauer. He's not Jon Stewart. He's a trained interrogator who's going to wring as much information out of you as he possibly can. He's also going to try to make you look like a bad guy. Like a liar and a scumbag. He's going to make you out to be a key player in the worst environmental disaster ever to hit the Gulf of Mexico."

He's gone pale. "I'm an accountant! I had nothing to do with the spill!"

"He doesn't care, Pete! His job is to make you look bad. During the deposition, the plaintiffs' lawyer can ask you whatever he wants. There's no judge there to stop him. The attorney defending you can object, but that's a legal formality—it doesn't stop the questions. Unless the plaintiffs ask about something privileged—communications between you and your lawyer—you have to answer."

Over the top? Sure. But it's doing the trick. His forehead is gleaming.

"Now you, Pete, are in a particularly awkward position," I continue. "The plaintiffs have gotten their hands on a few of your e-mails. Do you know which ones I'm talking about?"

He nods slowly, staring at me like a petrified gerbil.

"I'm here to help you, Pete. I'm going to guide you through everything, step by step. I'll teach you how to listen to the questions, how to think about them, how to answer. If you pay attention and do exactly what I say, the deposition will go very well."

I give him a wide smile. He smiles back. I stop smiling.

"But only if you work hard. If you give bad testimony? The case goes down in flames. EnerGreen loses, and it's all your fault. Twenty billion dollars. That's not loose change, even for the world's third-largest energy company. Imagine putting that on your résumé, Pete. Do you want EnerGreen to lose?"

"No, ma'am," he whispers. Even the backs of his pudgy little hands are sweating now.

I smile at him again. "Good. Let's get started."

I begin with the mechanics. The stenographer will sit here, to your right. Speak slowly and clearly, so that she has time to catch everything.

The camera will be here. When you speak, look into the camera, not at the attorney asking you questions. He will be to your left.

"Your attorney will be sitting next to the stenographer," I say. "His name is Philip Gardiner. Philip will be defending EnerGreen during the deposition on Friday. He'll object to questions and make sure you understand what's going on. He's there to help you."

"Okay," Pete says.

"If you don't understand a question, say so. Ask for it to be rephrased or repeated. The last thing I want you doing is guessing at what the plaintiffs' lawyer is trying to ask."

He picks out another doughnut. "Okay."

We run through some practice questions and answers, starting with the preliminaries: his education, his work history, the general duties of accountants, his job at EnerGreen. He's stiff and awkward at first, but slowly gets more comfortable.

"I'm going to let you in on a secret, Pete. There is one simple rule to acing a deposition. Learn it, and this thing is in the bag. Are you ready?"

"Yes, ma'am."

"Here's the rule. Listen to the question, and answer *only* that question."

"Those're two rules," he says.

"It's one rule. With two subparts."

"You should call it two rules," he says. "Easier to remember that way."

He reaches for another doughnut. I slap his hand away. He jumps in his chair and looks at me with startled eyes.

"I need you to focus here, Pete. What I'm saying is important. In order to answer the question correctly, you have to understand the question. You don't want to answer a question that hasn't been asked of you, do you?"

"No, ma'am."

"Right!" I say. "*Never* say anything beyond the bounds of what the questioner posed to you."

"Can I have a doughnut now?"

"No. We're going to do an exercise. Remember the rule," I say. "Listen to the question and answer only that question."

"Yes, ma'am." He pauses. "Was that the exercise?"

"No. This is it. Do you know what time it is, Pete?"

He checks his watch. "Ten forty-five."

"Wrong," I say.

"Sorry," he says. "It's ten forty-three."

"The answer is 'yes'!" I shout. "The answer to the question, 'Do you know what time it is?' is 'Yes'!"

"What if I'm not wearing a watch?" he whispers.

I put my head in my hands. "Let's take a break."

Pete scuttles out of the room. I text Will:

—get yr tuxedo?

—I just picked it up.

—try it on for me later?

—Bad luck!

—fine. just bowtie

Will doesn't answer. When Pete comes back, I remove the e-mails from my binder and place them in front of him. "Do you recognize these documents, Pete?"

He glances at them quickly. "I know those e-mails. I wrote 'em."

"Do you remember sending them?"

"Yes'm, I do."

"You are telling me, Mr. Hoffman, that you have a specific, clear recollection of sending these e-mails. You remember," I bore deeply into his droopy little eyes, "sitting down at your desk one morning, turning to your crumb-strewn keyboard and typing each and every one of these words?"

"My keyboard's not—"

"Under *oath*," I continue relentlessly, "under penalty of *perjury,* you are testifying here today that you recognize both of these e-mails, word for word, that you remember the date, the hour, the minute, the *second* your index finger hit 'send'?"

He looks frozen. "No?"

"Okay!" I say. "So you don't specifically remember sending these e-mails?"

He grins. "Sure I do!"

For once I'm glad I won't be defending this deposition. As second chair, all I'll have to do is keep an eye on the running transcript and hand Philip the occasional document. Watching how he deals with this yahoo will be good experience, at least.

"Let's talk about what you actually wrote here, Pete. What did you mean when you said that you were going to give certain figures a, quote, good old scrub-a-dub, end quote?"

"That's an accounting term," he tells me.

"'Scrub-a-dub' is an accounting term?"

"Scrubbing numbers, massaging numbers." He waves a dismissive hand. "It's standard CPA terminology."

"Is 'It's kind of a scam' standard accounting terminology, too?"

"Sure."

"What does it mean?"

"You know," he says, "that something's a little off. A little fishy. Not quite right."

I stare at him for a moment. "Pete? That's what 'It's kind of a scam' means in non-accounting terminology, too."

"Oh yeah," he chuckles. "Right."

I grip my pen tightly. "You need to avoid using that sort of language during your deposition. The plaintiffs want sound bites, pithy little quotes that they can put in a brief, or cite in their opening arguments, or plaster across the Internet to make EnerGreen look bad. Don't oblige them. If you find yourself about to give an answer that uses the word 'scrub,' or 'massage,' or 'scam,' or 'creative accounting,' or 'fraud,' or anything that those of us here in the *real world* consider negative, just— don't say it, okay?"

He looks chastened. "I'll try."

I drill him on the e-mails for a long time. I finally get him to a place where he can testify that what he wrote was a combination of imprecise wording, wonky CPA talk and playful irony. That the other accountants he was e-mailing would have understood that he wasn't actually suggesting that they commit fraud, lie to their auditors or hide anything from anybody. It's not great, but it's the best I can do.

We take another break, and I check my phone. I have a new e-mail.

> Hi honey ok know you dont want to hear it but we are worried you havent thought this thru! gran never told you the whole story about her husband (my dad) but maybe it'll help you understnad why we're making a big deal out of this. Gran grew up poor as you know the family having hit hard times and she had terrible teeth because they didnt have any money for dental care plus in those days people werent aware about flossing like they are now.

This is my mother's signature style. The woman changes the oil in her own truck, can fix almost any mechanical object and has an encyclopedic knowledge of tropical hardwoods. But she punctuates like a modern poet.

> she went up to Miami for law school she met a wonderful man. A dentist. The initial attraction having been due to her dental problems but she loved him and she married him very fast only to find out he was a TERRIBLE GAMBLER. Several times they would have to leave where they were living in the middle of the night as they didn't have the rent money. She got pregnant (me) and had to drop out of school. And then one night he didnt come home and she waited and waited sure that his debts had caught up with him but no.
>
> He ran off with his HYGIENIST!
>
> Now im not saying this is what Will is going to do (of course!!!) but that marriage distracted her from what she wanted to do and of course she got back on track but it was

HARD. People maek big life decisions without thinking and it
matters honey!

Love,
Mom

I start composing a snarky reply, but I hesitate. Mom means well.
She always means well. And I love her to pieces. She used to play with
me for hours when I was little—get right down on the floor with my
wooden blocks and dolls and dinosaurs, building fantastical structures,
inventing whole worlds. But as I got older, she had a harder time dealing
with me. Reasoning and argument were not her things. I could talk cir-
cles around her, tie her up in knots. She couldn't discipline me for shit.
Fortunately Gran was there to stop me from going totally off the rails.
Until she couldn't.

Why am I thinking about this now? I shake out of it and type a
quick reply:

Wow—crazy story! can't believe hadnt heard this one before.
talk soon—busy today with work. thanks mom! xxL

I toss my phone into my bag as Pete shuffles back into the room. It's
almost one. "Now, Pete," I say, for what feels like the millionth time,
"the plaintiffs allege that EnerGreen committed fraud in its financial
statements by inflating the projected costs of the oil spill in order to hide
losses racked up by the company's energy trading subsidiary."

"Yep," Pete says confidently.

I stare at him hard. "What do you mean, 'yep'?"

He suddenly looks super shifty. "I mean," he says slowly, "that I understand that what you just contended, right there, is that which the
plaintiffs also are themselves contending with."

Jesus, this is painful. I remove a few more documents from my binder
and spread them on the table. "Let's talk about the financial statements,
Pete. I'm going to pretend to be the plaintiffs' lawyer, okay?"

"Yes'm."

"Mr. Hoffman, do you recognize this document?"

"Yes'm."

"Can you tell me what it is?"

"This is EnerGreen Energy, Inc.'s 2012 annual report to the Securities and Exchange Commission," he says.

"Would you please turn to page forty-five?"

"Yes'm."

"Do you see at the top of the page, in Schedule 9, line 14, that the projected damages from the Deepwater Discovery oil spill are assessed at $55 billion?"

"Yes'm."

I finally snap. "Enough with the goddamned yes'ms!"

He looks cowed. "Okay."

"You're killing me with the yes'ms, Pete."

"Sorry."

"I'd like to show you a different document," I say, handing him another one. "This is the insurance claim that EnerGreen Energy filed with AIG, its primary accident insurer. Do you see that on page four, EnerGreen projects its total losses from the spill as only $25 billion?"

"Yes," Pete says.

"Mr. Hoffman. How do you explain that while EnerGreen was telling the SEC and its shareholders that damages from the spill were going to be over $50 billion, it was telling its insurers that the losses were only going to be $25 billion?"

Pete shifts in his seat. "I would say that when you're dealing with audited financials, which is an extensive process, a multifaceted process, there's always lots of moving pieces, balls in the air if you will. You've got various cost centers utilizing different metrics and rubrics to achieve your ultimate outcomes. Any discrepancies therein would be in the normal course caught and corrected in the standard processes of verification and reconciliation."

"That makes absolutely no sense," I tell him.

"Are you you right now," he asks, "or the plaintiffs?"

"I'm me," I say. "What's the truth?"

"We were using the spill to hide major losses from our trading division," he says.

I stare at him.

"Our traders had entered these long-term forward swaps that fixed the price of natural gas at year-end 2011 levels," Pete continues. "But the price plummeted when a new field was discovered out there in Uzbekistan. We were stuck in these godawful contracts, which they tried to hedge by entering into a different set of swaps pegged to the price of titanium—"

I wasn't following him, but I didn't have to. "Fraud," I say. "You're talking about fraud."

Pete looks taken aback. "I don't know that I'd call it fraud."

"What would you call it?"

He thinks a moment. "You're right," he says. "It's fraud."

He keeps explaining, and all I can do is gape at him. He's so nonchalant. He's just told me that his employer is committing accounting fraud, securities fraud and probably a dozen other kinds of fraud I've never even heard of. EnerGreen, a company responsible for one of the most horrific environmental disasters in history, actually saw that disaster as a convenient opportunity to hide other mistakes, a handy way to lie, cheat and steal so that it could keep making money.

And what's Pete doing? Sitting here serene as can be, eyeing the last doughnut.

"How big are the losses?" I ask him.

"North of fifteen billion."

My mouth drops open. "Fifteen *billion* dollars? That's enough to bring down the company."

"You bet. If the truth got out? Credit would dry up. We wouldn't have enough cash to cover daily operations. It'd be your classic run-on-the-bank scenario."

He pauses, glancing at the doughnut, then at me. I nod. He takes it.

"That's why we had to hide the losses," he continues, his mouth full. "What I said in that e-mail is true. The spill was a goddamned godsend, coming when it did."

A goddamned godsend. I take out my phone and text Philip:

—Big problems at the deposition prep. Can you please call me?
  Thanks.

Then I text Lyle:

—hoffman = nightmare. we have to postpone dep

I stand up. "We're done here, Pete."

"We are?"

"I think it's safe to say that your deposition is not going to happen anytime soon. My boss is going to call your boss's boss's boss's lawyer, and then somebody's going to write a big check, and we're all going to say good-bye."

Lyle writes back:

—Call me. Also pltffs want his empl records.

—dep cant happen, lyle!

—Just do it.

Unbelievable. "So there's one last thing," I say to Pete. "In the highly unlikely event that this deposition goes forward sometime in the very distant future, the plaintiffs want us to produce your employment records. It's a formality, but we have to do it or they'll yell and scream and accuse us of violating the rules. You said something about working for a subsidiary?"

"Right," he says. "EnerGreen Energy Solutions LLC. We just opened a branch office in Key West. I came down to help set up their accounting system and decided to bring the family. The office has a couple geologists doing deepwater testing around here."

"Hey," I say. "Awesome. Welcome to the Florida Keys, EnerGreen."

"There's a secretary there named Maria. She can get you what you need."

"Why do you work for an LLC?"

"It's a tax dodge," he explains.

Why did I ask? Why?

Pete looks worried. "They gonna ask me about that?"

"They're not going to ask you about anything. Ever." I hold out my hand. "It was really nice meeting you, Pete. Enjoy the rest of your vacation."

11

I dial Philip's number as soon as I step outside. Betty says he's on the other line. I tell her to interrupt him. She tells me, politely, to go to hell. I hang up and think. I need to call Urs, our in-house lawyer. There's no way he knows about the fraud—he's far too upstanding to have kept it from us. Which means EnerGreen employees lied to him—their own attorney—about what Pete's e-mails really meant. Insanity! I start dialing his number, but hesitate. Lowly associates aren't supposed to deal with the client directly. It would be a major breach of protocol to go over Philip's head like that. So I call Lyle.

"We have a problem," I say when he answers. "The plaintiffs are right. About everything. EnerGreen is committing fraud. Massive, crazy fraud. Hoffman told me everything. He's a disaster, by the way. He—"

"Slow down," Lyle says. "What happened?"

I take a deep breath and tell him everything.

"Jesus," he says when I'm done. "Jesus."

"This case has to settle, Lyle. Now. I tried calling Philip but I couldn't get through. He needs to talk to the client. He needs to convince them to settle. But first and foremost, someone needs to call the plaintiffs and postpone this deposition."

"Relax, Wilder. The deposition isn't going to happen. EnerGreen made a new settlement offer this morning. Philip is on the phone with the mediator right now."

So that's why Lyle sounds so calm. "That's such great news!" I say.

"I know. I'm drafting the paperwork as we speak."

I lean back against the hood of the car. The anxiety I felt moments ago begins to fade. "I'm so glad this case is over. EnerGreen. Ugh. What a bunch of scumbags."

"Alleged scumbags," Lyle corrects me. "And they're no worse than our other clients."

"Are you kidding me? They're criminals. You should have seen this guy sit there inhaling doughnuts and describing how EnerGreen is flirting with total financial collapse."

"It sounds rough," he agrees. "I'm sorry you had to deal with it alone."

It's nice to have a halfway civil conversation with him. The prospect of settlement must be putting him in a good mood.

"Will you be sure to tell Philip everything I told you about the prep? He needs to know how deep this hole is and impress upon Urs that EnerGreen really does have to suck it up and pay."

"I'll tell him," Lyle says. "In fact, that's him on the other line. I better go."

We hang up. I feel much better. The morning was a total waste, with some truly dire moments, but it's going to be fine.

Then something else occurs to me. Do I have a personal obligation to report EnerGreen to the authorities? I can't remember the exact ethics rule, but I know someone who will. I dial Gran's number.

"What's the rule about client confidentiality and the commission of a crime?" I ask.

"Florida Rule of Professional Conduct four dash one point six, subsection b, part one," she replies instantly. "A lawyer must reveal information pertaining to the representation of a client to the extent the lawyer reasonably believes such disclosure necessary to prevent the client from committing a crime."

"She's still got it, folks!"

"Who cares?" she grumbles. "I might as well be dead."

"So if the crime has already been committed, I don't have to reveal it?"

"Not only do you not have to," she says, "you can't. Client confidentiality."

"Sweet!"

"What's this about?" she asks suspiciously.

"Can't tell you! Duh!"

"Please give me something," she pleads. "I'm so bored."

I listen to her complain for a while about gardening and crossword puzzles and chair yoga. I consider asking her about the dentist. I'd always had a general idea of who he was and why they got divorced, but I'd never heard the full story before. Compulsive gambling and irresistible hygienists is one thing. But Gran deferring her career for a man? Impossible to imagine.

Instead I say, "Why didn't you tell me Teddy was back?"

There's a pause. "Is he?"

"Please, Isabel. You know everything that happens around here."

"Leave him alone, Lillian Grace."

"He came looking for me!"

"He's doing well," she tells me. "It's a miracle the state took him on, after . . . what happened. Being in the service probably helped."

"Sorry, *what?*"

"He was in the army," Gran says.

Teddy, in the army? There's no way.

"Let it go," Gran warns me.

"Fine," I say. "I'm letting it go. This is me, letting it go."

"I'm serious, Lily."

"So am I. Later, Gran."

I head back to Key West and immediately get snarled in construction traffic on Roosevelt. I see the sign for the EnerGreen Solutions office—the subsidiary Pete mentioned. I might as well get his employment file, dotting my i's and crossing my t's like a good little associate. There are a few protesters gathered in the parking lot when I pull in. I smile and wave at them as I go inside. I try to be pleasant whenever I run into people protesting the oil spill. They're generally pretty nice one-on-one, and their signs are hilarious. (EnerGreed! Obvious, but clever.)

I find Maria and arrange to have copies of Pete's employment records sent to the firm. I call my paralegal and tell her to send them along to the plaintiffs when they arrive. Pulling out of the parking lot, I spot my mom's truck going by. I honk, but she doesn't notice. I decide to follow her. Maybe we can grab a late lunch. She winds her way into Old Town and pulls up in front of a house covered with scaffolding and plastic sheeting. One of her signs is stuck in the yard: ANOTHER BANG-UP JOB BY WILDER CONSTRUCTION! So embarrassing. I used to steal them all the time when I was in middle school, on principle.

She hops out of her truck and disappears around the side of the house. I park and watch her. Mom's looking much more put-together than usual. Her t-shirt and shorts look clean. Her hair is combed and tied back neatly. Maybe she's meeting a client.

I try calling Will before I get out of the car. No answer. I try Philip again just to make sure Lyle conveyed the seriousness of the situation, but he's still tied up. I skim my work e-mail. My phone pings. It's Ana, texting me a selfie from a dressing room somewhere. She's modeling a goofy-looking, multicolored peasant get-up. She writes:

—ok?

I write back:

—youll be a huge hit at the harvest festival

—bitch!!!

I finally walk up to the house and follow a little brick path along the side. It winds between some overgrown bushes and leads to a weather-beaten kitchen door. I glance through the foggy glass.

Rusty old appliances, tools and boxes of building materials are scattered around the room. I see my mother, too.

But she ain't working.

Instead, she's lying on a pile of moving blankets, moaning and clutching the very attractive buttocks of the man who is stretched on top of her, screwing her vigorously.

I jump away. Then I look again. I know that sounds kind of sick, but it's not like I can see her or anything! I'm watching her friend. He's in really good shape. Nice ass, as I mentioned. Great back, too. Backs. They're underrated. You don't think about them until you see a really nice one and then it's like . . .

Wow, he has *lots* of energy.

I know, I know—this should appall me. But it makes me happy.

For her, I mean.

I should stop watching.

Should I, though? Let's face it. Men? They're not that hot. Not all-around, like women are. Men have random hairs and bad fashion instincts. Odd smells. They never exfoliate. Either they try way too hard, or they don't try at all. Of course, some are lovely, and most have a few good qualities, but sometimes you have to look hard for them. Like in those *Where's Waldo?* books. Or the cocktail menus of trendy Brooklyn restaurants, where it's all locally sourced moonshine and heritage groats and fermented parsnip shavings, and you really have to study the damn thing to find something drinkable.

My point: when you come across a handsome man, such as the one banging away at my mother right now, it's hard not to stare. You feel special. Honored. It's probably how bird-watchers feel when they've been sitting in a treehouse all day, with their binoculars and their water-resistant pants, and they finally catch a glimpse of a rare three-toed grackle or whatever. There's that same sense of wonder and delight.

Except they don't want to fuck the grackle.

Or maybe they do. Maybe that's the point of bird-watching. I don't know.

They are *really* going at it.

I'm going to stop watching now.

You know what, though? I'm happy that Mom has found someone. I tend to think of her as this sad old nun. She was so heartbroken when Dad left her. So bereft. She eventually recovered, but she never dated while I was growing up. She threw all her energy into two things: her business, and me. In her more maudlin moments, she would say that my father was the only man for her.

Oh.

Oh, *no.*

People sometimes refer to a man as "devastatingly handsome." It's an apt phrase. A truly gorgeous man can buckle your knees. Kill you a little inside. Because there he is, proof that perfection has existed out in the world, all this time, but it's not for the likes of you. All you can do is gaze, lingeringly, dream a little, and thank the gods for this little foretaste of heaven.

That becomes a little complicated, though, if you also happen to call that man—

"Dad!" I shout, pounding my fist on the window.

They fly apart. Oh, God—total nudity! I quickly retreat to the front yard.

My father is a devastatingly, painfully, ridiculously handsome man. He's pushing fifty, but he's got it all going on. A full head of wavy black hair, barely starting to grey. An athletic body. An unlined face with a pair of amazing green eyes. He would have been a great movie star, because he's charismatic as hell. He's also got this patrician, British thing going on that's pretty irresistible. If you're into that sort of thing.

Which, you know. Some people are.

Basically, Henry's like a minor deity, one of those cupbearers who were always bringing the gods of Olympus their coffee and snacks, and always causing fights.

I look just like him.

Ha ha! Nope.

I look like Mom. We're all right, but compared to Dad we're total trolls.

I hear the kitchen door bang. Here he comes, pulling on his shirt. "Little one!" he cries, opening his arms. "Let me have a look at you!"

I back away, hands up. "No touching, okay, Henry? I can't handle it right now."

I watched them for way too long. I should probably order up a marathon session with Dr. Boog.

"Darling," Dad says, all wounded. "Come inside. Let's talk."

I follow him reluctantly into the kitchen and take a seat on a folding chair. He pours some champagne into a Dixie cup and hands it to me.

"Where did this come from?"

"I brought it with me from the hotel," he says. "They make the most brilliant insulated bags nowadays. Shaped like wine bottles!"

I raise my cup. "To progress."

"Cheers." He taps his paper cup against mine. We drink.

My mother slips in from another room, eyes on the ground. They sit across from me on a couple of packing crates.

I take another sip and set my cup on the floor. "Well, children," I say, clapping my hands on my knees. "This *is* a surprise!"

"Oh, honey," Mom says. "I'm sorry you had to find out this way. I'm so embarrassed!"

Dad turns to her, genuinely surprised. "What on earth for?"

"Can we back up for a second?" I say. "You two haven't seen each other for years, as far as I know—although I'm beginning to wonder if I know as much as I think I know. Anyway, you don't get along. You've never gotten along. How did this even happen?"

"Things have been a bit frosty these past few years," Dad agrees. "I suppose the change was really thanks to you. A few months ago, your mother called me to talk about your engagement. We had this lovely conversation, didn't we, Kat?" He brushes a lock of hair behind her ear. "We talked about the wedding, our time together here in Key West, and you, of course." He turns his smile on me now. I feel my face getting hot. I quickly finish off my champagne.

"It was wonderful to catch up," Mom says. "After that, we started calling each other fairly regularly. Normal, parents-of-the-bride-type things."

"And then," Dad says eagerly, "we both happened to be in front of our computers one day, and your mother taught me how to use Skype. Do you know about Skype?"

"Skype?" I say. "Gosh, what's that?"

"It's only the most ingenious—"

Mom puts a hand on his leg. "She knows what Skype is, Henry."

"Then you know how *magical* it is!" He slips an arm around her waist. "To be able to see her again—it was incredible!" Mom rests her head on his shoulder. "We exchanged a few more e-mails and texts," Dad continues. "We did some more Skypes. Ultimately, we decided that I should come down early to see if something might happen." He smiles broadly. "And something definitely happened."

Mom buries her face in her hands.

"Nice, Dad. How long have you been here?"

"Two days." He lifts the bottle. "Shall I top you off?"

I hold out my cup. "So when you called me on Sunday . . ."

"I was trying to reach your mother," he admits.

"Mystery solved." I sip my drink. "How about this weather?"

"Magnificent," he says. "But then, it always is."

"February is sometimes iffy. When we were picking a date, we thought—"

"You really aren't bothered by this?" Mom asks.

"Of course not," I say. "Who am I to judge?"

And really, I'm happy to see her so happy. She's radiant.

"There you are, Kat." Dad pats her knee. "I told you she wouldn't mind."

"Do Jane and Ana know?" I ask.

Mom hangs her head again. Dad shakes his.

"I'm keeping out of it," I say. "I don't have a dog in this fight. Actually, all my dogs are in this fight. Comes to the same thing, I guess. Where's Trina?"

"She's in Vilnius," Dad says. "Her mother is rather ill."

"What's wrong with her?"

He frowns. "Cancer, I'm afraid."

"Cancer," I say. "Her mother is 'rather ill' with cancer."

"I know it seems awful," Mom says quickly, "but you have to understand—"

"Hey!" I cry. "Déjà vu! Dad—remember when I was sixteen, and you caught me and Charlie Hurst in the pool house in Montauk?"

"You were fifteen," Dad replies. "And yes, I remember."

We shoot the breeze awhile longer. It's really nice. I can't remember the last time the three of us hung out together like this. Dad opens another bottle of champagne. Eventually he walks me back to my car.

"So, what does this mean?" I ask him. "Are you getting back together?"

Dad frowns. "It's difficult to say. We're taking it step by step. I'm very fond of your mother, of course, but there are so many other factors to consider . . ."

He drapes an arm around my shoulder as he continues to talk. I close my eyes. He smells so good.

"But listen to me!" he cries. "Banging on about myself while this week is supposed to be about you. I've been neglecting you, darling, and I'm sorry. Are they still trying to talk you out of it? Shall I intervene?"

"Honestly, Daddy? You're probably not the most persuasive advocate for holy matrimony right now."

He actually looks hurt.

"Anyway, it's under control," I add. "There are only four more days until the wedding."

Four more days?

Oh, God.

He squeezes my arm affectionately. "Whatever you think best. But when am I going to meet this Will character?"

"Tonight's his bachelor party. Should I see if he can meet us for a drink beforehand?"

He grimaces. "Tonight's no good for me."

"How about dinner tomorrow?"

"No . . . I'm afraid tomorrow doesn't work either."

I stop walking and turn to face him. "You're in Key West, Dad. What could you *possibly* have going on?"

He scuffs a bare foot in the grass, looking abashed. "Oh, this and that. Seeing old friends. Catching up on paperwork."

Paperwork? Whatever—it's not worth interrogating him. "You'll meet Will on Thursday, at any rate. That's the night the families are getting together for dinner."

He's stopped listening. He glances back over his shoulder at the house. "Right," he says. "Well. I suppose I should . . . get back in there. If you don't mind?"

"Sure, Dad." I give him a big hug. "It's good to see you."

"You too, little one." He gives me a jaunty wave and sprints back into the house.

12

I drive back to the hotel. What a strange day. I sit out on the balcony and watch the sunset. I text Freddy:

—hiya

—holla

—will @ bachelor party

—bastard!

—right?

—we'll show him

For my second bachelorette party, we gather all the newly arrived guests and stake out space at the pool. Lights flicker in the palm trees. A jazz trio is playing at the bar. I settle into a lounge chair between Freddy and Nicole. Miraculously, Nicole's phone is nowhere to be seen. We chat about work, about the wedding. She actually seems to be enjoying herself.

A gorgeous guy walks past us. Freddy puts a hand over her heart. "Unbearable," I agree.

Nicole rolls her eyes.

"What," I laugh. "I can't look now?"

"Since when have you ever just looked?" Nicole is smiling, but there's an unmistakable edge to her voice.

"Lighten up," Freddy tells her. "We're having fun."

She shrugs. "If you say so. I think it's kind of sad."

I should have known her good mood wouldn't last. It's a shame. Nicole and I were so close in law school. She was always on the prickly side, but she was also cool and funny and wickedly smart. Lately she's turned all dour and judgmental. I think the breakup with her boyfriend made her bitter.

"What's sad about appreciating a good-looking man?" I ask.

"What's sad is that you only act this way when you've been drinking," she replies.

"Not true," Freddy informs her. "I've seen Lily check out guys when she's completely sober. Like while driving. Or at the doctor. Or at funerals."

"Hey," I say. "Don't want people to ogle? Don't have an open casket."

"I'm serious," Nicole says over our laughter. "It makes you seem like one of those women who goes out and gets hammered so that she can shed her inhibitions."

Does this person know me at all? "Alcohol lowers my standards, not my inhibitions," I say. "Big difference."

Freddy and I clink glasses. But Nicole won't let it go. "I'm concerned about you, Lily."

"That's very touching," Freddy says tartly. "But there are a couple of flaws in your argument."

"I'm not making an argument," Nicole says. "I'm only suggesting—"

Freddy interrupts her. "Of course you're making an argument. Why deny it? Lily drinks, and Lily screws around. You conclude that Lily screws around *because* she drinks. Isn't it equally possible that Lily drinks because she screws around? Or, what's far more likely, that the two have nothing to do with each other?"

"Possible, sure," Nicole says. "But most women aren't like that."

"Oh, okay," Freddy says. "So we're not actually talking about Lily, then. We're talking about 'most women,' and what 'most women' do. Interesting."

Nicole turns to me. "Am I so off base here?"

"Yes."

"The random hookups? The meaningless sex? Do you really enjoy it?"

"Yes."

Nicole shakes her head. "I don't buy it."

At which point I finally lose patience. "Why, because I'm a woman? And women aren't like that? They don't *really* enjoy sex? They don't lust?"

"No, but—

"I'm faking it, huh? It's all a big trap to catch a man and have his babies? Good to know, Nicole. Thanks. I love it when women explain other women to themselves. And when they top it off with a hefty dollop of condescension? That really warms my heart."

Nicole gets up and walks away. I set my empty glass down on the table. Freddy's watching me.

"Too harsh?"

Freddy shrugs. "When the scars heal, she'll probably appreciate the extra asshole. What's got you so worked up?"

"Long day. Weird day. For example, I caught my mom and dad doing it on the floor of an abandoned house this afternoon."

"Katherine? And Henry?" she cries. "Together?"

"Yes, yes and a big old yes." She begs for the gory details. I oblige. I haven't been able to stop thinking about it. My parents, together again. My father, cheating on his fifth wife with his first. The implications for my own marital future are . . . not great.

Freddy leans back in her chair contentedly. "Your father is a beautiful man. I would have watched, too. Hell, I would have joined in."

I shift uncomfortably in my chair. "But he's not your father."

"This would make an amazing country song! I caught my momma and my poppa on the kitchen flo'," she belts out, "but they sho ain't married to each other no mo'!"

"I think you're missing the point, Freddy."

"Hold that thought. I have to pee." She disappears.

I get up and wander around. The party is in full bloom. I greet old friends and meet some of Will's relatives and school buddies. It's a lot of fun, but I'm still troubled. I head for the bar. Before I can get there, my friend Diane comes screaming up and practically tackles me to the ground. I'm so happy to see her! We met as teenagers at the hospital. Now she's a psychiatrist herself, which is perfect because she's totally insane.

"I need some advice," I tell her.

"Don't do it," she says.

"Don't do what?"

"Whatever you were thinking about doing."

"Why not?"

"Because whatever it was, it wasn't your first impulse," Diane explains. "If it had been, you wouldn't be asking for advice—you would have just done it. And if it wasn't your first impulse, it's not in your nature to do it. So you shouldn't do it."

"I have absolutely no idea what we're talking about," I say.

"Good," Diane says. "Go with that."

Freddy has joined us. "So what if it was Lily's first impulse? She can change."

"People don't change." Diane points to the cocktail Freddy just handed me. "Are you going to drink that?"

I give it to her. "You're a psychiatrist, and you're telling me I can't change?"

"Maybe a little, around the margins," she replies. "But no, not really."

"I'm so screwed."

"You're not screwed," Diane says. "Your life is awesome. You're marrying Indiana Jones!"

I laugh. "Will is no Indiana Jones."

"He's so fucking hot!" Diane cries. "Does he wear the hat in bed?"

I put my arms around her. "Speaking of bed, I think we need to help you find yours, quick."

Instead, she staggers off, and Freddy brings me another drink. We sit down. Everyone is pink and tipsy, happily chatting about how they've been taking advantage of all that the island has to offer. My friends Leta and Caroline kayaked through the mangroves today. Another group went snorkeling. Will's Aunt Dahlia won't stop raving about the seafood. They're all talking about dodging some snowstorm that's barreling toward the East Coast, how relieved they are to be here in paradise, where it's all warm breezes, fruity drinks and shimmering pool.

My phone pings with a text.

—What up?

I reply:

—nada

—Bored?

—maybe

—Send me a picture

—what of

—Surprise me

Freddy looks over my shoulder at the screen. "Why is your dry cleaner texting you right now?"

"It's not my actual dry cleaner," I explain. "It's a guy I met there. That's how I keep track."

"Interesting," she says. "I thought that's why someone invented names."

"This way, Will won't get suspicious if he looks at my phone."

Dry Cleaner writes:

—I want u now

"Because that's not suspicious," Freddy says. She puts down her drink and takes the phone from me, scrolling through my contacts. "Nails, Hair, Hardware Store . . ."

I sigh. "Dumb, but so dreamy."

"Cleaning Lady, Pet Store." She looks up. "What were you doing at a pet store?"

I shrug. "I like to browse."

"Accountant, Dentist," she reads. "These are all fake?"

"No, Dentist is my actual dentist."

She drops the phone on the table. "I guess I should be relieved that you aren't sleeping with your dentist."

"No." I finish my drink. "Not anymore."

"Jesus, Lily!"

"What? It was great. Until it got weird."

She picks up her drink. "I don't get sexting. I've always found it skeevy."

"It's only skeevy if you're reading someone else's," I say. "But if you're the one doing it? And know who's on the other end, and what they can do? Sending one out, waiting for one to come back? Not sure what it's going to say or what it's going to show? There's nothing more exciting."

"Eh," Freddy says. "I like bodies."

"You're analog. You're lo-fi."

"I'm no-fi." The phone pings, and she picks it up. "Your dry cleaning is ready. What's the passcode?"

"9455."

She types it in. "9455," she says. "W-I-L-L. That's either very sweet, or very twisted."

She hands me the phone.

—where r u?

—1000s of miles away

—:(

"Boring!" Freddy says.

I toss the phone into my purse. "I think Will is hiding something," I say. "Something big."

Freddy stretches out her legs, crossing her ankles. "Here we go."

"He's been acting very agitated lately. Jumpy. Nervous. Not himself."

"Honey, if I were about to marry you, I wouldn't just be jumpy," she says. "I'd be shitting myself."

A waiter arrives with more drinks. "Get this," I tell her. "Will said he'd never been to Key West before, but he knew exactly where the cemetery was."

"An archaeologist knew the location of a bunch of old stuff?" Her eyes widen. "That is so fucked up!"

"And he lied about his name. It's not William. It's Wilberforce."

"No it isn't," she says automatically.

"Yes, it is."

"Wilberforce," she says. "Wilberforce Field."

"Oh my God," I whisper. "I didn't even think of that."

"He's a lost *Star Wars* character," she says. "A reject from the cantina scene!"

We about die laughing. Then Freddy stands and holds out her hand. "Come with me."

We go upstairs and sit on her balcony. We share a joint. She cracks open a couple of bottles of rum from the minibar. Then she positions her chair so that it faces mine.

"It's time for a little truth telling," she informs me.

"Oh boy."

"You know that I love you," she says. "I speak my mind, but I never judge. I support you one hundred percent. And I will defend you to the death from morons like Nicole and their bogus ideas about what all women think and how we should all behave. You are who you are, and you do what you do—the texting, the guy Sunday night, whatever's going on with your boss, *everything*—and it's just you. Your . . . whatever-you-want-to-call-it. Appetite for life. Blithe abandon. But, honey? I'm starting to get a little worried."

"I'm fine," I assure her. "Everything's under control."

"For the last three days, you bring up your doubts every time we talk. It's like you can't help yourself. But as soon as we start actually discussing them, you retreat. You deflect. You make a joke, or change the subject, or start spinning your ridiculous theory that Will is some nefarious gold digger. And I've played along. I didn't want to rush you. But it's Tuesday night. You're getting married on Saturday. Pardon my French, but Lily? It's time to shit or get off the pot."

I cover my face with my hands. "I don't know what I want, Freddy! I said yes, didn't I? It was so romantic. So sudden. He swept me off my feet. He's the kind of person a person like me should want to marry. He's interesting, and intelligent, and kind, and steady, and loving."

"So he's not a devious liar with a dark past?"

"Of course not. And here's the thing. When anyone suggests that I shouldn't marry him, or offers any impediment, I become convinced that it's the right thing to do. There's some part of me that really wants this."

"Just not all of you," she says gently.

What happened to all my certainty, my conviction last night that this was what I wanted? I stare out at the sea and watch the lights of a cruise ship move slowly across the horizon.

Freddy takes my hand and gives it a comforting squeeze. "You're such an honest person," she says. "You can speak your mind to anyone, about anything. But you can't seem to level with the one person who should know everything. I don't get it."

She doesn't get it? She should try being me for a while.

I finish my rum and lift my feet off the balcony railing. "Let's go."

"Back to the party?"

"No." I stand up. "Out. Just you and me."

13

As Freddy and I turn onto Duval, I see Teddy walking toward us, half a block away.

"Dammit," I mutter.

"What?"

He's with a girl. Not touching her, but walking close. His hands in his pockets. He says something to her. She laughs.

I look around, but there's nowhere to hide. He finally notices me. It's dark on the sidewalk, but I see him hesitate. Then he keeps walking.

"Lily." He nods. "Hi."

"Oh, hi!" I hold out my hand to the girl. "I'm Lily."

She smiles. "I'm Melanie."

She has long, strawberry-blonde hair. She's tall. Thin. Tan. Pretty.

Bitch.

What is *wrong* with me?

I turn to Teddy. "I can't believe we're running into each other like this."

"It's a small town," he replies. He's gazing at the ground, looking like he'd rather be anywhere but here.

"Right," I say. "Right." I'm still shaking Melanie's hand. I stop. "Are you guys on your way to dinner?"

She looks puzzled. "It's like one in the morning."

"No kidding!" I laugh. "That's late!"

"Yeah," she says.

"You shouldn't have left so quickly last night," I say to Teddy.

He looks up at me, and his face is grim. I turn back to Melanie. "It's not like that," I tell her. "We're old friends. We were talking at my hotel. Not *my* hotel—I don't own it. I'm staying there. And we were in the lobby, not my room or any—"

"Lily," Teddy says quietly.

"He was meeting someone else," I continue, not able to stop myself. "Not a woman, of course. A witness. Who could have been a woman, I guess. But not me!"

"Lily," Teddy says again.

"We're old friends," I say. "Did I say that already? So, yeah." I turn back to Teddy. "It was so good to see you, and to meet you—"

"And now we're leaving!" Freddy says, taking my arm. "Bye!"

We walk a few more blocks and come to a crowded bar. We go inside and find seats. The bartender comes over. "Two Jack Roses, please," Freddy says. She turns to me. "What was that?"

"What was what?"

"Your violent attack of extreme stupidity. Who was that guy?"

I don't answer. She waits.

"His name is Teddy," I tell her. "We were best friends when we were kids."

"Just friends?"

"Why does everyone keep asking me that?"

"Probably because of how you look at him," she replies. "Who else is asking?"

"Will. We ran into Teddy last night. How do I look at him? Wait," I say. "Don't answer that."

Our drinks arrive. We clink glasses.

"How come you've never told me about him?" she asks.

I raise my glass to eye level. I gaze at the cloudy red liquid inside. I turn my wrist, making it swirl gently.

"We fell out of touch," I say at last. "I haven't seen him in thirteen years."

I down my drink in three quick swallows and set the glass on the bar. Freddy waits, but I don't say anything more. I order another round. We turn on our stools with our fresh drinks and survey the crowd.

"Do you see that guy over there?" I say. "By the jukebox?"

She looks. "Dark hair?"

"That's my perfect man. Tall and thin. Slightly scruffy. Intelligent-looking. But drinking a beer. I like a man who drinks beer."

She squeezes my hand. "Is it hard, having such rarefied tastes?"

"I mean he looks intellectual, but he's doing something earthy. I like that," I say. "I like hidden depths. Someone soulful, but lusty. Cultured *and* crude. Someone who takes me to see some old French film, but we end up making out in the back row of the theater."

"That sounds more like hidden shallows," Freddy remarks.

"Hidden shallows," I repeat. "I want hidden shallows." I gesture to the bartender. "Two more, when you get a chance?"

"Here comes Perfect Man," Freddy says.

He walks up and grins at us. He's a little drunk. I grin back. "Howdy, pardner."

He takes my hand and kisses it. "You are the most beautiful woman in here," he says.

I look around. "That's not saying much."

"I can't believe you're alone. Wait." He looks at Freddy. "Are you two . . . ?"

"Hell no!" Freddy says.

"You never know these days," he says. "Two lovely ladies such as yourselves. You might be . . . you know. Which is totally fine. Awesome, in fact."

"He seems to have the right amount of shallows," Freddy observes.

I take his face in my hands and kiss him on the lips. "He certainly does."

"You're doing it again," she says.

"Please, Freddy. I don't want to talk about it anymore."

"Talk about what?" asks Perfect Man.

"You're distracting yourself so that you don't have to deal with what you know you have to deal with," she says. "You've done it over and over. Yesterday, the wedding finally became real to you, and what did you do? Got drunk and alienated your in-laws."

"In-laws?" Perfect Man says.

"Saturday at the club," she continues, "no sooner did we start talking about your impending nuptials than you headed in to work. Now you're messing around with this random guy, right after everything we've been talking about? I bet it happened Sunday night too, when you took off on your own. Am I wrong?"

I gesture for another round. "I have to tell you, Winifred, for someone who claims not to judge, you sound *awfully* judgmental right now."

Freddy takes my hand. "I'm *not* judging. Marry him, don't marry him. I don't care."

"Marry who?" says Perfect Man.

"You know I'll support you no matter what," she continues. "But I think you should actually decide, and not just let it happen."

She's right. Of course she's right. And I will decide. Soon. Just . . . not now. I take Perfect Man's hand and lead him through the crowd. We find a storeroom. I shut the door behind us. I grab him by the belt and pull him close. We stumble back against the shelves. An empty box falls on us, and we laugh. He's pressing his hips into mine, his hands cupping my face, but I pull back a little, making both of us wait. I like the anticipation. I reach up and run my fingers through his hair. He leans in again, but again I pull back. I kiss his eyes—left, then right. His cheeks. The line of his jaw. I take my time with his ears, biting the lobes. I press my cheek to his and inhale the scent of him. Swimming pool, lime, whiskey. I slip my hands under his shirt. I brush my closed lips against his, softly, right to left and back again. I kiss his top lip. I take his bottom lip between my teeth and tug on it gently. I kiss his throat. Finally I kiss him full on the mouth, opening his lips with mine. I give him my tongue. I taste his, which is sweet and smoky. I feel his hands on my hips, my waist, under my shirt and up my back. I put my hand between his legs and feel the hard outline of his cock. He presses into me. He bites my throat, then he's back at my mouth, kissing me deeply.

God, I *love* cute boys. They make all my problems disappear. I don't have to think about anything. Just this, these mouths and tongues and lips and teeth and hands. These bodies. We're crushing each other now, both breathing hard. He unhooks my bra and caresses my breasts, pinching my nipples gently with his fingers. I gasp a little, and he covers my mouth with his again. I'm about to ask him if he has a condom when he murmurs, "That was pretty funny, what you said."

I reach for his belt, begin to unbuckle it. "What?"

"That you're getting married." He pushes aside the collar of my blouse and kisses my shoulder.

"But it's true," I say. "I am getting married."

He pulls back. "When?"

"Saturday." I lean forward and kiss him again.

Such a look of puzzlement on his handsome face. "What are you doing with me?"

"What do you mean?" I laugh. "I'm doing . . . this. I'm having fun."

"But why?"

At that moment, a bartender walks in and kicks us out. I'm glad. It spares me from bursting into tears.

I lose Perfect Man and go back out front. Freddy's talking to a girl. I start chatting with the guy on my left, but he doesn't have anything interesting to say. I head for the bathroom. I trip and spill my drink on someone. "I'm so sorry!" I cry. I grab some napkins off a nearby table and offer them to him.

That's when I get a good look at him. He's in his late thirties, red-faced and balding, golf shirt stretched tight around his sizable gut. He's surrounded by three or four other drunk, sunburned men.

He reaches out and strokes my arm. "Honey," he says, leering, "you can spill a drink on me any day."

Suddenly, I'm filled with fury. Not at this random drunk, happy guy saying something dumb to a girl at a bar, but at myself. Still, I decide to take him up on his offer. I lift a full pint glass off a nearby table and throw it at him. He jumps off his stool and starts shouting at me, and his friends are upset, too. Then Freddy is at my side and hustles me out of the bar.

"Where to?" I ask.

"Home, love," she says. "Home."

We head back to the hotel. I shouldn't have thrown that drink. I shouldn't have made out with Perfect Man. Obviously. Still, it's okay. I had a hard day. Practically the whole thing consumed by work. Thank God I won't have to deal with EnerGreen and its sweaty little accountant any longer. What a bunch of crooks. Think they can do exactly as they please, with no fear of repercussions. Those poor seagulls. Ener-

Greed. The protesters are right. EnerGreen deserves to be brought low. Lying and cheating with . . . what? Blithe abandon, that's what.

No. No no no no no.

That's not . . . I'm not . . . I'm not *that* bad.

I trip on a root poking out of the sidewalk.

I wish I could talk to Teddy about all this. Wish I could talk to him about anything. But he doesn't want a thing to do with me. I don't know how I looked at him, but I definitely know how he looked at me. His eyes gone opaque, like they used to when he was angry. Teddy. And Freddy. Hey, I never realized that before! Will all my best friends rhyme? Will I be sitting on the porch of some old-age home seventy years from now, Hetty and Betty on either side, rocking in my rocking chair, swapping tales of the good old days with Eddy and Neddy?

Probably not. There won't be porches on old-age homes when I'm old. Or windows. The olds will be stuck in little pods, tiny televisions strapped to their eyeballs. Or spewed into outer space, like—

This is why I live in the moment. I think about the future and I become little-old-lady space garbage. I think about the past and . . . I don't. I don't think about the past.

We're back at the hotel. The party is over, all my friends dispersed. The band has packed up, and the bar is closing. As I stand next to the pool and look down into the turquoise water, the lights go off.

I shouldn't be doing this.

It's a huge mistake. The truth of it hits me like a physical blow. I wander away from the pool, out onto the beach. I kick off my sandals and step into the surf. The water is icy. I sit at the edge of the dry sand and stretch out my legs. The moon is so bright I can see everything.

Freddy is right. My family is right. I have no business getting married. I've known it for five months, deep down. It's not in my genes. It's not in the way I was raised. And whether or not I can change, I haven't.

But what about Will? He'll get over me quickly. Find someone more suitable. This is better for him, too, in the long run.

It's not going to be fun, what I have to do. In fact, it's going to kind of suck. I'll have to ask Freddy how she broke off all those engagements. What she said, how she said it. What happened after. She'll show me the way. She always does.

I feel better already.

No I don't. I feel awful.

What have I done?

A wave rolls in, pulling at the sand under my feet, dragging it back out to sea.

It's okay. Better late than never, right?

WEDNESDAY

14

Something's rustling in the closet. I look down the bed, but I can't see anything. Will is sprawled next to me, facedown, fully clothed. I hear a thump. More rustling.

"Whoever you are, just make it quick," I call out. "We won't put up a fight."

Freddy emerges with an armful of clothing. "Inspection time!"

"You." I let my head fall back on the pillow. "I should have guessed."

She dumps everything at the foot of the bed. She pulls a dress out of the pile, gazes at it with contempt and tosses it on the floor.

"That's for the rehearsal dinner!" I protest.

"Interesting. You didn't tell me it was a costume party." She picks up a sheer blouse.

"Don't be mean."

Will lets out a long, hoarse moan.

Freddy begins sorting rapidly. "No, no, fine, hell no, fine, whoa. *Whoa.*" She's holding up a jacket. "What the hell?"

"I bought that at Barneys!"

"Hope you saved the receipt, Colonel Mustard." She drops it and kicks it away distastefully. "We're taking it back."

"Lily?" Will croaks.

"Will's awake!" I leap on him and kiss his head. "Will's awake! Will's awake!" He rolls over and tries to push me away.

"Can we order croissants this morning?" Freddy asks.

"Did you have fun last night?" I ask him. "Where did you go?"

"Lily, I really—"

"Check it out." Freddy plucks a pale blue tunic out of the pile and holds it up. "Aunt Edna, playing Yahtzee in the dayroom."

"Were there strippers?" I ask him. "Were they hot?"

He covers his head with his arms. "Could you please not be in my face right now?"

"Help me, Obi Wan!" Freddy squeals, holding up a white maxi dress. "You're my only hope!"

"Shut up!" I holler. Will cries out weakly. I brush the hair away from his forehead. "Do you need some painkillers, honey? I have Vicodin. Percocet, too, I think. I might even have a couple of Oxy left over from my root canal."

"No, we took those," Freddy says, examining the seams on a pair of linen pants. I glare at her. "I mean, you gave them to me," she adds quickly. "For me to use. When I had . . . pain."

"Do you have any Advil?" he asks.

I look up at Freddy. "Can you check?" She disappears into the bathroom. I stroke Will's head. "What did you guys do last night?"

"Why are you screaming?" he whimpers.

Freddy comes back. "No OTCs." She picks up the room phone. "Is everybody on board with croissants?"

Will struggles to sit up. "My mom wants to have breakfast with you."

"No problem," Freddy says. "Have her people call my people."

"Not you. God!" Will clutches his head. "It hurts to breathe!"

"With me?" I say. "When?"

"Right now. She said she'd wait for you at the restaurant where we're having the rehearsal dinner. Anytime after nine."

It's nearly ten. I coax Will into drinking some water. Then he disappears under the duvet. I get dressed. Freddy follows me downstairs and through the lobby. She links her arm through mine. "I lost track of you after we got back last night."

"I went for a walk. I had a lot to think about."

"I was worried that I'd been a little too hard on you."

"With all that tough love? Of course not." I pat her hand. "You were right about everything."

She looks at me in shock. "I was?"

"Of course. You completely convinced me to call off the wedding."

"I did?"

"Yes." We walk through the doors of the hotel and into another achingly beautiful day. I take a deep breath of the salt-tinged air. "But now, I'm not so sure."

Freddy covers her face with her hands.

"I can't help it!" I cry. "I woke up next to him just now, and he was all rumpled and helpless and hungover? It was adorable. I wanted to be with him."

Freddy shakes her head.

"I guess I'm kind of like Hamlet," I continue.

Freddy uncovers one extremely skeptical eye.

"I mean, with the indecisiveness and all."

"Ohhh," she says. "I thought you meant because you're homicidal, Danish and insane."

"That too."

She takes my hands. "Lily, honey, all kidding aside—"

"We'll talk about it later," I say. "I promise. But I'd better go. I don't want to keep Will's mom waiting."

We've reached the sidewalk. Freddy straightens the neckline of my dress. "You're hopeless."

"Probably," I say. "But don't give up on me. I might surprise you."

In the twenty minutes or so that it takes me to walk to the restaurant, I come up with a little code of conduct for this meeting. I'm going to behave myself. No, better—I'm going to *crush* this fucking breakfast. I'm going to make Will's mom love me. For whatever reason, Will cares what his parents think. And I care what Will thinks. Fixing Monday seems like the least I can do. So I'll apologize profusely, of course. Compliment Will a lot—what mother doesn't love that? Talk about the wedding, so we can bond a bit more over planning. What else? I could do the starry-eyed-young-lawyer thing, pepper her with questions about her career as an ass-kicking federal prosecutor. Without using the word *ass-kicking,* of course. Or any curse words. It's going to be hard to carry on a conversation, but fine, no profanity. And no jokes about the wedding. Or work. Or sex. How about no jokes at all? I'll let her take the lead, and I'll listen and nod and smile.

And no drinking, of course.

Okay, one drink.

Willpower!

As I turn onto Whitehead Street, my phone pings with a text:

—I'll be there in 5 minutes, my darling. Wait for me in bed.

I swear to God with this guy.

—srsly, henry?

—Lily!

—pls learn how technology works

—lol!

—dont say lol, dad. just dont

—Sorry darling! Ttfn!

I walk through Blue Heaven's gates and into the cheerful courtyard, which is decorated with painted guitars, lobster traps and other Keys flotsam. Anita is sitting at a table under a torn canvas umbrella, looking prim and uncomfortable in the laid-back environment. But she gives me a warm smile as I pull out a chair and sit down across from her. "Good morning," she says. "Did you sleep well?"

"Like the fishes. And you?"

"Absolutely. We're having the most wonderful vacation. The sun and the sea, the food and the architecture. The amusing culture. It's all so restful and relaxing." She sighs contentedly. "It's such a shame we're not staying."

"What?"

The waiter appears. "Can I get you something?"

"I'd love one of your Bloody Marys," I say.

"Actually, she'll have coffee," Anita tells him.

I turn to her. "Sorry?"

The waiter leaves. Anita leans forward and snaps her fingers in my face. I'm so surprised that I gape at her for a few seconds. Then I burst out laughing. "Did you really just do that?"

"Be quiet," she says. "I want you to be quiet right now and listen to me."

Her nostrils are flaring. Her carefully made-up face is getting all blotchy.

Moms-in-law is *pissed*.

"I did not ask you here so that you could make another drunken spectacle of yourself," she says sharply.

"I wanted to apologize for that," I say. "It was totally—"

She waves it away. "Save your breath. Your behavior Monday, while deplorable, was at least true to your character."

What is going on? "My character? Are you—"

"Any apology would be a lie, and I'm not interested in more lies. I will say this, though." She starts jabbing at the table with one of her vicious red nails. "I expected a lawyer—a young lawyer, of all people—to treat a United States Attorney with a little more respect. I have *never* been as insulted as I was by you."

"Sure you have," I tell her. "Just not to your face."

Because why should I sit here and take whatever she has to say? If she's not going to play nice, neither am I.

For whatever reason, my sass seems to calm her down. "Let's keep this short." She removes a bulky white envelope from her handbag and places it on the table. "This is for you."

"No thanks," I say promptly. "Don't want it."

Here we are, having a nice mother-in-law–daughter-in-law spat, and she busts out a big old unmarked envelope? People don't do that in real life. Who does she think she is, Robert De Niro?

"Take it." She shoves it at me. I unfasten the clasp and pull out two thick manila files.

The first is a copy of my juvenile record.

I am vaguely aware that I should be shocked and furious and horrified right now. Probably scared, too. But I'm not even surprised. I think I knew this was coming. Ever since I saw Teddy on Monday night. Or stepped off the plane on Sunday. Or stepped onto one, thirteen years ago. Some part of me must have known that this would eventually happen.

Anita's eyes are on me, watching my face. She looks triumphant and expectant and smug.

"That's weird," I say. "I don't remember putting this on the registry."

She smiles.

The partners at my firm were right. She does have fangs.

I tap the folder. "I don't know how you got this. This was expunged."

She nods sympathetically. "Digital files can be *so* tricky, can't they?"

At this point, I know what's in the other folder. But I have to be sure. I push the first one aside so that I can see the name typed on the tab at the top: Lee DiFortuna. I don't open it.

"Don't you want to see the pictures?" Anita asks.

I return the files to the envelope and the envelope to the middle of the table. My coffee finally arrives. I take a sip and set the cup back down carefully. "I'd say this is some kind of sick joke, but you don't strike me as the merry prankster type."

"It's not a joke."

"In that case," I say carefully, "I'm pretty sure that what you've done is what we in the legal profession call *illegal*."

"You're hardly in a position to lecture me about what's legal and what's not," she replies.

I hold up my hands. "Can we stop, for a second? You're obviously very upset, and I'm sorry about that, but I have no idea what you're doing here. So I think the best thing right now is for me to leave, and later we can—"

"The best thing for you to do right now," she says, "is to end your relationship with my son."

No way. She cannot be for real. This cannot be happening.

"If you do not," she continues, "I will show him these documents."

Gran was right: this woman is a killer. But really, this is *so* typical for a prosecutor. They think they're masters of the universe. They threaten and strong-arm people into doing what they want. So confident, so certain that they're on the side of right and justice that they're entitled to frighten people by using all the power of the state, and then some.

She's a bully. And I hate bullies.

I tap the envelope. "Will is going to understand that the kid who did this stuff is not the woman I am now. So please, be my guest. Wrap it up in a big fat bow and give it to him." I raise my coffee cup and toast her.

"I will," she says. "And I will also send a copy to the managing partner of your law firm."

I freeze. She raises her coffee cup and clinks it against mine. She takes a sip of coffee, sets the cup down and smiles. "I take it, from your inability to formulate some flippant reply, that you didn't disclose your colorful past when they hired you."

I say nothing.

"How unfortunate. However, I can't say that it surprises me."

I finally find my voice. "You can't do this."

"No? Who's going to stop me?"

"How about the police?" I say, too loudly. Heads turn. I lower the volume. "How about a couple of your colleagues? How about anybody else who might be interested to know that you've broken, oh, half a dozen state and federal laws, which is the only *possible* way you could have gotten these records?"

"It will be so interesting to see which of us has more credibility," she says thoughtfully. "The decorated federal prosecutor, or the disgraced former attorney."

"Okay, look. I know that you don't approve of me, but—"

She cuts me off. "I can't tell you how thrilled I was when Will called me and told me about you. 'Mom,' he said. 'I'm in love. Lily is perfect. She's smart, and ambitious, and she loves the law.' I was overjoyed. But it happened so fast. You sounded too good to be true. So," she shrugs, "I did a little digging."

"Unbelievable."

"My thoughts exactly!" she retorts. "Because there you were," she waves a hand at the folders, "in all your glory. You can imagine my dismay. My horror. But do you know what I did? I did the right thing."

I have to laugh at this. "In what possible way could you have done the right thing?"

"I gave you the benefit of the doubt," she snaps. "I walked into that lunch on Monday with an open mind. I thought, I shouldn't prejudge. Maybe she's different now. Maybe she's changed."

"I am different," I say, almost pleading with her. "I have changed."

"I can see that." She leans forward, practically spitting at me. "You've gotten *worse*."

That's not true. I know that's not true, and it helps me pull myself together. I reach for my coffee, take a sip. I set my cup back down. I lean back in my chair and smile at her. "You know what I'm looking forward to? Christmases in Chicago!"

"You are going to call off this wedding," she tells me. "You have absolutely no choice."

"The person who doesn't have a choice here, Mama Bear, is you. This is Will's decision, and mine. Not yours."

"Will doesn't know who you really are!" she yelps. "My son is a wonderful man. He's brilliant. He's creative. He's sensitive. He's sweet and trusting. Far too trusting."

"And he has a mom that's *far* too into him."

"He deserves someone who can take care of him, support him. Not someone whose obvious moral failings will threaten to undermine everything he's worked so hard to accomplish."

"Let's not get too excited here, okay? Will is a great guy, but I haven't seen him heal any lepers lately."

I didn't think her face could get any more red, but it does.

"Your wonderful son," I continue, "is a man in his early thirties who's managed to graduate from college and hold down a job. As a bonus, he knows how to feed and wipe himself. Congratulations, Anita." I give her two thumbs-up. "You raised a winner!"

It is so satisfying to watch her struggle to control her temper. I can't resist twisting the knife. So I lean forward and smile at her. "Actually, let me revise that. Will is also *amazing* in bed. Did you teach him that, too?"

That's when she loses it. "How *dare* you?" she shrieks.

We now have the attention of the entire restaurant. I stand up. "Thanks for breakfast, Moms!"

"You have twenty-four hours," she calls after me.

"Love you!" I give her the finger and walk out.

15

I leave the restaurant and walk down to the marina behind one of the big new hotels. The thrill of combat quickly wears off, and I'm left feeling a little sick. What the hell happened back there? How did breakfast go from zero to crazy in two sips of coffee?

I sit on a bench and look up at an enormous cruise ship docked at the pier. The thing is four or five stories high—it's as if a massive apartment building just sidled up to my hometown. I'm trying very hard to keep my mind a blank. It doesn't work. Thoughts of Lee keep intruding. I'm usually good at blocking them. Even here, this week, Lee has barely surfaced. But my usual strategies aren't working. So I give up and close my eyes, and there he is.

After a while I call Freddy.

"Do you think I should buy a t-shirt that says My Wiener Does Tricks?" she asks.

"No."

"They're two for ten bucks," she says. "I haven't bought you guys a wedding gift yet."

"Can you come meet me?"

"What's wrong?"

I lean back against the bench and close my eyes. "Everything."

I wait for her at the entrance to the Hemingway museum. She appears around the corner and sees my face and throws her arms around me. I really don't know what I'd do without her.

"Jesus, Lily. You look terrible."

We buy tickets and walk into the main house, a square mansion of creamy stone with tall yellow shutters. About a dozen people are assembled in the living room, waiting for the tour to begin. Freddy and I hang in the back.

A clock chimes, and a little old lady in a tropical shirt and Bermuda shorts bustles into the room. She has a faded bowl cut and eager eyes. "Welcome, welcome, everyone, to beautiful Key West, Florida, and to the Ernest Hemingway Home and Museum!" she cries. "My name is Donna Kuntsmeister—"

"No way," Freddy murmurs.

"—and I'll be your guide as we go back in time, over *eighty years,* when the spot where we're standing *right now* was the home of one of America's most prolific, influential and *controversial* writers." She looks around dramatically. "Ernest *Hemingway.*"

"Why are we here?" Freddy whispers.

"Hemingway lived in this house for over *ten years* with his second wife, Pauline Pfeiffer, a journalist and heiress from *Parkersburg,* Iowa." Donna beams at us. "Are there any Iowans with us today?"

"I needed to talk to somebody," I whisper back.

"I'm all ears," Freddy says. "Like that baby over there. Jesus, the poor thing."

"—then let's get started!" Donna cries. "If anyone has questions along the way, please don't hesitate to pipe up."

The group shuffles into the hallway after her. "I have a problem," I tell Freddy.

"We are now standing in the Hemingways' dining room," Donna announces. "When they were in residence here in Key West, Ernest and Pauline *loved* to entertain."

"Let me guess," Freddy says. "You mouthed off, and Will's mom flew into a rage."

"That was definitely part of it."

"Why do you always do that?" she sighs.

"Why do I always do everything that I always do?"

"Nineteen forty," Donna says, answering a question. "But Pauline lived here until her death in 1951, which occurred after she learned that her son Gregory had been arrested for entering a ladies' restroom dressed in his wife's clothing."

Freddy blinks. "That is so not where I was expecting her to go with that."

"This is a sea chest made of Circassian walnut," Donna is saying. "Pauline used it as a writing desk."

A woman asks, "What's Circassian walnut?"

"Some type of wood," Donna replies.

"Sounds like something out of *Star Wars*," I say.

The woman nods. "Yeah."

"It's not from *Star Wars*," says Donna.

"Maybe it's what the Millennium Falcon was made out of," I say. "Circassian walnut."

Donna shakes her head. "It wasn't."

"I heard it was supposed to be called the Circassian Falcon," I say. "But George Lucas has a lisp, so he couldn't pronounce it. And he's the boss, so . . ."

The woman says, "George Lucas has a lisp?"

A man says, "What does this have to do with Hemingway?"

Donna says, "Let's move on, shall we?"

We all follow her into the library. Freddy nudges me. "Are you going to tell me what's on your mind, or are we here so that you can heckle the docent?"

"She threatened me," I whisper.

"Donna?"

"Will's mom! She's trying to blackmail me."

"Pauline bought this chandelier in *Paris*," Donna says. "She had it sent all the way *here*. By *boat*."

"That's impossible," Freddy says. "You must have misunderstood her."

"Trust me. I heard her loud and clear."

"—in Los Angeles, where Pauline stayed with her sister Jinny and her lover, the violinist and film producer Laura Archera. Laura and Jinny would later have a polyamorous relationship with Aldous Huxley."

"Are we on drugs right now?" Freddy asks. "Is this whole tour a hallucination?"

"Welcome to Key West," I say.

"No," Donna says, "I'm afraid I don't know where that lamp is from."

"Unless I call off the wedding, she's going to tell Will about something that happened when I was a kid."

"Something bad?"

I nod.

"Gregory met his fourth wife in the ladies' room of a bar in Coconut Grove," Donna says. "This was shortly after he had a single breast implant, on the left side. After the wedding, he had the implant removed."

"Hang on," Freddy says to me. She raises her hand. "Sorry, Donna? I'm going to have to ask you to stop."

"I beg your pardon?"

"You're making this up," Freddy says. "You must be."

Donna folds her arms and gives Freddy a look like, Google it, bitch. Freddy whips out her phone. So do a couple of other people.

"Well?" someone asks.

"It's true," Freddy murmurs, scrolling. "Every word."

"Where do you see that?" a man asks, staring at his phone.

"Try 'Gregory Hemingway boobs,'" Freddy tells him.

He types. His eyes widen. "Holy crap."

Freddy puts her phone away and smiles at our guide. "Apologies, Donna. Please proceed."

Eventually, Freddy and I drift away from the tour and head outside. We wander over to the carriage house and take the steps to the second floor to see Hemingway's study. We stroll through the gardens. Freddy is patient, waiting for me to start talking.

The swimming pool is sparkling in the sunlight. A dozen elephant statues stand around the perimeter, gazing at the empty water. I step over the white plastic chain and kick off my sandals. Freddy follows me. We sit at the edge and dip our feet into the warm water.

I turn to her. "Want to get something to eat?"

"Stop stalling," she says. "You'll feel better after you tell me."

"It's so hard to begin. I keep this stuff locked up." I kick at the water. "But I feel like if I tell you, I'll have somebody on my side. Somebody who knows everything."

"I'm always on your side," she says.

"I know, but . . . okay. Here goes."

Deep breath.

"This probably won't come as a big surprise, but I was a trouble-maker growing up. A real screwup. Not drugs or drinking or sex, be-lieve it or not. That was normal down here, and it didn't interest me. Not back then. I was just . . . wild. Disobedient, disruptive in school, al-ways mouthing off. A real pain in the ass."

"Like most kids," Freddy says.

"Most kids grow out of it. I only got worse. And I had a partner in crime."

"Teddy," she says.

"We were born only a few weeks apart. Our mothers were old friends from high school. After Dad left, they got really close—Teddy's mom was raising him alone, too. She was a nurse. Mom and Mrs. Ben-net used to take turns watching us when the other was working. I knew everything about him. He never had a lot to say, but I knew what he was thinking. Always." I dab a foot into the water, making ripples.

"And we were awful. We were well on our way to being complete delinquents before we even broke into double digits. We sprayed graf-fiti. Skipped school. Egged cars. Shoplifted. And we got away with it. I mean, we got caught occasionally, but we usually escaped real punish-ment. I could talk my way out of anything, and I had Gran to back me up. She'd rant and rave at me, and Mom would cry and ground me, but they'd get the school or the police or whoever off our backs. And Teddy was this . . . angelic child. He was so quiet and calm. Nobody ever be-lieved that he could do the things he did."

"You sound like quite the pair."

"We were so bored. Don't get me wrong—we weren't on some per-petual crime spree. We went to the beach, and we rode our bikes. We fished and swam and all that. But this island is so tiny. And it gets old fast. Causing trouble was exciting. And we had no fear. None."

"Sounds like you haven't changed."

This is about the last thing in the world I need to hear right now. "Please don't say that!"

"Okay, okay," Freddy says. "Sorry. Keep going."

So I do. I tell her how Teddy and I goaded each other, constantly. If I stole a bicycle, Teddy would steal a scooter. If he snuck into a strip club, I'd sneak into a massage parlor. As we got older, it got worse. We stole cars and drove them around in the middle of the night. We broke into vacation homes and made breakfast, or ordered AA literature, or repainted the walls.

Freddy bursts out laughing. "You did not!"

"We were crazy. When we studied the Vikings in school, we cut a sailboat loose from the docks and set it on fire. While we were on it."

"Wow," she says.

Wow is right. I take off my sunglasses and squint in the light reflecting off the water. We had so much fun. Every day was an adventure. I hate myself for enjoying these memories, because of what came after, but I can't help it. I close my eyes and for a moment, I remember. Me and Teddy, together.

"I don't know the particular moment when everything changed. When my . . . feelings for Teddy changed. It wasn't like a bolt of lightning or anything. There was no sudden realization that the boy I'd known all my life was actually way, *way* more than my best friend. But by the time I was fourteen, I couldn't hide it from myself any longer. I was in love with him. Totally and completely. Desperately. Worldendingly."

"As only a fourteen-year-old can be," Freddy remarks.

It was bad. When school let out in June that year, I went up to visit Ana for a week in DC, and then to see Dad and Jane in New York. I missed Teddy the entire time. I obsessed about what he was doing without me. Counted the days until I'd be with him again. Compared him to every other boy I saw, and found them all lacking—not as smart, not as funny, not as interesting. He wasn't a cute kid anymore—he was beautiful. His sea-grey eyes. His crooked smile. His sly wit. And he had such physical grace. Such presence, even at fourteen.

"I don't know what I expected to happen when I got back," I tell Freddy. "Maybe that he'd see me again, and a lightbulb would go off. But it didn't. I came home and nothing changed."

In no time I was a walking cliché—the personification of lovesick teenage angst. I was anxious. I was awkward. I said all manner of stupid shit. I burst into tears at no prompting. I couldn't sleep. I couldn't eat.

And Teddy didn't notice a damn thing. I was so desperate for his attention—the right kind of attention. I finally gave in to my mother's pleas and got a decent haircut. Teddy mocked it. One day I wore a skirt. He couldn't stop laughing.

How could he not see what was happening? How could he not feel it too? I was so tortured. It had to change. I had to *make* Teddy love me. All I needed was a weapon.

"His name," I tell Freddy, "was Lee."

He was from Jacksonville. His family had moved next door to Teddy while I was gone. Lee was our age, but nothing like us. He was sweet and well mannered. A little shy. He loved to fish. He had a gap between his front teeth and a big, honking laugh. He was always smiling. It didn't seem quite genuine—you got the sense that he was hiding something, presenting a carefully composed face to the world. Although maybe that's hindsight.

I was tired of being invisible to Teddy. I decided to make myself visible to Lee—very, very visible—and maybe Teddy would finally see what he was missing.

So I complimented Lee. Touched him. I copied the things I'd seen my father do—the way he looked at Jane, the way he flirted. I smiled at Lee and listened to him and laughed at his jokes. Always, and only, in the presence of Teddy.

Stupid, thoughtless, typical teenage bullshit.

And it worked.

Lee began responding almost immediately. He got nervous whenever I was around. Brought me presents. Made me a mix CD of awful country music. Invited me over for dinner with his weird, humorless parents. I managed to keep him on the hook while giving him nothing in return. I wouldn't even hold his hand. But I kept smiling and laughing and flirting.

In my mind, everything I did was okay because I was in love. It never once occurred to me to feel bad for using Lee.

Not that it mattered. My phony infatuation was having no effect. Teddy didn't seem to notice, or care. This only made me redouble my efforts, which made Lee fall that much harder.

Love made me a total asshole.

"You were fourteen," Freddy says. "All fourteen-year-olds are assholes."

"Let me finish, and then you can decide whether that excuses my behavior."

Lee was now part of our little gang, but he didn't get the thrill we got from being bad. His family was pretty religious, so he had these scruples. And he was afraid of his parents. He became our voice of reason, talking us out of the worst stuff. Most of the time. Not always.

In early August, I walked into Teddy's house to find him and Lee sprawled on the living room sofa, playing video games.

"Guess what?" I said.

"You're blocking the screen," Teddy said.

Lee sat up and made room for me. "What?"

"That house my mom is renovating? Her crew found a crate of dynamite in the carriage house."

Teddy finally glanced up. "For real?"

I nodded.

He threw down his joystick. "Let's go."

"She called the county already. A bomb disposal squad picked it up this morning."

He slouched back on the couch, defeated.

"But not before I liberated a few sticks," I said.

His slow, delighted grin made my stomach flutter.

"What would we even do with it?" Lee asked skeptically.

"Blow shit up," Teddy replied.

"Duh," I added.

Lee looked troubled. "I'm not sure that's such a good idea."

We ignored him, and he reluctantly followed along as we planned our next act of mayhem. We soon identified a target: the naval air station off Palm Avenue.

"Hang on," Freddy says. "A *naval* station?"

"We were fourteen," I say. "We were idiots. Lee wanted to set it off on the beach somewhere, or in the swamp, but he was overruled. And it's not like we were planning to take out a plane. We were just going to leave it outside the gates in the middle of the night. It was more the badass principle of the thing."

We did some research. I became so absorbed that I pretty much dropped my whole act toward Lee. He started trying to hide his feelings. It didn't really work.

One Sunday morning, Teddy and I began assembling the bomb at a rickety card table in his garage. The only light came from a couple of windows high up on one wall. It was outrageously hot and stuffy in there, but we had to keep the door closed to avoid attracting attention.

Teddy held up an old alarm clock I'd found in our attic. "Do we really need this?"

"Yes."

"Why?"

"Because it's cooler that way," I said. "Obviously."

"It's stupid," he muttered, but I ignored him. I was puzzling over the instructions I'd printed off the Internet at Gran's office.

"Where's Lee?" Teddy asked.

"Church, I guess. His dad makes him go."

"God," Teddy muttered. "Just kill me."

"Seriously."

He started poking through the jumble of screwdrivers in his toolbox. I was stymied by the directions about wiring the clock to the explosives. I remember thinking that it was too bad I couldn't ask my mom for help—she'd figure this out in no time.

In a voice I didn't quite recognize, Teddy asked:

"So are you and Lee like boyfriend and girlfriend now?"

My mouth was instantly dry. I kept my eyes fixed to the piece of paper in front of me.

"I don't know. Maybe."

"Do you like him?"

I pretended to search for something on the table. "Sure. Lee's great."

"Yeah," Teddy said, with withering contempt. "He's *great*."

I said nothing.

"He likes you," Teddy said accusingly. "He's always talking about you. Lily's so this, Lily's so that. It's annoying."

I swallowed my anger with difficulty. "I guess he sees things you don't see."

"Yeah," he snorted. "Because they aren't there."

I finally threw down the instructions. "What's your problem, Theodore?"

"Don't," he warned me. He hated it when I called him by his full name.

"Then stop acting like a jerk."

"*You're* acting like a jerk!" Teddy said. "The way you are around him makes me sick! It's all," he tossed his hair and adopted a girlish falsetto, "Oh, Lee, you're so funny! Ha ha ha! You're so smart!"

"What do you care?"

"Because you don't act that way with me!" he shouted.

The garage was silent. Outside I heard a truck rumble down the street, a lawnmower buzzing in the distance.

Teddy's eyes were full of hurt. They told me everything I needed to know. Everything I'd been dying to know all summer.

"I tried," I said at last. "I tried to be that way with you."

Teddy shook his head. "Not really."

"I tried," I insisted. "You laughed at me."

"Try again," he said softly. "I won't laugh."

I could only stare at him. Was he joking? Was this really happening—the thing I'd wanted so badly, for so long?

It was. Teddy put his hands on my shoulders, leaned in and kissed me.

It was the first kiss for both of us.

It was awful.

Freddy laughs. "Awful?"

"We didn't know what we were doing! His mouth was open, while mine was closed. Then I opened mine just as he clamped his shut. My lips were too dry. His were too wet. Our teeth clacked together." I shrug and kick at the water. "It was all very awkward and sloppy and weird."

Also?

Magical.

We finally broke apart. We looked at each other. And we both started to laugh.

We left the garage and went into his house, where we spent the next three hours on the sofa learning how to kiss. By the time we heard his mom stirring upstairs, getting ready for work, we were experts. Professionals. Future gold medalists.

Teddy and I began sneaking off together every chance we could get. Lee knew something was up. He kept trying to get me alone, but I made vague excuses. He'd call my house and I wouldn't answer. I didn't laugh at his jokes anymore. I was evasive. He was sad and worried. Frankly, he was becoming kind of a pain. We would have left him out of the plan entirely, but now he insisted on coming along. He was hyperenthusiastic and wouldn't stop talking about how awesome it would be when we set off our bomb.

All to impress me.

"You should tell him," Teddy said at one point.

We were in my room, lying together on my bed. I stared at the ceiling, at the knife marks we'd made when we were little kids. Teddy was right, but I was procrastinating. Now that I'd gotten what I wanted, I was feeling guilty.

"I'll tell him," I said. "Soon."

Two nights later, we met at midnight for our grand assault against the United States military. We sneaked up to the entrance to the base and set the bomb in front of a low concrete wall near the guard booth. I never did figure out how to incorporate the alarm clock, so we just lit the fuse, then hid behind a clump of palm trees about a hundred yards away.

I remember it all so clearly. The uncertainty, the fear that we'd screwed up and wasted the dynamite, or that it was too old and crusty to work.

When the bomb exploded, the sound was deafening. Flames shot up into the night, and the windows of a couple of buildings across the street blew out. We screamed with joy and danced in the light of the fire. Even Lee was thrilled.

Then we heard the sirens.

Somehow, we had failed to anticipate the possibility of a brisk response to an explosion near a military base. Lee started running toward the city marina. Teddy grabbed my hand. We ran through a modern housing development and back into Old Town. We raced through the narrow streets and lanes we knew so well, slipping over fences and through backyards, ducking behind parked cars, avoiding the streetlights.

We finally came to a conch house on Eaton Street. My mom had worked on it a few years earlier. I knew that it was empty most of the year. We found a loose shutter and pried it open. Inside, we took turns drinking straight from the faucet, long gulps of lukewarm, rusty water that ran down our chins. We didn't want to turn on the lights, but we found a few candles in the kitchen and lit them.

Then we went upstairs, found the master bedroom and started taking each other's clothes off.

I stop talking. Freddy is watching me.

"So," she says. "Did you . . . ?"

"We did."

"You were fourteen?"

I glance at her. "That surprises you?"

"I guess not." She pauses. "How was it?"

I stare at the water. "Amazing."

It shouldn't have been. It should have been like our first kiss, fumbling and uncomfortable. And it did hurt like hell for about three seconds. I cried out, and Teddy froze. "Are you okay?" he whispered.

"Yes," I whispered back. "Yes yes yes."

I was okay. I was more than okay.

He was inside me. I really, really liked it.

And we were really, really good at it.

We stayed there until close to dawn. Then Teddy walked me home and followed me up the almond tree and into my room. We undressed and did it again, moving slowly to keep the bed from creaking. Then he tucked me in and left.

I drifted off to sleep, perfectly content. Something had changed—I could feel it. I had no interest in causing trouble anymore. I had just discovered the best possible way not to be bored.

Too bad it was a little too late.

The police showed up at Lee's house around three that afternoon. Teddy came running to find me. The massive stupidity of what we'd done came crashing down on our heads. Dynamite, outside a naval base? Were we out of our minds? Why didn't we listen to Lee and take it out to the beach, or blow up an abandoned fishing boat? Why did we have to destroy *federal property*?

All of a sudden, the fun was over. We were potentially in real trouble—sent away to reform school, maybe actual prison. This was Florida, after all, where they love to try juveniles as adults.

Teddy and I went back to his house and waited. The police stayed at Lee's for a long time. We watched them leave. An hour or so later, Lee's parents left, too.

"Let's go talk to him," Teddy said. "Find out what they said."

I shook my head. "Let me go alone."

He was instantly suspicious, jealous. "Why?"

"Just let me do it, Teddy. I'll reassure him. I'll make him understand."

When I went to the back door, I could see Lee sitting at the table in his kitchen, staring into space. I knocked and walked in. He turned to look at me.

"They know," he said, in a hushed voice. "They know it was us."

Someone had seen three kids loitering in the area before the bomb went off. With our stellar history, we were automatically prime suspects. The police had probably gone to Lee first so that Gran wouldn't interfere.

"It's only a matter of time," Lee said. His words were tumbling out. He was panicked. "We have to confess. It'll be better for us. That's what they told me."

I took his hands across the table. "Lee, they're lying. They have no proof."

"My dad is going to kill me," he whispered.

He did have a crazy dad. Not abusive or anything, but super, super strict. A dad you don't disappoint. Lee was terrified of him.

I told him that we had to have a united front, that we couldn't confess, that we'd be fine, that my grandmother would take care of it. She knew the police, the lawyers. She'd get us off. They didn't have any solid proof that it was us. I smiled at him. I stroked his hands. I tried everything I could think of to manipulate him into doing what I wanted.

"They're trying to scare you, Lee. So what if they have an eyewitness? Gran always says eyewitness testimony is unreliable. And whoever it is couldn't have actually identified us, or the cops would have arrested us already. All we need to do is—"

"I thought you liked me," Lee said suddenly.

"What? Of course I like you." I gave him an encouraging smile, praying that it didn't look as phony as it felt.

"I saw you guys run off. Where did you go?"

"Where did we go?" I was thinking furiously. "We just, you know, we ran. We went back to my house."

Lee was staring at me, but he didn't seem to hear a word I was saying. "Do you like him?"

"What? No!" I reached out and took his hand, which he'd drawn away. "I want to be with you."

"You like him. You want to be with him."

"No! I don't even think of him that way."

"Have you ever kissed him?"

I didn't respond. Lee was leaning forward in his chair, watching me intently. One knee was bouncing up and down under the table.

"Lily. Did you kiss him?"

"He kissed me," I admitted. "I didn't like it."

"Did you do it?"

"What?" I tried to sound confused. But of course I knew what he meant. I knew what *it* was.

"I saw you. You left me behind on purpose."

"We didn't, Lee! We—"

"Did you go off somewhere and do it?"

"No!"

"Tell me, and I won't talk. I won't confess. I just need to know."

I felt trapped. Could I trust him not to talk if I told him the truth? Did I have a choice?

"What do you want to know?" I asked.

Lee swallowed hard. "Did you do it?"

I looked down, and then looked him in the eye.

"Yeah," I said.

His face was perfectly blank. And that's when I finally felt it, in my gut. He loved me. And I'd made him feel that way. I'd led him on. And now I'd broken his heart. Because he was fourteen years old, like me, and when you're fourteen, everything is a tragic opera, everything is either the beginning of the world or the end of it.

He had to stop looking at me like that. I couldn't stand it.

"It didn't mean anything, Lee. It was stupid. I want to be with—"

"Okay," he said. "It's okay."

"What's okay?"

"It's all okay. It's fine. I won't talk."

I said a few more things to him. I tried to explain that it wasn't for me, that it was better for all of us. But it was like he couldn't even hear me. So eventually I left. As the screen door banged shut behind me, I could feel my spirits rising. We were in the clear. We weren't going to get caught, everything was straight between me and Lee, and I could be with Teddy for real now, openly.

All of my problems had been solved.

A breeze puffs up out of nowhere, rippling the surface of the pool.

"Was that it?" Freddy asks.

"No." The breeze fades away, the water stills. "About an hour later, Lee went to his parents' closet, found his father's handgun, and shot himself."

Freddy inhales sharply.

I wish I could ease off the edge of the pool and into the water.

"When his parents came home, Lee was still alive." I pause. "He died in the hospital the next day."

I feel Freddy watching me, but I keep my eyes on the water.

"Teddy and I confessed everything. In one way, we were very lucky. This happened in August of 2001."

"Jesus," Freddy mutters.

"Jesus is right. If we'd pulled our little stunt a few months later I'd still be in jail. Instead, it was all over in a few days—the investigation, the lawyers, the social workers. My father flew down with his crack legal team, and Gran called in every favor she had. So did Ana. All my parents got involved—it's when they finally put aside their differences and bonded. I appeared before a judge and made all sorts of promises, and my parents made all sorts of promises, therapists and curfews and special classes, and my father paid a shitload of money, and then he took me to New York with him. I had a nice stay at a fancy psychiatric hospital on Long Island, where a lot of doctors tried to find out whether whatever was so obviously wrong with me could be diagnosed and medicated away, which, sorry, no. After that, I went away to school."

"What happened to Teddy?"

"His mom was furious—she blamed me for everything. My dad offered to pay for a lawyer for him, but she refused. Ultimately they made him go to some juvie school near Miami. We . . . we lost touch."

"You didn't see him again?"

"Not until two days ago."

She's silent for a moment. "It wasn't your fault, Lily."

"Lee had problems," I say. "He probably suffered from depression, but his parents refused to deal with it. They turned out to be bonkers. His mom came up to me in court, as we were leaving. She grabbed my arm, and she got really close to my face and said, 'I hope you have a child someday. And I hope you have to watch him die.'"

"Christ, Lily."

I shrug. "Can you blame her?"

"But—"

"No, I didn't pull the trigger, and yes, he was already messed up, but look, Freddy. If it weren't for me, and my recklessness, and my cruelty, Lee would be a twenty-seven-year-old with mild depression and a wacko family. Not a kid who's been dead for almost as long as he was ever alive."

Freddy puts her arms around me. A cat saunters up to the edge of the swimming pool and bats at the water. Another breeze ripples the surface.

I can still hear his voice. I thought you liked me, he said.

I thought you liked me.

16

Freddy and I watch the water for a while.

"Lily?" she says gently. "This is awful, I know. But let's focus on the present. Is Will really going to care about all this? You were just a kid."

I think about Monday night. About Will's concern that we don't know that much about each other. His specific questions about my childhood.

"Maybe not," I say. "But if I don't break up with him, his mother is also going to tell my law firm."

"Which makes her a total bitch," Freddy says. "But again, so what? They love you. You've been amazing for them."

I press my palms to my eyes. "When you apply for admission to the bar, which is basically a license to practice as a lawyer, you have to disclose any past criminal offenses. Even offenses that have been expunged. They won't necessarily stop you from being admitted," I pause, "but if it later comes to light that you failed to disclose anything . . ."

Freddy understands in an instant. "Lily. No."

"I screwed up! I screwed up, and if the firm finds out, they will fire me in a heartbeat. They could report me, and I could be suspended. Maybe even disbarred."

She thinks for a moment. "But you don't have to be a lawyer. Your family has money. You can do whatever you want."

It's sweet how she keeps trying to solve this. "I don't like my job," I say. "I love it. It's the one thing I've ever wanted to do—the one thing I really feel suited for. Law school, working at the firm—those are the only challenges I've ever felt were made for me. And the only things I haven't screwed up yet. If I can't do what I want to do, I don't know what will happen, Freddy. I might . . . finally, truly lose it."

We watch another cat stroll up to the edge of the water. This one dips a six-toed paw in, shakes it delicately and licks off a few drops of water.

"You need to let Will go," Freddy says.

I stare at her in disbelief. "And let his mom win? But she's a bully!"

"This isn't a contest, Lily. It's your life."

"It's a contest *and* my life. I won't let him go."

"But you have so many doubts already, and—"

I shake my head firmly. "Not anymore. I'm fully committed."

"Because you finally have some real opposition," she says.

"Be on my side, Freddy. Please."

"I *am*. You know I am. But no lie, my friend. You are in one serious motherfucking pickle."

This makes me laugh, finally. There's a sudden commotion inside the gift shop, and someone comes flapping toward us.

"Donna!" Freddy cries. "Join us, girlfriend! The water's *amazing*!"

Instead, she kicks us out. Freddy and I walk back to the hotel. She takes my arm. "I have to say, this feels like the key to all mysteries."

"What's that mean?"

She shrugs. "It's no wonder you have such a hard time telling Will the truth. Look what happened the last time you were honest with a boy about sex."

"It happened," I say. "And it was terrible. And I think about it every single day. But it didn't change me, Freddy. Look at what I was like before. Look at my dad. I was always going to be like this."

We walk through the lobby, heading for the elevators, but then I stop. "Do you really want to cheer me up? Let's go have a long, boozy lunch."

"We can't," Freddy says. "Your mothers are waiting upstairs to watch you try on your wedding dress."

"You're joking."

"Surprise?" she says.

I drop my head onto her shoulder.

Upstairs, I slip the key into the lock. "Game face," Freddy whispers. I open the door.

"Surprise!" Mom, Ana, Jane and Gran are lounging around the room, picking at a bowl of fruit like a bunch of dissipated empresses.

"Ladies!" I cry. "Wow!"

I think it's going to be hell, but it isn't. Whether by agreement or chance, nobody starts nagging me about how I shouldn't marry Will. They've probably given up and accepted the inevitable, at the very moment when it's all become so very . . . evitable.

Right now they're deep in the middle of their own gossip battle royale.

"Tell me," Ana is saying. "Just tell me his name."

"I'm not seeing anybody!" Mom cries.

"You're blushing, Kat." Jane peels an orange with her long, delicate fingers. "You couldn't deceive a child."

Freddy removes a garment bag from the closet. I pull my dress over my head. She hands me a blindfold.

"Seriously?"

I've never seen my wedding gown. Not a sketch, not a scrap of fabric.

"Last time," she promises. "I want it to be perfect before you see it."

I put on the blindfold. I hear Freddy unzip the bag.

"You're glowing," Ana accuses Mom. "You're nuclear."

"I'm not glowing!"

"You can't lie to me. I'm too perceptive. It's my Latina intuition."

Gran snorts. "You're about as Latina as the girl on the raisin box."

There's a swish of silk as Freddy removes the dress. Everyone falls silent.

"Jesus H. Christ," Gran says.

"My goodness," Mom whispers.

Ana laughs. "Freddy, you've got some balls."

"Shh!" Freddy tells them. To me: "You're going to step into it. Hand on my shoulder." She pulls the dress up around me, slipping the sleeves up my arms.

"You're the one who looks fabulous, Ana," Jane observes. "You've gained a little weight since the fall."

"Aha!" Mom cries. "You only eat when you're happy. Who is he?"

I hear a knock, and someone opens the door. "Mattie!" Mom says. "Come in! Freddy is showing us the dress."

Freddy buttons, prods, stretches and straightens. I pluck at the skirt. The fabric is so soft I almost can't feel it. She bats my hand away. Then she tugs at the neckline. "Where did your boobs go?"

"I loaned them to Gregory Hemingway."

Gran chuckles. "Did a little sightseeing this morning?"

"We have the walk-through at the Audubon House tomorrow," Mattie is saying. "I'm very worried about the structural integrity of the porch. I heard on the news this morning about a wedding where the dance floor collapsed, and *eleven* people died!"

"Good God!" Mom cries.

"Five of them were *children*!"

"That was in Pakistan," Ana says.

"Oh!" Mattie breathes a huge sigh of relief. "Thank *goodness*!"

Freddy is doing something complicated to the back of the dress. "In general, Lily has appalling taste," Jane observes, "but I can see that she was right about you, Freddy."

"I really was. You should give Freddy a bunch of money so that she can quit her job and start her own company."

"Perhaps I shall."

"She wouldn't need much. And anyway, you and Nerge are still rolling in it, right?"

"His name is Serge," Jane says. "As you know."

"Where is he, anyway?"

"Bonn. He arrives tomorrow."

Freddy tugs gently on the hem of the dress. "Can we return to the part of the conversation about someone giving me money?"

"You can't take Serge's money," Ana tells her. "It's tainted."

"His granpappy was a Nazi," I explain.

"He was a French collaborator," Jane says serenely. "It's entirely different."

"Here we go." Freddy turns me toward the mirror. She removes the blindfold.

I can't believe what I see. The dress has tiny sleeves and a low-cut neckline. It's fitted through the hips and then fans out to the floor, with a train in back. It's got all sorts of pleats and tucks and little things I don't even know the names of. It's glamorous, and elegant, and sexy.

Which is all great, but not the unbelievable part. That would be the color.

The dress is not white, or ivory, or even champagne.

It's a deep, rich, shimmering scarlet.

It's a red wedding gown.

I gaze at myself in the mirror, in my wedding dress, and I realize that this is the moment that every girl dreams of. The moment when the fairy tale comes together.

But for me, the fairy tale is falling apart.

And it's not because of Anita's attempt to derail the wedding. Or because I've just dredged up the worst events of my life for Freddy. No, I'm thinking about the present. About my uncertainty, my vacillation. My doubts about getting married. My lies, the way I behave.

What kind of bride acts like I do?

What kind of *person* does?

I burst into tears. Everyone gasps.

Freddy looks horrified. "You hate it!"

"I love it!" I wail. "I absolutely love it!"

"Lily," Freddy says softly. "Don't." She puts her arms around me.

"I'm sorry," I sniffle. "I'm probably ruining the fabric."

"Well, yes," she says. "But that's okay."

"Pre-wedding jitters." Mattie clucks sympathetically. "It happens to everyone." That only makes me cry harder.

Ana stands up. "Come on, ladies. Circle of love time."

They surround me and give me a big group hug.

"Don't cry, honey," Gran says.

"Izzie's right." Jane strokes my hair. "You know how your eyes puff up."

"It's going to be all right, Lilybear," Ana says. "Whatever the hell is going on, it's going to be all right."

I pull myself together, eventually. I take off the dress, and Freddy packs it away. My mothers want to take me out to lunch, but I beg off. I tell Freddy I'm going to take a nap, and she reluctantly leaves.

I do try to sleep, but I'm too restless. I leave the hotel and walk aimlessly. Duval Street to Angela Street to Thomas Street. Olivia to Emma to Petronia. Soon I'm standing in front of an ordinary house. White clapboard. Yellow shutters. Lee's old house. It used to be brown and tired, with curling linoleum on the kitchen floor, shaggy carpet, an overgrown front yard. Now it's another bland, pristine renovation, waiting for the next hurricane.

I open my bag and find the business card I filched from Teddy's wallet. I dial his number.

"Ted Bennet," he answers.

"Ted?" I repeat.

"Hi."

"Since when are you Ted?"

"People don't take a detective named Teddy very seriously," he says. "Strangely enough."

"You could use that to your advantage. You're named Teddy and they think they'll walk all over you, and you just come in and like, *pow!* Beat the shit out of them."

"Interesting idea."

"You're a vicious, evil brutalizer. Named Teddy."

"Is there something I can do for you?"

"Yes," I say. "Meet me somewhere."

"I don't think that's a good idea."

"Why not?"

"Why not," he says, like it's a challenge.

"Please, Teddy?"

He's silent for a long time. Finally, "Let me think about it."

He hangs up. I wander back to the hotel. I'm still restless. Agitated. I go up to the room. As I open the door I think—Enough. This is not me. I like to be happy. I am happy, all the time. I work very, very hard at it.

I throw myself on the bed. I need some distraction, something to lift my spirits. I'm about to look for porn on my computer when my phone pings with a text. Maybe it's Will!

Oh, even better. It's Lyle.

—Philip and I may need you on a call tomorrow. 1 pm.

—what for?

—Just make sure you're available.

I text him a few more times, but he doesn't answer. Maybe it's about our next case. If there is a next case for me.

I hear a key in the door. Will is back!

"Hey, baby!"

"Hi." He drops his wallet on the desk. He pulls a handful of sea grass out of his pocket and spreads it on the windowsill. I start to ask him about it, but he bends down and kisses me. I pull him onto the bed. He stretches out beside me. I reach for his belt. He helps me off with my dress. Things are progressing nicely. No fireworks, but that's okay. I'll take plain vanilla sex right now.

I reach inside his pants. Nothing's happening. I stroke him gently. Then harder. Still nothing. I go down on him. I get a tiny reaction, but . . . not enough. What the hell?

"I drank way too much last night," he says apologetically. "It's not going to happen."

"Can we keep trying?"

He pulls me up beside him. "I still feel awful."

"But . . ."

He takes the remote from the nightstand and turns on the television. He flips a few channels and then turns back to me. He strokes my hair and kisses my forehead. "Sorry. We can still cuddle for a while, can't we?"

On the television screen, flames are leaping out of a hotel window. People with '70s hair are screaming. I know how they feel.

Because *cuddle*? Cuddle? His psychotic mother is threatening to ruin my career. I've spent the day thinking over my very worst memories. I do not want to fucking cuddle!

Is this what being in a relationship is like? I guess I didn't notice when we were in New York. We both work long hours, we're busy people. Down here, on vacation? Will should want to have sex all the time, hangovers be damned. He should try harder. What gives?

I jump off the bed and get dressed. "I'm going for a swim."

He looks surprised. "Okay."

That's all he has to say? "Okay?" Not, "But you don't have your bathing suit." Or, "You don't have a towel." Is he really not going to notice this very obvious lie?

I open the door. "Bye!"

"Have fun," he says.

I walk out. The door slams behind me.

Frustration!

I stand in the hallway, considering my options.

The elevator dings, and Javier steps out. He's reading something on his phone as he walks down the hall, tripping once, almost running into the wall. He finds his door and fumbles in his pocket for his room key.

I walk up to him quickly, push him inside his room and close the door behind us.

"Lily!" he says, looking startled. "Hey. What's—"

"Got a minute, Javier?" I pull out a chair and sit down.

He adjusts his glasses and peers at me curiously. "Sure." He sits across from me.

"I want to talk to you about Will," I say.

He looks concerned. "Is he okay?"

"I was hoping you could tell me." I stretch my legs out under the table and look around the room. It's smaller than ours. Spotless. Javier must be very tidy.

He tugs nervously on one ear. "Is this about the bachelor party? I swear I had nothing to do with—"

I smile at him. "Do you have anything to drink?"

"I'm trying not to use the minibar," he says apologetically. "It's so expensive."

I open the refrigerator and grab a handful of bottles. Bourbon. Perfect. I unscrew one and drink it down.

"Will really wasn't kidding," Javier remarks.

I gaze at him in silence. He's cute. Geeky, but cute. Freddy shouldn't have given up so easily.

"Help me out, Javier. I've got a funny feeling about Will. I'm wondering whether he's really the person he says he is."

"He is." Javier nods vigorously. "He definitely is."

I open another bottle and take a sip. "I have a few questions for you."

Javier frowns. "I'm not sure I should be talking about Will behind his back like this."

I lean forward. "I need you, Javier. I need your wisdom. You've known Will since kindergarten."

"High school."

"Whatever. Here's what we're going to do." I'm improvising now. The bourbon helps. The bourbon always helps. "For every question you answer, I'll remove an article of clothing."

Javier looks shocked. "That actually makes me really uncomfortable."

"Fine. Then for every question you answer, I'll leave on an article of clothing."

"I really don't want to—"

I start unbuttoning my sweater.

"Okay okay okay," he says. "What do you want to know?"

"Tell me everything about Will. Tell me his secrets."

"I don't think he has any secrets."

I kick off a sandal.

"His grandfather died in prison," Javier says quickly. "He couldn't get into *Breaking Bad* because the science was too dumbed down. He got crabs once from a towel at the Yale gym."

"Tell me about his girlfriends."

"They were nice," Javier says. "Grad-school types, you know? Intellectual, serious."

"Much like myself."

"Um, yeah . . ."

"Does he have any bad habits? Any vices?"

"He tried dipping tobacco once, during exam week," Javier says. "It made him throw up."

This is useless. And I'm bored. "How does he feel about his mother?"

Javier looks startled. "His mother? Fine, as far as I know. I mean, normal. She's a little intense. I think he seeks her approval."

"Intense is right," I say. "Have you met her?"

"Mmm hmm." He crosses and uncrosses his legs. He stares at the floor, suddenly fascinated by the beige carpet.

I narrow my eyes. "When?"

"Will and I went to high school together, so . . ." He shifts in his chair uneasily. "And then, one summer during college, I got a job as a paralegal in her office."

"Did you have a lot of interaction with her?"

He bites his lip. "Not really."

I take another sip of bourbon, saying nothing. A good attorney knows when to slow down the questioning, let the pauses grow. Nervous people hate silence. They perceive it as a judgment, and fall all over themselves to fill it.

Which is exactly what Javier does. "I mean, Anita—that is, Mrs. Field—she was an Assistant U.S. Attorney at that point. She wasn't in charge of the whole office, like she is now. They all have their own cases, and in terms of working with paralegals like me—"

"You slept with her," I say.

"No!"

"Oh my God, Javier." I put my hand over my mouth. "You did. You bonked Will's mom!"

"It was a mistake!" he cries. "There was a softball game between our office and the local FBI. We went out for beers afterward. She drove me home!"

"The ride home after a sporting event." I nod approvingly. "Classic move."

He covers his face with his hands. "I was drunk! We did it in her station wagon. The same one she'd used to drive me and Will to quiz bowl tournaments!"

"How many times did it happen?"

He tries to compose himself. "Just that once."

"Stop lying to me, Javier."

"Seven!" he wails. "We did it seven times!"

"Javier, Javier," I say darkly. "Javier."

"I thought I wanted to be an attorney, but after that? No way." He shudders. "You people are out of control."

"You're in big trouble," I tell him.

His eyes widen. "Why?"

"Don't you know it's treason to commit adultery with a United States Attorney?"

His brow furrows. "No it isn't."

"Well, it's not very nice! And the mother of your best friend? I should tell Will."

He looks panicked. "You wouldn't do that."

I open the third bottle of bourbon. "Fine. I won't. Provided that you call Anita right now and tell her that you're going to confess everything to him unless she leaves me alone."

"Are you kidding? She'll have me put on a terrorist watch list or something. She's crazy, in case you haven't noticed."

Fair point. I finish the final bottle of bourbon and stand up.

"What's she doing to you, anyway?" he asks.

"It's not important." I take off my sweater and let it drop to the ground. "Let's get naked."

"What?" he cries. "No!"

"Why, I'm not good enough for you?"

"No, it's not that! You're very . . . but . . ."

"You only sleep with women who've been confirmed by the Senate? That's a short list, Javier." I kick off my other sandal. "And Condi and Hil are busy ladies."

"Will's my best friend!" Javier protests. "I couldn't do that to him."

I bend down and look him in the eyes. The neckline of my dress is loose—he doesn't want to look, but he can't help it. "Javier," I whisper. "Let's have some fun."

He looks away, then back at me. "It's wrong," he says.

"That's what makes it *fun*!" I pull my dress over my head and kneel in front of him. I rest my hands on his thighs. I part his legs slightly. "Tell me what you like."

"I can't," he says softly.

I lean closer. "Javier." I slip a hand around the back of his neck and pull him toward me. I brush his lips lightly with mine. "You can tell me." I kiss him again, lingering this time. I feel him respond. I slide my other hand up his leg. "What do you burn for but never get?"

He looks me in the eye. I can feel him wavering.

Then he says, "I think you should leave."

17

I'm shutting the door to Javier's room behind me as the elevator dings again. Freddy steps out. She sees me and stops dead.

I salute her. "What ho, my lady?"

She cocks her head. "Whose room is that?"

"Javier's."

"Javier," Freddy says. "Will's best man."

"No worries, Mother Superior. He shot me down."

Her eyes widen. She wobbles theatrically. "I feel a great disturbance in the Force."

"Can we be done with the *Star Wars* references, please?"

"As if a million souls just cried out in agony—"

I take her arm. "Shut up and buy me a drink."

We leave the hotel and walk into the warm, starry night. We pass a Mexican restaurant. "Margaritas!" we cry at the same time.

On the back patio, Freddy raises her glass. "To Javier. A man of rare fortitude."

"Please." I sip my drink. "I get rejected all the time."

"It really doesn't bother you?"

I shrug. "So some guy isn't interested in me. Who cares? Maybe he's married. Maybe he's gay. Maybe he prefers blondes. That's on him, not me."

"I guess you're the one with the fortitude. Or," she adds wryly, "it's the alcohol, masking all those inhibitions and insecurities."

"Don't forget my insufficiencies," I say. "My ineptitudes and imperfections."

"Your immaturities. Your infelicities."

I raise my glass. "To all of my ins. My ins and uns and disses." Freddy clinks her glass against mine.

We finish our drinks and keep walking. On the next block, she takes my arm and picks up speed. "Whatever you do," she says, "do not look up at the balcony of the building across the street."

So of course I do. It's a nice place, a romantic little seafood restaurant in an old island mansion. There are intimate bistro tables set out on the balcony, draped in white cloth, lit by flickering candles. Various attractive couples are drinking wine, holding hands, gazing into each other's eyes.

Including my father and Jane.

Jane?

I stop walking.

"Oh," I whisper. "Oh no."

"Maybe it's innocent," Freddy suggests. "Two exes grabbing a bite. Catching up."

His hand slips under the table and disappears under her skirt.

"Maybe she has a cramp," Freddy says, not able to tear her eyes away.

Dad raises Jane's hand to his lips. He kisses it. She's smiling at him indulgently, leaning toward him, toying with her gold necklace. He turns her hand over and strokes her palm with his fingertips, gazing into her eyes.

"I've seen *you* do that," Freddy murmurs.

Dad reaches out and traces the line of Jane's jaw. He brushes aside a few strands of her hair.

"He's going to kiss her," Freddy says, hypnotized.

His hand slips around the back of Jane's neck. He pulls her close. He whispers something in her ear.

He kisses her.

We back under an awning and watch. For a long time.

Then some intuition, some sixth sense, causes him to break off and look directly at me. His eyes widen. I grab Freddy's hand and yank her away.

On the next block, she stops and turns to me. "I think I'm in love with your father."

I pull her along. We pass the open door of a quiet wine bar and peek inside. Soft jazz is playing. The padded leather stools are mostly empty.

"This place is super tasteful," Freddy says. "Let's leave."

I drag her inside. The bartender wipes down the counter in front of us. "What are you ladies drinking?"

"The blood of our oppressors," I say.

"Or absinthe," Freddy says.

"Let's recap," I say. "My father is cheating on his current wife with his ex-wife, on whom he's cheating with his other ex-wife. How is that possible?"

"Parents," Freddy says. "They grow up so fast."

What is Jane thinking? She's married to a really nice guy (ancestry issues aside). Is she going to throw it all away for Dad, who cheated on her with her best friend? And what about poor Mom? She's going to have her heart broken all over again.

Our drinks arrive. They taste awful, but soon I feel a comforting glow. My phone rings. It's Henry. I ignore it. Freddy starts chatting up the girl on her right. I glance to my left. The seat is empty, which is a relief. I half expected to see the Ghost of Christmas Future sitting there, with his black cloak and skeletal hands and everything, saying, "Did you see what I saw back there? Were you paying attention? Because, sweet-heart? That's *you*."

I pluck at Freddy's sleeve. She turns to me. "How did you break off your engagements?" I ask.

She gives me a very loving look. She senses that I have finally made a decision.

"You can't think about it too hard," she tells me. "You just get it done. Walk in and say, 'Will? It's over. We're wrong for each other.' And then you leave. Quick and clean."

"Doesn't he deserve the truth?"

"The last thing that boy deserves," she says gently, "is the truth."

We order another round of drinks. My phone pings with a text:

—Please pick up your phone. We need to talk.

—this is yr daughter, fyi

—I know that!

—what the hell, henry? what are you doing?

—I'm afraid I don't know how to explain it.

—try

—I ran into Jane last month in Aspen. She was looking so well.
   We had coffee. We spent the entire time talking about you.

—oh no. this ones not on me

—That's not what I meant! These last few months have been
   very trying for me, darling. Trina's been back and forth to
   Europe. You know I don't like to be alone. I'm very dull
   company.

   . . .

—:(

   . . .

—I'm working it out. Truly I am.

   . . .

—In the meantime, it would be very helpful to me if you didn't
   say anything to anyone about this.

I think about that for a minute. Then I type:

—it would be very helpful to me if you bought me a jaguar
   convertible

Nothing for a minute. Then:

—Color?

—red pls!

—I'll have Fitzwilliam take care of it on Monday.

I put away my phone. Freddy pokes me. "Can you do me a favor?"
"Anything," I say.
"Loan me five hundred dollars."
"You need a quickie abortion or something?"

"I need my own room. Nicole is bugging the hell out of me."

"What is it now?"

"Honestly, Lily?" Freddy finishes her drink and gestures to the bartender. "I'm sick of how she talks about you. She doesn't approve of you, fine, that's her right, although I don't get why she considers herself your friend. Regardless, it doesn't justify the constant stream of nasty, passive-aggressive bullshit. This afternoon? She actually used the s-word."

"Socialist?" I say.

"No."

"Super special?"

"No."

"Seismically sexy?"

"Slut, Lily. She called you a slut."

New drinks arrive. I raise mine. "To Nicole. Truth teller extraordinaire."

"Oh, no," Freddy warns me. "You know we don't use the s-word in this house."

"I thought it was the c-word we didn't like."

"That too," she says. "And depending on context, the b-word. But we definitely, *definitely* don't like the s-word."

I shrug. "It's just a word."

Freddy holds up her hands. "Whoa there, Nellie. It is not *just* a word, okay? It's a vicious little judgment and sentence, especially when one woman uses it to describe another."

"Let Nicole judge," I say. "Let them all judge. I couldn't care less."

"You should care," Freddy insists. "It's not right. She wouldn't judge you if you were a man."

"It has nothing to do with whether I'm a man, and everything to do with whether Nicole is an asshole."

"It's both," she says. "If you were a man, Nicole wouldn't have the vocabulary to judge you. All the words for women who like casual sex are negative. All the words for men who like casual sex are positive."

"That can't be completely true."

"Slut. Whore. Ho. Skank. Tramp. What else?" Freddy pauses. "Floozy. Hussy. Now we have to get kind of old-timey. Trollop. Strumpet. Harlot. Can you come up with any positive terms—or even any neutral ones?"

I think about it. "No," I admit.

"But men who sleep around? They're Casanovas. Don Juans."

"Romeos," I say. "Lotharios."

"See?" Freddy says. "Talk about a double standard. Men get Shakespeare, and women get the gutter."

That's when someone taps my arm. I turn to him. He has dark hair. Blue eyes. Hot as hell. He leans toward me and smiles confidentially.

"I've always been fond of the term 'tart,'" he says. "It's a bit pejorative, but not extraordinarily so."

He's British.

I fall deeply in love.

He holds out a hand. "I'm Ian."

I take it. "I'm yours."

Freddy eyes him. "He's not the same one from Saturday night, is he?"

I take his face in my hands and kiss him on the mouth. "Nope," I say, breaking away at last. "He's new."

He smiles at me, a little dazed. "You took your time sorting that out."

"It doesn't do to be hasty in these matters, Ian." I pound my fist on the bar. "My good Lloyd! A jeroboam of your finest whiskey!"

The bartender looks up from his phone. "What now?"

"Give me a bourbon," I say. "This absinthe stuff is disgusting."

"Make that two," Freddy says.

"Make that four," I say. "We've got lots to talk about with our new friend here."

"Five, then," Freddy says. "Because what about him?"

"Five," I tell the bartender. "No, six."

"Six?" Freddy says.

"Well, if we each get two, and then he . . ." I pause. "Wait."

Freddy shakes her head. "Math."

Soon there's a row of glasses lined up in front of us. We each raise one. "To true love," I propose. We all laugh bitterly and drink.

"Do you agree with my friend Freddy?" I ask Ian. "Has the English language judged me and condemned me?"

"Absolutely," he replies, setting down his empty glass. "Language is a key part of the conspiracy, isn't it?"

"The conspiracy?"

Ian picks up another bourbon. He holds up the glass and gazes appreciatively at the amber liquid inside. He takes a sip. "The conspiracy," he says, drawing out the word, savoring it. "The grand conspiracy by which we all use sex to make each other utterly miserable."

Freddy and I exchange a look.

I say, "I was under the impression that we use sex to make each other happy."

"That's the great genius of the conspiracy," Ian says. "It hooks us with its promises of outrageously satisfying short-term pleasure. Long term? It completely fucks us over."

"I'm not trying to make anyone miserable," Freddy objects.

"Of course you're not *trying* to," he agrees. "That's the even greater genius of the conspiracy. We are all part of it, all victims and perpetrators, even as we are entirely unaware that it exists."

He picks up another bourbon. Freddy and I put our heads together.

"He's completely insane," I whisper.

"I know!" she whispers back.

"I really want to sleep with him."

"Me too."

"But you're gay!"

She looks offended. "Only most of the time!"

"You just want him because he reminds you of my father."

"Pots and kettles, Lillian," she warns me. "Pots and kettles."

"Whatever," I say. "We need to resolve this—he's drinking all our bourbon."

"Let's flip a coin."

She takes one out of her purse. I call heads.

I win!

I buy her three pink squirrels. "No hard feelings?"

She pats my arm. "Go get him, killer."

Our glasses are empty. I order another round and turn back to Ian. "Tell me how it works, this little conspiracy of yours."

He raises an eyebrow. "Do I detect a hint of skepticism?"

"I'm not a fan of grand explanatory theories," I tell him. "But go ahead. Persuade me."

He gets right down to it. "There's a message, right? And the message is everywhere. Sex is bad. Sex is wrong. Sex kills. We hear it at church, from our parents, in school, from our doctors, from the news. The message is simple, uniform, consistent and pervasive." He picks up another bourbon. "So what happens? We internalize the message, and we hold ourselves accountable to it, and we condemn anyone who thinks or acts or believes differently."

"Hold on," I say. "A pervasive message that sex is wrong? We live in a world that's saturated with sex. Television, movies, Internet porn, tween pop stars. Hell, look around you." I point out the open doorway to the revelers staggering by on Duval. "You're sitting in Sexy Sexville, USA."

Ian drains his glass. "Of course we're surrounded by it. The conspiracy needs opposition to flourish. Disagreement sharpens the message. Seeing sex everywhere and thinking that everyone else is doing it and loving it, while we believe it to be shameful and wrong—yet all the while secretly still wanting it ourselves? That makes us all the more conflicted and tormented about it."

I glance over to see what Freddy thinks of this. She's talking to the girl next to her again. "I guess I never got the memo," I tell Ian.

"Beg pardon?"

"I don't think sex is bad."

"Of course you do," he replies. "You're a woman, aren't you?"

I place my glass on the bar and gaze at him coolly. "You were doing so well, Ian. Don't piss me off now."

"Just listen," he says. "Men don't have it easy. We're taught that sex is wrong, but also that we're selfish pigs helplessly in thrall to our dicks. If we try to restrain our baser instincts, we're self-castrated weaklings. If we give them free rein, we're vile rapists. The result? Misery. But for women, it's far worse."

"How so?"

He picks up another bourbon. "You have to be made to feel worse about sex than men, because whatever pleasure you derive from it must always be secondary to ours."

"You don't want us to enjoy it because you're afraid of being cuck-olded," I say.

"I'm thinking of something far more elementary. If men actually had to worry about pleasing women, we'd be doomed. It would be curtains for us as a gender. Our penises would permanently shrivel up and retire to a Buddhist monastery in California."

I laugh.

"I'm quite serious," he says. "Not about the monastery, of course, but about everything else. Having to take responsibility for sexually satisfying a woman? That's a terrifying prospect for the vast majority of men. Our solution? To make sure that your desire for satisfaction is extremely limited. So you are taught from the earliest age—even more than men—that sex is dirty and disagreeable and something that good girls don't do. You've been persuaded that you want intimacy, stable re-lationships, children. You want sex only insofar as it provides you with those things. If you accept the message, you don't enjoy sex that much. Result: misery. If you don't accept the message, you're branded a filthy nympho. Result: misery." He clinks his glass against mine and smiles at me cheerfully. "Diabolical, isn't it?"

Freddy pokes her head back into the conversation. "Thanks. We'd forgotten about 'nympho.' But what about us gays? How do we fit in?"

"You have your own set of problems," he replies. "But fear not: the conspiracy is working hard to initiate you into the realm of comprehen-sive sexual dissatisfaction." He raises a glass to her. "For example: wel-come to matrimony."

"Hang on," I say. "This isn't the Dark Ages. There are plenty of women out there who enjoy sex."

"Yes, and they aid and abet the conspiracy," he says. "Women who freely explore their sexuality, and take pleasure for pleasure's sake? They exist to be punished and judged. More importantly, they've been con-tained. Explained. They're as enslaved to the conspiracy as the rest of us. I take it you're one of them. Therefore, you're a slut, and others—men and women, especially women—will shame you to make you an example to others. You're an affront to everything they've been taught and a reminder of everything they secretly want but won't let themselves have. Which takes us back to your original point. Why are there no positive words for a woman who happily, unashamedly screws around? We don't need those words. We don't want those words. We don't want that woman to exist."

He stops talking and picks up another drink. I look around. The bar is emptying out.

Like I said, I don't care much for grand theories. I think they're bull-shit, by and large. Ian pretty much lost me as soon as he started talking about capital-W Woman. What Woman is. What Woman wants. What Woman is taught, and what She thinks, and how She feels. She's such a convenient reduction. Such definitive proof of the validity of every crack-pot theory. Such a pervasive justification for the staggering amounts of unfairness in the world.

Whatever. It's late. Time to move on.

He's finishing another drink. I lean close and put my hand on his arm. "Ian?"

"Yes, darling?"

"Let's go make each other miserable."

I say good-bye to Freddy, who's so absorbed in her new friend she barely notices. Ian and I leave the bar and walk up Duval. We happen to be staying at the same hotel. Serendipity! We get into the elevator and he pushes me against the far wall. The doors close. He immediately kneels in front of me and lifts my dress. He yanks down my panties and puts his mouth on me. I feel his tongue push into me, his hot breath, his lips. I can barely stay upright. I close my eyes and bury my hands in his hair. And yes, this is happening in a hotel where I know probably eighty of the other guests—one of them my fiancé. At this moment, I couldn't give a damn.

The doors open at the top floor. He pulls me out and we stumble against the wall, kissing and clawing at each other. I try to pull away, to make him wait, but he's insistent, forcing my mouth open with his, pressing a leg between mine, holding me so tight it almost hurts. Some-how we make it inside his room, and things slow down. He pulls my sweater off my shoulders. He unzips my dress and lifts it over my head. He unhooks my bra and lets it fall to the floor. Slides my panties down my legs. Slips my sandals off my feet. Kissing me the entire time, every-where. It feels unbearably good.

I unbutton his shirt. "Human beings are terrible to each other, aren't they?"

"Monstrous," he agrees. He lifts and kisses my breasts as I pull his undershirt over his head. His chest is broad and strong, lightly freckled. He's wearing some sort of cologne. I inhale deeply, loving the scent. I bend my head and catch a nipple between my teeth. I feel it harden. We sink to the floor. I kiss his rib cage, his belly, the bones of his hips. He's pushing up against me now, his heels digging into the floor, his hips rising. But I take my time.

"Why do you think men and women mistreat each other so badly?" I ask.

He takes my face in his hands and kisses me deeply. "You've a very funny notion of foreplay."

I unbuckle his belt. I unbutton his jeans and pull them down. I run my hand up and down the hard length of him. "And you've a very beautiful cock."

"I bet you say that to all the boys."

I smile at him. "Yes, but I don't always mean it." I kneel and take him in my mouth. His hands are in my hair, gripping my head and pushing it down.

"Your friend is wrong," he gasps. "There are so many good words for women like you."

I look up. "Give me some examples."

He pushes me back down. "Later, love. Later."

After a while I find his jacket and search through the pockets in the hopes of finding a condom. I do. I put it on him and then lower myself, slowly. He groans. I put his hands on my breasts. I move up and down, taking all of him inside me. I kiss him, my teeth catching his tongue and biting gently.

"Lascivious," he says. "There's a word."

"Give me another."

He wraps his arms around me and we roll over. "Licentious, of course." He enters me again, deeply. "Lecherous," he says. "Carnal."

"Carnal is good." I push up against him. "I like carnal."

"Lewd," he says. "Lusty." With each word he thrusts deep inside me. "Smutty. Filthy."

I grab his hips and pull him into me. I smack his ass. He pins my arms to the ground. "Wicked," he says. "Very, very wicked."

We end up on the balcony, our skin prickled by the night air. He has me up on the railing. My legs are wrapped around his waist. He buries his fingers in my hair and forces my head back as he moves in and out of me. He kisses my neck, my breasts, my shoulders. The metal is wet with spray from the ocean. I could slip and fall, but I don't care. Instead I come, endlessly. He does, too.

He draws a bath. We sit in the steaming water, facing each other.

"Ian?"

"My dear?"

"Your theory is ludicrous."

He looks wounded. "I didn't convince you?"

"No," I say. "But it might be the most effective pickup strategy I've ever heard."

He leans back contentedly against the tiled wall. "I've spent a lot of time working on it."

"As a conspiracy, though, it doesn't make any sense." I move my foot so that it's resting between his legs. I start playing with him. "Why would we choose misery?"

"We like it," he replies. He lifts my foot out of the water and examines it. He kisses my big toe. "Misery is safe. It's more comfortable than happiness."

"More comfortable?"

"Certainly." He kisses another toe. "We never have to worry about losing it."

"I don't like misery," I say.

"No? What do you like?"

I sit up and move toward him. "I'll show you."

Soon I'm on top of him again. "I wish I'd met you months ago," I say breathlessly.

"I agree." He kisses me. "I thought it such a shame when you missed the holiday party."

I stop moving. "What?"

He laughs and kisses my breasts.

"The holiday party," I say, trying to think. "The holiday party."

Oh, shit.

I struggle to get up, but he's holding me tight.

"Ian!" I say, striking my forehead with the heel of my hand. "Ian from the museum!"

He's one of Will's coworkers.

Technically, his boss.

And one of his groomsmen.

He laughs softly, kissing my neck. "I've heard so much about you."

I try to get up again, but he doesn't let me.

Just when I thought I'd gotten over feeling guilty about everything.

He's watching me, smiling.

What's the harm at this point, though? I mean, seriously? What does it matter?

I stop struggling. Ian's hands are stroking my back lightly. "Will's a lucky man," he says.

"You think so?"

He laughs again. "Oh, absolutely."

THURSDAY

18

I open my eyes. I'm lying in bed, staring straight out the window at the shimmering sea.

I am perfectly sober. My mind is clear.

I'm going to tell Will. I'm going to call it off, right now.

I take a deep breath. I roll over.

He's not there.

I sit up and look around. The room is empty. When I get out of bed, I see a note on the desk.

You look so peaceful—didn't want to wake you.
See you at the Audubon House at 11.

The Audubon House? Oh, right—we're meeting Mattie there this morning for a walk-through. Of the wedding that's not going to happen.

I order breakfast and eat it while I get dressed. I start berating myself about last night, but I stop. It doesn't matter. I mean, it does matter—seeing my father, that nonsense with Ian? Further proof that I have no business getting married.

I leave the hotel and head down United Street. This little wedding preview is going to be gruesome. With all of Mattie's talk about wanting the event to be such a storybook affair, a fairy tale come to life? I'm picturing showers of rose petals, roving ice sculptors. Runaway kids in fluffy wings.

No doubt in my mind: there will be doves.

Maybe I can pull Will aside before she arrives and get it over with.

I turn onto Whitehead Street. Will is waiting by the picket fence in front of the Audubon House. Standing beside him are his mother and father. I freeze.

He comes up and kisses me. "Morning, sleepyhead!"

"What are they doing here?"

"My parents? They're interested. Especially my mom."

Who's smiling at me right now in her special, special way.

"Will?" I say. "We need to talk."

Then Mattie tears up in her car, one wheel bumping up onto the sidewalk. She tumbles out, hair a mess, dragging an overstuffed tote bag and an enormous binder and dropping her phone and losing her glasses and calling out "Hello! Hello there!" and waving frantically, even though we're all standing about ten feet away.

"I'm so sorry I'm late! Oh, look—*parents*! I'm Matilda Kline—delighted. Just delighted. Delightful. And how is everyone this morning? Fine? Fine? *Fine*. I was checking the weather report, and it looks like we're in good shape for the next few days. Very good shape. Nothing to worry about on the meteorological front. Not down here, anyway. The rest of the country, well . . . Now, let me . . . there's a . . ." She fumbles through her tote bag, spilling papers onto the sidewalk. "Oops! Alrighty then. The house and gardens are open to the public today—they'll close early on Saturday so that we can set everything up, of course. Right now we'll pop in so that I can show you around and give you an idea of what's going to happen in just two days!"

Mattie hustles us through the small gift shop, waving to the woman at the ticket desk, and leads us into the garden along a winding brick path. Sunlight sparkles on the lush greenery all around us. We end up at the back of the mansion, in a courtyard circled by tall palms.

"Here we are!" she cries. "Now then. Let me see if I can help you visualize it." She drops her things on a bench and steps into the courtyard, turning to face us. A calm seems to settle upon her. She smiles beatifically. "The guests will be seated in rows of white chairs, down *here*. The ceremony will take place on the back veranda of the house, up *there*." She points to the steps that lead up to the wide, wood-planked porch. "You two will have a good view of the crowd," she explains. "People often forget that part—that a wedding ceremony should be as much about you seeing your loved ones as it is about them seeing you."

Will squeezes my hand. Mattie goes on to explain various things about flower arrangements and bunting and how the parents will walk down the aisle and be seated.

"Now, Lily. Your bridesmaids will emerge from the garden over *there*—the irises are in bloom, so I think it will be beautiful. They'll walk down the aisle, and you'll follow them. Dusk will be falling, so as you proceed we'll turn on the lights in the trees and around the garden. It's a little theatrical," she concedes, "but then, it *is* a wedding."

"Sounds beautiful," Harry remarks. Anita is staring at me, arms crossed. I turn away. It's all very lovely, and much more tasteful than I expected. But so what?

Mattie leads us to another open space in the garden, beside a rectangular pool thick with lily pads. "The dinner tables will be scattered throughout the garden, but the heart of the reception will be right here. We'll start with champagne and a little music immediately after the ceremony, when you two will be busy with the photographer. I found a bluegrass duo—a husband and wife. I think you'll like them."

Will grins. "That sounds great!"

"I thought you'd like it. You know," she wags a playful finger at us, "I feel like I've gotten to know you both pretty well in the past week. It's helped me incorporate a few fresh ideas."

Fresh ideas. That's what I'm talking about. Bring on the cracked-out cupids!

"For example, I've noticed how much you love spending time with your friends. So I called around and found . . . *this*." Mattie opens her binder and shows us a picture of a vintage photo booth, with a red velvet curtain and a stool. "Your guests can use it all evening and take home the photo strips as souvenirs. The machine keeps copies so that you can make an album out of them. What do you think?"

Will laughs. "It's awesome, Mattie."

She beams at us. "I'm so glad you like it. Now over here, we'll set up a standard bar. And beside it," she gestures to a little nook next to the lily pond, "is where we'll station your wedding mixologist."

"Our mixologist?"

"I met the most wonderful young man last week. His name is Joseph. He recently moved here from Brooklyn, and he knows *hundreds* of drink recipes. He invented one recently that he thinks will be perfect for your signature cocktail. It has champagne, key lime juice, some French liqueur I've never heard of and then, what was it? Oh, yes—a gin-soaked strawberry. You drop the strawberry in the champagne, and it fizzes up! It's delicious," she says, giving me a wink.

Mattie is *on fire*.

She found an amazing swing band. An award-winning cake baker. At the end of the night, an ice cream truck is going to pull up and pass out key lime Popsicles to departing guests.

Popsicles!

No question, this would have been a great party.

"What happened?" I ask her. "You're so . . . with it, all of a sudden. No offense."

She smiles bashfully. "This always happens a few days out. I'm in the zone now."

We continue strolling around the garden, listening to her describe more details, more little touches. Then she stops and strikes herself on the forehead. "Goodness! I nearly forgot." She pulls two little booklets out of her tote bag. They're made of creamy card stock. Champagne-colored ribbon ties the pages together. "The programs," she explains. "I just picked them up from the printer."

She hands one to each of us. The cover reads:

The Wedding of

Lillian Grace Wilder

and

Will Clayborne Field

February Twenty-Third, Two Thousand and Fourteen

QUOS AMOR VERUS TENUIT, TENEBIT.

I stare at the phrase in Latin. I read it maybe three or four times. I turn to Will. "Did you tell her?"

"She asked me how we got engaged," he says. "But I didn't know she was going to—"

"No no, this was my doing," Mattie says eagerly. "Will told me about it, and I thought it was so lovely. True love . . ." She turns to Will with an embarrassed laugh. "I've forgotten the rest of the translation. What does it mean?"

"It means . . ." He hesitates, then clears his throat. "It means, 'true love holds fast to those it once held.'"

Mattie puts a hand over her heart. "Beautiful! And who wrote it?"

"Seneca," Will says. "A Roman philosopher."

I tear my eyes away at last and look up at Will. He's still staring at the program.

"What do you think of the font?" Mattie asks.

I don't say anything. I can't. I'm caught up in the memory of a night in the middle of September.

It was a Wednesday. Will called me at the office and asked me to meet him at eight o'clock outside the museum. I'd spent a more-than-usually-insane amount of time at work that week, and I was tired. "Does it have to be tonight?"

"Yes," he said. "The moon is out."

Mysterious. I texted him when I arrived at the imposing steps on Fifth Avenue. He directed me to a side door, where he was waiting to usher me inside. I followed him through several dim, hushed galleries, into the Great Hall. The only illumination came from the half-moon windows high above us, and the emergency lights over the doorways. The room, which I'd only ever seen filled with hundreds of people, was empty. Our footsteps echoed across the marble.

We passed the entrance to the gift shop and the main staircase, where Will waved to a security guard. I was secretly hoping he'd invited me here so that we could do it in the Temple of Dendur—a long-standing dream of mine—but instead Will led me into the Greek and Roman wing. We walked through a long gallery filled with statues and urns and pieces of mosaic, until we came to a glass-covered courtyard, with columns spaced around a central fountain.

Will was right: the moon was out. The statues filling the room glowed in its light. The torso of a man, a centurion, a satyr, an armless nymph. The head of an aristocratic woman. A sarcophagus carved with scenes of battle. In the silence and emptiness of the room they were no longer dead pieces of art, but living things. Not part of a collection, but each existing in its own space, as it must have thousands of years ago.

I turned to Will. "They're beautiful."

"There's something else I want to show you." He unhooked a rope across a small doorway. "We just finished restoring this. Come in."

I stepped into a tiny room. The only illumination came from the courtyard and from a small frosted window set high in one wall.

"What is this?"

"A cubiculum nocturnum," Will said. "A bedroom. From a Roman villa that was buried by the eruption of Mount Vesuvius."

I squinted in the dim light. The walls were covered with images I couldn't make out. "This is from Pompeii?"

"Close. About a mile away."

I stood in the middle of the room and turned slowly. My eyes were adjusting, and the frescoes on the walls slowly appeared. Blue skies. Cliffs in the distance. A birdbath—no, two. Birds splashing in the water. Columns twisted with vines. On the two long walls, buildings towering up to the ceiling, piled one on top of the other. Frescoes of a city, for a house in the country. The colors were so bright. Blue, crimson, green, yellow, ochre. I made out temples, statues, urns and burning pyres.

A bedroom, buried for two thousand years. Was anyone in here when the volcano erupted? Sleeping, or making love? Waking up to the explosion, the thermal blast, the rain of ash outside the window?

I expected Will to be doing his standard museum patter—interpreting the iconography, describing how the villa was discovered, how the frescoes were restored. But he wasn't saying anything.

"You're awfully quiet," I said, turning around.

That's when he stepped forward, took my hand and got down on one knee.

He was holding a ring.

"Do you remember the night we met?" he said. His voice was a little shaky. "You asked me to say something to you in Latin, and I did, but I wouldn't tell you what it meant." I nodded. I couldn't speak. He slipped the ring onto my finger. It was a simple, engraved silver band. "*'Quos amor verus tenuit, tenebit,'*" he said, tracing the letters slowly. Then he translated it for me. "I first read that years ago, when I was learning Latin. I loved the rhythm of it. It sounds better in the original, doesn't it?" He repeated the phrase softly as he turned the ring on my finger. "When I read it, I thought, I'm going to remember this. If I ever fall in love, this is what I'm going to say to her. And so I said it to you, that first night. Because I knew. I knew it was true love, and I knew that it held me, and would keep holding me, forever." He looked up at me. "Will you marry me, Lily Wilder?"

And that's when I dropped to my knees and said, "Yes."

"Yes?" he said, hopeful, half disbelieving. "Yes, really?"

"Yes!" I cried. "Yes really! Yes of course!"

And then we kissed, and we cried, and we laughed and kissed some more. We walked around the rest of the Greek and Roman gallery, holding hands, stopping to kiss, and embrace, and laugh. Then we went home and went to bed.

And it was like those first three days, passionate and true, and afterward, I looked into his eyes and saw all the way into him. But I wasn't just seeing him. I was seeing us. I was seeing where I was supposed to be. I didn't want to leave. And I wouldn't leave. I understood all this, at once. And I accepted it. I didn't hide from it or run away. It wasn't until the next day, or the day after, that I started denying, doubting, explaining it all away.

But there's only one explanation for that yes. And for so many other things. For why I feel happy every time I walk into a room and find Will there. Why I've resisted breaking off our engagement against everyone's advice, against my better judgment, against my own self-interest. Why I call him, and text him, and e-mail him, and generally pester him to death. Why I'm always touching him, and kissing him, and playing with his hair. Why I love to talk with him, and joke with him. And go out with him. And come home to him. Why I am constantly trying to get into his pants. Why I get that fluttering feeling in the pit of my stomach every time he touches me, or smiles at me, or just looks at me.

I said yes because I fell for him the moment I saw him. I said yes because I want to marry him.

Love.

I love him.

Oh, shit!

"Lily?" Mattie says. "The font?"

I look up. "The font is fine, Mattie."

What am I going to do? How can I realize this *now*? How can I suddenly discover, at the least opportune moment, that I do in fact love the man I've spent days and weeks and months wondering whether I love?

Okay, wait. Calm down.

I can fix this. I can figure out a way to stop his mom from stopping the wedding.

How? Not sure. Really not sure about that.

I need time to think. I have no time to think.

We've started walking again. Will has his hands in his pockets and is gazing at the ground thoughtfully. His parents are ahead of us. As we circle back toward the front gate, he moves ahead to say something to his father, and Anita drops back to walk beside me.

She skips the pleasantries. "You're out of time."

"Why do I have to do this?" I ask. "You found what you found—why not tell him yourself?"

She smiles at me pleasantly. "Shall I tell him about your infidelities, too?"

And there I was, thinking things couldn't get any worse.

"I know a number of people in New York. Fellow prosecutors, friends from law school." She raises her eyebrows. "You have quite a reputation."

"You have a lot of nerve, talking about infidelities."

After an infinitesimal pause, she replies, "I have no idea what you're talking about."

My phone pings with a text. I glance at it—something silly from Diane. I'm about to drop it back into my bag when . . . I don't.

Anita keeps talking. "Isn't it better this way? You can't want this, not really. A fancy wedding? A marriage to someone so obviously unsuited to you, a marriage destined to fail? It's not worth throwing away your career."

"How did you know my career would matter to me?"

She shrugs, twirling the stem of a leaf between her fingers. "I asked around."

"Of course you did." I glance down at my phone again.

"I thought I knew my son," she continues. "But he's a complete mystery to me. He's such an intelligent person. He must be blind not to see who you really are."

That's about as much as I can take. I stop walking and turn to face her. "Javier says hi."

Her expression is innocent, slightly puzzled. "Javier? Will's friend?"

"Yes, that Javier. He told me quite a story about the summer he worked in your office."

"Did he work there?" She tilts her head, as if she's making a real effort to recall him. All good trial lawyers are gifted actors, and Anita is no exception. "Now that you mention it, I do vaguely remember . . . Goodness, that was so long ago!"

"Goodness, wasn't it? Still, Javier remembers it well. How tired he would get after softball practice. He was *always* so grateful when you would give him a ride home."

She gazes at me levelly. "I'm not sure what you're driving at."

"Aren't you, Anita?"

"No. I'm not."

"That makes sense. You probably had lots of affairs with subordinates over the years. This was the only opportunity Javier had to screw a United States Attorney."

Her face contorts with rage. "How *dare* you?"

"A married one, too," I continue. "And the mother of his best friend. I can see why that would be a lot more memorable for him than it was for you."

"This is absolutely outrageous!"

"What did he say? It lasted for months. You couldn't get enough of each other. Night after night after night."

"I have *never*—"

"Sometimes you couldn't even wait until the office was empty. You called him in, closed the blinds in your office, and did it right there on your desk." I widen my eyes. "A lowly paralegal and Chicago's chief federal prosecutor. Sounds pretty hot, Anita. The big boss, and her cute, submissive little underling."

"That's completely untrue!" she snaps. "I was only an Assistant U.S. Attorney at the time. And it didn't happen dozens of times. It was more like four or—"

In the sudden silence, I can hear a bird chirping merrily in the tree above our heads. Will and his father laughing about something. A rooster crowing on a nearby rooftop.

Anita is staring at me, her mouth compressed into a thin line.

"That was almost too easy," I say. "But then, that's a prosecutor for you. You guys just *love* to tell people when they're wrong. It's like you can't help yourselves."

"I am warning you," she says in a low voice. "If you try to smear me with this, you will be very, very sorry. I will deny everything, and I will be believed. My reputation is impeccable. In fact, it's safe to say that—" She breaks off in frustration. "Are you even listening to me? Stop playing with your phone!"

It's true—I've been fiddling with it the entire time she's been talking.

"You young people are all alike!" she snaps. I guess she has to vent her rage on something. "Obsessed by these pointless distractions! Texting, and social media, and those moronic games. Will behaves exactly the same way. You're wasting your lives."

"It's not all texting!" I protest. "My phone does a lot of other things. For example, this application right here?"

I hold my phone up to show her.

"It's called Voice Memo."

Anita stares at the blinking red dot on the screen.

"It's very handy," I add. I stop recording and press Play.

We hear her say: "That's completely untrue! I was only an Assistant U.S. Attorney at the time. And it didn't happen dozens of times. It was more like four or—"

I press Stop and smile at her.

"Your expression right now? Priceless. In fact . . ." I snap a photo and show it to her. "That's definitely one for the wedding album, am I right?"

She grabs for the phone, but I hold it out of reach. Her dignity doesn't allow her to tussle for it.

"You'll never get away with this," she hisses. "No one will believe you."

I nod thoughtfully. "It will be so interesting to see which of us has more credibility. The U.S. Attorney battling sexual misconduct allegations? Or the woman with the audio file."

She looks murderous. "You can't possibly—"

"Lily? Anita?"

We look up. Will and his father are waiting for us.

Harry grins. "What are you two girls gabbing about?"

"Nothing!" we say at the same time.

We catch up with them. "I'll get you for this," she mutters.

I give her a friendly pat on the rear end. "Sure you will, Mom. Sure you will."

We're back at the front gate. I take Mattie's hands in mine. "I cannot thank you enough. You've planned a truly amazing wedding."

She blushes and beams at me. "I'm so glad you're pleased. But really, you made it easy, my dear."

"Did I?"

She cocks her head. "Well, no. But that doesn't matter now, does it? We're on our way!"

She starts giving me a lot of instructions about the rehearsal tomorrow. I don't really listen. I'm too happy. Eventually she disappears, trailing receipts and farewells. Will's parents head back to the hotel, Anita's head hanging low.

I turn to Will. "I have a quick call for work in a little while. Wait for me, and then we can get some lunch."

He frowns, running his hands through his hair. He looks a little downcast.

"Is everything okay, baby?"

"Oh, yeah," he says, shaking out of it. "Definitely. But I told Javier I'd help him practice his best-man speech. I'll have to catch up with you later."

"Okay. Have fun!"

He kisses me good-bye, and I watch him walk away. I turn and stroll in the other direction. I get a text from Freddy:

—u ok?

—everythings great!

—??

—im in love with Will!

—???

—and I thwarted his moms evil plot to ruin my life!

—??????

—wedding on, bitches!

My phone rings. "What are you smoking?" Freddy demands.
"Love!" I cry. "I'm smoking *love*!"
"I was afraid this might happen," she says. "We drank way too much absinthe last night."
"It's not a hallucination. It's for real. Really, really for real."
She sighs. "Can we take this step by step?"
"Sure!" I'm practically skipping down the street. I pluck a flower from a vine trailing along a picket fence and put it in my hair.
"So . . . you love Will," she says doubtfully.
"I loved him all along, Freddy. I'm over the moon about him." I tell her about my epiphany. I tell her I know it's love because I've spent all my time trying to reason it out—I should marry Will because of *x* and *y* and *z*, I shouldn't marry Will because of *a* and *b* and *c*—instead of examining how I feel. I've tried to deny what I felt for him, to do everything I could to reject it. Because I lost love once and didn't think I deserved it again. Didn't think I was wired for it, capable of doing it right.

But when you stop denying the truth, and open your eyes and see it? It has a solid quality. You just know.

When I'm done explaining, she doesn't nag me or doubt me—she gets it. "So the wedding's on?"
"Yes! His mom can't rat me out anymore." The flower falls out of my

hair. I put it back in. "I secretly recorded her admitting that she had an affair with Javier."

"Wait—*what?*"

I forgot to tell her about that. I guess I've had a lot on my mind. I give her a quick recap.

"And that's enough to stop her?"

"If this got out, it would be a huge scandal. It would ruin her career, just like she tried to ruin mine. I blackmailed the blackmailer, Freddy!"

"It does have a certain poetic justice to it," she agrees.

Call-waiting beeps. It must be my one o'clock with Philip and Lyle. "I've got to go, Freddy. I'll call you back."

Everything is so perfect right now! I'm going to get married. I saved my job. I'll have this call with Philip and Lyle to find out what interesting new case awaits me on my return, then enjoy to the utmost the last two days before my amazing, fun, Popsicle-strewn wedding to the man I love.

It's been a difficult few days. Or months. I wish I'd conducted myself a little differently with respect to . . . well, pretty much everything.

But I didn't know I loved Will! It makes all the difference.

Everything is going to work out. A life of ease, contentment and happiness awaits me.

I click over to the other line. "Good afternoon, gentlemen!"

"Wilder?" Philip says. "We have a problem."

19

"Problem? What problem?"

"The settlement fell through," Lyle says.

"The EnerGreen settlement? Why?"

"Because our client refuses to listen to reason," Philip says irritably.

I turn onto Duval Street as Philip explains that EnerGreen's board is balking over the proposed method for distributing the settlement to the plaintiffs. Everything sounded so certain on Tuesday. The deposition canceled, the papers all but signed. And now they're hung up on some trivial procedural point. Ridiculous.

"I take it the deposition is on for tomorrow?"

"It's on," Lyle confirms. "I've already called Hoffman. He's ready to go."

"Wait until you meet this guy, Philip. He's a real piece of work."

"I'm not coming," Philip replies. "You'll be handling this one on your own."

I stop walking. A woman bumps into me from behind—at least, I think it's a woman. I'm too focused on what Philip just said to know for sure.

"Whoa, whoa, whoa. What are you talking about?"

"It's the storm, Wilder. The entire city is shutting down."

"What storm?"

"You really are in vacation mode, aren't you?" Lyle says. "There's a blizzard bearing down on the East Coast. They say it's going to be the biggest in years. The airports are closing as we speak."

A blizzard? A little snow and ice? So what? Our firm is famous for the insane lengths its lawyers go to in order to help their clients when the stakes are high. Working for days without sleep. Ignoring serious illnesses. Risking jail time. Bad weather has never stopped us before. What is Philip thinking?

"You need to be here," I tell him. "There's no way I can defend this deposition by myself." Someone else bumps into me. I start walking again, turning onto a side street.

"What do you mean?" Lyle says, his voice dripping with fake big-brother cheer. "You're going to be great!"

"You can handle Hoffman's e-mails," Philip says. "I'll tell you exactly what to do."

"It's not just the e-mails I'm worried about, Philip. It's what he has to say about the financial statements. If he starts testifying about the fraud it's all over for EnerGreen."

"The alleged fraud," Philip corrects me.

"Not alleged," I say. "Actual. The actual fraud."

"What on earth are you talking about, Wilder?"

"Didn't Lyle tell you?"

Silence on the line.

"Tell him what?" Lyle says innocently.

For an instant, my mind goes blank. I stop and lean against a store-front. I can't quite take in the magnitude of what's happening.

"Lyle," I say. "Oh, Lyle. You useless, useless piece of shit."

"Wilder, please," Philip chides me.

"She's hysterical," Lyle says to Philip. "I told you she wasn't ready."

"One of you needs to tell me what is going on," Philip says. "Immediately."

So I sit down on a curb, in the shade of a banyan tree, and I start talking. I describe Pete's prep. I explain that the wild allegations in the complaint, the overheated stuff we thought was just rhetoric, is, in fact, true. That EnerGreen lost billions and billions of dollars in bad trades and used the oil spill to try to cover it up. I tell him how Pete will fall apart if questioned about it. I say that not only will EnerGreen lose the case, but because of the size of the fraud, the company could very well go under.

Then I finish talking, and I wait.

There's a long silence. Philip clears his throat. "Explain something to me, one of you, please," he says. His voice is calm, level. Extremely ominous. "Explain to me how it is that I, the partner in charge of this case, am learning this information now. Today, one day before the deposition of this witness. How is that possible?"

"This is the first I'm hearing about it, too," Lyle announces.

"He's lying, Philip."

"I'm not lying! She never told me any of this."

"He's lying through his teeth."

"Stop," Philip says. "Both of you. Stop."

There's a long pause. Lyle starts to say something, but Philip must gesture to him to be quiet. Finally, he says, "I am going to make some calls. We'll get back to you shortly, Wilder."

We hang up. I pace around for a little bit, marveling at Lyle's treachery. This is a new low, even for him. I should be enraged, beyond irate, but I can't muster anything more than mild annoyance. Why bother? There's no way Philip is going to let me fly solo here. He'll solve the problem, one way or another.

My phone pings with a text from Teddy:

—I can meet you at 3. Green Parrot.

I'm responding when Philip and Lyle call back. I can tell right away that the news is not good. Philip sounds agitated, distracted. Unlike himself.

"I've just gotten off the phone with Daniel Kostova," Philip says. Kostova is the plaintiffs' lead counsel. "He is refusing to postpone the deposition. Kostova is—he claimed that he is already in transit to the Keys. And if—he stated that if we try to delay, he will file an emergency motion with the court—a motion for sanctions—attaching Hoffman's e-mails as evidence of our supposed bad faith."

"Then it's simple," I say. "We don't show up. No witness, no deposition."

"That won't work," Lyle says. "Kostova will still move to have us sanctioned, and it gives him an even better excuse to put the e-mails in front of the judge."

"I have been unable to—to reach Urs," Philip continues. "I will keep trying, but I don't think we can depend on EnerGreen acceding to the settlement, not even if we—if they—if we can impress upon them the urgency of the situation." He exhales heavily. "Wilder is right. I need to be there."

He continues talking, reeling off to Lyle a whole bunch of instructions about documents he needs, transcripts of other depositions, copies of court orders. I've never heard him so rattled before. The seriousness of the situation has sunk in. If EnerGreen goes down because of a bad deposition, the firm's reputation will take a serious hit. As will his.

"Betty will make my travel arrangements," he says. "She will—I will have her call you with the details, Wilder. Lyle, I want you to reach out to Hoffman and tell him to be ready to meet with me first thing in the morning." He pauses again. "Try to convey the message correctly this time."

Lyle protests, "Philip, I didn't—"

"Shut up," Philip says. "Not another word out of your mouth."

Lyle and I are both shocked into silence. At a firm with some real screamers, Philip is famous for his courtesy. I've never heard him raise his voice or utter an angry word to anyone. He is the epitome of gentlemanly detachment. Breaking through that façade is part of what makes sleeping with him so much fun.

Was. *Was* part of what *made* sleeping with him so much fun.

We finally wrap it up. I check my messages. Nothing from Will. I have a little time to kill before meeting Teddy, so I decide to get my hair done. Do a dry run for Saturday. I find a salon, and soon a nice gay man is doing all the complicated and painful things I've always wanted done to my hair. I sit back in the chair and relax.

It's kind of a bummer that I'll have to spend most of tomorrow working. But second-chairing this particular deposition will be unlike anything I've ever done before. Professionally, I mean. Philip is amazing at this sort of thing, and from what I've heard, Kostova is no slouch, either. There should be lots of fireworks.

Then I think about my upcoming honeymoon with Will. We're going to have so much fun. I'll make sure that we get to the bottom of this sex business. Really hash it all out. I'll open up and be honest with him—you know, within reason—and we can start our married life with a clean slate.

It feels stupid to keep repeating it, but I really am so happy right now. Bliss!

I leave the salon about an hour later, stopping to admire my reflection in a shop window. Not bad. Not bad at all.

I'm not the only one who thinks so. A guy stops behind me, watching me.

I turn and smile at him, touching my hair. "You like?"

He smiles back. "I like. A lot."

What the hell am I doing? I turn and hurry away. I can't flirt like that anymore—I'm taken!

But you know what? It's not a big deal. I caught myself. It's just a habit I have to break.

My phone rings. It's my good buddy Lyle!

"Hey, loser! Did he fire your ass yet?"

"I think I'm safe for the time being," Lyle replies. "Philip isn't going to be firing anybody for a while."

Something in his tone stops me.

"He was just admitted to the hospital," Lyle adds.

I move closer to the curb, out of the main stream of pedestrians. "That's not funny, Lyle."

"Betty heard a crash in his office and found him lying behind his desk. Fortunately, the EMTs managed to stabilize him."

"Watch out!" someone cries, grabbing my arm. I was about to walk into traffic. I turn onto a side street.

"Too early to say whether it's a full-blown heart attack, but I saw him as they were wheeling him out." Lyle whistles. "He was *not* looking good."

It's true. I can tell from his voice, his barely concealed glee. Philip isn't coming. The deposition is going forward, and he won't be here. I'll be on my own.

And I *know* the professional significance of this should be sinking in for me right now, filling my soul with horror and fear and trepidation and all that. But honestly? All I can think about is how many times—and in how many ways—Philip and I have had sex. Intense, strenuous, *crazy* sex. In his office, in mine. At the Waldorf. On the—well, you get the point. Once he gets going, the guy is like a bull. All that, but present him with a little staffing problem on a deposition and he keels over like some delicate flower?

Men.

I'll never understand them.

"Needless to say, you'll be defending the deposition," Lyle says.

Of course it's not just a little staffing problem. It's a major crisis, with a major client, on a major case, with—most important—major repercussions for my life.

"Can't the firm send someone else?"

"Nope."

"We have eighty litigation partners." I can hear the panic in my voice, but I can't stop it. "You're saying that every single one of them is busy with something more important?"

"I'm saying that none of them is particularly eager to get dragged into this shitshow," Lyle retorts. "Philip did his best to rope somebody in, even as they were loading him onto the gurney. But nobody wants to slog through a blizzard, fly halfway across the country and defend a losing deposition in a doomed case. Philip asked me to go partner by partner until I found someone willing to take his place, but . . . I realized that I'm a little busy at the moment."

"You . . . you . . . oh Lyle, you are one . . ." I can't even come up with an adequate insult.

"Kostova's going to crush you," he continues helpfully. "He's good, Wilder. Decades of experience. You'll probably learn a lot from him. Not that it'll do you any good."

I hate having to do what I'm about to do, but the situation is truly desperate. "What about you, Lyle? Can't you come?"

He's silent for a moment. "I might consider it," he replies. "But you'll have to say please."

I bite my lip, close my eyes and cross my fingers. "Please?"

"Please what?" he says.

"Please will you . . ." This is killing me. I try again. "Please will you come down here and help me?"

His laughter rings through the phone. "Not in a million years."

"You asshole!" I shout. "This is going to be terrible for the firm. Doesn't that bother you?"

He snorts contemptuously. "I'm not a partner. I'm getting paid either way. Our clients are scumbags—you said so yourself. Why should I stick my neck out for them? This humiliating loss will have no effect on my reputation." He pauses. "Unfortunately, the same can't be said for you."

"This is all your fault!" I cry, in a helpless rage.

"Maybe," he says. "But you're the one who's going to be blamed. When it's all over, Philip might not actually fire you, but you'll always be tainted by this. Inside the firm and out. You'll be the lawyer who single-handedly lost the largest environmental class action in history."

He's right. As far as the legal profession is concerned, it won't matter that EnerGreen committed the actual crimes, and not me. It will be my name, and my name alone, listed on the transcript as the attorney defending the deposition. My voice in the video recording, objecting in vain as Hoffman gets destroyed. The whole thing will probably end up getting a lot of media attention, not to mention interest from the government. Choice bits might show up on YouTube.

I'll be famous. Infamous.

Sure, some people will understand it wasn't my fault, that there was nothing I could do. Some people will pity me.

But what they'll never, ever do is hire me.

I'm gripping the phone so tightly my hand hurts. "You're lucky I'm not standing in your office right now, Lyle."

He ignores me. "But who knows? Maybe Philip will fire you outright. I guess it just goes to show you."

"Show me what, Lyle?"

"That fucking the boss doesn't always pay off," he replies.

"Jesus Christ!" I shout, losing my temper at last. "I wasn't fucking him because he was my boss! I was fucking him because I wanted to fuck him!"

There's a sudden silence. I look up.

The sidewalk ahead of me is blocked by about a dozen toddlers. They're wearing name tags and matching green shirts. Holding hands in an adorable little chain.

I know those shirts. I know the middle-aged woman leading them. It takes me about three seconds to place her.

"Mrs. Carter?"

My preschool teacher shakes her head. "Lily Wilder. Your *language*."

I close my eyes. "Sorry. I'm just . . . sorry." I turn and walk in the other direction.

"So it's a coincidence?" Lyle says. "You would have slept with Philip even if it didn't help your career, even if you wouldn't get anything out of it? That's what you expect me to believe?"

"I don't expect you to believe anything, Lyle. But think about what you're saying, and compare it to reality. You review my hours. You see how much I bill. You know that I work as hard as you do, and that I get my share of shit assignments. Right?"

He's silent.

"I have some news for you, Lyle. When a woman chooses to have sex, there's not always some ulterior motive. We're not necessarily seeking power, or procreation, or relationship security, or career advancement. Sometimes, we just want sex. I've gotten one thing out of sleeping with Philip. I've gotten *sex* out of it. This is probably hard for you to understand. It's probably a little scary, because it doesn't align with your extremely limited understanding of how women work. It doesn't cohere with the message you've heard all your life."

Whoa. The message? I need to be careful. I'm starting to sound like Ian.

"Look, Wilder," Lyle says. "I don't care—"

I cut him off. "You do care. Obviously you do, or you wouldn't be jeopardizing a twenty-billion-dollar lawsuit just to fuck me over. You care, and so I'm explaining this to you, in the hope that you will see how wrong you are. Here's the basic point, Lyle. There is no capital-W woman. No standard model who explains us all."

My voice is rising now, and I'm gesturing wildly with my free hand. An elderly couple approaching on the sidewalk gives me a wide berth. Can't say I blame them.

"You want to know why I slept with Philip? Because I *felt* like it, Lyle. Maybe I gravitate toward older men because I have a thing for grey hair, or because most men my age are boring, or because I have some serious, *serious* daddy issues. But you know what? Actually, I don't gravitate toward older men. I like younger men, too. I like all sorts of men. And I will continue to like them, and sleep with them—or *not* like them, and *not* sleep with them—based on *my* preferences, and not the preferences of presumptuous, narrow-minded people like you. Bottom line, Lyle? You're wrong. About me, and about everything else. Is that clear? Any questions? No? Good. Then why don't you and your puny, tyrannical, terrified little penis go fuck yourselves, okay? Because nobody else ever will."

I hang up. I'm breathing heavily.

So this is what ease, contentment and happiness feel like.

Awesome.

I check the time and run to the Green Parrot.

20

I don't know what the hell I'm doing, in the middle of a work crisis, two days before my wedding, meeting Teddy at a dive bar on Whitehead Street. But here I am, and there he is, a beer in front of him, looking guarded and bored and restless and irritated.

I sit down across from him. He glances at my elaborate hair, and I immediately feel self-conscious. A stray curl grazes my cheek, and I hurriedly tuck it behind my ear.

"I thought you couldn't drink on duty," I say.

He picks up his beer and takes a sip. "I'm not on duty."

He gives me a patient smile that doesn't extend to his eyes.

"I just ran into our old preschool teacher," I say.

"Mrs. Carter?"

"She's still not a fan."

"Surprise, surprise." He glances around like he's checking for the nearest exit.

"Gran told me you joined the army."

He nods.

"Why?"

He takes another sip of his beer. "Love of country."

"Come on."

No answer.

"Did you go overseas?"

He sets his beer down. "Is this really why you asked me here, Lily?"

"I wanted to see you," I say. "To catch up."

I cringe. That was completely the wrong tone. Teddy knows it, too. He spreads his arms wide like, Here I am.

"Why are you mad at me, Teddy?"

"I'm not mad at you."

He's acting so cool and collected. He's doing it to irritate me, like he always did. And it's working. So I start needling him, like I always did.

"You've been mad at me since we saw each other on Monday. Don't lie. I still know when you're lying."

"Don't be so sure," he says.

The bartender comes over. I ask for a glass of water. I turn back to Teddy. "Why are you mad at me?"

"I'm not." He won't look me in the eye.

I try a different tack. "Do you like your job?"

"Yes."

"Are you good at it?"

"Yes."

"Is Melody your girlfriend?"

"Melanie," he says. "And yes."

"Do you love her?"

He doesn't answer.

"Why are you mad at me, Teddy?"

"I'm not."

"How's your mom?"

"Fine."

"Why are you mad at me?"

"Because you left!" he shouts, slamming his hand down on the table. I jump. His beer tips over and crashes to the floor. The bartender looks over. A few people glance up from their drinks.

"Happy now?" he says.

"They made me leave," I say quietly. "I didn't have a choice."

"I wrote to you," he says in a low, angry voice, "over and over and *over*. You never wrote back. You never called me. You were supposed to come back. You promised."

It was always this way with him—he'd hold it in and hold it in, and then the dam would burst.

"Things got complicated," I say.

"No *shit* things got complicated, Lily! But you got to leave. I went to prison."

"It wasn't prison," I say, instantly regretting it.

He laughs in disbelief. "Are you kidding me?"

"Sorry," I say. "I'm sorry. That's not what I meant. I just—I don't know, Teddy. I was fourteen. I freaked out. I didn't know how to deal. Lee was—"

"This is not about Lee."

"Of course it is! If I hadn't acted the way I did, he'd still be alive."

Teddy leans across the table toward me. "Lily, this is *not about Lee*. Lee was fucked up long before you got to him. This is about you and me. How you loved me, and I loved you, and you abandoned me."

"I didn't—"

"You got to start over up north with your rich dad. And I went to jail. Sorry," he raises his hands in mock surrender. "Let me correct that. I was involuntarily enrolled in the Avon Park Youth Academy. Funny, though. It didn't seem like much of an *academy* at the time, what with the gangs, and the drug dealers. The frequency with which I got the shit kicked out of me. The way my mom couldn't stop crying every time she visited. But yeah, that was high school. Go Raiders."

Now I'm the one who can't look him in the eye.

"You want to know why I joined the army? I had no fucking *choice*, Lily! And boy, was *that* a fun four years. Afterwards, I came back and joined the FDLE—not an easy task, thanks to my juvenile record, but having almost been killed twice in Afghanistan, and having collected a few wounds and a few medals, I was lucky enough to impress people in high places."

I feel a tear roll down my cheek. I wipe it away.

"So, Lily, old friend, that's what I've been up to," he continues relentlessly. "It sure is nice to catch up with you after all this time. Now it's your turn. Remind me—how long were you in that fancy hospital?"

"Nine weeks," I say in a small voice.

"Nine weeks. And then on to boarding school, right? And college. And law school. Where do you work now? Some big firm in New York City, right? Sweet. How's your office? Got a nice view of the park?"

"I'm sorry," I say. "Teddy, I'm so sorry."

"You. Deserted. Me. You didn't write to me *once*. To hear from you would have meant the world to me. Because you meant the world to me.

But you were gone. And you've always been gone. But now you're back, to get married. And I'm supposed to be happy about that. Happy to see you."

"You hate me," I say.

He sits back in his chair, suddenly deflated. All the anger gone. We look at each other across the table. "If it's any consolation," I say, "you couldn't possibly judge me as harshly as I judge myself."

He leans forward, furious all over again. "Oh no? Guess what, Lily. Judging yourself—knowing you're doing something wrong but doing shit about it? That doesn't make everything okay."

I hold up my hands. "Fine, Teddy, you win. You don't want to hear it. So what's the point of all this?"

"You're the one who wanted to see me! Let's have a drink, like old friends, right? I never wanted to see you again! Monday night, okay, that was me. I don't know what I was thinking. I heard you were back, and I acted on impulse. I'm so sorry I did. Because I saw what you were doing. You looked at me, and you decided to play it like nothing ever happened between us. Like we were just two old friends, two pals, just palling around. I saw you make that decision. I saw it in your eyes. And that means you know. You know what you did. And don't tell me you don't, because I always know when you're lying, too."

I've been looking down, but now I look at him, and suddenly he's a boy again, with a boy's hurt, angry face.

"I loved you," he says. "I loved you, and you threw it away."

I reach across the table for his hand, but he pulls back.

"No way. You're too late." He stands up and walks out of the bar.

I watch him go. Then I put my head down on my arms.

He's right, of course. I abandoned my best friend in the whole world. My best friend, and my first love. I ran away because it was easier to run than deal. I left a trail of destruction in my wake and pretended not to notice. Then I acted like I could charm my way back here, into his life, and everything would be fine between us. I could tell him my problems, and he could help me.

Will's mom nailed it. I haven't just changed—I've gotten worse.

I think about work. How I love to mock and criticize my terrible client, distance myself from it in my head. Attack it as a purely selfish organism that's using one crime to perpetrate another, doing whatever it can to promote itself and its own interests above all else.

Sounds familiar.

I finally realized this morning that I love Will. That I want to get married. And I managed to beat his mom at her own game, clearing the way for my own happiness.

But what did I win, exactly? The opportunity to keep lying. And lying and lying and lying. To the one person in this situation who hasn't lied. The one person who has always told the truth.

"Excuse me?"

I lift my head. The bartender has come over to sweep up Teddy's broken glass. "You can't sleep in here," he says, smiling apologetically.

"I'm not sleeping, Lloyd. I'm marshaling my extremely limited resources."

"Would you like a drink?" he asks.

"No thanks," I say. "I have to go."

21

I leave the bar and go back to the hotel. I have a little time before the big family dinner, so I sit out on the balcony, thinking. Then I take a long shower. I put on makeup and adjust my hair. I iron my favorite dress. I'm suiting up, putting on my armor. Only I'm not sure who I'll be fighting. Maybe just myself.

When I get to the restaurant, I linger for a moment in the doorway of our private dining room. They're all in there, arranged around the table like a painting. It's not a staid family portrait this time, though, but one of those big, splashy scenes by Caravaggio or some other Baroque artist. You know the ones—set in a gambling den or tavern, filled with color and movement, capturing an assortment of thieves, brigands and loose women in the moment right before the knives come out.

Dad is at the head of the table, consulting the wine list with a baronial air, pausing from time to time to smile at the waitress fawning over his shoulder. Ana is to his left, scowling and muttering to herself as her thumbs fly rapidly over her phone. On her other side, Will's dad is desperately trying to impress Jane by relating some convoluted legal anecdote. She's nodding politely and playing with a large sapphire ring on her right hand, clearly wishing it was filled with poison. Mom is next to Jane—or would be, except that she's on her knees, hair in her face, trying to stop the table from wobbling. Across from them, Gran is holding forth about the colossal stupidity of the Supreme Court while Anita is tapping her fingernails impatiently on the table, trying to get a word in edgewise.

And there's Will, glancing at his phone, looking around anxiously. Waiting for me.

It's so easy to see how this night could have unfolded. After the first rush of introductions and hasty conversations, everybody would relax. Settle in. Wine and food would loosen us up. Dad would charm Will's parents. Ana would fascinate us with political gossip. Gran and Anita would manage to find common ground. Harry would tell funny stories about Will as a kid. We would begin the slow, rocky process of getting to know one another, of forging the big, messy, fractious union that surrounds every marriage.

I bet it would have been fun.

Will finally spots me in the doorway. He jumps up and comes around the table. He kisses my cheek. "Wow. You look beautiful."

"Thanks. You look great, too." I've never seen him in a suit and tie. He even shaved. He looks so handsome. I swallow hard. "Will? We need to talk."

"Let's get a drink," he says. "Just you and me."

He leads me back down the hallway and into the bar of the restaurant, where he picks a table in the corner. A waitress comes over, and Will orders a beer.

"Anything for you?" she asks.

I shake my head. It's time to do this.

"Will, there are a few things I need to talk to you about."

"Actually, can I go first?" He takes a deep breath and exhales it shakily. He runs his hands through his hair. "So I've been thinking about it all day, and . . . it's kind of funny. When we were at the Audubon House this morning? The wedding became so . . . so *real* to me all of a sudden. In a way it never had been before. I knew it was going to happen, obviously, but . . . and all day, I've been thinking, you know, that . . ."

He trails off. He looks down at the floor and wipes his hands on his pants. "You know what? I'll cut to the chase." He looks directly at me. "I know everything, Lily."

I stare at him, speechless.

His beer arrives. He picks it up and takes a long drink.

"I know you've been unfaithful to me," he continues. "Repeatedly."

My stomach drops. My face is hot. I feel like all the air in the room has been sucked up.

"How?" I ask. "How did you know?"

"I've always known," he says simply. "Almost from the very beginning."

"What are you talking about?"

"Lily," he says. "You come home from 'work' in the middle of the night, drunk as hell, your hair a mess. You're always floundering for explanations about where you've been and who you've seen. I see how you look at other men when you think I'm not paying attention. And some of the things you do in bed make it clear that you haven't spent the last decade in a convent. Finally?" He smiles at me almost pityingly. "You leave your phone lying around, with that rookie contacts list of yours. I'd have to be a moron not to suspect something."

He takes another long drink of his beer. How can he be so calm right now? I am completely at sea, until I manage to latch on to a single detail. "You figured out my texting system?"

"Two phones, totally separate," he tells me. "It's the only way to go."

"Would you like another beer?" the waitress asks. He nods. She turns to me. I shake my head. I haven't taken my eyes off Will.

"What do you mean, two phones?"

Will sits back in his chair. "That brings me to my next point." He looks me right in the eye again. "I've been doing the same thing."

I stare at him blankly.

He stares back.

"What?" I say.

"I've been unfaithful to you, too."

"No, you haven't," I say.

"Yes, Lily. I have."

"Is this a joke?" I say in an unsteady voice. "Some twisted way to salvage your pride? Because listen—what I do has nothing to do with you."

"I know," he says. "Believe me, I understand."

"No!" I cry, a little too loudly. "You *don't* understand. You can't. You're not me. You're Will Field. You're thirty-two years old. You have, like, three Ph.D.s. You work at the Metropolitan Museum of Fucking *Art*! You're funny, and dorky, and sweet. You love me. You can't be me."

"I love you, and I sleep with other women," he says.

"That's impossible."

He leans forward. I look away, but he reaches out and lifts my chin, forcing me to look him in the eye. "Not impossible, Lily. True. Remember the waitress Monday night? The one you teased me about—you said she thought I was cute? She did. She gave me her number when you went to the bathroom. I met up with her the next night, after my bachelor party. And again on Wednesday afternoon."

I pull back, but I can't look away.

"That night, when I came back to the room and you wanted to have sex but I couldn't get it up? I wasn't hungover, Lily."

"Why are you saying this?" My voice sounds small.

Now he takes my hands in his. His eyes are eager, imploring. "Because I don't want us to lie to each other anymore! It's killing us. I tried to tell you the truth Monday night, but I chickened out."

Monday. The night of our long, strange discussion about the past. I thought he was pumping me for information. Not working up his courage in order to make a big confession of his own.

I pull my hands away. "I don't believe you."

He gazes at me for a moment, perplexed. Then he takes a phone out of his pocket and sets it on the table between us.

"What's this?"

"My work phone," he replies. "Quote-unquote."

"Why are you—"

"Read the texts," he says.

I look down at the phone. "It's locked."

"The code is 5459."

I type it in. The screen activates.

"It spells L-I-L-Y," he says. "I hope you keep that in mind, after."

I look up at him. "After what?"

He takes the phone from me, opens the messaging application and hands it back.

"After now."

I scroll through the log of conversations. There are hundreds and hundreds of them. Weirdly, it doesn't show the names of whoever Will was texting—only phone numbers. I open one at random. Someone writes:

—where ru

Will responds:

—In bed.

I click on another conversation. Someone else writes:

—whatre you doing right now?

Will responds:

—I'm at work.

—take a break.

—Impossible.

—ill make it worth yr while

—My while is worth a lot.

—haha how much

I choose another:

—cant wait to see you again

—Don't wait. It could be dangerous.

—lol give me an hr

It's dated yesterday morning.

The waitress places another beer in front of Will. I pick it up and take several long swigs. I start to choke. Will tries coming around the table to pound me on the back, but I wave him off.

"This is not your phone," I gasp. "It can't be."

I read:

—tomorrow nite?

—How about right now?

—srsly?

—I'll be there in 20 minutes.

Sent two weeks ago.

"These texts are so dumb," I say. "You're much wittier than this. I—"

—want u to tie me up and—

No no no. No way. I check his contacts folder. It's empty. "Why are there no names?"

"I memorize the numbers," he says. "It's safer that way."

"You made this up. You doctored it somehow."

But then I stop talking. I just clicked on a text with a photo of a girl. A redhead. She's naked, smiling at the camera, stretched out on a bed with one hand behind her head.

It's Will's bed in his old apartment. I recognize the headboard.

I look up. He takes the phone from my hand. I can't breathe. I feel all hollowed out inside. Is this actually happening? Can this really be Will?

A yawning pit has opened up below me, and I'm falling through a world that I had no idea existed. Everything is new. Everything is strange.

"There's one more thing you need to know." He's scrolling through the texts. Then he hands me back the phone. He's opened a conversation from Saturday night. It begins with a message from a Brooklyn number:

—where r u?

He responds:

—At home. You?

—club. So bored

—I'll meet you at your place.

—haha

—I mean it.

—I cant.

. . .

—wait. Shes leaving.

. . .

—shes going to work. Ill be there

"Saturday night?" I say. "During my party?"

Will taps the number, and the phone dials. He puts it on speaker and sets it on the table between us. We hear the tinny ringtone through the speaker. Then someone answers.

"I said I didn't want to hear from you again."

I know that voice. That sharp, slightly nasal intonation. It's the voice of a thousand late-night conversations whispered in the library over books and coffee. The voice of dozens of study sessions, when we crammed for final exams. The voice that was the first to call and congratulate me when our bar exam results were posted.

"Hello?" Nicole says. "Will?"

I look down at the phone. Will ends the call.

Nicole. And Will.

My friend Nicole. And Will, my fiancé.

The man I love.

I lunge for him across the table.

He grabs my wrists before I can claw his eyes out. "Lily!" he cries. "Stop!"

"You *whore*!" I scream.

I try lunging again, but he's holding me tight. The entire bar has gone quiet. I struggle—all I want to do is get at him, to make him feel some fraction of the pain and fury that I feel right now. I want to bite and kick and scream.

"Did you know her apartment has bedbugs, Will? If you gave me bedbugs I will fucking *kill you*!"

"Everything's fine," Will says to the waitress, who's approaching us hesitantly. "We're okay." To me he says, "Lily. Calm down. You can't be mad." Slowly, cautiously he releases me.

"Can't be mad!" I say loudly. "How interesting. I can't be mad!"

"Lily, stop."

"And yet, here I am," I say, a fresh gust of rage filling me with energy. "Feeling the teeniest bit . . . mad. Isn't that odd? Isn't that astonishing? You should put it in one of your academic papers. Assuming that you are, in fact, an archaeologist, and not a fucking *garbage man*!"

I lunge at his face again, but he catches me. "Stop!"

"How *could* you, Will? She's one of my bridesmaids!"

He brings his face close to mine. "That's what bothers you—the fact that she's in the wedding party? Are you sure you want to go there, Lily?"

I stop struggling. I'm leaning toward him over the table—I try to pull back, but he won't let go.

"You're not angry," he says again. "You're surprised. You're shocked. But you can't really be hurt by this. Not you."

I look at him. My fury is gone, vanished as quickly as it came. He must sense it, because he releases me and sits back warily, waiting for another assault.

But all I have left is a single question, and I ask it calmly and quietly.

"Why did you ask me to marry you, Will?"

He leans forward and takes my hands. "Because I love you."

I pull them away. "That's impossible."

"Lily Wilder," he says. "I have been in love with you since the first second I saw you. When you walked up to me at that bar and put your hand on my arm, and I turned to you, and you smiled at me? My life started. Everything that came before was . . . preparation. Spring training." He smiles. "Foreplay. You walked in, and it was like the world went from black and white to color. You heighten everything. When you're around, music sounds better. Food tastes better. You make alcohol completely superfluous. I never know what you're going to say or do, and that's so exciting. Sometimes I have a hard time breathing when I'm near you. I'm worried that my heart is wearing out from beating so fast. You're smart and beautiful. We have real conversations. You're sweet and caring and funny. I love you so much that it makes me a little crazy. And if I can't spend the rest of my life with you, I'm going to have a really hard time figuring out what to do with myself."

I feel my eyes fill with tears.

We're going to sort this out. We'll fix it. We'll find a way.

"But I still want to sleep with other women," he adds.

I slap him as hard as I can. The sound rings through the restaurant. All the people who weren't already staring at us turn to look. Will says nothing, holding his burning face.

His phone is on the table. I pick it up and drop it in my bag. "I'm going back there," I say, jerking my head toward the room where our families are waiting. "Don't follow me."

I pull off my engagement ring, my beautiful, romantic ring, and I set it down in front of him. Then I turn and walk away.

22

I enter the private room and walk right up to Anita. "The wedding is off," I tell her. The room falls silent. "Your son is waiting outside."

She rises. Harry is staring at her. "Anita," he says. "What did you do?"

She doesn't respond, so he turns to me. "What did she do?"

"Please go," I say. And they do.

I pull out a chair and drop into it. I pour myself a healthy glass of wine and knock it back. I nod appreciatively.

"Isn't it lovely?" Dad smiles. "Try the white."

I set my glass on the snowy tablecloth and look at each of them in turn. Gran. Mom. Jane. Ana. Dad. There's so much love, so much sorrow and sympathy and compassion in their eyes.

Not for long!

"You are a bunch of miserable, lying scumbags," I tell them, "and you've ruined my life."

"Lilybear," Ana says gently, "you must feel awful right now, but you did the right thing."

Mom adds, "I'm sure this has been difficult, but don't take it out on us."

"Difficult?" I cry. "You're sure that this has been *difficult*? How the hell would you know? You're all wrapped up in your own dramas. I have some *major problems* here, people! I also have about seventeen parents, and it would be nice if I felt like I could turn to any of them for advice or encouragement. But no!" I wave my hands in the air wildly. "Oh, *no*! I only hear from you when you want to berate me, or give me suggestions on seating arrangements, or when you accidentally text me instead of your booty call!"

I look pointedly at Dad. He's giving me a look like Please no please no please no.

"I know you!" I cry, pointing at each of them in turn. "I know you all! You are guilty, guilty, guilty!"

"The hell I am!" Gran snorts.

"You're fine," I concede. "Although you coddled me. You let me run wild. I should have been thrown in chains as soon as I could crawl. No, it's the rest of you I'm talking about. What a stellar collection of role models. You, Mom." I point at her. "Spending my entire childhood mooning around after a man who abandoned you. And Jane." I turn to her. "You're a soulless, social-climbing vampire." I look at Ana next. "And *you*. Possibly the worst of the bunch." My lip curls in disgust. "A member of the United States House of Representatives."

Ana throws down her phone angrily. I raise a hand. "No. You're not the worst. Not by a long shot. No, the hands-down winner here is Henry." I train my sights on Dad.

"Darling, you're going to make yourself ill," he says soothingly.

"Do any of you know why I'm in this mess?" I shout. "Do you have the slightest clue?"

They're all pissed at me now, so they have a few suggestions.

"Deficient genes?" Gran says.

"Overactive libido?" Jane suggests.

"Chronic substance abuse?" Ana adds.

"Okay, yes!" I cry. "Yes to all that! But more importantly, I was never given a *strong moral foundation*. Children learn by example. Look at my examples! We're all a bunch of big, fat liars. It's got to change. We need a new family commitment to honesty. Henry?" I point at Dad. "You're on."

Dad is looking at me with panic, but then something happens. Comprehension dawns. I see him transform from a pleading, helpless, hunted creature into someone resolute, brave. He squares his shoulders and stiffens his upper lip. He turns to his ex-wives.

"I'm sleeping with all of you," he announces.

Dead silence. They stare back at him, then turn and glance at one another.

"Ana too?" I say.

He gives her a sidelong glance. "I'm afraid so."

"You're unbelievable!" I cry. "I suppose this one's also my fault. You and Ana ran into each other and started talking about the wedding, and—"

"Oh no." My father chuckles. "Ana and I have been sleeping together for years."

I gape at him.

"We never really stopped," Ana adds. Then she turns to Jane. "What about you?"

"It's only been a few weeks," Jane replies. "Kat?"

"A couple of months," Mom says. "Mostly via Skype."

I stare at them. They really don't mind? I glance at Dad. He seems as shocked by their attitude as I am.

I turn to Mom. "But you're in love with him! You've been pining away for decades!"

"Oh, honey. That was over a long time ago."

"It was?" Dad says.

"Of course, Henry." Mom smiles. "Now I'm just using you for sex."

More silence. Then there's a chortle. I'm not sure who from—maybe Ana. A giggle from Mom. Someone guffaws. Soon, all three of them are roaring with laughter, clutching at one another, gasping for breath. Ana is bent over, pounding the table. Mom is wiping the tears from her eyes. Jane is actually emoting.

Dad and I gape at them, astonished. Gran looks disgusted.

"Darlings," Dad says, "are you truly not upset?"

This sends them into fresh gales of laughter. "Darlings!" they howl. "Darlings!"

I just wanted a nice big family blowout, okay? A huge, screaming fight, wherein I could whip up the rage of all my mother figures as a kind of proxy for my own. Where I could watch somebody else being attacked and punished for his extremely bad behavior.

But this? I have no idea what the hell to think of this.

They finally begin winding down, collecting themselves. I manage to get their attention. "It had to be a surprise at least, right?"

They all look at one another and start giggling.

I turn to Gran. "What about you?"

She sighs wearily. "Nothing surprises me anymore, honey. I'm too fucking old."

This sets them all off again. Even Gran chuckles. Dad is still flummoxed, but clearly relieved. Eventually I slip out, and they don't even notice.

I leave the restaurant and call Freddy. I don't even know what I say to her, but she's there in ten minutes and whisks me away. At a bar down the block she sits me on a stool and holds my hands and looks into my eyes. "What's wrong? What happened?"

"The wedding's off," I say.

She grips my hands tightly. "For real?"

"For real," I say, stifling a sob. "Really, really for real."

Freddy gestures to the bartender. "Two Sazeracs, please." She turns back to me. "I thought you loved him. I thought you worked everything out."

"I do love him, but . . . a bunch of things happened." She hands me a napkin, and I wipe my eyes. "I realized I couldn't go through with it. It's a long story. But that's not why I'm upset. Or, it is, but that's not all."

"What is it? What's wrong?"

The bartender brings our drinks. I burst into tears. Freddy wraps her arms around me, and I weep onto her shoulder for a long time. After a while, I straighten up and wipe my eyes again. I tell her everything. She doesn't believe me. I show her his phone.

She scrolls through the texts. "Will. Of all people."

"I thought he was the only person who was telling the truth," I say sadly. "The only one who was being completely honest. I was so wrong."

I said I loved surprises. I said I wanted hidden shallows.

Did I ever get them.

"He seemed so normal," Freddy marvels.

"He still does! It was the strangest thing, Freddy. He was sitting there across from me, confessing everything, laying it all out, but he was the same person I knew yesterday. I kept expecting it to be like one of those big reveals in the movies, you know? Where the guy you thought was the good guy turns out to be the bad guy, and suddenly there are all these subtle changes, like his clothes fit a little better, and his smile is somehow sinister, and he has evil, messed-up hair?"

"He's got messed-up hair in this picture," Freddy remarks. She glances at me. "Sorry."

"Anyway, none of that happened. He was still Will. My Will. But now that I think about it, everything makes sense. Women are always falling all over him. He brushed it off in my company."

"I never thought he was quite as nerdy as you made him out to be," Freddy says. She clicks on another text and her eyes widen. "But I had no idea he was like this."

I look at the screen, then quickly away. How could I have been so blind? There's something so genuine about Will. It's what drew me to him, after all. And drew others, too. I think about Diane, going on and on about him Tuesday night. How cool it is that he's an archaeologist. How he's so hot, he's just like—

"Oh my God," I whisper. "Will really *is* Indiana Jones."

Freddy clicks on another text. She looks up and nods.

This is unbearable! Will, with all those other women. Even my moms were crazy about him. I thought he was being friendly with my mother on Sunday—all that bullshit about historic renovation? He was *flirting* with her!

The bastard.

So much for my ability to read people. So much for my intuition, my confidence that I always know when someone is lying.

"He slept with Nicole," I say.

Freddy almost drops the phone. "Sorry, *what*?"

I explain. Freddy is appalled. "That's so heinous!" she cries. "I mean, Nicole is pretty and everything, but—"

I look up. "You think she's pretty?"

"Not as pretty as you," Freddy says quickly.

"Oh, God!" I clutch my head in my hands. "What is *happening* to me!"

"She's got a lot of goddamn nerve, attacking you for sleeping around," Freddy observes. "What a c-word."

I pick up Will's phone and start scrolling through the texts again. I click on another picture, another beautiful woman. I open his photo album and swipe through it. Girl after girl after pretty, pretty girl. And the texts themselves? Full of long, flirtatious exchanges, assignations, passionate gratitude.

That's when it hits me.

Will is capable of all this. All this passion and lust and fun. And he did it with other people.

Not with me.

I throw the phone, hard. It flies across the room and smashes into the wall.

"Hey!" says the bartender.

"Sorry! My hand slipped." I turn to Freddy. "I'm going to find him and cut his dick off."

"Lily, wait," Freddy says. "You wanted out of this wedding, remember? All week you've been full of doubt. Will has done you a favor."

Perfectly true. Perfectly reasonable. I start to cry again. She sighs and strokes my hair. She hugs me and tells me that it's going to be okay. She chastises me and mocks me. She orders ridiculous drinks and distracts me with funny stories about her own disastrous engagements.

She's in the middle of a good one about Norman when her phone buzzes. "It's Leta. She wants to know where we are." She begins to type a response. "I'll tell her you're busy with your family."

"No." I put a hand on her arm. "Let's meet her somewhere. Let's invite everybody."

"Are you sure you're in the mood?"

"What else am I going to do?"

"Eat?" she suggests. "Sleep? Get the hell out of town?"

"Can't!" I sing. "Work tomorrow!" I tell her about my doomed deposition. Then I tell her what happened with Teddy. Then I'm tired of talking, and since she won't do it, I take out my phone and round up the usual suspects, and soon my third and final bachelorette party begins in earnest. Nobody but Freddy knows anything, so I have to pretend to be happy. I think I do a decent job.

We have a lot to drink. We dance. We go to a strip club. We do a couple of lines in the bathroom. We watch the male strippers hurling themselves around the stage.

"What is it about balls?" Freddy says, as a stripper wags his package in her face. "What makes them compelling to people like you?"

"I can't explain it," I say. "It's one of the mysteries of life."

Diane squeezes in between us. "I can explain it," she says. "It looks like all these women are really into it, right? Really excited? They're not. They're in a state of complete psychosexual terror. See Janelle over there?" My friend Janelle is receiving some very personalized attention from one of the dancers. "She can't look away because at any moment that little g-string could break and a pair of long, waxed testicles could flop into her face and slap her silly."

"You're crazy!" I laugh. "She's having a blast."

Janelle turns to us. *Help me,* she mouths.

We move on to another bar. And another, and another. We dance and drink, we drink and dance. Our group grows as other friends join us, people who think that this is the first wedding-related event of the weekend, when actually, ha ha, nope. We find a dive bar near the water and drink beer and eat French fries on the patio. We try a drag bar. A lounge with fancy cocktails. At some point, I stop pretending to be happy, and I am happy. Sort of.

Until Nicole walks in with a few other friends from law school.

Freddy sees her and stands up. "I'll take care of this."

"Don't." I rise slowly. "I want to talk to her."

Freddy puts a hand on my arm. "What are you going to say?"

I toss my drink back. "By 'talk to her,' I mean 'punch her in the face.'"

"Lillian. Be the bigger person."

"But I want to be the smaller person." I take a step forward. "I want to be really really fucking small right now."

"You're no good in a brawl." Freddy is actively holding me back now. "Remember that night in Greenpoint last year?"

"Brooklyn." I sit down again. "It defeats me every time."

"Wait here," she says, and I watch as she marches up to Nicole. With a few brief words, Freddy has her running. After a while I calm down, and I can't help but reflect. What right do I have to confront Nicole, anyway? What did she do that I haven't done, over and over and over again?

We're in a big, noisy bar on Duval when my phone pings with a text:

—Can we please talk?

I stare at it for a minute. Then I respond:

—no

—I know it was a shock, but you can't really be angry.

—why dont you text some other girl. you have so many to choose from

—Please, Lily. I'm trying to understand why you're so upset.

Freddy sits down hard, sloshing her drink. She's a little tipsy. I show her my phone. "Why am I upset?"

"Because you thought you knew him, and you didn't," she says. "Because you were blind. Because your pride is wounded. Because even liars don't like being lied to, and players don't like being played. Because—"

"God, Winifred. Enough."

—i dont know you. you arent the person i thought you were

—Yes I am! This is only one part of me. Like it's only one part of you.

. . .

—Lily?

—stop writing to me. youre a scumbag. youre a pickup artist, with that little scrapbook of conquests on your phone and all those stupid texts

—You won't let me explain.

. . .

—So your infidelity wasn't a problem, but mine is? It was okay when I wasn't enough for you, but not okay when it turns out that you weren't enough for me?

I stare at the screen. I wasn't enough for him. There it is, in black and white.

It hurts. God, does it hurt.

Freddy is reading over my shoulder. I glance at her, hoping for some sympathy. Instead she says, "It's a fair point. You aren't exactly being consistent."

She's right. And I can't help but think back to my big, rousing speech to Lyle this afternoon. I'll screw whoever I want to screw, and anybody who judges me for it can go straight to hell. I'm a woman, hear me roar!

Still. This is different.

"Why do I have to be consistent?" I demand. "I'm being honest about how I feel for once. Isn't that what matters?"

"Of course," she says. "But—"

"No, I get it," I say. "What goes around comes around. Karma's a bitch. I'm being punished for my—"

I stop talking.

"Lily?"

Sins. I'm being punished for my sins.

Ian was right!

"The conspiracy of sexual misery!" I clutch my head. "It's got me!"

My phone pings again.

—Please keep talking to me.

He wants to talk? Let's talk.

—nicole, will? NICOLE? are you fucking kidding me?

—3 words for you, Lily. Ian. Javier. Tom.

"Who's Tom?" Freddy asks.

I toss back another drink and gesture to the bartender. "I think he might mean Tim."

My phone pings again.

—I'm sorry about Nicole, okay? That was a mistake. I told her on
    Sunday night that it couldn't happen again. She didn't take it
    well.

I think back to Sunday. Will was so agitated at the last Hemingway bar. And Nicole seemed more hostile than usual after that. Of course.

Freddy goes to the bathroom. I stare at my phone. My anger has disappeared—it seems to come and go in bursts—and now there are a few things I want to know.

—if cheating isnt wrong, why did you hide yours from me?

—I didn't want to lose you.

—hahaha

—It was a mistake. I should have been honest. But I could tell you were having doubts about getting married. I was afraid of losing you. I'm so in love with you.

—in LOVE with me? lol bitch pls

—Don't you remember what I said to you Saturday night? What I'm always saying to you? I love you exactly the way you are. I know you, inside and out, and I love you.

—i remember. now i know it was all a lie

A few seconds later my phone rings. I don't give him a chance to speak.

"You didn't mean it, Will. You didn't mean any of it. The Latin. My ring." A sob rises in my chest, but I manage to fight it. "The night we got engaged. All lies."

"You're wrong, Lily! I love you. Yes, I've slept with other people. But those two things aren't mutually exclusive."

"Yes, they are! You can't love me and sleep around. You can't send skeevy texts to random women and also want to marry me."

"No?" he says. "Then explain your own behavior over the past six months."

"That's easy. I didn't know I loved you, you fucker!" I slam the phone down on the table. I know that's not the whole picture, that it's more complicated than that, but at this point I'm too drunk and sad and pissed off to care.

The phone rings again. I don't answer. I have another drink. A guy sits down next to me. We talk for a while, but all I can do is compare him to Will. Count the ways in which he's inferior. Not as witty. Not as smart. His eyes not as beautiful. His smile not as—

I start to cry again. The guy mumbles something and disappears.

A few friends come over to comfort me—it's clear to everyone by now that something is wrong—but I downplay it. Pre-wedding jitters! Nerves about the dress! I don't want to be consoled. I thought I was going to be punished by having to tell Will the truth about myself. I thought my agony was going to be in admitting my lies and losing him. I had no idea what was headed my way.

—Come to the hotel.

. . .

—Lily. Don't go quiet like this.

I turn off my phone and drop it into my bag. Freddy is eyeing me cautiously.

"What?" I demand, a little more harshly than I probably should.

"Give him a chance to explain himself," she says. "In person."

I nod slowly. "I bet you're loving this, aren't you?"

"Lily. How can you say that?"

"You were right, and I was wrong," I continue. "About everything. I bet you even knew that I loved him, didn't you? You knew that there was only one possible explanation for my indecisiveness, for my wondering and worrying, my stubbornness in the face of serious opposition— that I was head over heels for him but couldn't even recognize it. Deny it, Freddy. Please. Tell me I'm wrong."

I watch her closely. She can't lie to me.

"The thought did cross my mind," she admits.

"It crossed your mind. Isn't that nice. Hey, thanks for sharing."

"Lily—"

"You know what? This has been delightful, but I have to bail. I have work tomorrow." I stand up and walk away.

As I'm heading for the door I pass a couple sitting at a small table. I noticed them earlier—they're so attractive and friendly looking, young and tan, happy and relaxed. I change course and sit down with them.

"Greetings," I say. "I'm Viktor Boog, eminent psychotherapist."

Their names are Sandra and James. They're from Laguna Beach, California.

"We've been watching you for a while," James says. "Looks like you're having a tough night."

I wave away his concern. "Let's talk about you."

They're celebrating their fifth wedding anniversary. They hold hands and cuddle while we talk.

"You seem so happy," I say. "How do you keep the magic going?"

"Communication," says James.

"Threesomes," says Sandra.

I laugh.

"No, really," she says.

"Threesomes have always been tough for me," I say. "I'm not that great of a planner."

"You don't always have to plan them out," James replies.

"Interesting." I stand up. "Will you excuse me? I need to use the ladies' room."

Sandra rises. "I'll join you."

She follows me down the hallway and into the bathroom, where we find an empty stall. She closes the door behind us and her hands slip around my waist.

I have only hazy memories of making out with girls in boarding school, but I'm pretty sure it was nothing like this. Because if it had been, I never would have switched to boys. This? This is incredible. Our mouths fit together perfectly. We begin to kiss, softly at first, but with increasing urgency as we open up to each other, our lips soft and hot and seeking out the other's. She smells amazing, all lush and flowery—I lower my head and brush my mouth along the line of her smooth throat. I want to devour her—her lips and tongue and face and neck. Her skin is unbearably soft, and I want to touch every part of her. I kiss her wrist, her hand, each finger. Her mouth is on my mouth, her hands running down my body. She puts one between my legs and presses hard. I gasp. She kisses me again, her sweet tongue in my mouth, tasting like champagne and strawberries.

And breasts! They're so much *fun*. Who knew? Okay, lots of people, but not me! Sandra's are small and round and perfect. I cup them in my hands. I bend down and kiss one through the thin fabric of her sweater. I feel her nipple harden as I tug on it with my lips. I bite gently, and she cries out. She takes my face in her hands and kisses me again. I bury my fingers in her silky hair. I feel one of her hands reach up my dress. She pushes the cloth of my panties aside and slides a finger inside me.

"Let's stay in here forever," I whisper, my mouth on her ear. "Let's never go back out there."

"We're leaving my husband out," she murmurs. "It's not fair."

"You're right," I say feverishly. "Let's go get him."

We come out of the bathroom. Sandra nods to James. He quickly pays for their drinks and we get ready to leave. Freddy is suddenly at my side.

"Lily," she says. "Don't do this."

I smile at her. "It's fine! Also? I get the whole girl thing now. You're *so* right!"

"Lily, please. You're in no condition."

She puts a hand on my arm. I shake it off roughly. "Leave me alone."

She looks stricken. I feel a twinge of guilt, but I let it go. I'm so sick of thinking.

"I'll call you later," I tell her. "Stop worrying so much!"

We leave the bar and walk down Duval. I hold Sandra's hand. There's a breeze that tastes like the ocean. Their hotel is even fancier than mine. James kisses me in the elevator. He's good, too. I wish I could leave everything and go back with them to Laguna Beach. I wish I could marry both of them. That would be a pretty nice life.

We get out of the elevator and walk down the hall. James's arm is around my waist. Sandra puts the key in the door.

I start shaking my head.

She turns back to me with surprise. "Honey, what's wrong?"

"I can't do this," I say.

"That's okay," James says quickly. "We don't want you to do anything you don't want to do."

"I want to, but I can't," I sob. "I think . . . I think I should go to bed."

Sandra puts her arms around me, and I weep on her shoulder. "Oh, sweetie."

"I was supposed to get married on Saturday. I thought he was a wonderful man. But it turns out he's a philandering asshole. Just like me!"

Sandra pats my back. "Shh. It's okay. Shh."

They're very understanding. James walks me downstairs and waits with me for a cab. When one arrives, he opens the door. He gives me a hug.

"Don't worry," he says kindly. "These things have a way of working out."

FRIDAY

23

An alarm is beeping somewhere close to my head. I feel around under the pillow, find my phone and silence it. Why did I pick 7 A.M.? I have eleven missed calls from my mother figures. I also have a new text message from Will:

—Check your e-mail.

I write back:

—go fuck yourself

I toss the phone onto the nightstand and roll over. Freddy is lying next to me.

"You're really addicted to that thing," she whispers.

"I'm sorry I was mean to you last night," I whisper back.

"No worries, love."

"Where are we?"

"My room. I kicked Nicole out."

"My life is over, Freddy."

"No it isn't. You just need a makeover. You look like the girl who crawls out of the television set in *The Ring.*"

"What's the point? And anyway, I don't have time."

She strokes my hair. "That's okay. We'll do a makeover montage."

She's already made me appointments at the hotel spa. I slowly get dressed. All my anger is gone. Now I'm just sad. Profoundly sad.

We're about to head downstairs when my phone pings.

—I think I've figured out why you're so upset.

Why can't he leave me alone?

—It's not because I lied. It's not because you feel like you don't
 know me.

. . .

—You must think what we do is wrong. You must feel guilty. I
 want you to know I understand.

That thing about me not being angry anymore? I'm over it.

—you understand, will? gosh, what a RELIEF! i feel SO much
 better. i dont fucking hate your guts anymore!!!

—Read my e-mail, Lily.

My phone rings as Freddy and I get into the elevator. I answer.
"Leave. Me. Alone."

"I'm in Javier's room," Will says. "Let's talk this out."

"I should meet you why?" I say heatedly. "So that you can lecture
me about how I'm the last person in the world who should be throwing
stones right now? So that you can tell me all about the 'guilt' that I supposedly feel? Do you torture all your women like this?"

"Lily. Please."

"Explain Monday morning," I say. "Explain our first three days together. And then explain all the other times. How sex with you was
amazing and mind-blowing one moment, and then *completely* boring
the next. Were you spent? Were you holding back? Seriously, Will—I'd
like to know."

Silence. At last, he says, "It's complicated."

I laugh. "I bet it is."

"Why didn't you say anything before now?" he retorts. "Why didn't
you ever bring it up?"

"Nice try, but we're not talking about me right now. We're talking
about you."

"We're talking about *us,* Lily. You didn't speak up because it made
you uncomfortable, right? You didn't want me to know the real you.
The one who really loves to have sex. Because you were ashamed."

It's infuriating how little he understands. "I've never felt ashamed about sex, Will. I only felt guilty about lying to you."

"And you lied to me because you thought what you were doing was wrong! But it's not. We're not bad people. What we do is normal. We're perfect for each other, Lily. We're practically the same person. Don't you see that?"

That is about as much as I can take. "I don't want to marry myself!" I shout. "I want to change!"

There's a long silence.

"If you don't feel ashamed," he says at last, "then why do you want to change?"

I end the call. Freddy stares straight ahead, pretending she didn't hear anything. I guess she's playing it safe after last night. I start to dial Will's number again. I want to tell him he doesn't get it. That I misspoke. I don't want to change, exactly. I want . . .

To hell with it. I don't have to justify myself to him.

We leave the elevator, cross the lobby and enter the hotel spa. The woman behind the sleek, minimalist bamboo desk has a wide pink smile and skin as smooth, plump and flawless as a newborn's ass. She inclines her head graciously and greets us with a not-at-all pretentious "Namaste."

I immediately turn to go, but Freddy takes my arm. "Trust me. You're going to feel better."

Doubtful. Namaste leads us to a dressing room, where we change into fluffy white robes. She returns and shows us into the main waiting area, a hushed, dimly lit room where dippy Eastern music trickles out of hidden speakers and low sofas are arranged around a fountain.

Lounging on several of these sofas are Mom, Jane and Ana, swathed in spa robes and sipping green tea.

I turn to Freddy. "Are you *serious* right now?"

"They were worried!" she says defensively, sidling among them and sitting down.

"You weren't returning our calls," Jane adds. Her hair is wrapped in an enormous white towel, and she already has some toxic-looking orange goo smeared all over her face.

Ana slips her phone into the pocket of her robe. "We finally got in touch with Freddy. She told us what happened."

I walk over to a side table and pour myself a glass of water with a few slices of cucumber floating on top. "Then you all know that congratulations are in order. You won. I'm not getting married."

"That's why we're here, honey," Mom says. "We've changed our minds. We think you should marry Will."

At which point my head explodes, splattering all over the nice teak walls and embroidered Indian pillows.

"We didn't think you really loved him," she explains. "We were concerned that you were deceiving him, and that you would both be horribly unhappy when he found out the truth. But it turns out that you *do* love him, and he knew everything, and he still loves you. So . . ."

I look around. "Where's Gran?"

Ana frowns. "She refused to come. She thinks spas are unhygienic."

Namaste is passing through the room with a stack of towels. She pauses, looking affronted, then disappears into a treatment room.

Ana gazes after her. "Does anyone else find something unsettling about that woman's skin?"

"She's extraordinarily well hydrated," Jane says approvingly.

I pour myself another glass of water and settle onto a sofa opposite them.

"Let me make sure I understand," I say. "A bunch of divorced women—who are each currently carrying on an affair with a married man, a man to whom they were each married, and whom they divorced because of his chronic infidelities—these women are now counseling me to get married?"

They exchange a glance.

"Women who know me better than anyone else," I continue. "Women who know everything about me. These are the women who are now urging me to pledge my faith and fealty to *one man*—a man I have repeatedly cheated on, and who has repeatedly cheated on me? This is what's happening right now?"

"Pretty much," Ana says.

"You have to understand something, darling," Jane says. "Infidelity in a marriage is inevitable."

Mom looks taken aback. "I don't know if that's true."

"Of course it is," Ana says, glancing at her phone.

"It's inevitable and irrelevant," Jane continues. "Cheating wasn't the real problem that each of us had with Henry. It was basic incompatibility."

"Your mom was a homebody," Ana says. "She wanted to stay in Key West, while your father longed to travel the world. I wanted to go into politics, and Henry was not going to be the kind of spouse I needed. Jane was socially ambitious, and Henry is anything but. You and Will are in the same place in your lives. You love your careers. You want to be in New York. You enjoy doing the same things."

"Obviously," Jane murmurs.

I lean back on the couch. "Infidelity is no big deal. That's what you're saying."

"It *is* a big deal, because it's universal," Ana says. "Think about it, Lilybear. Why is it that everybody in this country claims to hate cheating, to find it horrifying and wrong, but at the same time everybody in this country is screwing around, or dreaming about screwing around, or screwing around on the phone, or the computer, or in their heads? Men, women, colleagues of mine in Congress—in the most sick and demented ways—celebrities, ordinary people, newlyweds, the elderly. Everybody," she concludes. "Everybody cheats, and everybody lies about it."

"That's a little extreme," Mom says.

"We're animals," Ana says. "We need to accept it and get over it. There's so much more to marriage than sex. People let it get in the way of otherwise healthy relationships." She glances at her phone. "Why, thanks for responding, you useless bastard!"

"Put that thing away," Jane sighs. "We're in a spa, for God's sake."

Namaste is leading a client into a treatment room. She puts a finger to her lips. We ignore her.

"What if I want to be faithful to one person?" I say. "What if I want to change?"

"You *want* to change?" asks Ana.

This has been nagging at me since I blurted it out to Will. I must have had a reason for saying it. "Maybe 'want' is a strong word. I feel like I should."

"That might not be a bad idea," Mom says.

"Why should she change?" Ana demands.

"The population of Manhattan is shrinking," Jane observes, gazing at her gleaming nails. "Eventually she's going to run out of men."

"Lily doesn't need a man to complete her," Ana says. "Nobody does. We're all proof of that."

"I worry about my little girl," Mom says. "Her lifestyle is so . . . unconventional."

Freddy perks up at that. "Unconventional? Is that code for 'wrong'?"

"No!" Mom cries. "I mean—"

"Seriously, Mom," I say. "You're one to talk. What I saw going on Tuesday afternoon was pretty unconventional, wouldn't you say?"

"Let's stay focused," Jane says. "Marry Will now. You can change your mind later if you want."

Mom looks affronted. "He's not a pair of shoes. She can't just return him if she changes her mind."

"Why not?" Ana says. "That's what each of us did."

"Ladies!" Namaste cries, exasperated. "Spa voices, please!"

We turn to her slowly. She looks frightened and backs out of the room.

"Let me ask you all this," I say. "What is the purpose of marriage?"

"Love and family," Mom says.

"Partnership and companionship," Ana says.

"Wealth and social legitimacy," Jane says.

"You guys need to get your stories straight," Freddy remarks.

Mom clasps her hands and leans forward. "I saw how you looked at each other when you walked into the restaurant last night. You two love each other."

"You're both smart and successful," Ana adds.

"He's so *tall*," Jane says.

"All reasons why he'd make a good boyfriend," I say. "But are they reasons to marry him?"

Nobody responds.

"Lily?"

Namaste is standing at the door.

"Your masseuse is ready for you," she says.

As I follow her out, the room erupts in passionate argument.

Over the next three hours I am exfoliated, peeled, steamed and wrapped in seaweed. I am Reiki'ed and biotherapeutically drained and craniosacrally realigned. I am weighed down by hot stones. It does make me feel better—but just barely.

The alarm on my phone beeps, and I pull it out of the pocket of my robe. The deposition starts in an hour. I check my e-mail. Maybe the plaintiffs have agreed to a postponement. Maybe Philip has had a miraculous recovery, or some other partner is riding to the rescue.

No such luck. The only message in my inbox is an e-mail from Will, sent at 5 A.M.

I Am Not A Scumbag, And Neither Are You.

Catchy. I drop the phone into my pocket.

Back in the room, I get dressed for work. Freddy is sitting on the bed. "I need a favor," I tell her. "Call it off. Officially. Get in touch with Mattie, and my parents, and just . . . stop the wedding."

Her face is full of concern. "Are you sure, honey?"

I nod unhappily. "I'm sure."

It's raining when I leave the hotel. So much for Mattie's promises of sunshine. Poor Mattie—she's going to be disappointed about a hell of a lot more than the weather today. But I don't have time to worry about her, or the wedding, or Will. I need to focus on work. I spent some time thinking about the deposition while I was in the spa. I came up with one minor procedural argument for postponement, but I'm afraid plaintiffs' counsel will laugh in my face if I bring it up. And if I demand that we call the court and ask for an adjournment, the judge will surely deny me—and be furious that I even raised it. I need a substantive reason for stopping the deposition, but so far I've got nothing.

I pull up in front of Gran's house and run to the front door. I find her in the kitchen reading the paper, her hair in foam rollers.

"I need you to second-chair a deposition," I say. "I'll explain everything in the car. But you have to hurry."

The paper's on the floor and she's headed upstairs before I even finish speaking. I have nothing better to do while I wait for her, so I start reading Will's e-mail.

Dear Lily:

There are many things about me that you don't know. That's my fault, and I want to correct it. I'm hoping that if you get a better understanding of who I am, and why I am the way I am, we can fix this.

Please read all the way to the end.

Some of these things I've never told anyone.

For as long as I can remember, I've adored women. My dad says that when I was three I would regularly confess my love to waitresses in diners and women at bus stops. I had my first girlfriend at four—we would walk around the playground together, holding hands. I loved how women looked and how they moved. Their hair, their voices. My kindergarten teacher was an elderly woman named Mrs. Echternach. She was short and stumpy, with a hairy upper lip. But such beautiful blue eyes. I thought she was a goddess.

Unfortunately, I was no god. As I got older, I went from cute toddler to awkward adolescent. I had braces, bad skin, played French horn—you name it. I became shy—painfully so. I still admired girls, but from a distance. Remember how I told you about the library and all the time I spent there? I remember one book in particular—a study of Greek and Roman sculpture. When I was feeling low I would pull it out and pore over all those lines and curves, those necks and shoulders and breasts and faces. All representations of beauty, real beauty, that once existed in the world.

Was I sexist? Was I viewing women solely as objects? I suppose. But I was a kid. I didn't know what "objectification" was, or why it might be bad. Ultimately, I knew that what I thought or didn't think about women and their bodies didn't matter. I didn't have a prayer of ever being with a real one. So I looked and worshipped, convinced that I would never touch.

Or so I thought. Over the next few years—

Christ, this is a dissertation! How long would his vows have been? I hear Gran clomping down the stairs. She appears in the doorway in a navy suit and some nifty orthotics, a handbag the size of Rhode Island dangling from her arm. I drop my phone in my bag, and we head out to the car.

Will can't help himself. He's always been this way. How original. I forgive him for everything.

On the way to the EnerGreen office on Flagler, I fill Gran in on what we're facing.

"This deposition is part of the Deepwater Discovery oil spill litigation," I tell her. "You've probably read about it—it's the class action arising from the drilling platform that exploded in the Gulf two years ago?"

"Of course," she growls. "Those incompetent bastards."

"Those incompetent bastards are now your clients, Gran. Our witness is an accountant who wrote some terrible e-mails that appear to implicate EnerGreen in a massive fraud—basically, they suggest that EnerGreen used the costs of the oil spill to hide huge financial losses. Helpfully, our witness is also a complete idiot." I describe the e-mails and tell her about the prep.

"Jesus," she says. "Can he explain why he wrote them?"

"Unfortunately, yes. He was telling the truth. The fraud is real. And it's huge. If the plaintiffs put those e-mails in front of Pete and he testifies about them, EnerGreen will lose the case. Even worse, the SEC and the DOJ will find out about the fraud. The entire company will go down in flames."

"Then there's no question," Gran says. "You can't let him testify."

"I don't know how to stop it! I've racked my brain, but I've got nothing."

"In that case, you'll just have to contain the damage. Sometimes that's the best you can do."

"I know, Gran, but that means I'm screwed. I'll be the scapegoat for all the awful things that are going to happen at this deposition. The firm is likely going to fire me—to placate the client, if nothing else."

"Why is all this up to you?" Gran demands. "Where's the partner in charge?"

As quickly as I can, I explain about Philip's heart attack. I expect Gran to be flabbergasted, astounded, furious at Lyle's outrageous behavior.

Instead, she says, "Philip? That's his name?"

"Uh-huh." I keep my eyes on the road, but I feel her snappy black eyes boring right through me.

"What are you hiding?" she says. Her voice is quiet. Dangerous.

I shake my head vigorously. "Nothing."

"You're sleeping with him, aren't you."

"Oh, Gran!" I try to laugh, but it doesn't come out right.

"Lillian Grace Wilder!" Gran cries. "For *shame*!"

"It only happened a few times! It doesn't mean anything."

"Oh, fine!" She throws her hands in the air. "As long as it doesn't mean anything."

"Will you please focus on what's important?" I turn into the lot in front of the EnerGreen subsidiary on Roosevelt and park the car.

"And what is that?" she asks. "Given all that you've told me, I'm not sure how I can help you."

"I don't know. Just . . . back me up. Give me moral support. Stop me from doing anything blatantly stupid. Beyond that, I'm not sure there's much you can do."

We get out of the car and head inside. A receptionist directs us to the conference room where the deposition will take place. The court reporter, a young woman with green nails and a mouth full of chewing gum, is already setting up her equipment—a stenograph machine connected to a laptop that will translate her shorthand into a running transcript. The videographer, an older man with a long grey ponytail, is readying his camera and microphones. The plaintiffs' attorney, Daniel Kostova, is seated at the table, organizing his documents. We all smile and shake hands and exchange pleasantries.

And I think, this is right. The plaintiffs are going to win. And they should. They're the good guys. Just look at this one. Kostova is a schlubby, Pooh-looking guy in his mid-forties, with frazzled hair, a bad suit, papers flying everywhere. Passionately devoted to environmental causes. He's spent his entire career suing polluters and toxic waste dumpers, and winning a lot of the time. Sure, he's made a pile of money doing it, but he's helped a lot of people. He's good, too—all southern courtesy and razor focus. I wouldn't be able to stop him if I tried.

"I'll go find our witness!" I say brightly.

As I walk down the hall, I get a text from Mattie.

—I jsut had an extremely disturbing convrsation with your maid of honor. Could you call me?

Not a chance. I step into a vacant office, where Pete is waiting. He jumps up from his seat when he sees me.

"Boy, am I nervous!" he says. He's already sweating.

"It's going to be fine," I tell him. "Just remember everything that we talked about on Tuesday. Listen to the question. Answer only the question that's asked. If you don't understand the question, ask for clarification. Pause before answering, so that I have time to object. Got it?"

"Yes, ma'am." He nods vigorously, then stops. "Could you repeat that?"

I do. He leaves to use the bathroom. I check my phone, and I can't help it—I open Will's e-mail.

Or so I thought. Over the next few years, things changed in a big way. Puberty hit. My appearance improved. Girls began to notice me. I was so shy I never would have dared to walk up to a pretty girl. Fortunately, I didn't have to. Don't get me wrong—I know I'm no movie star. But I think they were responding to something I was giving off. My reverence, I guess you could call it. My adoration. I didn't lie or flatter them. I wasn't a pig or a pickup artist. And I'm not now, either. Women come to me, Lily. And they've taught me a lot. Like what you can do with bodies that's even more amazing than looking at them.

Pete returns. "I think I'm all set."

I drop my phone in my bag. "Let's go."

24

We enter the deposition room, and I introduce Pete to Kostova. Gran has settled herself at the conference table and is rummaging through Rhode Island.

I show Pete to his seat at the end of the table. He looks troubled. "Aren't you going to be next to me?"

"I'll be right over here, next to the stenographer," I tell him. "Your face is the only one people want to see."

I sit down, and Kostova gives me a genial smile. "We're waiting on Philip then?"

"He wasn't able to get out of New York before the storm hit," I explain.

Kostova looks surprised. "I thought he was exaggerating. So it's just you and me today?"

"And my local counsel," I say, gesturing to Gran.

Kostova looks at me closely. "I don't remember seeing you at any of the other depositions."

"This is my first time defending."

"A rookie!" He smiles indulgently. "I'll go easy on you."

We clip on our microphones. Gran pokes me. "Why did you tell him that?"

"Because he asked? I don't know, Gran. What does it matter? He seems all right."

She shakes her head grimly.

The camera starts rolling, and the stenographer swears Pete in. I glance at my e-mail.

So basically, my teenage years were consumed by academics
and massive amounts of sex. But as I got older, it began
to bother me that I never fell in love. Why could I adore a
woman's body but have no romantic feelings for her? Had my
book of sculptures warped me? I liked many of the girls I slept
with, but I never felt a strong emotional connection. Was I a
bad person, some sort of sociopath?

It worried me. A lot. Ultimately, I didn't find an answer to the
question of why I couldn't fall in love, but I found a way to
make peace with it.

We all have, as far as I know, one go-round on this planet.
One chance to experience what it means to be human. And I
know people will disagree, but for me, being human is about
enjoying sex. It's what stops the nagging internal voice. It's
what makes us feel both alive and immortal. And there's
nothing wrong with anyone—man or woman—who enjoys
having sex with lots of different people. I started doing some
research into the subject and found a wealth of scientific
evidence that humans aren't engineered for monogamy. It's
a myth that has been perpetuated by all our sociocultural
institutions—religious, political, artistic. We've been taught to
believe—

Is this what museum curators do all day—sit around concocting
elaborate sex conspiracies? Shouldn't they be, I don't know, unearthing
priceless relics and writing little informational placards to stick on walls?

I skim a few paragraphs about hunter-gatherer societies and polyamorous primates. Then:

Everything I read was consistent with how I felt. I couldn't
see any reason why I shouldn't have the freedom to do as I
pleased, as long as I didn't hurt anyone else. As long as I was
honest, as long as I didn't deceive any of my partners into
thinking that love was on the table, what I was doing was
okay. More than okay. It was right.

But then I met you.

"Counsel will now state their names for the record," the stenographer says.

"Daniel P. Kostova of Kostova, Carey and Gray, LLP, representing the plaintiffs."

It's almost laughable. I mean, count on an academic to come up with a high-flown justification for sticking his dick into every available hole, right?

"Ms. Wilder?"

I look up. "What?"

"You need to introduce yourself," Kostova tells me. "If you want something to appear in the record, you need to make sure it shows up on the transcript."

"Of course," I say. "Sorry. Lillian Wilder, of the firm Calder, Tayfield and Hartwell, attorneys for defendant Energy, Enter—EnerGreen Energy, Incorporated. With me is Isabel Curry, local counsel for the, uh, the defendant."

A rookie? Who, me?

Kostova turns to Pete. "Can you state your name for the record, sir?"

"Peter A. Hoffman," Pete says nervously.

Kostova leans back, crosses his legs, smooths his tie down over his belly and smiles at Pete. "Mr. Hoffman, we were introduced off the record, but let me introduce myself again. My name is Daniel Kostova, and my firm represents the plaintiffs in a class action pending before Judge George Forster in the United States District Court for the Eastern District of Louisiana. I'm going to be asking you a series of questions about that case today, but first I'd like to run through a few ground rules with you, which I think will make this deposition go real smoothly. The sooner we're finished here, the sooner we can get out there and enjoy some of that beautiful Florida sunshine. Of course," he chuckles, "it's raining right now, but with any luck that'll soon change. So, Mr. Hoffman, what do you say?"

He is utterly focused on Pete. His every gesture is leisurely, friendly, relaxed.

Pete nods. "All right."

Kostova beams at him. "Now sir, have you ever been deposed before?"
My phone vibrates.

—Did you read my e-mail?

—i cant talk right now

—It's important, Lily.

Kostova is running through the basics, the things every lawyer says at
the beginning of a deposition. I glance over at the transcript scrolling on
the stenographer's computer screen.

> Q: Now, Mr. Hoffman, I would ask that you please
> answer all my questions verbally. A nod or a shake
> of your head won't show up on the transcript.
> A: Yes, sir.
> Q: If you need a break at any time, you let me
> know.

I look down at Will's e-mail.

> At first, I tried to tell myself that there was nothing different
> about you. But when I woke up beside you after that first
> night, I didn't want to leave. So I stayed. For the best three
> days of my life.

> Then work separated us, but I was still so happy. This is it,
> I thought. I'm in love, at last. I was wrong about sex and
> emotions and monogamy—about everything. This is what
> people mean when they say that you just know.

> When we got back together, I knew immediately that you'd
> strayed. I could see it on your face. I was instantly filled with
> an immense, jealous rage. I wanted to find the guy and hurt
> him. It was terrifying. I was so furious with you. For two
> weeks I'd been with no one, looked at no one, thought of no
> one but you. And you betrayed me.

> I was in love, but I didn't know what to do. It seemed
> hopeless.

Don't laugh, but the Stoics helped me figure it out. I realized that I was suffering because I was trying to control something that was out of my control. You. You and your desires and preferences and impulses. You and your body. I was never going to be happy, never at peace, until I let go of that urge to control you.

I'd made an error by assuming that love was incompatible with freedom. But my love for you didn't give me the right to deny you the pleasure you sought. You should be free to do what you want. And so should I.

And so I did, terrified but curious. And it was <u>fine</u>. It didn't change my love for you at all. The two coexisted, and it was you, Lily, who taught me this.

I asked you to marry me because I want to be with you forever, enjoying life to the fullest and letting you do the same. But I made a mistake. I didn't tell you any of this. At first I didn't think it was necessary. Based on the way you lived your life, I assumed that you understood—that you got the freedom thing. I soon realized that it wasn't that simple—that there was a lot more going on inside your head than you were letting on. But things were going so well between us that I decided I could tell you later, ease you into it.

Yesterday morning, it all came crashing down. I realized we were going to have this wonderful party, this glorious celebration. We were going to say our vows in front of our families and friends, and be united in their eyes. But there would be no marriage of true minds, because of everything that I knew and you didn't, and everything you knew and thought I didn't.

So I told you. I really did think that after the shock wore off, you'd understand. That it would make sense to you. I see now that I was wrong.

Talk to me, Lily. I have a lot more to say.

Love,
Will

I stare at the screen for a long time. When I look up, everyone is staring at me.

"Sorry, what?"

"I said," Kostova says carefully, "shall we do the usual stips?"

I feel myself turning pink. "Um . . ."

"The usual stipulations," he explains. "The rules that we've agreed to for all the depositions in this case. That objections need not be stated on the record, except objections as to the form of the question. That the court reporter is relieved of the obligation to maintain the original transcript." He pauses. "That sort of thing."

I don't know how to respond. My mind is half on Will's e-mail. I don't want to agree to something just so that I don't look ignorant and inexperienced, but unfortunately I *am* ignorant and inexperienced, so . . . Also? I'm not a golden retriever, and I'd kind of prefer that Kostova not talk to me like one.

Meanwhile, the seconds are ticking away while everyone is waiting for me to answer, and I'm sitting here like a . . . a golden retriever.

"It's fine," Gran mutters.

"Very well," I say. "We agree."

"Could you speak up?" the stenographer says. "I'm having trouble hearing you."

"I said, we agree."

My goddamn phone vibrates again. This time it's Philip.

—Wilder. Are you at the deposition? What's happening?

—we just started. are you ok?

—I'm perfectly fine. These doctors are catastrophists. Who's with you?

—nobody

—Lyle didn't find someone to fly down?

I'm about to tell him the truth, but I hesitate. What if I do and he kicks the bucket for real? I can't have that on my conscience. So I pick the first name I think of—a scary-brilliant female partner who I have a secret crush on.

—i meant im alone right now. raney moore is coming. shes on her way from the airport

—Good. She's excellent. Let her take the lead.

—ok

—Do exactly as she says. And keep me updated.

—ok

Kostova is starting with the basic stuff—Pete's education and work history. He's so amiable, so very pleasant. I'd tell him every bad thing I ever did. He has turned his body toward Pete, shoved a hand in his pocket. Just us folks sittin' around on the porch, havin' ourselves a lil ole chat.

> Q: I'd like to ask you about your preparation for
> this deposition. Did you meet with counsel?
> A: Yes.

Kostova asks Pete several more questions about the prep: how long did we meet, when, who was present. Then: "Did you review any documents in preparation for your deposition?"

I intervene. "I'm going to instruct the witness not to answer that question."

Kostova breaks off to stare at me. "On what ground?"

"Attorney-client privilege," I reply. "My discussions with Mr. Hoffman in the course of preparing for this deposition are privileged."

"Of course they are," Kostova says. "Which is why I didn't ask about discussions. I asked a yes or no question, seeking facts. Did he look at documents. Not, what were the documents? Not, did your counsel select them? Did you—"

He's right. I jumped in too soon. "Fine," I say. "I just don't want—"

"Don't interrupt me, Counselor! You've accused me of attempting to invade the privilege, a serious impropriety. I'm entitled to defend myself."

He goes on and on. When he's finished, I say, "I beg your pardon. I misunderstood you. Mr. Hoffman, you may answer."

"Can you repeat the question, please?" Pete says in a small voice.

They proceed, and slowly the heat drains out of my face. I glance over at Gran. She's glowering at me.

My phone vibrates. I have a new e-mail, subject line: Addendum.

> You asked me this morning about our sex life. Honestly, I
> don't know if I can explain it, except to say that what we have
> between us is new to me. I'm not used to caring. I'm not used
> to feeling so strongly. Sometimes I can let go and enjoy myself.
> But other times I get nervous. Overwhelmed. I wanted to talk
> to you about it, but ... I thought there would be time later. For
> everything. It's another example of why I should have been
> honest. Why we both should have been honest. Love, Will

Kostova is trying to soften Pete up. It's working. Pete's answers are becoming longer and longer.

```
Q: What was your job title at Allied Gas?
A: I started as a payroll specialist. Eventually I
was promoted to assistant director of finance.
Q: Did your duties change?
A: They sure did. Before I left I was overseeing a
team of, oh, about six other accountants responsible
for managing payables.
```

Kostova moves on to the duties of accountants at publicly traded corporations. "Would you say, Mr. Hoffman, that accountants play an important role in ensuring that the information disclosed about a corporation to its shareholders is essentially accurate?"

"Objection," I say.

Kostova turns to me. "What is the nature of your objection?"

This catches me off guard. I've never seen a lawyer interrupt his own line of questioning to challenge an objection. "I'm objecting to the form of the question."

"Obviously. And what, in your opinion, is the defect in the form of my question?"

"Why are you—"

"If the question is truly objectionable," he continues, with elaborate patience, "I wish to correct it. I assume that you are not interposing objections simply to coach your witness, or to otherwise disrupt this deposition. So I would like you to tell me the basis for your objection."

"I'm not coaching my witness," I retort. "The question was vague. I don't understand what you mean when you use terms like 'important' and 'essentially accurate.' I don't think—"

"You don't understand 'important' and 'essentially accurate'?" He laughs. "Why don't we let the witness decide whether he has a similar problem with basic vocabulary? He is the one whose comprehension matters, after all."

"Mr. Kostova, it's my job to object when I feel that the question is flawed."

"Let's move on," Kostova says. "Madam Stenographer, would you read back the question?"

The stenographer peers at the computer screen and reads Kostova's last question in a monotone: "Would you say, Mr. Hoffman, that accountants play an important role in ensuring that the information disclosed about a corporation to its shareholders is essentially accurate?"

"Yes," Pete says.

Kostova asks a few more questions and gets a few more answers. Then he asks, "Would you say that the primary purpose of an accountant at a publicly traded corporation is to ensure that information disclosed to the public is accurate?"

"Objection," I say.

Kostova sighs. "And the basis for this objection?"

"Mr. Kostova," I say, "why don't we go off the record to discuss this?"

I would like to know why he's giving me such a hard time, considering how easy I'm making this for him. But he looks at me like I've just suggested that we all pull our pants down and take a collective dump on the conference table.

"If you have anything to say to me, Ms. Wilder, you can say it on the record. I have no intention of stopping this deposition in order to try to understand your mystifying objections."

Oh, *I* know why he's giving me a hard time. Here I was, thinking he was a hero, a fighter for the little guy. I forgot that he's still a lawyer, and therefore a total—

"Kindly state the basis for your objection, or withdraw it."

"The question is vague," I say. "You're asking the witness's opinion about—"

"I can't ask his opinion now?" Kostova laughs. "This is ridiculous."

Gran raps on the table with her knuckles, startling everyone. "I see no need for this colloquy," she says sharply. "Either you are confident that your manner of questioning this witness is correct, Mr. Kostova, or you are not. Stop wasting time."

Kostova shrugs. The stenographer rereads the question. Pete answers. My phone vibrates.

—Here's what kills me. You love sex. You take such pleasure in it. I can tell that when I'm inside you. And it's not because you like transgression, or were fucked up by your adolescence. You just like it. And you know why?

—leave me alone! im WORKING!

—Because you're human, Lily. You're supposed to like sex. With lots of people.

. . .

—Early humans had multiple sexual partners. Monogamy didn't arise until the advent of agriculture.

—shit, will. no wonder you score so big with the ladieeezzzz. that is some sexy talk!!

—I'm trying to tell you that you're normal. You obviously don't think you are. You felt like you have to hide your true self from me. You had to lie.

—hold on just a goddamned minute. who lied to who here, wilberforce? we hid the truth from EACH OTHER, remember? we both lied

—True. But you've also been lying to yourself.

. . .

—You've bought into the fantasy that relationships have to be monogamous to work. You've bought into it even as you've proven yourself, time and again, to be COMPLETELY incapable of being faithful. How awful is that? To believe, truly believe, in a rule you can't follow. A rule that says that because you love me, you must become numb to the pleasures of other people.

I put my phone away and tune back in to the proceedings. Pete is still rolling over. I try to signal to him to slow down, to say less. He's looking at me like I'm a stranger. Kostova notices me fidgeting and smiles smugly.

"Can we take a short break?" I say.

"After I finish this line of questioning," he replies.

Q: It sounds as though you played an important role in the review of EnerGreen's financial statements prior to their being sent to the auditors.
Ms. Wilder: Objection.
A: Well, I don't know about that.
Q: But, sir, you just said that you were in charge of ensuring that the figures from the various divisions were entered correctly into the documents sent to Ernst & Young. Isn't that right?
Ms. Wilder: Objection.
A: That's right.

Kostova smiles at me. "Let's take a break."

As we leave the room. I check my phone. I have an e-mail from Urs.

> Lily. I have received startling news that Philip is in hospital
> and you are covering important deposition of Mr. Hoffman
> today. Please call me immediately. I would like to participate
> by conference call.

The last thing I need is the client listening in on this trainwreck. I write back:

> I'm afraid the phone lines in this room are on the fritz.

He writes:

> I am confused. Who is Fritz?

For God's sake.

> I mean the phones aren't working, Urs. You can't dial in. I'll call
> you when it's over.

Just after I hit send, my phone rings. I start talking before Will can say anything.

"What a hypocrite you are. You were upset with me on Monday afternoon because of how I acted in front of your parents. You were afraid I was going to blow your cover. They don't know you at all, do they?"

"No," he admits. "Not this part of me, anyway. They think I'm their high-achieving, upstanding son. Which I am, but also . . . I'm not."

"Hey, don't underestimate your mom. You two have a lot more in common than you might think."

"She told me what she did to you, and I am so sorry," Will says earnestly. "She's always been overprotective, but that was beyond the pale. She promised me that she's not going to try to harm your career."

"Wow, that is *so* generous! Can you thank her for me?" I'm pacing the hallway now—I lower my voice as I pass the open door of the conference room. "Let's talk about your mom, Will. And your dad. You accuse me of being in bad faith, of acting like I'm unfettered by convention while secretly feeling shame, right? Look at you. You talk a good game about how we should all screw whoever we want to screw, but you're too scared to let Mommy and Daddy know who you really are."

"There's nothing wrong with being private about it."

"Private? Is that what you are? Because it sounds like you've developed a whole interdisciplinary theory of fucking, what with the science, the philosophy, the art history. Hey, you should write a book. How to Screw Women and Infuriate People, by Will Field, Ph.D."

"I'm sorry, okay? I didn't mean to sound like I was lecturing you. I mentioned the philosophy and the science because I think they support some of the things we do."

"I don't *care* what science supports, Will! This isn't about shame and freedom and Neanderthal man. It isn't about the cultural 'fantasy' of monogamy. It's about you and me. How you lied to me, and I lied to you. Perfect for each other? We're a *disaster* for each other. And it's over."

I hang up. I walk into the office where Pete and Gran are waiting for me and immediately start laying into him. "Why are you being so goddamned chatty?" I holler. "That guy out there? He's not your buddy! He's not your friend!"

"He seems all right," Pete says defensively.

"He's not all right, Pete! He's out to nail you to the wall. He wants EnerGreen to go under. He wants you to lose your job. Do you want that?"

"No!"

"Then listen to the question, and answer *only* the question that's asked. That's all I want you to do."

Pete scurries off to the bathroom. I turn to Gran. "Why is Kostova bullying me?"

"Because you're letting him."

"I am not!"

"You are acting weak, Lillian Grace, and he's capitalizing on that. If you want to stop him, you need to be more assertive."

"Really, Gran? I should just be more assertive, and magically everything will be better? I don't know what I'm doing!"

"I'll tell you what you're sure as hell *not* doing, and that's acting like a lawyer!" she snaps. "Every time I look at you, you're playing with your damn phone. Every time you challenge the man, you end up retreating in terror. You're sitting quietly like a good little girl and staying out of his way, which is *exactly* what he wants you to do." She scowls in disgust. "I raised you better than this."

"Why don't you help me?"

"Because every time I step in, it makes you look weak. You're the one defending this deposition, not me."

"But how, Gran? How do I do it?"

Her expression softens a little. She folds her gnarled hands over her purse. "Do you want to know the number one mistake young lawyers make when they have to do something public, like appear in court or take a deposition? They aren't themselves. They're suddenly thrust into the spotlight, and they either lose confidence, overwhelmed by everything they don't know—which seems to be what's happening in your case—or they think they have to play a role. They have an idea of what a lawyer is supposed to be, of how a lawyer is supposed to behave, and they try to fulfill it. Either way, it never works for them. You can't fake it, Lillian Grace. Deep in all that education, and in your gut, you know how to get this done. You have to figure out your own way."

Pete comes back from the bathroom, and we all return to the conference room.

25

When we go back on the record, Pete does his best to follow my instructions, answering in monotones. Kostova looks at me pityingly and turns up the charm. In no time Pete becomes comfortable and expansive again.

> Q: Before we get in any deeper, I should ask you
> what your official title is.
> A: I'm a deputy director of the financial services
> division.
> Q: And where is the financial services division
> situated in EnerGreen?
> A: Oh, we aren't a part of EnerGreen directly. I
> work for EnerGreen Energy Solutions.
> Q: That's not the same thing?
> A: No sir. It's a subsidiary. EnerGreen Inc. is the
> parent.

Kostova starts delving into Pete's job description. I object from time to time, but he doesn't give me a hard time. I glance over at Gran. Disappointment is coming off her in waves.

My phone vibrates.

—I need an update.

—everythings fine, philip

—Please call me on a break. I want to talk to Raney.

—ok

I set down my phone. Then I have an idea.

—raney wants to know how you want her to handle hoffmans
   emails

—It should be obvious to her.

Shit! I try again.

—she traveled all night to get here. i think shes pretty jetlagged,
   so . . .

I don't get a response.

Kostova is handing Pete a document. "Mr. Hoffman, I'm showing
you a document that has been marked Plaintiffs' Exhibit H-12." He
passes a copy to me.

I flip through it. It looks like a bunch of pages printed off some website and stapled together. "Excuse me, Counselor," I say. "Where did this
come from?"

"I beg your pardon?"

"I'm curious as to what this exhibit is," I say. "We don't appear to
have produced it."

"I'm entitled to question a witness about any document I choose,"
Kostova replies. "I'm not limited to documents EnerGreen has produced."

"And I'm not suggesting you are," I say carefully. "But I am asking
you, as a professional courtesy, to tell me where you obtained it."

He smiles at me. "If you want to ask me questions, young lady, I suggest you take my deposition."

The room falls silent.

"Young lady," I say.

We stare at each other across the table.

"Really," I say. "Young lady."

He nods. "Really."

I look at Gran. She looks back at me.

I stand up. "We're taking a break."

"We just took a break," Kostova says, but I'm already out the door.
Pete and Gran follow.

In our empty office, I pull out a chair and sit down. Pete looks worried. "Am I screwing up?"

"Yes, but it doesn't matter."

"Should I—"

"Quiet! I need to think."

And I do think.

I think, Thank you.

Thank you, all you men.

All you thoughtful, well-meaning, considerate men, who have taken time out of your busy, *busy* schedules to correct my errors, to teach me about who I am, and to tell me what to do.

You are all so very kind.

But I am so very tired of you. You confident, self-satisfied, know-it-all men, doing your best to help me learn how to think. How to behave. How to understand why I am the way I am.

Take Will, for example. He's been totally obnoxious. The ponderous, self-serving justifications. The enlightened theories. The smug presumptions. He's the perfect parody of a stuffy, navel-gazing academic.

And then there's Kostova. Bullying me. Condescending to me. Tossing out a "young lady." Making perfectly clear that I am not, and never will be, his equal.

However . . . I haven't exactly been acting like his equal. Texting like a teenager? Allowing my romantic problems to distract me from my job? Letting a man push me around?

Fine. Time for a change of plans.

What did Gran say? I have to find my own way.

Pete is staring into space. I snap my fingers. "Did you already testify that you were employed by a subsidiary?"

He blinks. "Whuh?"

"He did," Gran says. "EnerGreen Energy something or other. Why?"

"Because there's an argument that this deposition is procedurally defective."

"What argument?"

It's the one I thought of in the spa. I explain it to her. She says, "That's the most hypertechnical load of bullshit I ever heard in my life."

"Hello? We're lawyers, Gran. Hypertechnical bullshit is what we live for."

"You want to try to adjourn the deposition on that ground? Honey, the judge will crucify you."

"What if I can get Kostova to call the judge?"

Judges hate it when parties pester them to settle petty squabbles. And they're always harder on the one who insisted on calling.

"How would you do that?"

I smile at her. "By being myself."

I clap my hands together. "Okay, Pete, we're going to try something new. Whenever I tap my finger on the table, like this," I tap the desk, "I want you to say, 'Can you repeat the question?' Okay?"

"Sure," he says dubiously.

"Let's practice." I tap my finger, very lightly.

"Can you repeat the question?" he says.

"Perfect." I hand Gran my phone. "Don't give this back to me until the deposition is over." It disappears into the vastness of her handbag. "Let's go."

We return to the conference room. "Thank you for joining us," Kostova says.

I give him a grin and hitch my chair up to the table. "So sorry. I had a few lady things to take care of."

The tape starts rolling again. Kostova begins a series of questions about EnerGreen's corporate structure. Then he moves on to Pete's specific responsibilities.

    Q: What are your duties as deputy director of the
    financial services division at EnerGreen Energy
    Solutions?
    Ms. Wilder: Objection.
    A: I would say that I have three primary areas of
    responsibility.
    Q: Tell me about the first area of responsibility.

I listen to a bit more. Then I scribble on a yellow Post-it. When Kostova turns to consult his notes, I slide the Post-it to Pete, making sure Kostova catches me doing it.

"I'd ask that the record reflect that counsel for the defendant has passed a note to the witness," he says. "In clear violation of the rules of the court."

"How dare you state that on the record!" I say hotly.

"What does it say?" Kostova asks Pete.

"Don't read it," I tell him.

"Read it," Kostova says. Pete looks from Kostova to me, terrified.

"I instruct you not to read it," I say.

"On what possible ground?" Kostova demands.

"On the ground of attorney-client privilege." I roll my eyes. "Obviously."

"It's not privileged if you hand it to him during a deposition," Kostova says, controlling his irritation with effort.

"It's privileged to me," I inform him.

"This is ridiculous! Either the witness reads the note into the record, or I'm calling the court."

"I'm calling the court!" I repeat in a high-pitched whine, waving my hands helplessly in the air. "Oooh!"

Kostova starts berating me. I glance at the transcript running on the stenographer's computer.

```
Mr. Kostova: This is ridiculous. Either the witness
reads the note into the record, or I'm calling the
court.
Ms. Wilder: I'm calling the court. Oh.
Mr. Kostova: Counsel, I would strongly advise you
to . . .
```

The video would have picked up my mocking tone, but the transcript doesn't. Most stenographers capture only the plain text of questions, answers and objections. And that's what this one was doing, exactly as I'd hoped.

"Fine," I say. "Read the note please, Mr. Hoffman."

Pete looks down at the Post-it. He clears his throat. "I hear the grouper special is excellent."

Kostova turns to me, completely baffled.

"We're making dinner plans," I explain. "Please continue your questions. We're wasting all that beautiful Florida sunshine."

Kostova peers at me for a moment, then resumes his questioning. It takes him a little time to pick up his rhythm. And he's lost a bit of his geniality toward Pete.

```
Q: Were there any other employees of the financial
services division who had responsibilities similar
to yours?
Ms. Wilder: Objection.
Mr. Kostova: Ms. Wilder, I must ask you to state
your objections in a normal tone of voice.
Ms. Wilder: I am stating my objections in a normal
tone of voice, Mr. Kostova.
Mr. Kostova: You know very well that you are
singing.
Ms. Wilder: Singing, Counselor? Be serious. This is
a deposition, not America's Got Talent.
Mr. Kostova: Ms. Wilder, you are singing. Please
stop singing.
Ms. Wilder: Please stop littering the record with
your extraneous remarks.
Mr. Kostova: Let's move on.
```

I try a number of different styles: rap, country. Beyoncé. Tom Waits really aggravates him. The stenographer is looking at me with her eyebrows raised, which, fair enough. But each time I object, the transcript simply reads:

```
Ms. Wilder: Objection.
```

I'm irritating Kostova, I'm distracting him, but most important, I'm wasting his time. By court order, these depositions have a fixed length. Once the day is over, so is Kostova's time with Pete.

He moves on to the financial statements. "Mr. Hoffman, let's talk about your involvement in EnerGreen's 2012 financial reporting process."

"Objection," I say.

"I haven't asked a question yet," Kostova says sharply.

"I know. You're cluttering the transcript with unnecessary speeches. If you have a question, please ask it."

It takes him a minute to find his place in his outline. "Mr. Hoffman. At the time that EnerGreen Energy was preparing its 2012 financial statements, which were publicly filed with the SEC, were you deputy director of the financial services division of EnerGreen Energy Solutions?"

"Objection," I say. I tap the table very softly with my finger. Pete glances at me. I give him a tiny nod.

"Could you repeat the question, please?" he says.

Kostova does. I tap the table again.

"Could you repeat the question, please?" Pete says.

"What don't you understand about the question?" Kostova asks.

I jump in. "It's so rambling and discursive that I don't think any of us have any idea what you could be possibly driving at."

"Ms. Wilder—"

"You mention EnerGreen Energy, you mention EnerGreen Energy Solutions, something about the SEC—"

"Ms. Wilder, will you—"

"—some vague time in the past that seems designed to trap the witness into taking a position on something about which he may have no recollection—"

"I demand that you stop talking!" Kostova says loudly. "You are coaching your witness, and that is impermissible. As I said earlier, you may state your objection as to form, and then—what are you doing? Stop doing that with your face."

"I'm not doing anything with my face."

"I would like the record to reflect that, that counsel for defendant is . . . she's moving her lips while I'm speaking in a, in a . . . mocking fashion."

I finish mouthing the words *mocking fashion* and smile at him. He knows that he sounds like a complete fool, and now it's in the record. I tap the table.

"Could you repeat the question, please?" Pete says.

Kostova is lost. He asks the stenographer, who glances back into the transcript and reads out the question.

"Yes," Pete says. "I was deputy director at that time."

"And were you involved in the drafting and review of those financial statements prior to their being sent to EnerGreen's auditors?"

I tap the table.

"Could you repeat the question, please?" Pete says.

Kostova repeats it.

"When you say involved—" I begin.

"Ms. Wilder!" Kostova snaps. "I will have no more of your speechifying!"

"Speechifyin'!" I shout, startling the entire room. "You call that speechifyun', Mistah Fletchah?" I start mimicking his southern drawl. "I do declayuh, I have *nevah,* in all my boan days, been called a speechifyuh, and I—"

"If you do not stop immediately, I will—"

I pound the table. "I reject your insinuation that I am a speechifyah, and I say unto you that—"

"—have no choice but to call the court and—"

I tap the table with my finger.

"Could you repeat the question, please?" Pete says.

"Water," Gran whispers.

I pretend to reach for my pen and knock my glass over. Water flows across the table toward Kostova's papers.

"Dammit!" he says, sopping it up.

Gran gives me a wink. The few times I've dared to glance at her since we came back into the room, her expression has been completely impassive. Now I realize that she's just trying to conceal how much she's enjoying herself.

Kostova composes himself and continues. I dial back on the objections. Pete is warier now that Kostova has started in on the financial statements—his answers are nice and terse.

"Mr. Hoffman," Kostova says, pulling some documents out of a folder. "I'd like to show you a document marked Plaintiffs' Exhibit H-14." He hands a copy to Hoffman and passes one to me. "Are you familiar with this document?"

I tear off the first stapled page with a flourish and lay it flat on the table. This catches Kostova's eye. I fold down the top two corners toward the center. He watches me, puzzled, then turns back to Pete.

"Now, Mr. Hoffman," Kostova says. "Please turn to page five and take a look at the fifth bullet point. It discusses the issue of potential discrepancies between company data and the reported figures, does it not?"

"Yes, sir," Pete says.

I fold the paper in half and bend the wings up. I make additional folds. I test the points with the tip of my finger. Kostova is staring at me.

"And—and Mr. Hoffman, what was the company's procedures as to such—as to such discrepancies?"

"Objection," I say, continuing to fold the paper.

"Well," Pete says, "I would say that when you're dealing with audited financials, there are always a lot of moving pieces, a lot of balls up in the air—"

Kostova is watching me and trying to listen to Hoffman's absurd answer. He can't focus.

"—and you've got various persons and cost centers utilizing different metrics and rubrics to achieve your ultimate outcomes. Any discrepancies would in the normal course be caught and corrected in the standard process of verification and reconciliation."

I hold up a perfect origami swan and present it to Kostova with a grave bow.

"Ms. Wilder!" Kostova fumes. "Your behavior is very distracting."

"I don't know what you're talking about, Meesturrr Kostovvvaaahhh."

Kostova turns to Hoffman. "Could you repeat your answer, please?"

I tap the table.

"Could you repeat the question, please?" Pete says.

"Could you repeat your answer, please?" Kostova says.

Pete chuckles. "This is like Who's on First?"

Kostova struggles to control his temper. "Perhaps we should take a break."

"I don't need a break," I say. "Do you, Mr. Hoffman?"

"No'm."

"We'd like to keep going," I say. "We're eager to get out there and enjoy that beautiful Florida sunshine."

Kostova is enraged but manages to swallow it and continue. He knows he's running out of time. With every question, I now interpose an objection. I do a French accent, an Italian one. I do a robot voice. Robert De Niro. Kostova tries to ignore me, but he can't. Every time he has to deal with my nonsense, he loses his rhythm. He can't focus on Pete's answers.

> Q: Mr. Hoffman, what was EnerGreen's standard—Ms. Wilder, I must ask that you stop that.
> Ms. Wilder: Stop what, Counselor?
> Q: You are humming. I must ask that you stop humming.
> Ms. Wilder: Don't be ridiculous, Counselor. I'm not a llama.
> Q: I was not suggesting that you are—
> Ms. Wilder: I don't think a deposition is an appropriate venue for making hurtful remarks about other people's appearance.
> Q: Ms. Wilder, as you know very well, I was not—
> Ms. Wilder: I accept your apology. Let's move on.

"Mr. Hoffman," Kostova says. "What was EnerGreen's standard practice regarding discrepancies between internal documents and drafts of its financial statements?"

"Objection," I say.

He can't let that pass without comment. "On what possible ground is that question objectionable?"

"The question is vague and ambiguous, contains an improper characterization and is compound," I reply.

"Stop," he says. "Just—"

"It's argumentative. It's leading. It incorporates hearsay."

He's getting very worked up. He's all red and sweaty, and his hair is sticking up.

"You're badgering the witness," I continue calmly.

He is outraged. "I am not—"

I tap the table.

"Can you repeat the question, please?" says my good little parrot.

Kostova loses it. "You shut up!" he says.

We're all silent for a moment.

"Let's take a break," Kostova says.

"You don't want to finish your line of questioning?" I ask innocently.

He pulls off his microphone and walks out of the room.

In ten minutes, we resume. Kostova has calmed down. The back-and-forth is smooth.

> Q: Mr. Hoffman, was EnerGreen Energy careful
> in ensuring that all of its financial statements
> accurately reflected the financial state of the
> company?
> Ms. Wilder: Objection.
> A: Yes.

I make a few noisy objections, a few more speeches, but Kostova only smiles at me. He's picking up speed again, getting into a rhythm with Pete.

> Q: Mr. Hoffman, did EnerGreen ever have any internal
> discussions about the impact of the Deepwater
> Discovery oil spill on its projected gross revenues
> and earnings?
> Ms. Wilder: Objection.
> A: Yes.
> Q: Were you a part of those discussions?
> A: In a way, I suppose.

Did I really think this would work? Kostova is too good. Any minute now, he's going to present Pete with the financial discrepancies, Pete is going to collapse, they're going to get to the e-mails, and then it's over.

What would rattle this guy? He's a fighter for the little guy. A David, always battling corporate Goliaths. He has a deep conviction that what he's doing is right.

How can I *really* piss him off?

Kostova is questioning Pete about specific items in the 2012 financial statements. "And on page 4 of Exhibit H-21," he says, "does Table 3 accurately represent EnerGreen's gross revenue for fiscal year 2012?"

"Trying to figure out your cut?" I say.

Kostova looks at me over his reading glasses. "Excuse me?"

"You're representing the plaintiffs on contingency, right? What's your fee? Thirty percent of whatever you recover for the people who were actually harmed? Or is it forty percent? To cover your expenses, quote-unquote?"

"This is outrageous!" Kostova snaps. "I'm asking the questions here."

I whistle. "That's a nice chunk of change. No wonder your firm fought tooth and nail to be appointed lead counsel."

"Young lady," Kostova says, "I have spent over twenty-five years fighting for—"

"You're smart," I say. "That's why you only sued EnerGreen. You didn't sue the manufacturer of the oil platform, because they went bankrupt—no good to you guys. And you didn't sue the individual supervisors—the guys who were bribed to falsify the inspection reports, who are now in jail. That would have complicated matters. It would have messed up your story that EnerGreen, and EnerGreen alone, is responsible for everything that happened."

"Ms. Wilder, I must ask you one more time—"

"Focus on the deep pockets, right?" I smile at him. "You know what, Kostova? You would have made a pretty decent lawyer at a real firm."

That's when he loses it. "Your behavior is out of line!" he shouts. "I want a ruling!"

"Fine," I say. "Denied."

"I want a ruling from the judge, you idiot! We're calling the court."

"Great idea." I close my binder. "Who's got his number?"

26

We call the judge's chambers on speaker phone and learn that he's finishing up a hearing. We wait for over an hour, which Kostova spends glaring at me, Gran spends fidgeting with suppressed excitement and Pete spends sweating profusely.

Me? I'm busy taking notes.

Finally the phone crackles, and we hear muffled voices and the shuffling of papers.

"Six fifteen on a Friday, people," the judge growls. "This better be good."

"Your Honor," Kostova begins, "I apologize for disturbing you, and I assure you that I would not have done so if I didn't feel that the circumstances compelled me—"

"Your point, Counselor," says the judge.

I've attended a handful of conferences and hearings in Judge Forster's courtroom since this lawsuit was filed. I've always liked him. He's prickly and no-nonsense, but generally pretty fair. I've never actually spoken to him before, though, and the prospect is suddenly terrifying.

"Your Honor," Kostova says, "I have nothing but respect for the firm representing EnerGreen in this litigation. But in twenty-five years of practice I have never been so appalled at the conduct of counsel in a deposition as I have been today. Ms. Wilder's behavior has been juvenile, offensive, demeaning and hugely inappropriate. She has made speeches on the record, blatantly coached her witness and otherwise behaved in a manner utterly unbecoming an officer of the court. Her aim appears to be to disrupt the deposition and to conceal her witness's utter lack of preparation."

He goes on like this for a while, speaking in general terms, as I'd hoped he would. No experienced lawyer really wants to go crying to a judge that his opponent made singing objections and mocked his accent and was otherwise mean to him. Kostova seems confident that his towering outrage will convince the judge to punish me.

"In conclusion, Your Honor, I would ask that you order the witness to answer the questions I put to him without obfuscation, and that you order counsel for the defendant to follow the court's rules and comport herself professionally. I think sanctions would not be out of order, but that, of course, is in Your Honor's discretion."

I hear some whispering from the judge's clerk. Finally, the judge says: "Counsel for EnerGreen. You're on."

Everyone in the room looks at me.

I can do this. I'm totally in control!

I clear my throat, lean toward the speaker phone, and say something that sounds like, "Yuhaarrgh huuuuhnnurr?"

"Pardon?" Judge Forster says.

I'm nervous, okay? I get a grip and try again.

"Your Honor, this is Lillian Wilder. Thank you for the opportunity to respond. As I will explain in a moment, Mr. Kostova's complaints about my conduct are without foundation. However, I have a more pressing matter to raise with you first. The record has established that the plaintiffs' request for Mr. Hoffman's deposition was defective. I therefore move that it be adjourned."

Kostova's mouth falls open. "What?"

"Mr. Kostova has elicited testimony establishing that Mr. Hoffman works for a subsidiary of EnerGreen, not the corporation itself," I tell the judge. "That subsidiary is not a party to this lawsuit. Under this court's rules, the plaintiffs should have issued a subpoena for Mr. Hoffman's deposition. They did not. Accordingly, this deposition should be postponed until the plaintiffs correct their error."

Kostova immediately begins to sputter. "This is ridiculous, Your Honor! EnerGreen consented to this deposition!"

"Is that so, Ms. Wilder?" the judge asks. "Did you consent?"

"Yes, Your Honor."

"You have also permitted it to go forward for several hours today, have you not?"

"Let me explain our thinking on that, Your Honor. We have sought to abide by this court's rules that the parties work together in good faith to resolve discovery disputes. Plaintiffs were eager to depose Mr. Hoffman, and in the interest of professional courtesy, we agreed. That professional courtesy was not reciprocated when we attempted to re-schedule the deposition because of the blizzard on the East Coast. Plain-tiffs refused our request, which meant that Mr. Gardiner, the partner in charge of the case for EnerGreen, was not able to attend." I pause. "And that, Your Honor, takes me to my second issue: the abusive behavior Mr. Kostova has demonstrated toward myself and my witness."

"What?" Kostova cries.

"Mr. Kostova has bullied me for making perfectly appropriate ob-jections, has lectured me at length over trivialities and has chastised me for trying to do my job. I could take all that if it were not for the rude-ness and abuse he has heaped on my witness. With your permission, Your Honor, I am now going to do something that Mr. Kostova, in his lengthy attack on my alleged conduct, did not do. I'm going to give you some examples." I turn to the stenographer. "Could you please read page forty-three, lines twenty-four through twenty-six?"

The stenographer reads in a monotone:

    Witness: Could you repeat the question, please?
    Mr. Kostova: Dammit!

Kostova says, "Your Honor, what the transcript doesn't show is that a glass of water—"

"You'll have your turn in a moment, Mr. Kostova," the judge says. "Right now Ms. Wilder has the floor."

"Madam Stenographer," I say, "could you now read from page sixty-two of the transcript, lines twelve through fifteen?"

The stenographer obliges.

Witness: Could you repeat the question, please?
Mr. Kostova: You shut up!

"Your Honor," Kostova says. "This is not—"
"And could you read page seventy-six, line nine?"

Mr. Kostova: I want a ruling from the judge, you
idiot!

"Your Honor," I say, "I understand that Mr. Kostova is frustrated that he is not able to elicit the testimony that he wants from my witness. But that's no justification for this sort of behavior. As Mr. Kostova knows, this is my first time defending a deposition. I can't help but think he's taking unfair advantage of my inexperience."

There is a long pause. Kostova is purple with outrage. "Mr. Kostova," the judge says at last, "why didn't you agree to postpone the deposition?"

"Your Honor, I was already en route to the Keys when counsel for the defendant called and demanded that the deposition be delayed. To be frank, given the explosive nature of some of the documents pertaining to this witness, I suspected that they were using the weather as a pretext."

"A pretext?" the judge says incredulously. "Have you been watching the news, Counselor? They're calling this the storm of the century. It's stretching from Boston down to the Carolinas. The Weather Channel has even named the darned thing. What are they calling it?" We hear some whispering on the other end. "Pluto!" the judge cries. "They're calling it Pluto! The ninth planet! Ruler of the underworld, Mr. Kostova. This snow is serious business!"

"Yes, Your Honor," Kostova says uncertainly.

"You couldn't accommodate a reasonable request to delay the deposition?" The judge is getting worked up now. "Instead, you decide to come running to me, late on a Friday, with a bunch of complaints about a junior associate who's supposedly making your life difficult?"

Kostova protests. "Your Honor, Ms. Wilder is deliberately interfering with my ability to question this witness. Her citations to the record completely fail to provide the context for what has happened here today."

"Do you have anything specific that you wish to cite in support of your contention that it is Ms. Wilder, and not you, who has behaved with an extreme disregard for decorum and professional courtesy, both before and during this deposition?"

I smile at Kostova. Go ahead, I think. Tell him I made faces at you and gave you paper animals. Tell him that you let a lady lawyer rattle you, and that you lost your temper. Let's see how well that goes over.

Kostova doesn't have time to go through the transcript and look for examples. The judge is waiting.

"She hummed, Your Honor," Kostova says at last. "And there was a . . . she made a swan—"

"Am I to understand, Mr. Kostova, that you are seeking my intervention in a deposition because opposing counsel was *humming?*"

"Your Honor," he says, "if you will give me a moment, I will try to find some examples of her distracting behavior, and the long speeches that she has made, but—"

"Speeches, Mr. Kostova?" The judge chuckles. "My, my. If I were to sanction every attorney who made speeches on the record, the whole lot of you would be in jail."

"Yes, Your Honor," Kostova says.

"Probably not a bad idea," the judge adds. "Now, give me a moment." Silence.

I close my eyes and pray.

"I'm adjourning this deposition," he says.

"I'll be damned," Gran mutters.

"You should have agreed to the postponement, Mr. Kostova," the judge continues. "It would have been the professional thing to do."

"But Your Honor," Kostova protests, "we've already started, and—"

"I'm not going to get drawn into some he-said-she-said here," the judge continues. "It sounds to me as though everybody needs to cool off. I suggest that you sort out your procedural issue and reschedule the deposition for a few weeks from now. I have no doubt that EnerGreen's counsel will be both accommodating and professional. Isn't that right, Ms. Wilder?"

"Absolutely, Your Honor." I smile broadly at Kostova.

"Your Honor," he says, "I would ask—"

"Save it, Counselor. I've made my ruling. Have a good weekend, everyone," the judge says, and hangs up.

The stenographer's fingers are hovering over her machine. "Are we done?" she asks.

"We're done," I say, not quite believing it myself. She types in a few final lines and begins packing up her things. The videographer is already wrapping up his cables. I unclip my microphone.

Kostova is staring at me with murder in his eyes.

"You said you wanted a ruling," I say innocently.

"If he knew half of what went on here," he says.

Gran says, "If you want something to appear in the record, you need to make sure it shows up on the transcript."

"I'm going to get the video of this deposition in front of the judge immediately," Kostova tells me. "I'm going to seek sanctions against your firm and against you personally. You're in for a world of trouble, young—"

He stops himself. I smile at him. "Say it again. Wait until you see what I've got for an encore."

He throws his papers into his briefcase and storms out.

"Is it really over?" Pete asks.

"For now," I say. "But don't get too comfortable."

"I sure won't."

"You should think about updating your résumé."

"I sure will."

"You might want to hire your own lawyer."

"Can I hire you?" he asks hopefully.

"Hell no! But you can hire her." I point at Gran.

She looks up from her handbag. "What?"

"Give the man your contact information, Izzie. You're back in business."

Pete takes her number and says good-bye and scurries out the door. Gran and I turn to each other.

"Lillian Grace Wilder," she says slowly. "That was reckless, dangerous and almost entirely unethical."

I sigh. "I know, Gran. I know."

She hugs me hard. "I haven't had that much fun in years!"

I open my laptop and call Urs on Skype. Soon his round face, framed by severely parted coal-black hair, is peering back at me through the screen. As quickly as possible, I tell him everything. Pete's e-mails. The truth about the fraud. Urs's pale face gets paler. I go step by step through the deposition, concluding with the call to the judge. His wide eyes get wider. When I'm finished, he gawps at me for a long time.

Gran taps the screen. "Is it frozen?"

"This fraud," Urs says slowly, in his precise, accented voice. "This fraud is . . . how big is this fraud?"

"Fifteen billion dollars," I say.

Urs seems to wobble, but it could be the Wi-Fi in the conference room. "This witness, Hoffman," he says. "He is prepared to testify about it?"

"He's too dumb to be stopped."

Urs begins, quietly, to hyperventilate. Then he drops off the screen. Gran and I exchange a glance. I hope I'm not causing cardiac arrest in yet another lawyer.

In a moment, Urs reappears, smoothing his hair back into place with one hand. "Now, you say you paused this deposition, and you made an argument to the judge, and with this argument you provided citations to the transcript that were . . . how would you characterize them? Somewhat misleading? Very misleading?"

"Misleading-ish?" I suggest.

He gazes at me hopelessly. "This is normal litigation practice in America?"

"Normal or not, she saved your ass!" Gran cries, getting all up in the screen so that the only thing visible is her scary old-lady eyeball.

Urs rears back. "Lily? Who is this fearsome person?"

"My grandmother," I say. "And your local counsel."

Urs clutches his head. "I am very confused."

"Listen, Urs. Here's the point. What I did worked—for now. But as soon as the plaintiffs get the video of this deposition, they're going to file a motion that will show the judge how I misled him. Our credibility will be shot, we'll be heavily sanctioned and the judge will order the deposition to resume. EnerGreen has to accept the current settlement proposal. Immediately."

"As you know, I have little influence over my superiors. I cannot guarantee that they will listen."

"You have to *make* them listen, Urs. I just put myself on the line for a bunch of crooks, and they have to make it right—for the plaintiffs and for me. Tell them that if they don't settle right away, I'm going to resign and tell the court everything I know. And I know a lot."

Urs nods slowly. "Yes. Yes, that should persuade them."

"They also have to fix their accounting problems, or I'm going straight to the DOJ."

"Very well," he says. "All will be relayed."

"I think that's it. Any questions?"

Urs shakes his head. "This has been a distressing call for me. But thank you, Lily and Lily's grandmother. You have done excellent work. I will praise you to Philip when he recovers."

The screen goes dark. Urs is gone.

We pack up and get ready to go. Gran hands me my phone. I have eighteen texts.

Philip: I'm troubled that I haven't heard from you, Wilder.

Mattie: Is ths another one of your jokes???

Will: Please don't go silent like this.

Mattie: I've wokred very hard to make this weddign perfect and thsi is what I get in return?

Ana: Where are you, Lilybear?

Mattie: How could I expect you to taek it seriously, though? You haven't taken anything seriously this week. Its been all f this and f that.

Mattie: I'm so tired of it!!!

Philip: I emailed Raney Moore. She tells me she's in Knoxville, not Key West. What is going on?

Freddy: yr wedding planner might kill me

313131: Your appt with Dr. Gibbons is scheduled for 03/02/14 at 10:00 AM Reply Y to Confirm, N to Cancel

Mattie: I have news for you younge lady. When you have to keep saying no offense to someone, youre probably offending them!

Jane: We all feel terrible, darling. Please call me.

Pharmacist: whats up girl?

Mattie: I quit!

Philip: Going into surgery now. Please call Betty with any updates.

Will: I guess you've made up your mind.

Freddy: pls call i hve no limbz!

Will: I never meant to hurt you.

I drive Gran home and park in front of the house. She turns to me. "I'm proud of you, honey."

"I just followed your advice and played to my strengths. Acting stupid and enraging people."

"I'm not proud because you won. I'm proud because you showed up. A lot of people would have abandoned ship. You saw it through to the very end, and you did your best for your client, even though it deserves to rot in hell." She puts her hand on my shoulder and squeezes. "You're a damn fine lawyer."

Nobody's praise could mean more to me. Jesus, my eyes are welling. "Thank you, Gran."

"Now," she continues, "you also made a shitload of mistakes. Let's start with your manner of addressing the court."

She proceeds to spend the next forty-five minutes critiquing everything from my voice to my body language to my knowledge of the rules of evidence.

"All in all," she concludes, "I'd give you a B. Maybe a B-minus, considering the blatant ethical improprieties."

"Gee, Gran. Thanks for the positive reinforcement."

She pats my knee. "You're welcome. Now come inside and I'll make you a sandwich."

"God, no!" I say quickly. "I mean, I'm exhausted. I'm going to head back to the hotel and crash."

She gives me a look full of love and sympathy. "What's your plan after that?"

"Pack up, I guess. Go back to New York."

She gathers Rhode Island from the floor of the car. "Will you come by and see me before you leave?"

"Of course."

She gives me a big hug. "Thanks for the referral, hon. I feel like myself again. Take it from me —retirement's a bitch."

She hops out. I pull away, watching her in the rearview as she waves good-bye.

27

I am bone tired. My mind is still whirling from the deposition, not to mention my back-and-forth with Will. His last text was hours ago. I wonder where he is.

I park the car at the hotel and sit there for a long time. If nothing else, the last few hours have been a welcome distraction from the complete fiasco that is my personal life. I'm not angry at Will anymore. Not even irritated. But I can't think about it anymore. I'll have plenty of time to sift through the wreckage tomorrow. Maybe Freddy and I can honeymoon together. That would give Will time to pack and move out. We wouldn't have to see each other again.

I finally get out of the car and head inside. I walk through the doors and stop short. Teddy is sitting on a sofa. He sees me and stands up.

"Hey," he says. "Can we talk?"

I am so goddamn tired of talking. But he looks anxious, and when he sits back down, gesturing to me to join him, I do.

"I wanted to apologize for yesterday afternoon," he says. "I was a dick to you. I'm sorry."

"Don't be. I deserved it."

He reaches out and takes my hand. "You didn't. I've spent a lot of time over the years blaming you for things. Too much time. I thought I'd stopped. I thought I'd accepted what had happened to Lee and to . . . to us. It was so long ago, and we were so young. But then you came back, and everything got stirred up again. I felt ridiculous for being upset, and that made me even angrier. I took it out on you." He releases my hand but is still gazing at me intently. "I'm sorry."

"There's something you need to know," I say. "I thought about you constantly. I missed you every single day. I was lost without you, Teddy. But giving you up was my punishment to myself. I thought I deserved it for what I did."

He nods.

"I didn't mean to punish you, too," I add. "I should have told you."

"It's okay. It's all in the past."

"I'm leaving tomorrow."

"What about the wedding?"

I just shake my head. He looks surprised but says nothing. He feels sorry for me. And I am suddenly struck by how different everything might have been. My life and his. If I hadn't stolen the dynamite. If we hadn't built the bomb. If I hadn't gone to Lee's house. If I'd written Teddy back, and kept writing and writing and writing.

Would we have calmed down? Would we have straightened out? Could we be sitting together right now, here or in some other place, together in a completely different way?

I stand up at last. So does he. "I'm thirteen years too late," I say, "but can I write to you now?"

He smiles. "Sure."

I suddenly feel awkward. Should we hug? Shake hands? Teddy solves the problem, like he always did. He steps forward, leans down and kisses me full on the mouth, gently, sweetly. I put my hands on his shoulders and pull him close. His body feels the same, he tastes the same, his lips move the same way.

One last time I'm fourteen again, and I'm in the only place I ever wanted to be.

It's magical.

And then it's over.

He steps back and smiles at me. "Good-bye, Lily."

I raise a hand. "Good-bye, Teddy."

He turns. He's walking away, he's pushing through the door. He's gone.

I hear the elevator ding. I turn and see Freddy walking unsteadily across the lobby toward the bar. I follow her. She picks a stool and climbs aboard. I take the next one. The bartender comes over.

"Vodka," Freddy says thickly.

"And?" he asks.

"More vodka."

I clutch Freddy's arm. "Oh God. What's wrong?"

She looks at me all wide-eyed. I'm not sure she recognizes me.

"Little-known fact," she says, slowly and distinctly. "Little. Known. Fact. It is *surprisingly easy* to hypnotize a chicken."

"She's already three sheets," the bartender remarks.

Freddy raises a finger. "Step one. You press its little beak to the ground. Step two. You draw an X in the dirt in front of it." She draws an X on the bar with her finger. "You do that over and over again, and the chicken follows the motion with its beady little bird eyes, until . . . *voilà!* You have yourself one goddamned hypnotized chicken."

The bartender places drinks in front of us. Freddy downs hers in one gulp. Then she takes mine and downs it too.

"I have spent the day," she announces, way too loudly, "dealing with your wedding planner."

"Was it bad?"

She waves the question away, but the motion throws her off balance and she starts sliding off her stool. I haul her upright again.

"I found myself facing an impossible choice," she says. "Either destroy myself with drugs and alcohol or murder the crazy bitch." She gestures to the bartender for another round. "I chose the latter."

"You killed Mattie?"

"Oops!" she cries. "I mean 'the former.' I get those mixed up. Former, latter. Left, right. Up, down." She picks up her new drink. "Me, the rest of the world."

"I'm sorry I put you through all that."

"Heyyyyyyy." She throws an arm around me and hugs me, a little too tightly. "Imma maida honor. 'Swhy I'm here, right? To help plan wedding, help unplan wedding. Whatevs, babyloves. I'm here for *you*."

"Guess what?" I say. "I think I saved my job."

"Praise Jesus!" She slaps the bar. "I was worried we were gonna have one less lawyer in the world."

She downs another drink, which, oddly, seems to sober her up a little. She turns to me with serious eyes. "He's waiting for you upstairs."

I set my glass down carefully. "He's still here?"

She nods. "What are you going to do?"

"No idea. What do you think I should do?"

"I don't know, honey."

This is unprecedented. "You have no advice?"

"Champagne!" she cries.

The bartender places a flute in front of me.

I shake my head. "Thanks, Lloyd, but I don't think she meant to order it."

"No, but he did," the bartender says, pointing behind me.

Freddy and I turn. My father is sitting at a table in the corner. He raises his glass to us.

"Well whup me with a hickory stick!" Freddy cries, touching her hair. "How do I look?"

I slip off my stool. "I'll be right back."

Dad looks wonderful, as usual. Fresh and well rested, although maybe a bit melancholy.

He kicks out a chair for me. "Have a drink with your old father."

I sit down. "How was your day, Dad?"

He gazes into his champagne. "To be honest, little one? It's been a bit of a trial."

"Last I checked you were doing fine."

"Oh, you mean the business with your mother and Ana and Jane? That's all been sorted out. But I'm afraid Trina has asked me for a divorce."

"What? She adores you!"

"She did." He tops off our glasses, shaking his head gravely. "But it seems I recently e-mailed her a snapshot that was rather . . ." He hesitates. "Unfortunate."

"Oh, Dad."

"I know, darling, I know." He pauses. "I'm afraid this one is going to be expensive."

"No prenup?"

He glances away.

"You're a true romantic, Henry."

"It has always been my weakness." He gestures to the bartender, who brings another bottle of champagne. My father pops it open and pours. We raise our glasses, clink and drink.

"Well, enough about me!" I say. "What's going on with you, Dad?"

He puts his glass down and leans forward, taking my hands in his. "I'm sorry, little one. You've been having a hell of a time, haven't you? Is there anything I can do?"

I look into his beautiful green eyes. Should I ask his advice? This is usually a terrible idea, but maybe in this case it's the right thing to do. After all, I'm basically sitting across from my future self here.

What the hell? It's worth a shot.

"There's so much I don't know, Dad. Can a person change? *Should* a person change? Can a solid relationship be built on a foundation of lies? Am I doomed to repeat your mistakes, only backwards and in high heels? Is the purpose of sex to make each other miserable? Can marriage ease that misery? Can one person ever be enough? Are we all just animals? If you want to help me, answer these questions. It's pearls of wisdom time, Henry. Give me everything you've got."

My father looks totally befuddled.

"Let me simplify," I say. "Should Will and I get married, or should we go our separate ways?"

Henry fills his glass again and waits for the foam to settle. He sips thoughtfully. "Do you love him?"

"Yes. But it's more complicated than that."

"I'm not sure it is, little one. You met someone, and you fell in love. Will it last forever? That question, like the others you posed, is interesting but ultimately unhelpful. I think you said it best yourself, last night. We need a new commitment to honesty. I was never truthful with any of my wives. And if you can't be honest with the person you chose to be closest to in the entire world, why did you choose them? How real can that closeness be?" He takes another sip. "If, on the other hand, you *can* be honest, if you can show Will your true self, which must be a very, very difficult thing to do, you have a real chance. But only you can know if any of that is possible."

Henry actually said something meaningful. I can't believe it. "Dad!" I cry. "You nailed it! Thank you!"

"You're welcome, darling." He pats my hand. "Regardless, whatever decision you come to, I'm sure it will be the wrong one."

"What?"

"Sorry, sorry!" he laughs. "I misspoke. The *right* one, I meant to say. Whatever decision you make will be the *right* one. I apologize, darling. I'm a bit . . ." His hand flutters to his temple.

I put my head down on the table.

"Is that your little friend from university?" he says.

I look up. He's staring at Freddy, who's pretending not to notice.

Dad smiles at her. "She's grown rather attractive, hasn't she?"

I finish my drink and set the glass on the table. I stand up and pat him on the shoulder. "Henry? I don't know what I'd do without you."

But I've already lost him—he's gesturing to the bartender. "Same here, darling," he murmurs. "Same here."

I walk back to Freddy and put my arms around her.

"I need a favor," I whisper.

"Anything," Freddy whispers back, gazing over her shoulder at my father.

"Whatever happens tonight? I never, *ever* want to know about it."

She nods. The bartender sets a flute in front of her and pops open a dusty bottle. I kiss her cheek and walk out of the bar.

SATURDAY

28

Inside the room, a couple of votive candles are burning on the desk. The doors to the balcony are open. Through the sheer curtains I see Will. He's sitting with his feet propped on the railing. Holding a drink, looking out at the water.

The door slams shut behind me. He stands and comes into the room, stopping a few feet away. He hasn't shaved. He's wearing jeans and a t-shirt. His feet are bare.

"Hi," he says.

"Hi."

"How was your day?" he asks.

"Fine. What have you been up to?"

"Writing to you." He's watching me warily. "Talking with you. Thinking about you."

I nod slowly. "Is that it?"

"That's it."

I drop my bag on the floor. "Prove it."

I throw my arms around his neck and kiss him so hard I taste blood. He staggers and we fall onto the bed, me on top. I hike up my skirt and straddle him. His lip is bleeding. I lean over him and kiss it softly.

"Poor baby," I whisper. "I hurt you."

He smiles. "That's okay! I—"

I put a finger to his lips. I say, "Time for a little truth telling."

I start unbuttoning my suit jacket.

"I've had a hard day, Will. A hard week, in fact." I slip the jacket off my shoulders and let it fall to the ground. "I've spent a lot of time fretting about whether or not you and I should get married. A lot of time feeling guilty about the way I was treating you. A lot of time wishing I could change."

"But you don't have to—"

"Shh." I unbutton my blouse and take it off. I unhook my bra and let it slide down my arms. I place Will's hands on my breasts. I lean over him and he takes them in his mouth, lavishing attention on them with his lips and tongue and teeth. He tries to roll me over, but I pull back. I start unbuckling his belt.

"Now you, Will, have spent a lot of time telling me that I must feel shame. That I must regret who I am and how I behave." I tug at the buttons of his jeans, and he lifts up his hips so that I can slide his pants down his legs, then his boxers. I stroke his cock with one hand. "And according to you, I feel this way because I've been brainwashed into thinking that monogamy is the only right way to love. Right?"

"Can we talk about this later?" he asks breathlessly.

I stop unzipping my skirt. "We need to talk about it now. If you want, we can get dressed and go downstairs to discuss it."

He puts my hand back on his cock. "Please keep talking."

I wiggle out of my skirt and panties. I help Will off with his t-shirt. I stretch out on top of him. I kiss him deeply on the mouth. Then I stop and look him in the eye.

"The thing is, Will? You don't have the full picture." I kiss his throat and shoulders and chest. "Like I said, it's complicated. Sometimes I feel shame. Sometimes I feel guilt. Sometimes I want to change. But sometimes," I kiss his throat and shoulders and chest, "I don't."

We're both naked now. I move down his body and take his cock in my mouth. I slide my hands down his strong, slender legs. "You know what Emerson said about this, right?"

Will stares down at me. "Emerson?"

I look up at him. "Ralph Waldo Emerson."

"I know who Emerson is. I'm just . . . not really sure why we're talking about him right now."

"He said, 'A foolish consistency is the hobgoblin of little minds.'" I stroke Will's balls gently with my fingertips. "I don't have a little mind, Will. I have a big mind. I'm complex, and contradictory, and messy, and inconsistent." I kiss his cock. "I'm not an archetype, or a stereotype. I'm not a capital-W Woman, or a capital-H Human. You've oversimplified me. You've failed to see me as an individual. I find that extremely frustrating." I put my mouth on him again.

Will gasps. "My thinking was very reductive!"

I look up at him, and through the tangle of my hair I can see him watching me. After a while I sit up, wipe my mouth with the back of my hand and smile at him. I trail my hand along the length of his body, admiring it. I straddle him again and lower myself slowly, feeling him fill me as he strains upward to reach as far into me as he can. I begin to move on him, pulling up so that he almost escapes me, then letting myself fall. He reaches for me again but I pin his arms to the bed.

He says, "Lily?"

And I say, my mouth close to his ear, "Shut up."

I kiss his mouth. "I don't devote a lot of energy to wondering why I am the way I am. We spend so much time talking about men and women—what they want, what forces shape them, blah, blah, blah. Life is short, Will. People are unknowable. Enough with the pointless theorizing. We should enjoy ourselves."

"I couldn't agree more," he whispers.

I release his arms and put his hands on my hips. "I wanted to tell you all that today, but I was busy."

He pulls my face down to his and kisses my lips.

"I couldn't figure out how to put it all in a text."

He covers my face with kisses.

"I guess I'm not as talented at texting as you are."

That's when he stops kissing me and smiles. He throws me onto my back. He grabs a handful of my hair and thrusts deep inside of me. I wrap my legs around his waist and my arms around his neck.

It's like the first three days all over again, but better, because I know who he is now, and he knows me. I know why it's so good, why we're so good together. We move to the sofa, where we knock over a lamp and it falls onto the floor. To an armchair. Against the wall, where we accidentally rip down the curtain.

"You must think you're really something," I whisper. "All those women, falling all over you?"

His lips are on my throat.

"Is it the archaeologist thing? Is that catnip to the ladies?"

"It doesn't hurt." He clears the top of the desk with a sweep of his arm and lays me across it. I pull him into me.

In the bathroom he enters me from behind, standing so that we can see ourselves in the mirror.

I say, "I was with a girl last night."

He rests his forehead on my back, groaning softly.

"I could have had a threesome, with her and her husband," I add. "But I was too heartbroken to go through with it."

He pulls out of me. I turn around and hop onto the edge of the sink. As he enters me again, he says, "Well you're a fool, aren't you?"

I laugh. "Do you want to hear what happened?"

"Yes," he whispers.

I smile at him in the mirror. "Yes what?"

"Yes please. Please please yes!"

So I tell him about Sandra, how I touched her and she touched me. I whisper it all in his ear. When I run out of things to say, I start inventing, all the things I would have done with her, and that she would have done to me, and that her husband would have done to both of us, and what we would have done to him. I keep talking. I tell Will all the things about me that he doesn't know. What I like. What I love. What I've tried. What I haven't. About the worst times and the best. I tell him my fantasies. I tell him how I do it when I'm alone. I tell him how sex makes me feel and why I love it. That another person's hands on my body, or their mouth on my body, or their tongue, or their cock, makes me absolutely present, feels like something true and knowable and honest in a world that is otherwise totally unreal.

We end up on the bed, our bodies twined together, crying out at the same time. He collapses on me, his head on my shoulder. He kisses my hair. We're quiet for a long time as our breathing slows and our hearts stop pounding.

I close my eyes. That was exactly what I needed. And exactly why I came upstairs. Maybe that was obvious. It was obvious to me.

My mind drifts for a while. God, Will lasted *forever*. I close my eyes. I think about young men. They're all right. They're all so very, very—

"Lily?"

"Hmm?"

He kisses my ear. "I'm glad you came back."

"Me too." I open my eyes and push him off me. "And now I'd better be going."

"What?"

I stroke his arm, from shoulder to elbow. I bend down and kiss his cheek. "I'm leaving."

"No!" he cries, sitting up. "We're getting married."

I smile at him sadly. "We're not."

He grips my hands tightly. "I thought we worked it all out. What about . . . what about what just happened?"

"That was amazing. But it doesn't mean we should get married."

"Don't you—"

"We can still see each other in New York," I say. "We can date."

"I don't want to date you! I want to spend the rest of my life with you."

"We can't, Will. Even if we wanted to. I called off the wedding."

I try to pull my hands from his, but he won't let me. "You didn't! I talked to Mattie. I called off the calling-off. Please, Lily. I want to marry you. I want nothing more."

"You're out of your mind."

"Don't you love me?"

"You know I do."

"Then what's the problem?"

"What's the problem?" I get out of bed and start searching for my clothes. "We're the problem, Will. Everything you said today makes a lot of sense. Freedom, enjoying life to the fullest, refusing to control the one you love—all great principles to live by. And excellent reasons not to get married." I find my blouse on the floor and shake it out.

"No, they're not! We're—"

"Just listen." I start buttoning my blouse. "There's a lot of stupid debate out there about who should be allowed to get married, right? But with the exception of a few wackos who think four people should be able to marry each other, or a man and his goat, there's not a lot of debate about *what* marriage is. It's an agreement between two people. Two people who say, 'You know what? It's you and me, babe. Just the two of us, against the world.' And if, at this late stage in human history, we can't promise till death do us part, we can at least say that it's for the foreseeable future. If that's marriage—if marriage is about unity and togetherness and security—I think you need monogamy."

He starts to speak, but I raise a hand to stop him.

"Life is full of uncertainty." I reach under the coffee table for my skirt. "Full of peril. You don't know when you're going to get crushed by a telephone pole, or blown up in a terrorist attack, or run over by a truck. Or lose your job, or fall into a depression, or be diagnosed with cancer. Marriage is about safety. About having a port in the shitstorm of life. And I think that for a minimum level of comfort and happiness, you need to promise each other that your own bed is a sanctuary, that your partner's body is yours, and yours his. I don't think a marriage can work otherwise."

Yes, I am arguing for complete, total, full-on sexual fidelity.

Turns out I'm a very traditional sort of person.

Self-knowledge!

"We can have a marriage that works," Will says. "I know we can."

"We're incapable of being faithful! You said so yourself, all day. What exactly do we have to offer each other in marriage?"

"Everything that matters," he replies.

I step into my skirt and zip it up. "You only want to get married because it's romantic."

"Wrong," he says. "I want to get married because it isn't."

He's sitting cross-legged on the bed now. He gestures for me to join him, but I don't.

"Listen, Lily. Your parents' marriages all failed miserably, right? Ninety-nine percent of all marriages fail, whether the people in them admit it or not. Do you know why? Because marriage, as it's commonly conceived and understood, is kind of a scam."

I'm searching for my underwear, but this gives me pause. "Interesting phrasing."

"It's true," he insists. "You start out, and you don't want to be alone. So you pick someone who attracts you. Someone who makes you hot, who makes you laugh. Who you can imagine spending your life with.

And you fall in love. And it's a swooning, blissful, fairy-tale romance. You expect the honeymoon to last forever, as you've been led to believe it will. But it doesn't. It can't. We have lives. Work. Family obligations. People talk a really good game about sharing a life, for better or for worse, but they don't think past the honeymoon to the hard times and the routine. A good spouse is someone you can say anything to. Who you want to have kids with, share a house with. The person who will listen to your dreams and google your weird symptoms and call you on your bullshit and hold your hand as you die. That's what marriage should be. Not some ridiculous fantasy of happily ever after."

I reach under the bed for my shoes. "You didn't listen to a thing I said today, did you? I'm not interested in grand theories. I'm not interested in the big 'We.' This is not about all of mankind."

"Fine, but—will you please stop getting dressed?" He's holding out a hand. I sit on the edge of the bed. "It's about you and me," he says. "But your own ideas about marriage are drawn from what you see around you, right?"

"Sure."

"As are mine. And I know my mother has a lot of flaws, but she and my father have an amazing marriage. They are true partners. And somehow, they've managed to make it work for thirty-five years without straying."

"Uh," I say.

"What?"

"Nothing. Go on."

"But even if one of them had an affair, I have no doubt that their bond could see them through. They communicate. They work out their problems. They make accommodations for each other."

"Let's assume you're right," I say. "We can be a good couple. A great team. Why should we get married?"

"Because it's hopeful," he says. "Because it's romantic. Because it's fun to have a party. Because there's value in making a public promise. In standing up in front of everyone you love and saying, I take you, and hearing me say it back to you. It means something. Maybe everything."

"What about fidelity, Will? It might be a whatever-you-call-it, a cultural construct, a social invention, but people believe in it. People freak the fuck out about it. Don't we need to make the promise, even if we ultimately can't keep it?"

"What I'm talking about *is* fidelity," he says. "True fidelity. Look, Lily. I love women, and you love men. We love their bodies, and the way they move, and the way they smell and sound and taste. It's normal. It's not right or wrong. But we've all accepted this idea that one person is supposed to be enough, for all time. We're so convinced of it that when we aren't enough for our one and only—and very few people ever are—we feel obliterated. We're more committed to sexual fidelity than to marriage, since we regularly rip apart entire families to avenge our own sense of betrayal from minor lapses. You and I have something more. Something bigger. In bed and out. There have been a few times when we've been together and we've made some kind of strange connection. I know you've felt it, too."

I don't reply.

"Sex isn't all one thing," he continues. "It's not always meaningless, and it doesn't always move the earth. Consistency is for little minds, right? There's nothing wrong with us having something amazing while still feeling these urges to be with other people. I don't want to stop you from being happy. Our love, our relationship, is about so much more than sex. Because here's the real truth, Lily. I may want to sleep with a lot of people. But I only want to be intimate with you."

"So what are you suggesting? An open marriage? Those never work."

"Sure they do," he replies. "But I actually think we should give monogamy a try."

I gape at him. "What are you *talking* about?"

"We didn't start this relationship off right. All the sneaking around, the dishonesty, the deception? And we still haven't spent a lot of time together. I think we should focus on each other. Keep other people out of it." He smiles at me. "We've got the fairy tale right now. Why not enjoy it while it lasts?"

"But you just said—"

He reaches up and brushes the hair from my forehead. "The freedom to act is also the freedom not to act, right?"

I laugh. "You spent the day spamming me about free love, and now you want to give monogamy a try?"

He pulls me toward him. "What I want is you. Almost losing you made me realize what I'm willing to give up to keep you."

I think about this for a minute. "You make me sound like a real drag."

He kisses my shoulder. "The last thing in the world that you are is a drag."

"What if we can't do it?"

"As long as we're honest with each other, and talk it out, and love each other? We'll be able to deal with whatever happens." He's stroking my arm. "Who knows? Monogamy might be hot. Constraints could be interesting . . ."

I try to move, but he's holding me. He buries his face in my neck.

"Marry me," he says.

I need a minute to think. But Will is kissing me, so it's hard.

It really has been a hell of a week.

For the last few days, I've been pretty sure that I was going to lose the job I loved. Today, I'm still employed after blackmailing my black-mailing mother-in-law, as well as committing numerous ethical impro-prieties in the service of saving a heinous client from certain destruction.

God. When it's all down in black and white like that, it really doesn't look good.

Will lifts me onto his lap, and I wrap my arms around his neck. He tugs at my blouse, freeing it, slipping a hand underneath.

What else? I dredged up a lot of unhappy emotions for my oldest friend this week. But Teddy's okay. He's fine. I learned that I need to be more honest with myself. That I shouldn't hide from the past.

Then there's my family, whose marital advice I ignored and who I unfairly attacked as being the root of all my problems. But my mother figures seem to be doing fine. As for Gran, I got her back in business, didn't I? Overall, I get a gold star for family relations this week, although I should stop blaming Henry for the bad genes and bad example. And teach him about Will's two-phone system.

Finally, there's Will. At the beginning of the week, I had a sweet,

generous, wonderful fiancé who loved me. Now, I have a sweet, generous, wonderful fiancé who loves me *and* who is also a gifted and uninhibited sex maniac. I thought he only loved me because he didn't know
me. Turns out he loves me *because* he knows me.

And how do I feel about him, now that I know him?

I love him, of course.

I love him, and I don't think I can live without him.

The upshot? I've done everything wrong, and everything's going to
be fine.

I beat the conspiracy of sexual misery! The slut wins!

But one question remains. Should Will and I really get married?

A breeze off the water is making the curtains billow. The sky is
growing light outside. Dawn is coming.

"I almost forgot," Will says. He reaches over to his nightstand and
shows me four little strips of braided grass. "You wanted to know why
I was collecting all that sea grass." He takes my left wrist and kisses it
on the inside. He ties one of the grass braids around it. "It's an ancient
Celtic custom. The night before the wedding, the groom makes bracelets of grass for the bride's wrists and ankles." He takes a second braid
and ties it around my right wrist, kissing that too.

"Is this from *American Archaeology* or something?"

"Nope." He pulls my ankle toward him and ties a braid around it. "I
found it on a website called Weddingzone.com."

I burst out laughing.

"It's probably apocryphal," he adds. "But I like it. Apparently the
Celts thought these grass bracelets would keep the bride's soul from flying out of her body." He smiles at me so sweetly I can barely stand it.

"My soul's not going anywhere," I tell him.

He ties the final bracelet, bending down to kiss the inside of my
ankle. "Souls are tricky things. The Stoics thought they had eight parts.
There was the *hegemonikon*, the—"

I pull him up and kiss him on the mouth. "Enough with the fucking
Stoics, Will."

"Is that a yes?"

"Do you really think we can be honest with each other?"

"We don't have much of a track record," he admits. "But I think we can."

"Do you think we can be faithful?"

He shrugs. "We'll never know until we try."

I laugh out loud and he kisses me. Then I break away and look at him. Suddenly, it *is* like a scene in a movie. There's been some minor adjustment to the camera lens, a slight change in perspective, and I see Will for who he really is. He's not a bad guy or a good guy. He's smart, and funny, and nerdy, and sexy, and passionate, and kind, and earnest, and dirty, and thoughtful, and loving, and degenerate.

He's perfect.

And a disaster.

And he's mine, all mine.

"Will, I love you!" I cry. "I love you so, so much."

"Then say yes," he whispers.

"Promise me that we'll never fight, and always love each other."

"I promise."

"Promise me that you'll send me filthy text messages day and night."

"I promise."

"Promise me that we'll always tell each other the truth."

"We will always tell each other the truth," he says, "and we will always stay together."

I shake my head. "It's impossible."

"Maybe," he says. "But let's give it a shot."

I laugh. "Who *are* you?"

"Marry me," he says. "Marry me, Lily Wilder, and find out."

ACKNOWLEDGMENTS

I owe thanks to many people for bringing this book to life. I am very lucky to have such a brilliant and fun agent as Suzanne Gluck. Thank you, Suzanne, for turning to page one and starting to read. Thank you also to Bill Clegg, Laura Bonner, and everyone else at William Morris Endeavor for your help. My editors Lindsay Sagnette and Beth Coates improved this book enormously with their incisive comments and perfectly apportioned doses of love—thank you, both, so much. Thank you also to Julie Barer and Reagan Arthur for all your encouragement and advice.

Thank you to my father, Brendan Kennedy, whose unflagging devotion gave me the confidence to start writing, and whose ceaseless hounding induced the guilt necessary to finish. Thank you to my mother, Cynthia Kennedy, whose constant love and support resulted in a book that any mother would be ashamed of. To my brother, Dave, I need only say: Good times.

Thank you to Daniel Socolow, my wonderful mentor and friend, whose pointed critiques of gender inequality caused me to think about the issue early, often, and more creatively than I might otherwise have done. And thank you to the Honorable Miriam Goldman Cedarbaum, who set an example for me not only with respect to intelligence and personal integrity, but for what true accomplishment is in the world.

I never would have been able to create a friend like Freddy if I didn't have the following gifted, loyal, and vivid women in my life: Emily Chiang, Elena Goldstein, Andrea Jedrlinic, Diane Macina (it's alphabetical, get over it), and Dru Moorhouse. Thanks, ladies!

And of course and above all, thank you to Joshua Ferris, whose enthusiasm, unwavering faith, and gentle yet relentless criticism made this book possible, and to whom I am so very happy and so unbelievably privileged to be able to say "I do" every single day of my life.